H

Desire glimmered in his eyes and her breath quickened.

He ran his finger gently down the side of her neck and around her mouth, caressing her lower lip and sending a responding desire racing through her. He planted soft kisses on her cheek while his hands played provocatively across her skin. Her pulse hammered. Her whole body ached for more.

He raised her in his arms and lowered her to the blanket. She sighed with pleasure. The smell of grass and the fragrance of pine mingled with the scent of his cologne. Heat soared through her, almost like a fever.

He poised his body above her, his gray eyes demanding and controlling her green ones. "I want to ravage you so that you'll never forget this place, or me, so that our time together will be forever stamped into our memories. I don't want you ever to forget," he whispered.

Harper
Monogram

OUT OF THE PAST

SHIRL JENSEN

HarperPaperbacks

A Division of HarperCollinsPublishers

This is a work of fiction. The characters, incidents, and dialogues are products of the author's imagination and are not to be construed as real. Any resemblance to actual events or persons, living or dead, is entirely coincidental.

HarperPaperbacks *A Division of* HarperCollins*Publishers*
10 East 53rd Street, New York, N.Y. 10022

Cover illustration by Bill Dodge

First printing: March 1993

Printed in the United States of America

HarperPaperbacks, HarperMonogram, and colophon are trademarks of HarperCollins*Publishers*

❖ 10 9 8 7 6 5 4 3 2 1

My special thanks to my family and to my friends, Carol Carpenter and Debbie Weaver, for their support; to my critique group, Joan, Jerry, Chris, and Debbie, for their hours of work; to Pat Teal, who believed in me; and to the wonderful Katie Tso, who took a chance on this purely fictional and unusual book.

Most of all, my thanks to my husband, Roe, who helped and encouraged me to go for my dream.

PROLOGUE

"*Cressie . . .*"

Hearing the eerie murmur, the old woman stopped dusting the cherrywood table and asked, "What you wantin', Miss Kate?"

"The time draws nigh."

"You mean she's finally a-comin'?"

"Yes . . . it's been so long, Cressie."

"And what are you needin' from me?"

"There's wickedness about . . . evil that could ruin everything . . . evil that has killed before and might kill again."

"Then it must be stopped. Sal and I will help."

"Yes . . . and I'll be there for her as well." The voice paused. "The house will work its magic and will give her the roots she needs while healing her pain. But there are those who may cause her harm. We must protect her until she's ready."

"And if the wickedness holds sway?"

"Then the evil will breed more evil, and I'll find no peace."

1

"Do you believe in ghosts, Ms. Dillon?" Norma Peters asked, breaking the long silence. Her strained smile formed creases at the corners of her mouth.

Debbie forgot her tiredness and her irritation that the real estate agent couldn't produce a suitable place for her to settle into and lick her wounds in private. "I beg your pardon?"

Norma straightened the edges of the stacked papers on her desk. Her brown eyes met Debbie's gaze.

"I asked if you believe in ghosts," the agent repeated in a firm voice.

"No, I do not believe in ghosts. But what does that have to do with finding me a home? Oh . . . now I get it. You have a total reject you want to unload on me."

"Then I can assume you aren't easily frightened by wild stories about spirits and supernatural hauntings?"

"Spirits? Supernatural hauntings?" Impatiently

Debbie shifted position on the uncomfortable wooden fan-back chair. "Norma, I'm a level-headed woman who teaches practical business courses. That's one of the reasons Stephen F. Austin University hired me."

"I assumed that."

"Don't waste my time on ghosts or try to pawn off some wretched house no one wants. If you don't have anything decent to show me, say so, and I'll go somewhere else."

Norma cleared her throat. "You're missing the point."

"What is the point?"

Leaning forward, Norma said, "I believe you've seen that even though Nacogdoches is an important center in East Texas, it's still a typical small college town. Students flocking here take up every available rental space. They fill the dorms, the apartments, and they cram into the few rental houses."

"We've been over all of this. In fact, we've wasted the whole day looking at unsuitable catastrophes."

"I did warn you in the beginning—"

"I'm hot and tired."

"I understand, but I wanted you to see for yourself."

Debbie forced a smile to coax some cooperation. "I start teaching at the college this fall. Since I want to be settled by then, that means I have one month to find a place and ship my things here. Not very long considering everything."

"I agree, but—"

"I lived in a small college town in Vermont. I know there has to be something available. There always is."

"That's what I've been trying to tell you," Norma said. "I know of another house that's a few miles out of town. No one has lived in it since Sarah Muller died about two years ago. I think you might like this one."

"A derelict house that's rumored to be haunted and probably riddled with termites and decay doesn't seem much improvement over the horrors I've already seen."

Norma relaxed. "Actually, the house is in good shape. It may need a few repairs, a paint job, and the landscape needs trimming. However, this house is a real bargain, and with a little work and fixing up, you would make a nice profit should you decide to sell later. An investment, you might say."

The ringing telephone interrupted them. Debbie waited for Norma to answer it.

"My assistant will get that," said the sharply dressed real estate agent.

"This Sarah Muller who owned the house. Is she supposed to haunt it now?"

The door opened behind Debbie, and a woman said, "Sorry to interrupt, Norma, but I think you may want to take this call." When Norma frowned, the assistant added, "I was told it's important, and it's personal."

Norma smiled politely. "Excuse me a moment." She rose from the worn leather chair and hurried to the next office.

Sitting back, Debbie considered Norma's last presentation. A steal on a house would be a smart buy, and fixing the place up would certainly help fill the lonely times ahead. Still, something wasn't ringing true, and Norma's edginess along with the topic of ghosts didn't exactly make the house seem like any prize.

The agent's voice floated into the office. "Yes, I received the flowers. They're beautiful, but I can't talk now. I'm with a client."

Debbie crossed her legs and inhaled the sweet scent of the late-blooming pink roses sitting in a large vase on the desk. Their aroma was overwhelming in the small pink-and-gray office, and she waved her hand in front of her nose.

"Tell me quick. It'd better be important." Norma's voice rose with impatience.

Even if the house wasn't in great shape, it couldn't hurt to listen to the whole pitch, Debbie decided. The day was wasted for anything else, anyway.

"Damn. Why did she have to come here?"

At these words Debbie turned slightly on her chair. Through a small crack in the door, she saw Norma's back. Then the agent turned, and Debbie watched her wrap the telephone cord around her right hand.

"You have to learn to deal with her. If you don't, we could all wind up in a mess of trouble."

Disturbed but not wanting Norma to catch her curious stare, Debbie looked away. Sunlight filtered through the pink-flowered drapes and cast prongs of light on the wooden floor. Dust motes danced in the rays.

"Believe me, Gloria's dead. She's history and not part of our lives now. Teresa will come around when the money breaks loose. Don't let her throw you."

Debbie glanced through the crack again, wondering what money Norma was talking about. Somehow this conversation didn't exactly promote confidence in the woman.

"Jenny will accept whatever decision you make. She has no choice. You're her guardian."

Debbie wiped the perspiration from her palm and grimaced at the sight of her wrinkled clothes. The slim, dark green skirt and light green blouse shared their rumpled deterioration with her frazzled nerves.

"Listen, I can't stand here talking. I have someone waiting. But remember, Gloria's dead. You're running the show. . . . Oh . . . okay. I'll call you back as soon as I can."

Norma entered the room, and Debbie uncrossed her legs and straightened her back against the rigid webbing.

"Sorry about that. My friend is having a few problems that couldn't wait. Now where were we?" Norma asked, sitting down behind the desk.

"Still trying to find a house for me to either rent or buy."

"Oh, yes, the Muller place."

"You never did say, is Sarah Muller supposed to haunt the house now?"

"As far as I know, Sarah Muller rests peacefully in her grave."

Debbie considered Norma's comment. "I don't know. Two years seems a long time to remain vacant if something isn't dreadfully wrong with it."

"Not really. Probating estates tie property up for a period, and then the heir tried to break the will. That meant more time."

"Lawyers can be a pain," Debbie agreed, rubbing her throbbing forehead. She tried to wipe away the enormity of the vast changes in her life and the resulting decisions she faced. She pictured her last house, the one she had shared with her husband, Charles. The delightful brick home had nestled in a grove of maple and pine trees near the Vermont

college, and people were forever dropping by to
visit and enjoy the homey atmosphere. That's how
the beginning of the end of her marriage started:
with a casual visit by a beautiful young coed who
wanted to extort some advice from Debbie's too
popular husband.

Debbie pushed back the unhappy memories and
focused her attention on Norma. "Why do I have the
feeling that there's something you haven't told me?"

"The house sits on eighty acres. You might find it a
bit lonely with no close neighbors, but you should
certainly consider it. You can't beat the price. Sarah's
nephew, who's also the heir, badly wants to sell, as is."

"I would enjoy the privacy, but if it's such a great
buy, why hasn't it sold? Surely someone should have
snapped it up long before now."

Norma Peters tapped the eraser of a pencil on the
desk. "This house wouldn't suit most people, that's
why I didn't mention it sooner."

"Because of its condition or the rumored spirits?"

"Some people claim the house is haunted. Even
Sarah Muller said so. That's why I asked if you
believed in ghosts."

Debbie leaned forward and deliberately locked
eyes with Norma. "Why hasn't the house sold before
now?"

Norma pursed her lips. "If you think you might be
interested, why don't you take a look at the property.
There's still enough time to see it this evening. Then
we can discuss the details, and I can answer any questions you may have."

"And if I'm not interested in seeing this house?"

"Trust me. Go. You won't be sorry. In the meantime I'll call around for whatever else might be avail-

able. If I'm wrong about your reaction, we can always look at more tomorrow."

"You aren't taking me this time?"

"No. I have something else I need to do. Besides, if you view the house without me, you can make up your own mind about the property. I won't be able to influence you in any way."

Recalling the unfinished phone conversation, Debbie had a pretty good idea what that "something else" was. But that's none of my business, she chided herself. She had enough problems of her own, what with moving and starting her life over again, without nosing into local affairs.

Maybe she should do as Norma suggested. The more she considered the Muller house, the better it sounded, with or without ghosts. Living in what was claimed to be a haunted house would certainly be an unusual way to exorcise the bitter taste of a marriage gone bad. If the house needed work, she could vent her frustrations on repairs. "Is the ghost supposed to be a man or a woman?"

"I thought you didn't believe in ghosts."

"I don't." Debbie smiled in response to Norma's low chuckle.

Norma hastily drew a map. "Here are the directions." Removing a labeled key from her desk drawer, she continued, "Take this with you. You can call me later from your motel and let me know what you decide."

Debbie hesitated, then grabbed the key and the map. Tiredness and irritation forgotten, she left the office and walked to her Nissan, her steps light and bouncy. The sun warmed her face, the breeze brushed against her skin. She tingled with the thrill of the unknown, the first she had felt in a long time, and suddenly she laughed with spontaneous pleasure.

"Ghosts," she muttered. No one could be foolish enough to let the rumor of ghosts keep them from taking advantage of a good buy. Again a familiar uneasiness tugged at her enjoyment. There had to be something wrong with the place. There had to be something Norma wasn't telling.

Debbie unlocked her car and climbed inside. This was probably a waste of time, and she'd discover the agent had manipulated her. But she needed a place to live, somewhere she could settle into for the time she made Nacogdoches her home. Besides it wouldn't hurt to look, especially since Norma had nothing else to show her at the moment.

Debbie looked in the rearview mirror and saw Norma standing in the office doorway, her pink suit catching the full light of the afternoon sun. The agent looked as though she had just won the million-dollar lottery. Debbie's smile faded.

A quarter of an hour later, Debbie wondered if she had made a wrong turn. She had passed no cars on the narrow country lane, nor had she seen anyone. When she passed the drive to a large brick two-story house that displayed meticulous care but obvious affluence, she sighed and glanced down once more to the paper in her lap. Surely she must be close to the Muller house.

The clear, sharp fragrance from the pines filtered through the car's air-conditioning and brought back nostalgic memories of the small private college she had left behind. She caught sight of two squirrels staring down at her from a branch of a large oak that extended over the side of the road. She could learn to appreciate this peaceful atmosphere.

Rounding a bend, Debbie gasped and slammed on the brakes. Two horseback riders, a man and a girl, emerged from the edge of the thick woods. They weren't all that close, but their sudden appearance startled her. Maybe all the talk of ghosts had made her jumpier than she'd realized.

The two were dressed similarly, in jeans, colorful knit shirts, and the cowboy boots that were so popular in the area. Engrossed in their conversation, they didn't seem to notice her.

The man riding the chestnut stallion appeared to be in his middle thirties with dark brown hair and broad shoulders. He smiled at the teenage girl riding the gray beside him, but judging from the girl's stiff body and sullen expression, she clearly wasn't enjoying the absorbing conversation. Neither rider reacted to the dust the horses kicked up or the stallion's nervous twitch when Debbie accelerated and drew closer.

She halted again near the pair and, expecting them to look over at her and inquire what she wanted, rolled down the passenger window. They kept talking, ignoring her. Frustration grabbed Debbie, the same mounting irritation she'd felt sitting in the real estate office thinking about Norma's inability to find her a decent place to live.

The two turned their horses onto a path that wound between the big pines and tangled growth of untamed forest. They were going away, disregarding her entirely. Damn it, she wanted directions to the Muller house, and these two buffoons were the only people she'd seen for miles. She pressed her palm against the horn.

The long, continuous blare from her Nissan pierced the quiet with the force of resounding thunder. The chestnut stallion reared instantly. Thrashing forefeet flailed at the air, nicking the nearby vines. The rider tightened his legs against the horse's sides while he fought for control. Muscles in both man and beast bulged in the struggle. The horse bucked, twisting and turning, determined to be free. The man cajoled, adapted, and maintained his mastery.

The girl tugged on the reins of the gray horse until she managed to get out of the way of the battling pair. Watching the fight for supremacy from a safe distance, she bent low over the horse's neck and crooned reassuring words.

Horrified, Debbie stared at the result of her action. Her heart pounded as the man and his horse struggled. Quietly she urged, "Stay on. Stay on. Oh, please, stay on."

Like a bolt of lightning, the stallion took off, streaking down the path. Debbie's last sight of horse and rider was a vision of the man bending low in the saddle while he glanced back over his shoulder. He had finally noticed her, but the force of his anger made her shiver. Then the woods enveloped them, and only the diminishing sound of pounding hooves broke the silence.

"That was a dumb thing to do," the teenager said, walking her horse close to the open window.

"I'm sorry . . . I didn't think . . . Will he be all right?" Debbie followed the girl's gaze down the path.

The girl laughed. "Keith? Of course. He'll let Samson run himself out. He's been pulling at the bit since we started. No one's ridden him in a while, and Samson isn't one to let an opportunity go by. Besides, it'll get Keith's attention on someone else for a change."

Surprised at the girl's comment, Debbie decided her best action was to say nothing. The girl had short brown hair that curled around her elfin face, but it was her blue eyes twinkling with mischief that reminded Debbie of her brother, Scottie. She was probably around sixteen, as well.

"Actually, I should thank you," the girl said.

"Oh, why?"

"He was bitching at me again. Of course, he wouldn't call it that." The girl shrugged before peeking at Debbie through her dark lashes. "You know how it is. Older people are always uptight about something and full of advice. They think they know what's best when really they don't."

That sounded exactly like something Scottie would say.

At Debbie's silence, the girl continued, "Although to be fair, Keith's better than most."

"Well, I'm glad my thoughtlessness served some purpose." Debbie turned on her best smile. "My name's Debbie Dillon, and I'm looking for the old Muller residence. I was hoping you could help me. That's why I honked the horn."

The girl stopped patting the gray's neck. Her eyes widened as her gaze fell to scrutinize Debbie's attire.

Debbie, knowing what the younger girl must see, shifted uncomfortably in the thickening silence. Gone was the usual tasteful, businesslike appearance she had acquired in her twenty-eight years. In its place remained what might pass for an escapee from a drudgery farm. Her wrinkled clothes belied her slender frame; the lack of makeup highlighted the wrath of the hideous day and the vulnerability the divorce had created in her fragile appearance; and her shoulder-length blond hair lay in disarray from the breeze.

Debbie picked up the map from her lap and waved it to catch the girl's attention. "The real estate lady gave me instructions, but I must have missed the house somehow."

"No, you haven't. The driveway's around the next bend. What do you want with the Muller house?"

"I understand it's for sale, and I'm looking for a place."

"You're kidding. Don't you know the place has been empty ever since Miss Sarah died? They can't give it away. It's haunted."

"If that's the only thing that's wrong with it, I'm not worried. I don't believe in ghosts."

"You should be. I know what I'm talking about. My name's Jenny Winthrope, and I live down the road. You probably saw our place as you passed it."

Debbie nodded, her curiosity growing. Norma had mentioned a Jenny during the telephone conversation.

"Keith's a psychologist. He writes about people who claim they've seen ghosts or other weird things. He says people get all kinds of funny ideas and tell way-out stories to get attention. They exaggerate, and when he finds a perfectly logical explanation, they get mad. He doesn't believe in ghosts. But for what it's worth, he hasn't made up his mind about the Muller house yet."

"Keith? The man that was with you?"

"Yeah, Dr. Keith Douglas, the man on the runaway horse. Haven't you ever heard of him?" Jenny asked.

When Debbie shook her head, the teenager contin-ued. "My family's known him for years, and my sister thinks he's the greatest. He even dates her some-times."

A small smile tugged at Jenny's mouth, but sadness deepened her blue eyes. "Keith's even been known to spend some of his valuable time giving me advice when someone thinks my imagination is running wild again and I need help."

Debbie didn't know what to say, but the misery, loneliness, and desperation ringing in the girl's voice pulled at her heart.

Jenny's hands were clenched so tightly around the reins that the knuckles whitened. "I'm an overly emo-tional, immature teenager, you see. I have serious problems."

Overly emotional . . . wild imagination . . . serious problems. Charles had thrown those same accusa-tions at Debbie when she had first accused him of being unfaithful. Only she had been right, as she eventually learned to her bitter dismay.

"That's what Keith was doing today . . . picking me apart."

The girl was obviously repeating things she had heard and unconsciously exposing the way she felt. Debbie had so wanted to have someone to confide in and support her when her world had disintegrated around her, but there had been no one. She had felt isolated in her pain, just like Jenny. At that moment Debbie wanted to help this teenager. But how? And could there be some truth in the suggestion that she needed counseling?

Still watching for her reaction, Jenny said, "Keith's teaching at Stephen F. this year, but he travels to all sorts of neat places."

"Maybe I'll see him. I'm teaching there myself." Debbie didn't add that when she did meet him, she might go the other way, if his parting glare was any indication of the temperament she would encounter, and if Jenny's unhappiness was any measure of his companionship.

Jenny looked down the path and giggled. "Boy, I bet he's furious. I'd better go." She turned her horse, then stopped. "You really shouldn't buy the Muller house."

"I need a place to live." Seeing Jenny's guarded expression, Debbie added, "Don't worry. Supposed haunted houses don't frighten me a bit."

After a long pause Jenny said quietly, "It's not only Kate's ghost you have to worry about."

Before Debbie could respond, the girl spurred her mount and raced off down the path. The horse's pounding hooves raised a dusty screen between them.

Debbie tightened her hands around the steering wheel and, feeling exhausted, rested her forehead against them. What was Jenny alluding to? Was this the missing item Norma had failed to mention? Maybe she shouldn't look at the house after all.

The call of a blackbird filled the warm, lazy afternoon. Debbie raised her head and shook off her discouragement. She was letting both her own imagination and a teenager's fancies shake her. Ghosts didn't exist. Anything else she could handle. The image of Scottie filled her mind, and she laughed. If anything could redeem her in her brother's eyes, buying a haunted house would certainly do the trick.

The sun's rays reflected on the car's metal, making it gleam like a silver bullet. While she shifted gears and started up the engine, the strain of the last few hours vanished. Without even seeing the Muller house, she knew the place would be special.

After turning the curve, her remaining reservations dissipated with the subtlety of smoke. She stopped at the roadside, her gaze clinging to the large, white structure standing defiantly against a backdrop of tall pine trees. In style it resembled an old southern mansion, with a wide porch and columns. The house called to her senses as clearly as if it were speaking to her. Debbie felt a welcoming peace.

Admittedly the house showed signs of deterioration, she saw as she drove down the rough dirt driveway. The woodwork's white paint peeled in places, grayed in others. Boards covered several upper windows, and the large front door displayed a smattering of mud.

Still, the house beckoned.

As she parked in front of the porch, she studied the landscape. The tall, thick grass matted into a sea of green. Vines and bushes ran completely out of control, making her wonder if the yard had been tended since the owner died. The clean fresh air, the pink-and-yellow tones that meshed with the blue of the late afternoon sky, the large oak that shaded the front of the house, all touched a nostalgic note of homecoming within her. Debbie hungered to possess this house.

She sat there and reveled in the idea of installing this place into her life. She fantasized how it would look freshly painted, its brightness proclaiming her new beginning.

Finally she knew she couldn't wait another moment. She had to see the inside, see if it could begin to match the fever of excitement the outside brought.

Eager with anticipation, she walked up the three steps of the wide porch. She inserted the key, but before she could turn the lock, the ornate door swung open. Momentarily startled, Debbie stared.

In the foyer stood a tall, slender woman wearing an old cotton print housedress. Wrinkles lined her thin neck and furrowed around her blue eyes. Several strands of graying hair slipped from a confined knot at the back of her head. She brought a hardworking hand to cover her heart. "You came."

While Debbie's heartbeat slowed to normal, she expelled a relieved breath. "Yes, Norma Peters sent me. Did she call you?"

"No."

Filled once more with apprehension, Debbie looked past the woman and down the hallway. "I came to see the house. I'm sorry if I frightened you, but I didn't think anyone would be here."

"I've cleaned the house for forty years. Why wouldn't I be here?"

Debbie licked her dry lips. More evasiveness. First from Norma, and now this woman. . . . Only Jenny had blurted out the truth. Then again, if this Dr. Douglas was giving the girl counseling, who could say whether she occasionally skirted the truth. "I understood the owner died two years ago."

When the cleaning lady continued to stand silently in front of her, Debbie gave a small shrug. "I guess I didn't consider that someone would come in to clean."

"I wouldn't let Miss Sarah's house become unsightly, 'specially since both she and Miss Kate told me you would come."

Debbie blinked several times before the woman's unwavering stare. "I don't understand."

"Before she died, Miss Sarah said you would come. Miss Kate told me last month. My name's Cressie." The woman turned and headed back down the hall. "You look around the parlor; I'll put the teakettle on."

Too disconcerted to speak for a moment, Debbie stared after her. She called out before Cressie escaped, "But Sarah Muller died two years ago. You must have misunderstood something. She wouldn't have known I was coming here. I didn't know myself."

Cressie turned and locked eyes with Debbie. "She knew."

Debbie swallowed slowly. She couldn't believe any of this, and she didn't know what to say. And who was Miss Kate?

"She knew," Cressie reaffirmed in her reedy whisper.

Debbie tried to decide whether to follow Cressie and pursue the strange conversation or do as the woman had suggested and start looking over the house. From the foyer, a clock chimed five. She had come to see the house; the strange housekeeper could wait her turn.

Debbie turned and stepped into what Cressie had referred to as the parlor. Her heart raced with excitement when she looked at the lovely cherrywood furniture. The shining oak floor and soft short-napped rug recalled memories of vacations with her grandmother.

She passed the sofa and ran her fingers lovingly

along the back of the colorful printed fabric before stopping in front of a big window that looked out onto a large field with a grove of pines beyond. Scattered about were several stately oaks and some dogwoods. At another window she discovered a large pecan tree. The exterior of the house seemed to thumb its nose at the world, while the interior displayed love of possession.

And Debbie wanted to possess.

Suddenly she inhaled the scent of jasmine, and although she hadn't heard Cressie return, she sensed someone else in the room. She turned. No one. The room was empty.

She chuckled at her own foolishness. She was exhausted, and all the wild stories had her imagination playing tricks.

Debbie left the parlor and followed the course Cressie had taken. The white kitchen glimmered with modern equipment. Blue trim shone at the edge of the Formica counter and in the flecks of the vinyl floor. Even blue flower pots adorned small shelves at the side window, while apothecary jars filled with spices and herbs resided in the window over the sink. The gentle blending of convenience and homeyness was irresistible.

Cressie wiped her hands on a terry-cloth towel. "Tea won't be long. Do you want to sit in here?"

"This is fine." Debbie walked over and peered out a window at the open field behind. "Is that a graveyard at the top of that rise?"

"There's been buryin' there since the first settlers. Nacogdoches is the oldest town in Texas, you know. Back before the War Between the States, even. The Mullers were among the first to settle."

Debbie didn't want to discuss the dead. She had heard too much about the dead already today. "What is the large building behind the house?"

"Garage. Servants quarters on top." Cressie set two china cups together with spoons on the round oak table.

"Do you live there?"

"No. My husband and I have our own place 'cross the road and down a ways. There isn't any milk or lemon for the tea." The older woman's hands trembled slightly when she set down the sugar bowl.

Debbie moved to the table and curled her fingers over the back of the chair. She felt the need of support, and the smoothness of the wood provided her with a sense of stability. "What did you mean earlier when you said Miss Sarah told you I would come? And who is Miss Kate?"

Cressie's blue eyes seemed to look right through her, as if she didn't exist. Debbie shivered and glanced behind her.

The kettle began to sing, and Cressie rose slowly to take it from the burner. "Miss Sarah had the power. Same as I do." She poured hot water into a lovely old teapot. "We both could communicate with Kate."

"Kate?"

"Kate Muller. She roams the house. Searchin'. Always searchin'." After setting the dainty pot on the center of the table, Cressie straightened. "She's one of the ghosts. Then there's her father. Mean man, he was. Cold and hard-hearted. He don't like it 'cause Kate won't forget and rest. He's even madder that the devil's advocate has brought evil to his land."

Debbie understood how Alice must have felt after

falling down the hole and finding herself in Wonderland. She rubbed her pounding temples, trying to bring sanity back into the room. Catching Cressie watching her, a strange half smile on her lips, Debbie snapped, "I don't believe in ghosts."

"Dr. Keith don't, either, but I notice he's not quite so sure when people ask about this place. I wonder what he's going to say when he sees you."

Debbie remembered the man racing away on the stallion and decided not to pursue the subject. "Is the tea ready yet?"

"Not quite." Cressie brushed back a strand of hair as she swished the teapot. "You said Norma sent you out. Where do you come from?"

"I've been living in Vermont the last five years, but my mother and younger brother live in Houston. That's one of the reasons I came back to Texas."

"Come with me," Cressie said abruptly, and walked toward a staircase in one corner of the kitchen. "I think you'll find one of the upstairs rooms real interestin'."

Debbie hesitated at the lower step, and the older woman stopped and looked back down at her.

"You did come to see the house, didn't you?"

"Yes. . . ."

"Of course you did. You really didn't have much choice."

Debbie resisted the impulse to throw up her hands in exasperation. She followed Cressie upstairs. When the older woman glanced over her shoulder, her eyes glowing like blue crystals, Debbie stumbled, once more awash with uneasiness.

At the top of the stairs, Cressie emerged into a long hall flanked by several doors. She opened the one closest to her right and waited for Debbie to enter first.

An old-fashioned canopy bed decked out in white muslin occupied the space opposite the door. Two large rag rugs adorned the oak floor on either side of the bed. The jasmine flowers pictured in the crisp curtains looked so real, Debbie could smell their scent. The room even had a small fireplace on one side.

She glanced at Cressie and, seeing again the faint smile on the housekeeper's face, felt new waves of uneasiness. "Are all the bedrooms as lovely as this one?"

Ignoring the question, Cressie walked farther into the room and pointed to the portrait that hung over the cedar chest on the far side of the bed. "That's Miss Kate."

The picture portrayed a young woman with honey-blond hair and deep green eyes that tilted at the corners. She had a creamy complexion highlighted by pink lips that curved into a secret smile. Her delicate white muslin gown suited the styles of a hundred years earlier, and in her hand lay a twig of jasmine.

Debbie gave a small disbelieving laugh and sought for words to express her stunned feelings. Finally she turned to Cressie. "My family moved from Dallas to Houston, but that picture . . . that girl."

Cressie nodded sagely. The older woman's eyes slowly covered Debbie from her toes to the top of her head, leaving a trail of apprehension behind. When at last she met and locked with Debbie's green eyes, she said softly, "Miss Sarah on her deathbed promised the past would rise up with the comin' of the new owner."

Was the old woman as crazy as she sounded?

"And Miss Kate told me you was a-comin'," Cressie added.

Confused, Debbie returned her gaze to the portrait. Except for the clothes, the young woman in the picture could very well be Debbie herself.

2

The portrait touched Debbie in a way she couldn't explain. Surprise, excitement, discomfort, each took its toll. But what was worse, the young girl in the picture seemed to be trying to say something to her. The words were important. Debbie sensed it in every tingling nerve. What were they? She bent closer. She wanted to hear.

Or did she?

A draft of cool air brushed her arms, breaking her from her trance. What was the matter with her? A picture couldn't speak. She straightened, chiding herself for such foolishness. She was letting Cressie twist her good sense and manipulate her imagination.

Debbie laughed, although there was no hiding her discomfort. "I've heard of people having doubles, but this is the first time it's happened to me. I'm not certain I like it."

"Sometimes the spirits lead us in ways we can't control. When that happens, we can only do our best 'til we know what's 'spected."

Cressie's crooked, knowing smile sent a trail of unsettling shivers down Debbie's spine. She met the nonsense head-on. "And you think because I resemble the girl in this picture, I'm this person Miss Sarah and this Miss Kate told you would come?"

"A few years back, somethin' dreadful happened. Miss Sarah suspected what took place, but she was old, couldn't get around very good. She couldn't do what she wanted, and it worried her."

"What was it?"

"She would never say. She thought if I knew, I could be in danger. But she worried and fretted. On her deathbed she finally told me it would be up to the next owner to set matters straight." Cressie, lost in her own thoughts, gently smoothed the cover of the large fluffy pillow that decorated the bed.

The ensuing silence stretched on, and Debbie began to wonder what kind of weird situation she'd entered by walking into the Muller house. Normally she wouldn't entertain the wild ideas this crazy old woman suggested, but in spite of herself, she was intrigued.

"Miss Kate told me someone was comin' to release her restless spirit so she could find peace. Whoever came would have to solve Miss Sarah's dilemma as well. I figure that be you."

"Because I look like the portrait," Debbie finished for her. "As I said before, I don't believe in ghosts. Since I tend to mind my own business and not mix in things that don't concern me, I'm afraid if I should buy the place, your Miss Sarah and Miss Kate will have to wait a little longer. Now, can we see the rest of the house?"

Cressie gave that sly knowing smile Debbie was learning to detest.

"You belong here. You'll see." Turning, she led Debbie out of the room and down the hall.

As they wandered through the other bedrooms, Debbie refused to say any more about Sarah and Kate or their expectations. Instead she concentrated on inspecting the house. And whenever any niggling uneasiness crept in, she reminded herself that her resemblance to Miss Kate was only coincidental.

She stopped in a yellow bedroom and ran her fingers across the fine antique highboy. "I can't believe all this marvelous furniture was just left here."

Cressie sniffed. "Miss Sarah's nephew called it all old junk. Even when the lawyer told him he should sell the furniture separate, the fool couldn't be bothered. He said there wouldn't be any market in Nacogdoches for such pieces since everyone here had lived in these parts forever and had their own junk. He didn't intend to waste good money shippin' the stuff to Oklahoma. Besides, he figured if the furniture stayed, he'd get more money for the house."

"He's right about that. The furniture helps make the house, but I still can't believe he left it." Debbie didn't bother to hide her glee. "The furniture that I kept from my marriage will blend beautifully with what's here."

"Some of these young moderns don't have the sense God gave a goose. 'Yuppies' is a good name for 'em, and that young man leads the gaggle."

Debbie laughed. "Come on now, Cressie, I'm a young modern, and I love fine old things."

"You're different. You'll see."

Cressie opened the door to the spacious master bedroom. Absolutely delighted with the large walnut four-poster bed and dainty, frilly dressing table, Debbie forgot everything else and grinned like a school girl with her first love note. She strolled past the stuffed wing-backed chair and rocker to feel the smooth surface of the rectangular marble-topped table beside the bed. A few dog-eared books and an ornate glass-and-brass reading lamp were placed on top. Taking her time, she gazed at all the personal pictures and bric-a-brac that probably belonged to Sarah and adorned the walls and the top of the huge walnut dresser. She couldn't resist stroking its delicate surface, drawing pleasure from the feel of the polished wood. The room was enchantingly perfect.

Seeing a smug expression on Cressie's face, Debbie determinedly ignored her. She wouldn't let the housekeeper's attitude diminish her enjoyment. It reminded her too much of Charles's petty ways, and she'd left him in Vermont with his new wife.

The crowning touch in the room was the small fireplace. Since she was a little girl, Debbie had dreamed of having a bedroom fireplace, but she'd always known it was a romantic touch of foolishness. Now she ran her fingers lovingly over the white brick and let her imagination soar to once cherished dreams of a deep and lasting love.

A deep and lasting love. Was there such a thing?

Once she'd believed in it. Not anymore. Her divorce had taught her a lot, and it had left her on her own. She had no man in her life, nor did she want one, not for a long time.

She walked over to the front window and looked out. The wide expanse of lawn swept to the cluster of trees by the roadside and made her feel like a queen surveying her tiny kingdom.

She stepped over to a side door and peered into a private modern bathroom. It was decorated in the same shades as the bedroom, predominantly green with a dash of dark blue and a slash of pure white.

Cressie patted a huge bath towel that hung over a brass towel bar. "Miss Sarah liked her conveniences and could afford to indulge herself."

Cressie and Debbie left the room and descended the large curving front staircase to the main floor. Debbie smiled with delight. The house was indeed a prize—one she intended to possess.

"The house suits you," Cressie said as they reached the bottom of the stairs.

"I can't believe someone didn't snap it up immediately."

"Well, both Frank Johnson and Michael Townsend want to buy the land, but no one locally would move into the house." Again she cast Debbie that irritating half smile.

"Who are those men?" Debbie asked, refusing to let the woman unsettle her further.

"Neighbors. Johnson owns the land to the north, and the Winthrope estate lies to the south."

"I thought you said a man named Townsend was the neighbor."

"Same difference. Townsend married Gloria Winthrope."

Disturbed, Debbie paused. So many names continued to emerge—names she had overheard Norma mention on the phone. Gloria and Jenny, both Winthropes and both neighbors.

Cressie walked through a door off the main hallway into a library containing shelves of books and comfortable leather chairs. A modern typewriter and a small calculator graced the polished surface of the oak desk. "Miss Sarah used this room for her book-keepin' and such."

Debbie glanced around. The scent of lemon oil mingled pleasantly with the papery must of old books. "I'll have to mention to Norma how well you've kept the house. It looks lived in, and not like the other houses I saw for sale."

"Do what you like, but I don't keep the house for Norma Peters. The Mullers and Slavanias go back more than a hundred and fifty years together. I do this for Miss Sarah."

"Are you a Slavania?"

"Yep. Actually it's my husband's family name, but we've been married thirty-five years. Same difference now."

"After thirty-five years, I agree. You said you live down the road."

Cressie nodded and opened another door to reveal the downstairs bathroom for Debbie to see, then led the way to a small parlor at the back of the house. Cressie retraced her steps down the hall, into the large dining room behind the front parlor. Finally they were in the kitchen again. "Sal, that's my husband, can do the cuttin' of the grass and weedin' for you. He did for Miss Sarah. But when she died, he had to find other work."

Debbie wasn't certain she wanted to continue any housekeeping arrangements with Cressie, but since the older woman looked expectant, she asked, "How often do you come?"

"Just once a week now, but I'll come every day when you move in. Sit down. We'll have our tea and then look over the rest."

Debbie gratefully pulled out the kitchen chair and

sat. "I'm afraid I can't afford to have full-time help."

Cressie poured the tea. "We'll work somethin' out."

Before Debbie could respond, the doorbell rang. Setting down the pot, Cressie asked, "You 'spectin' someone?"

"Not unless Norma decided to stop by after all."

Cressie frowned and left the room.

Debbie sipped her tea slowly. Sighing with pleasure, she closed her eyes and let the soothing drink calm her. Such a simple panacea, hot tea. Such a disturbing day. Had she done the right thing in coming to Nacogdoches? She'd thought so in the beginning, but so many unsettling events brought uncertainties, and she did have other alternatives. These doubts weren't at all like her. She must be more unraveled than she'd realized. Probably thanks to Cressie; she was enough to rattle anyone.

Cressie's greeting rang with pleasure when she opened the front door. A man's voice responded and carried through the house. Their footsteps drew closer. Debbie, curious to meet a friend of the bizarre Cressie, looked up expectantly.

At the sight of the man standing behind the older woman and glaring grimly at her, Debbie lowered her cup carefully to the saucer, wishing for a place to hide. The man who had wrestled with the runaway stallion wasn't any more delighted to see her than he'd been at their last encounter.

"Dr. Keith stopped by," Cressie explained, turning toward the cupboard and taking down another cup. "Dr. Keith Douglas is the one I told you about . . . he doesn't believe in Miss Kate either."

"Oh, I believe in Kate," Keith protested, still staring at Debbie. "But not her ghost. I don't believe in the supernatural."

After setting a cup in front of the new arrival, Cressie placed her hands on her hips and added contentedly, "And this is Debbie Dillon. She's goin' to buy the property."

Debbie was glad of Cressie's chatter when not so much as the glimmer of a smile at the introduction broke past Keith's set expression. She knew most women would consider his narrow face, dark hair and eyebrows, and piercing gray eyes attractive, but he reminded Debbie of a hawk ready to pounce.

A thin sliver of a scar pierced through the shadow of his beard and ended with a small indentation at the firm end of his chin. A dimple almost, that begged to be touched, or a battle scar that admonished the bearer should be treated with caution.

And if Jenny was to be believed, this man held a doctorate in psychology. From the broad shoulders neatly displayed by the knit shirt and the muscled thighs tightly encased in jeans, Debbie felt certain he could bend more than minds, if he so desired. It was apparent Keith was not a man you wanted for an enemy, especially if you were a newcomer. Rubbing the side of her neck, she again regretted her action at their first meeting.

She cleared her throat. "I'm sorry I frightened your horse earlier. I didn't realize—"

"From what I understand, I imagine there's quite a few things you don't realize. That's why I decided to stop when I saw your car."

"I don't think I understand."

"I really didn't expect to find you still here. Jenny said she told you the house was haunted, and I knew

Cressie would be here today. Her predictions frighten people who have known her all their lives. I didn't think you'd last more than a few minutes before running for your life."

Debbie looked at Cressie for help, or at least a reaction, but it was obvious the woman intended to sip her own tea and watch. Suddenly Debbie decided to ignore her initial decision. She had wanted to start out on the right foot with her new neighbors, but there was always a bummer somewhere. Dr. Keith clearly filled the local honor.

She refilled her cup in order to have time to compose what she wanted to say. "Since you had to stop when you saw my car, I can't wait for the other little tidbits you think I should hear. But first I should warn you, Cressie and I haven't finished our own business. So, say whatever it is you have to get off your mind. That way we can return to important matters."

A shocked silence followed, and then Keith threw back his head and the room rang with his low, rich laughter. "I believe I owe you an apology, but Jenny was sincerely concerned about you," he said when he finally stopped. "And by the way, I accept yours for frightening my horse."

She had been beaten by an expert. There could be no gain in carrying on with the quarrel. "I would have felt dreadful if the horse had thrown you," she said.

"Humph," Cressie sniffed. "Not likely. Sticks like a burr, he does."

Keith grinned. "Cressie is one of my fans. You'll have to make allowances."

"And is Jenny one also?"

"Jenny's young and impressionable. She's immature for a girl of sixteen. Because she can't find answers at home, she frequently turns to me for advice."

Debbie wondered if Dr. Douglas had any idea how truly miserable Jenny felt or that she considered his advice an intrusion. Still, complaining about being bitched at was normal for a teenager. And as for Jenny's claim that people thought she had a wild imagination . . . well, Debbie had to admit she didn't know all the circumstances. What did impress her was that while Keith made light of his explanation, no amusement showed on his face at the young girl's expense. He took her problems seriously.

Turning to Cressie, Debbie asked, "You mentioned earlier that Michael Townsend was one of the neighbors who wanted to buy the land. How is he related to Jenny?"

"He's her stepfather," Keith interjected before Cressie could reply. "He married Jenny's mother. They live in the big house you passed just before you honked your horn at us."

Seeing the guarded look that Keith and Cressie exchanged, Debbie wondered what they had silently agreed not to disclose. When they remained quiet, the uneasy suspicion grew that the phone conversation she had overheard in Norma's office might give a clue. Debbie couldn't resist. "And Jenny's mother, does she live there, too?"

After a brief pause, Keith asked, "Where else would she live?"

Embarrassment warmed her cheeks. Debbie picked up her cup and drained it.

After a quick look at Cressie, Keith continued. "Gloria made a trip to Dallas. She's been missing since."

"That be six years ago," Cressie interjected.

Since everyone clearly wanted to end that subject, Debbie pushed back her cup. "So, Dr. Douglas, what was so important that you had to stop and talk with me?"

Keith's lips twitched. "You don't mince words, do you?"

"I'm sorry if I seem rude, but it's been a hard day. I want to finish seeing the property and get back with Norma. You stopped because you saw my car, so you must have something important to tell me."

She refused to look away from Keith's steady gaze. When he applied it, this man had the same charm and magnetism as her ex-husband, and she wasn't in any mood for more games.

"I think I've changed my mind," Keith said softly, and continued to hold her eyes. Then he smiled at Cressie. "You still make great tea."

Cressie chuckled. "You won't scare her away. She's like you, not afraid of anythin'."

"Well, you'll have to admit it could have been a real disaster if she had turned out to be the delicate type."

"Will the two of you stop talking as though I weren't here? I can speak for myself," Debbie snapped.

"You're right," Keith agreed, "it was unforgivable of us." He rose from the chair, and after shoving it back under the table, he placed his hands on the chair rail. "You appear to be fully aware of what you're doing. But let me tell you—this house is out in the country. The neighbors are friendly, but not close by, should you have any trouble."

"Like what sort of trouble?" Debbie demanded.

"Oh, like a break-in or fire, or you became frightened."

"As you said, Dr. Douglas, I'm a big girl and can take care of myself. I don't scare easily."

"Don't be too sure of yourself. We all need a little help now and then, and it's never wise to turn our backs on a friendly hand."

"I'll keep your advice in mind," Debbie said politely, and rose as he began to leave. He stopped when she called after him. "Oh, by the way. Is that all you wanted to say when you stopped? To warn me the house was considered haunted, and I might become frightened?"

Keith turned, his expression grim once more. The kitchen light reflected on the small dimpled scar. "Actually, I was trying to help out a colleague who might be getting in over her head."

"Jenny told you?"

Keith nodded. "When Jenny also mentioned you were new in the area and that Norma had sent you to see the Muller place, I thought you should be warned."

"But I thought you didn't believe in ghosts," Debbie said, glancing at Cressie for confirmation. Cressie's mouth pursed as though savoring a mouth-watering sweet.

"Oh, I wasn't going to warn you about any of Cressie's prophesies or Miss Kate's ghost. Cressie won't harm you, and I don't believe in the supernatural. But if you intend to buy the house, I didn't want you to get caught in the crossfire between your neighbors." Keith's gaze covered her thoroughly.

Debbie's insides tightened. "I don't understand." Was he using his charm to deceive her in some way, or had he actually been concerned about her?

He shrugged. "When you proved yourself green to

country ways by blowing your horn around horses, I thought Norma might be taking advantage of you, in a business sense."

"Does Norma take advantage of people?"

"Don't fret about it. I think you can handle whatever this small town dishes out. If anyone gives you too big a problem, just sic Cressie or the ghost on them." His smile broadened. "If worse comes to worst, you can always open your green eyes wide and give one of your gorgeous smiles." Turning, he strode down the hall.

Give one of my gorgeous smiles? She hadn't smiled once at the man. Debbie heard the front door shut behind him and turned to Cressie. "Is he always like that?"

Cressie picked up the empty cups and set them on the counter. "Dr. Keith has a way about him. But then most successful people do. Don't you agree?"

"I suppose so," Debbie said hesitantly. He wasn't like anybody she'd ever met, successful or otherwise. Although in a way he reminded her of Charles. Her ex-husband had stolen her heart at first glance, but she was older now and definitely wiser in the ways of manipulating males. Yet maybe she was being unfair to Keith. He had seemed sincere in his concern, and he couldn't know she was avoiding men. Especially those who looked to be on the prowl. If it came up again, she'd set him straight.

Noticing the time on the kitchen clock, she asked, "Can we see the rest of the place now?"

Two hours later, after talking with Norma, Debbie cradled the receiver on the bedside table in her motel room. The real estate agent would pick her up in thirty minutes for dinner. Unfortunately, Norma's final promise to have Debbie in the Muller house immediately had unsettled her all over again.

As she relaxed against the back of the queen-size bed, her legs stretched out in front of her, Debbie had to wonder why Norma wasn't telling her everything. She'd mentioned the rumor of ghosts but had said nothing about possible problems with the neighbors. Or about having to deal with an eccentric housekeeper.

Debbie frowned and picked at the orange pattern on the bedspread, her uneasiness mounting as she recalled Cressie's last melodramatic words: "The spirits grow restless. You be careful. Right must prevail. Like Miss Sarah said: No matter what anyone wants, the past will win out."

Exasperated, Debbie slapped her hand down on the spread and shifted her gaze to the printed draperies covering the room's large window. All towns were riddled with intrigue, but in small towns the machinations of secrecy loomed larger. Perhaps because there was less to distract from them.

This same sort of vague innuendo had triggered her decision to resign from the private college in Vermont. The pitying looks and insincere smiles had irritated her, as had running into her ex-husband at college functions. Even reverting to her maiden name hadn't helped because too many people knew her. But the worst part of all was that life no longer seemed simple and straightforward, with exciting plans and hopes.

Norma had exhibited this same elusiveness in their dealings over the Muller house. Why would an apparently level-headed businesswoman resort to such tactics?

Debbie sighed with the futility of worrying about it all. "I need to tell you a few things before you sign the contract," Norma had said. "Since we might be neighbors, it would only be fair." Debbie could only guess at the woman's meaning.

Suddenly needing to hear a friendly voice, Debbie picked up the phone and punched in her mother's number in Houston.

"Hi, Mom, I think I've found a house."

Debbie related her initial futile search and then told her mother the good points about the Muller house. Distracted at first by her own enthusiasm, she finally noticed a huskiness that normally wasn't in her mother's voice.

"Mom, what's wrong? Have you been crying?"

"Oh, Debbie, I don't know what I'm going to do about Scottie. He was out all night again last night. I was worried sick."

Debbie closed her eyes, hoping to hide from the guilt created by the unspoken accusation. She knew her widowed mother worried constantly about her teenage brother. Since fifteen he had been more than a handful. Because Debbie thought Charles might be a steadying influence on Scottie, the boy was supposed to have spent the summer with them in Vermont. Then came the divorce last spring, which effectively canceled the trip. At sixteen Scottie was almost out of his mother's control.

"Have you tried getting him to a counselor?" Debbie asked.

"He won't go. It's those terrible boys he's running around with. I don't know what he's going to pull next, but there's always something. And each time it's worse."

"You can't blame other people for Scottie's weaknesses. You need to find the root of the problem."

"It's peer pressure. What else? He has a good home here, I work myself silly trying to give him everything, and all he does is run around and party, staying out till all hours."

"Have you thought of making Scottie go to work to earn his own spending money? Then he wouldn't have time for those friends."

"Oh, Debbie, he's so good in sports. I'm hoping he'll get a football scholarship. He can't work and play ball, too, and I can't afford to send him to college like we did with you when your father was alive."

More guilt. Debbie knew her mother didn't intend to throw a guilt trip on her, but the fact was that twelve years ago, when she was Scottie's age, money had not been a problem. Now it was, and the knowledge hung around Debbie's shoulders like a heavy mantle. "Why won't you accept my offer to help out so you won't have to work so hard?"

"No, that's not fair to you."

"I'd rather do that than worry about you and Scottie. What if you got sick? What would happen to him then?"

"Well, it's not my health I'm worrying about. Besides, I have insurance. I only wish there was some way to make Scottie see how he's throwing his life away."

"Scottie's young, Mother. A few wild escapades is normal. He's got good stuff in him; he'll come around. But if you'd like, I'll talk to him the next time I'm down."

"That'll be fine, dear. I know you'll do whatever you can. Now, tell me more about Nacogdoches and the college. How did you find—"

Her mother's words were drowned out by a knock on the door. "Listen, Mom, the real estate agent's here now. I have to go. I'll talk with you later."

Again a twinge of guilt washed through her at the relief she felt when she hung up the phone. She wanted to help her younger brother, but how did you convince a six-foot-four, two-hundred-and-twenty-pound sixteen-year-old he didn't know everything?

Norma refused to discuss the sale until they'd finished their steaks and the waitress had poured coffee. Although eager to get down to business, Debbie enjoyed learning about the town's various specialty shops, the best cleaners and other juicy bits of knowledge that would make life easier once she settled into her new home.

Norma sipped her black coffee and finally said, "I understand you met Keith Douglas and Jenny Winthrope. What did you think of them?"

"You might say we got off to a boom." Seeing Norma's quizzical look, she explained about the horn honking incident.

"Keith didn't mention that when he called. He did say you asked directions, and later he talked with you and Cressie at the house. He pointed out how unsportsmanlike I would be if I didn't explain some of the neighborhood problems you might be facing if you buy the house."

Debbie grimaced. "That man really has a mania for interfering. You'd think after I almost dumped him from his horse, he'd want to stay as far away from me as possible."

Norma picked up her spoon and began turning it end upon end on the table. After a long silence she snapped down the silver utensil. "Dr. Keith Douglas carries a great deal of influence. People listen to him all over the country, and especially here in Nacogdoches. The college considers it quite a plum to have him on staff."

"Really? I had no idea he was so prestigious." College professors rarely achieved that much influence at such an early age; Keith could only be in his early thirties. Debbie wondered what she had missed.

"Keith feels very strongly about fair play. When he was in high school—he's from some town in Illinois— his parents were swindled out of a great deal of money by a pillar of the community. Keith's father has never been the same since."

"Well, I was beginning to think I had acquired a watchdog, and at the moment I'm not particularly high on men." Seeing Norma's suddenly raised brows, Debbie laughed. "Enough about Dr. Douglas. Right now all I want to discuss is how to buy the Muller house."

"Considering how you feel about men, I think I should warn you that he might not be so easy to slough off."

"Believe me, I have become very adept at getting rid of nuisances."

Norma chuckled. "I've heard a lot of women say many things about Keith, but this is the first time I've heard him called a nuisance." When Debbie didn't respond, she continued. "Don't be misled by his need to see fair play. He's a very ambitious man, and when it comes to something he wants, his tactics can be quite unsettling, even ruthless."

"I assume you're referring to females?"

"Women he can take or leave. No, I'm talking about his research for his books. Someone actually living in the Muller house, who might disclose goodness knows what, is like dangling a tempting fly over a hungry trout."

"Believe me when I say no man will ever make use of me again unless I want him to. Now, please, about the house."

Norma placed her elbows on either side of her cup and folded her hands so that she could rest her chin and look straight across at Debbie. "You saw the likeness of yourself in the picture of Miss Kate?"

Debbie nodded. "A matter of coincidence."

"Sarah was Kate's niece. Both lived to be quite old, and Sarah had her aunt's looks to some degree, but the resemblance between you and Kate is uncanny." After taking a deep breath, Norma went on. "You've met Cressie, and may have found her . . . uh . . . different. But Sarah was extremely eccentric. Not only was she herself convinced Miss Kate visited her on occasion, but Sarah also convinced everyone around. She said Kate wants to right a wrong from the past."

"What does that have to do with me? I told you I don't believe in ghosts."

Norma paused while the waitress refilled their cups. When they were once more alone, she said, "I don't know how you'll feel about it, but your similarity in appearance will certainly add fuel to the local tales. You should understand that ahead of time."

"That makes sense. Is this what Dr. Douglas wanted you to discuss with me?"

"Part of it. You see . . ." Norma's words trailed off as she looked toward the room's entrance, her eyes widening in response to what she saw. "Speak of the devil . . . there's Keith now, with Teresa."

"Who's she?" Debbie resisted turning to see the pair.

"Jenny's sister. Shush, they're coming this way."

Picturing Jenny's short brown hair and sad blue eyes, Debbie was almost speechless when she looked up at the couple stopping beside their table. Teresa had striking blue-black hair and violet eyes, and her clinging dress matched the ivory of her skin. Surprisingly, she was closer in age to Debbie's twenty-eight years than to Jenny's sixteen.

But it was Keith who took Debbie's breath away. He had been appealing in a virile, masculine sense that afternoon. Tonight he looked every inch the enterprising cosmopolitan. His charcoal suit fit to perfection, as only fine tailoring could accomplish. His white silk shirt provided a sharp background for the light gray tie patterned discreetly in red. A woman responding to such a man could find herself in deep trouble, Debbie mused. And she wasn't about to take the plunge, no matter how attractive he was. Charles had been good-looking, too, she reminded herself.

"Ladies," Keith greeted them pleasantly. "Enjoy your dinner?"

"Dr. Douglas," Debbie acknowledged.

"You know, continuing to address me as 'Doctor' might give me the impression you were trying to butter me up for some reason. Tell me, Ms. Dillon, what is it you want?"

Debbie couldn't think of an appropriate retort.

Reluctantly she had to admit he'd made his point.

Amusement still in his expression, he turned to Norma. "I assume you took care of that little matter we discussed?"

The realtor clenched her jaw briefly before replying, "Would I dare do otherwise?" Without giving Keith an opportunity to say more, she introduced Debbie to Teresa Wymans.

Teresa acknowledged the introduction with a half smile in Debbie's direction, then looked into Keith's face intently. "We're keeping the maître d' waiting, darling."

Annoyance flickered in Keith's eyes, then he shrugged. "If you'll excuse us, ladies . . ."

Teresa immediately tucked her arm through his, and the two walked off.

"Teresa Wymans?" Debbie asked, watching them cross the room. "Now I'm thoroughly confused. Jenny's last name is Winthrope, and Cressie mentioned the property to the south of the Muller land belongs to the Winthrope estate. Then she said Jenny's stepfather's name is Michael Townsend. Now you introduce Jenny's sister as Teresa Wymans."

Norma glanced at Keith and Teresa, who were seated at a table across the room. "Confusing, isn't it? Teresa still uses her married name, but she's in the process of getting a divorce. A truly ugly affair."

"And in the meantime she's passing her time with Keith?"

"At one time she was quite serious about him. That was when he used to visit his aunt and uncle here in the summers. She was in high school then. When Keith went back east to college, Teresa started dating and eventually married a boy she met at the college.

He took her back to Dallas, his hometown. His family's quite wealthy, actually, but I don't know if all that money helped Teresa find what she was looking for."

"And now both Teresa and Keith are back in Nacogdoches. I gather Keith's not married."

"No, nor do I think he's even considering it. Right now he's more involved with chasing down ghost tales and disproving them."

Glancing briefly across the room, Debbie found Keith looking at her. Embarrassed, she turned back to Norma. "A very enterprising man."

"Also an ambitious man. His classes are packed and have a long waiting list. He has written a book entitled *Fact and Fiction of Ghost Hunting.*"

Debbie's mouth dropped open before she gathered her wits. "He's *that* Keith Douglas?" When Norma nodded Debbie said, "That book made the best-seller list . . . for weeks. It's marvelous." Looking back at Keith, she could see amusement written all over his face and knew he must have heard her words. Then he winked.

Damn the man, Debbie cursed silently, and concentrated on Norma.

"He's been investigating houses in Galveston, Navasota, and other Texas towns while he teaches." Norma paused. "He's working on another book and has commented several times that the tales he heard years ago about Kate and the Muller house brought him back. Naturally, the college is delighted."

A waitress whisked by, trailing the odor of charcoaled meat. Debbie sipped her coffee. If Keith thought she would provide fodder for his publications, she would simply have to set him straight. He'd learn quickly. Relegating him to the back of her mind, she smiled at Norma. "So tell me. Is there anything else I should know before we sign the papers on the house?"

Relief flashed in Norma's brown eyes. She pulled a card from her purse and handed it to Debbie. "Here's the name of a banker who'll take care of the financial part. Since you plan to make a fair-size down payment, you shouldn't have any problem."

Debbie glanced at the card. "Should I see this Eleanor Farmsworth personally?"

"Yes. I talked with her this afternoon and mentioned you might be in. I'll meet you there, of course, in case there should be any last-minute problems. Eleanor said we could come in any time between nine and three tomorrow."

"Ten o'clock sounds good." Debbie tapped the card against her fingernail and thought back to the tea conversation in the Muller house. Before she signed any papers, she wanted to know one more thing. "I gather that I might expect some problem with the neighbors. Is it anything I should know about?"

"No, not really. Michael Townsend would like to purchase the Muller land. He wants to expand his horse facilities. I believe he plans to make you an offer later."

Debbie hesitated. She suspected there was far more to the story than Norma intended to tell. Could it have been Michael to whom Norma was talking on the phone? "Why didn't Michael Townsend either buy the place from Sarah herself or buy it from you after Sarah died?"

"Sarah Muller's will expressly forbids the sale of her property to anyone living in Nacogdoches at the time of her death. Her nephew took it to court, but the terms were airtight. That's another reason why you're able to buy at such a good price. He's glad to finally get his money."

"Why would Sarah do that?"

"During the last few years she didn't get along with her neighbors. Her eccentricities became more pronounced toward the end. She even isolated herself. Eventually she claimed the rightful heir should have the house."

Norma's pointed gaze raised goose bumps on Debbie's skin. After hearing about Sarah's claim, Norma's belief that Debbie's likeness to Kate's picture might cause comment became more understandable. "Why didn't Sarah get along with her neighbors?"

Norma shrugged. "She and Gloria Winthrope were good friends, but Sarah didn't think Michael was a particularly good husband or stepfather. Sarah was rather stubborn and opinionated. Once she made up her mind about something, you could stand on your head, and she wouldn't change her beliefs."

From the bitterness in Norma's voice, Debbie sensed Norma had crossed with Sarah herself. "What about the other neighbor?" she asked.

"Frank Johnson? He's a strange one, doesn't mix much. Surprisingly, he and Sarah got along okay . . . at least until the last few years Sarah was alive. She didn't want him to turn her land into a resort when she was gone, and didn't appreciate his persistence."

Debbie pressed her temples with her fingers. Confusion . . . nothing but confusion and cobwebs of local intrigue. "Why a resort?"

"You have a stream and a small lake at the back of your land that touches your property and his. Frank wants to take advantage of that."

"You know, the more I hear about this, the more surprised I am at the price. I know what we paid for a house in Vermont, and I know what my mother's house is worth in Houston. I'm getting a big house and a marvelous piece of land for about the same cost."

Norma reached across and patted Debbie's hand. "Don't question your luck. Just enjoy it."

"And the ghosts be damned," Debbie added cheerfully.

"Ghosts? I thought there was just Kate."

"Cressie mentioned another ghost today. She thinks it's Kate's father. He wants Kate to quit haunting. Cressie also said something about the devil's advocate bringing evil to the land."

Suddenly Norma was laughing, becoming almost hysterical before she pulled herself together.

Puzzled, Debbie asked, "I'm just repeating Cressie. Is anything wrong?"

"No, but I wouldn't mention those little gems to Eleanor tomorrow if I were you."

"The banker?"

Norma nodded. "She's not into ghosts, either, and she'd be more than happy to have your spooky housekeeper locked away if she could."

"Cressie is strange, but she seems harmless."

"You wouldn't say that if you'd been here six years ago when Eleanor's husband disappeared. Some suspected foul play at the time, but his body has never turned up, and no one has ever heard from him since."

"How terrible. But what does Cressie have to do with that?"

"At the time, Cressie was bandying about one of her wild predictions. She claimed that the sins of evil never vanished, but waited for revenge, and that the bad blood of our forebears always surfaced. Eleanor, of course, told Cressie to keep her disgusting mutterings to herself. From what you're saying, it sounds like she's at it again."

With her mind full of half-truths, unknowns, and suspicions, Debbie couldn't wait to get back to the motel. She'd given Norma a check for escrow and had signed the contract. Had she made a mistake? She could still change her mind.

Nacogdoches wasn't like any small college town she'd ever heard about. But then no town could be. There was so much intrigue and mystery here. Or maybe it just seemed that way, because she was hearing it all at once.

In the comfort of her own room, Debbie changed into her gown, knowing full well sleep would be impossible. She had just pulled the covers back when the bedside phone rang. The unexpected noise caused her heart to hammer in her breast. Her first thought was that her mother must be having more problems.

The stranger's voice on the other end was muffled. Debbie couldn't tell if it was a man or a woman.

"Are you the person thinking about buying the Muller residence?" the caller asked.

"Who's this?" she demanded.

"I suggest you think twice before you buy the Muller place. You might not live long enough to enjoy it."

Debbie's hand tightened around the black instrument, and a chill skittered down her spine. "Who is this?"

The dial tone hummed steadily in her ear.

3

After a restless night, Debbie drove to her ten o'clock appointment the next morning. Spotting the pitted red-brick building standing defiantly among the modern structures surrounding it, she realized the bank had probably seen sixty years of change. It oozed stability.

Norma's blue Chevrolet was already in the parking lot, so Debbie hastily locked her car and hurried off. She was at the entrance to the bank when a man bumped into her from behind.

"Sorry," he barked, his hand grabbing her arm to steady her.

When he didn't let go, Debbie said, "You seem to be in a great hurry. Don't let me keep you."

Thick, wavy blond and silver hair topped his weathered face, and a matching mustache adorned his upper lip. Sharp blue eyes scanned her before he spoke. "You must be the new young lady in town. You thinking of buying the Muller place?"

"That's right, but how on earth did you know?"

Debbie considered the great shoulders of the husky frame and the protruding stomach hanging over his jeans.

"The minute you hit town word spread that Kate's copy was here looking at houses. Hearing you was with Norma, I figured she'd show you the Muller place. Sarah said once that you'd be living there when you came. My name's Johnson. My property's to the north."

"I believe Cressie mentioned your name." Debbie wondered if she'd have to jerk her arm free. Then his words registered fully. "You did say Sarah told you? The dead Sarah Muller?"

"That's right. It's because of her I'm going to give you a little friendly advice. I'd think twice before considering living there. You have no idea what you'd be getting into."

"Cressie said Sarah told her about me."

"And I wouldn't let Norma or Elizabeth talk you into anything, either. You have to be careful around those two. They don't do anything for anyone unless they're going to get something out of it."

"Elizabeth? The banker?" Debbie had never felt so confused.

Without saying any more, he dropped her arm and hurried into the bank.

Watching the door close behind him, Debbie blinked. Several times. Although not as serious as the mysterious phone call, the warning he'd given her was explicit. Which made three in less than twenty-four hours. If she didn't know how ridiculous it sounded, she would call it a conspiracy. Maybe she shouldn't buy the Muller place. After all, she'd been through enough stress with the divorce. She'd hoped to find peace and quiet and a new beginning when she left Vermont.

And how could Sarah have known, two years ago, that she was coming here? At that time she'd been happily married. Probably Sarah had said something about "the next owner," and because Debbie bore a resemblance to Kate, everyone was jumping to conclusions. There was no other logical explanation.

Debbie's chin shot up with determination. She didn't know what was going on, but these people needed to realize she couldn't be pushed around. After talking with the banker, she might not buy the Muller house, but it would be her decision. Wherever she lived, these people needed to realize she was here to stay.

The clean, even lines of the marbled floor gleamed in the light inside the bank. Solid walnut desks dotted the central floor, and Mr. Johnson stood in front of one of the modern teller cages that lined one wall. A young lady smiled at him over the high marble counter.

The inside of the bank impressed Debbie even more than the outside. It conveyed a forward-thinking attitude usually linked with the large financial institutions of big cities, not the relaxed, cozy atmosphere associated with a small town.

From a nearby desk an attractive secretary looked up at Debbie's approach. When Debbie gave her name and explained her appointment, the secretary escorted her across a large open space and knocked on a stained-oak door bearing a gold-plated inscription: "Eleanor Farmsworth, President."

Debbie stepped from the marbled floor of the lobby to the thick gold carpet of the executive office.

The woman seated behind the polished mahogany desk conformed with her surroundings. Her navy blue designer suit added a needed touch of color and drew the attention of anyone entering.

After the secretary introduced Debbie, the woman behind the desk stood and extended her hand. "Good morning, Ms. Dillon. Please call me Eleanor."

Debbie hesitated, chilled by the banker's scrutinizing eyes, then crossed the carpet to shake hands. She nodded a greeting to Norma, who sat quietly on one of the visitor chairs.

"Did you have any trouble finding the bank?" Eleanor asked.

"None at all. Am I late?" The gold watch on her own left wrist pointed straight at ten o'clock.

"No, you're right on time."

The banker's small talk was clearly an attempt to remedy the first impression, but instead it solidified Debbie's discomfort.

With a furtive glance at the banker, Norma said, "I hope you don't mind, but I've already explained to Eleanor the financial information you gave me yesterday. I thought we'd finish quicker . . . and . . . it would make getting the loan easier for you."

At a temporary loss for words, Debbie made herself comfortable on the other visitor's chair and said simply, "Thank you."

"I've ordered us some coffee," Eleanor explained as the door opened again. "It always makes these matters more pleasant."

Debbie smiled noncommittally. Caffeine would only irritate her already nervous stomach.

The secretary set out blue-rimmed bone china cups and saucers. As she carefully poured coffee from the silver pot, Debbie compared the two businesswomen responsible for her being here.

At dinner the evening before, Norma had explained that although Eleanor was the older, both were from prominent Nacogdoches families and frequently attended the same social functions. Seeing the banker, with her graying dark hair, magnolia skin, and impeccable appearance, Debbie found it easy to believe that Eleanor dictated the social inclinations of the influential community the way she ruled her bank.

Norma, on the other hand, dressed in a crisp white suit and pink blouse, probably found time for fun and caused many a raised eyebrow. But the confidence the real estate agent had exuded yesterday now seemed forced. Johnson's description of the women echoed in her mind, though Debbie sensed he had his own agenda. He hadn't been able to hide the bitterness from his voice.

"We're delighted that you've decided to make Nacogdoches your home, Debbie," Eleanor said as she settled back in her large brown leather chair.

"Thank you," Debbie said simply. The whole affair bore a strong resemblance to friends' descriptions of their ordeal when sitting for orals in order to acquire their doctorates. No wonder she'd never been in a hurry to acquire that exalted title.

"Are you finding our small town to your liking?"

"Yes, and the people are quite friendly." God did forgive you for telling little white lies, Debbie told herself. "I think I'm going to like living here very much."

Eleanor looked briefly at Norma before continuing. "Are you certain you really want to buy a house so soon after your arrival?"

"No, but I like the Muller place."

"It's large, and it's stood vacant quite a while. You may find with time that our little town may not offer as much entertainment as you would like or your job may not meet your expectations. As I understand, you don't even know how long you'll stay here."

"To be truthful, I did plan to rent at first."

"That would seem wiser."

"Now wait a minute, Eleanor," Norma said, but fell silent at a glance from the banker.

"I assume you have the usual one-year contract at the college?" the banker stressed, once more concentrating on Debbie.

"Yes, but with a six-year tenure available."

"And what happens should you decide you don't like Nacogdoches or the college before that time? How will you support yourself and meet your financial obligations if you took out a loan?"

"I intend to make certain I like both. I've always thought that how well you succeed depends on the attitude you start with and whether you maintain a positive approach." Debbie settled back more comfortably. She liked teaching and had left her previous position by her own choice only because of the divorce. There should be no such problems here.

"I understand . . ." Eleanor glanced briefly at her manicured nails. "I understand that you remained at your last college position for only five years."

"My decision to leave Vermont has nothing to do with my ability to buy a house in Nacogdoches. I thought the purpose of this meeting was to arrange a loan."

Eleanor's eyes flashed with anger before she lowered her lids. In order to regain her composure, Debbie counted silently to ten. She was letting her own resentment of Eleanor's questions expose her bitterness from previous prying friends, and this wouldn't do, not when she wanted to borrow money. "I'm sorry. My leaving Vermont is still a bit painful, but I'm trying to put the divorce behind me. I think the down payment I'm willing to make should provide ample protection for the bank, should it agree to lend me the balance. At least that's what Norma thought."

Color stained Eleanor's cheeks. "I wasn't pressing to be rude or to bombard you with obstacles. I was speaking out of concern for your welfare."

Debbie didn't believe her. Maybe it was because the woman made her nervous; maybe it was because Norma appeared under such a strain and had shifted on her chair; or maybe it was because others had already suggested she shouldn't buy the house. Whatever the reason, Debbie didn't believe Eleanor's expression of concern. She said, "We did see the available rentals. None of them met my needs."

"Perhaps you didn't see all of them." Leaning forward in a confidential manner, Eleanor said, "I'm certain that I could put a nice house at your disposal. It's one you could lease until you feel certain you intend to stay."

"I understood Mrs. Peters showed me everything available." Debbie looked at the shut face and tight lips of a very angry Norma, but the real estate agent remained quiet.

Eleanor placed her elbows on the solid arms of the chair. She folded her hands so that her two index fingers touched and, as one solid cudgel, tapped against the edge of her desk. "I personally might have something you would find suitable."

"I'm afraid I don't understand."

"There's nothing complicated about it. I own a house that probably would fill your needs. I'm willing to let you rent it until you find whether or not you want to remain here."

"If the house is empty, why didn't Norma mention it or show it to me?"

"I doubt that she knew about it."

Eleanor's softly spoken words seemed false, as though for reasons of her own she was bypassing Norma and cutting her out of a possible sale. Norma's flushed, angry face seemed to agree.

"Doesn't the bank want to finance my purchase of the Muller place?" Debbie asked.

"If you have the down payment Norma mentioned, and if you have good credit, the bank would be more than happy to make you a loan. It's just that once you buy the house, should you not be happy living there, you might not be able to find someone else to take it off your hands."

"But I've already explained—"

"Then you could find yourself in a financial bind which could not only be devastating to you, but might affect the bank. I do have to consider these matters, you understand."

Norma sat quietly, her hands clenched around her purse. Eleanor sipped her coffee and waited.

The decision was Debbie's—to buy or to lease. And without ever seeing the house Eleanor offered, Debbie accepted its suitability. Despite Johnson's warning, Eleanor inspired that much confidence. Frustrated at the turn of events, Debbie pushed back a strand of hair.

Crossroads had dominated her life the last year.

She could have turned her head to her husband's infidelity and suffered a silent pain in return for a known financial security—or kicked him out and gotten a divorce. The latter meant an upheaval, an obscure future, possibly alone, and the certainty of innumerable repercussions from the academic world.

Once she filed for divorce, she faced a second decision: whether to stay in familiar surroundings with a job she enjoyed, but with friends she and Charles shared, and watch her ex-husband with the woman he had replaced her with, or to move to a new beginning, in a new area—maybe closer to her mother and brother.

Then she'd had to choose between standing on her own two feet and making her own decisions, moving alone to Nacogdoches, or bringing her brother for companionship and support, and giving him the break he wanted from their mother. Coming alone meant that she had to break her promise to Scottie that he could spend the summer with her. But she'd felt the need for this necessary time by herself to regroup, so Scottie had stayed in Houston, and her mother now suffered the consequences of Scottie's reaction. Still, Scottie was not Debbie's child to raise, only a younger brother who pulled at her heartstrings.

Now, again, she must choose her future, and Eleanor Farmsworth was presenting her with a viable alternative. But why? She didn't know Debbie; she didn't owe her any favors. The only thing that made sense was that Eleanor's offer must be connected to Norma in some way, and Debbie didn't like the idea that she might get caught in the middle.

She thought of the warnings, the frightening

phone call, and knew that the safest choice would be to rent from Eleanor.

Then she considered the Muller house, the sense of welcoming, of coming home.

Drawing a deep breath and praying her decision was right, she said, "Thank you. I appreciate your offer, but I believe I'll buy the Muller property as planned."

"You're certain?"

Debbie nodded.

"And Norma has warned you about the rumors of ghosts? While ridiculous, the talk has still prevented the sale of the house these last two years."

"Yes, Norma told me and so have Jenny Winthrope, Keith Douglas, and Cressie. But you see, Mrs. Farmsworth, I don't believe in ghosts, and I'm not afraid of the supernatural."

"I see."

Recalling the phone call and Mr. Johnson's words in front of the bank, Debbie added, "The only thing that might make me hesitate would be if the established families of Nacogdoches didn't welcome me for some reason. Small towns, particularly college towns, can be quite brutal if the people get down on someone. I shouldn't want that to happen to me."

Eleanor's raised brows acknowledged the gauntlet Debbie had subtly tossed her way. If the banker, in both her official capacity and as a social leader, intended to make Debbie's life miserable should she buy the property, she wanted to know up-front.

After a long silence, Eleanor smiled. "Well, you seem to be a young woman who knows her mind and isn't afraid to speak it. Shall we get on with the business of the loan?"

Emitting a long sigh, Norma jumped up and grabbed Debbie's hand. "You won't regret your decision, and we certainly won't let you feel uncomfortable moving into our town. After you ship your things and settle into your house, I'll give you a get-acquainted party. You can meet your neighbors. Once you make new friends, you'll feel quite at home."

"Oh, Norma, you don't have to do that," Debbie exclaimed, while feeling a warm rush of relief at the offer.

"Why not? Besides, it's time we had a party again. We haven't had a neighborhood get-together in . . . six years . . . hasn't it been, Eleanor?"

The other woman nodded in tight-lipped agreement.

"And what better occasion to start once more, than one to welcome you," Norma gushed.

The last party must have been before the disappearance of Eleanor's husband, Herman. Debbie replied sincerely, "That's nice of you, Norma. I think a party would be fun."

"You'll come, Eleanor?" Norma pressed, clearly striking back at the banker for her own earlier treatment.

A strained pause followed. "Yes," Eleanor agreed. "That would be lovely. I shall look forward to it."

"I didn't realize you would be a neighbor also," Debbie commented thoughtfully. "How far do you live from the Muller place?"

"My house is about a mile past there."

"I didn't know," Debbie said, surprised. Considering that she was a complete stranger in town and had only seen the house for the first time the day before, it seemed that she had already met many of the people who lived on the same road.

"Where do you live, Norma?" Debbie asked impulsively.

"On the other side of the Johnson property."

"And Dr. Douglas?"

"Keith rents one of the small houses I have on my land," the banker inserted smoothly.

The lease house was probably another of the same small houses. Curious, Debbie said, "I somehow thought Dr. Douglas lived in one of the apartments or with relatives here."

Eleanor smiled wryly. "I gather Norma has been filling you in on our most sought-after eligible bachelor. Well, he rents from me because he wants the peace and quiet to write. You can't do that surrounded by people, particularly if you already carry a certain amount of notoriety."

Opening the file that sat on the corner of her desk and momentarily ruffling the papers, the banker said, "You do realize I had your best interests in mind when I offered to lease you a house? But I shall look forward to having you as a neighbor with as much pleasure as I'm sure I would have had with you as a tenant."

Eleanor's words sounded sincere, yet . . . Debbie smiled as she took the papers the banker handed her, unable to shake the sense of falseness she felt with Eleanor. After reading the papers, she picked up the pen. This was her last chance. Once she signed, she was committed. She couldn't ignore that she had been threatened, but not by any ghost. Almost as an act of defiance, she slashed her signature across the bottom of the paper.

❀   ❀   ❀

Debbie climbed down from the ladder and inspected her work. She had been scrubbing and scraping the outside of the house since the day after she'd moved in two weeks ago. Every muscle in her body ached, but the results of her backbreaking work were beginning to show.

A carpenter had mended loose boards and replaced the broken windows. A roofer had inspected and tarred the area that leaked over the back porch. Now all that remained was applying the white paint, and Debbie had started that today. She herself wanted the pleasure of completing the face-lifting job on her new home.

Her heart swelled with the pride of ownership when she looked up at the two-and-a-half-story structure, the strength of the building lines, the workmanship of the gingerbread along the top of the wide front porch, and the gleaming white of the freshly painted pillar she had just finished.

She turned and studied the lawn, now trimmed and edged, its green texture reaching down to the trees near the road. Cressie's husband, Sal, had managed to complete a miracle in the two days he had worked. Yesterday before he left, he'd mentioned he would be starting on the flowers and shrubs next, readying them for the winter ahead. Looking around at the scraggly shrubs and the wild growth of flowers and weeds intertwined with vines, Debbie envisioned next spring's colorful landscape. She still wasn't certain what changes she wanted to make, she just knew she had to make them and that she would have to let Sal know next week. Anything would be an improvement.

At first she'd protested when Sal and Cressie had simply arrived and proceeded about their work. She wasn't certain she could afford their help, even with Sal working only once a week and Cressie two days. Now she had given up, knowing she would manage some way.

The Slavanias had given her little choice. Their families had worked for the owners of the house for more than a hundred and fifty years, and their loyalties went undisputed. They made that quite plain. Yet sometimes their quiet, studied looks made her uneasy. And when Cressie would mutter, "Kate's up to something," it was all Debbie could do not to scream.

Despite Cressie's predictions and all the rumors about ghosts, Debbie had seen no signs of Kate or her father, unless she considered the eerie feeling of being watched that came over her or the unexplained drafts. The former she chalked up to her imagination due to all the talk. And as far as the drafts, everyone knew old houses were famous for them.

The worst part of moving in had occurred the first several days. Debbie woke constantly during the night, waiting for the caller to act on his threat.

Strangely, it had been Cressie who had brought reassurance. Noticing the circles under Debbie's eyes and hearing about the phone call, Cressie had said, "Now don't you fret. Nothin's going to happen to you, not with Miss Kate around. It was probably someone's idea of a joke, but I'll ask around. It won't happen again, I promise you."

And whether Cressie's interference had stopped the caller, whether it was truly only a bad joke or he was simply waiting for the passage of time, life had been extremely peaceful. Looking around now at her domain, Debbie sighed with contentment.

It was funny, though, how the past could reach out and affect people in the present. Charles and her life in Vermont were ended, part of her past; but the arrival tomorrow of her personal belongings, together with the furniture she had chosen to keep, would bring memories associated with each. Part of her past remained as part of her future.

Debbie looked up once more at the Muller house and felt the same sense of belonging. The Slavanias made this new beginning more of a challenge. Lifting her face to feel the warmth of the bright sun and the touch of the light breeze, she brushed back a stray wisp of hair and smiled.

After rubbing the small of her back, she lifted down the bucket of paint from the shelf and moved the large metal ladder halfway to the next pillar. Once she was certain it sat firmly in place, she took the paint and brush and climbed up to continue whitening the ornate fascia across the front.

The sound of an approaching car broke her concentration, but she didn't look away from the curlicue she was painting. Hoping to finish this particular section before greeting her visitor, she ignored the slamming of a car door and continued painting toward the next ornament.

"Don't tell me you plan to paint the house yourself?"

Keith's implied criticism reminded her of Charles, and the bitterness momentarily stayed Debbie's brush. Despite the angry buzzes in her stomach, she resumed painting and even managed to reply calmly, "Why not? I'm capable."

"Why not? Because this isn't your normal vein of expertise."

"That doesn't mean I'm not capable of painting my house."

After a momentary silence Keith asked, "Have you considered the odds of falling and possibly breaking your neck?"

"No."

"What about when you're at the top of this monstrosity? That's a long way up there, and there aren't even many men who would take on the job."

Instinctively Debbie ground her teeth. She straightened and painted with the steady concentration of a gambler in front of a slot machine. "It's my house. It's my neck."

"It may be your neck, but it will still be some innocent bystander who'll have to call an ambulance to take you to the hospital."

Debbie glared down at the stern upturned face. With his hands resting on his denim-clad hips, the red-and-gray-striped knit shirt stretched across his broad chest, and his feet spread in a wide stance, Keith reminded her of a pompous dictator. He wore the smug confidence of an egotistical male who knew all the answers. He obviously didn't give a mere female credit for any intelligence.

Although eight feet separated them, she wanted to lash back. That taunting scarred dimple in his chin begged to be filled with paint. It would take only a single thrust of her brush. She clenched her hand to keep from taking action. Her brain worked frantically while she reminded herself that a mature, adult woman should not, must not, respond with the same basic outrage as a child.

As she twisted on the ladder, the metal legs suddenly rocked. Keith's mocking taunt still ringing in her ears, Debbie grabbed the fascia with one hand and reached for the top of the ladder with the other. In the process her fist struck the bucket of paint. Feeling the jar of contact and hearing the thud of flesh against metal, she hung on determinedly and watched as the bucket tipped and followed the path of the white paint pouring from it.

"What the . . . !" The quiet of the beautiful afternoon was broken by the clanging of the paint can as it crashed to the ground.

Debbie closed her eyes. "Please, God. Please, no."

"Of all the damned fool stunts . . . !"

Debbie drew her elbows close against her body and hung on for dear life. Slowly she forced herself to look down. Paint gleamed on Keith's dark hair, whitened his face like a clown's, and dripped down his knit shirt to puddle on the ground. Two furious gunmetal-gray orbs peered back at her, reminding Debbie how David must have felt as he faced Goliath.

She cleared her throat. "Are you hurt?"

Keith wiped the paint from his mouth with an angry swipe. "If you're asking if I'm still standing and in one piece, then the answer is yes. If you're inquiring if I'm considering turning you over my knee and whaling the daylights out of your backside, then again the answer is yes."

Stunned, Debbie swallowed. Distantly she could hear a horse approaching. And although she prayed silently for rescue, she refused to back off from any man, not even a justifiably angry one. She began to descend the ladder.

When a scant foot separated them, Debbie halted, taking her time to study the paint damage from the ground all the way to the top of his dripping head. Slowly she took the rag from her back pocket and handed it to him. "I am sorry, I really didn't mean . . ."

As his glare threatened to peel the newly painted pillar, Jenny's voice chimed in like a hand from heaven.

"I saw you two and thought I'd come and see what's up."

As Jenny climbed down from her horse, Debbie said, "We've had a small accident here."

"I wouldn't call it so small," Keith growled, and began to wipe the paint from his face and hair.

"Maybe you'd better go inside and wash up," Debbie offered, doubting he would ever get all the paint out of his clothes. She winced as she again met Keith's glower.

Jenny giggled. "I think you'd better hose off out here first. Otherwise you might track paint inside the house." Her giggles grew louder until she was laughing so hard she had to hold her stomach.

"It's not funny, Jenny," Keith growled again.

"I've always wanted to do something like that," Jenny exclaimed, and again broke into laughter.

"I thought you liked me," Keith complained.

Jenny shook her head. "Not to you, Keith. I've wanted to do something like that to Michael. Golly, Debbie, whatever did Keith say to make you so angry?"

Debbie's lips began to twitch. "I didn't mean to. It was an accident . . . really." Deciding it might be best to calm a rapidly angering Keith, she suggested to Jenny, "Why don't you go inside and see if Cressie can give you some rags."

"Did you tell her about the party?" Jenny asked Keith, obviously stalling.

"No," he snapped. "There hasn't been time."

Jenny made a hasty retreat, her laughter filling the air behind her. And it was then that Debbie's control began to slip. Because Keith *did* look ridiculous. No way would anyone recognize him as a pompous authority on ghosts *or* women. Debbie chuckled.

No matter how hard she tried to contain the noise or keep from meeting Keith's eyes, her amusement grew. So did her laughter. Then she heard the low musical sound of a male chuckle. It grew louder as, finally, she looked up at Keith. "I truly am sorry. I didn't mean to do that," she said after she'd caught her breath.

Keith shook his head. "I know. I guess I did aggravate you a bit. I forget how independent some of you career-minded ladies are. You'll have to chalk up my outburst to inborn male protectiveness."

Her ex-husband would never have admitted even to partial responsibility for such an accident, and he certainly would never have been able to laugh at himself.

She met Keith halfway. "You see, I want to do something myself to give the house a new look. Cressie has kept the inside immaculate, and Sal is doing the landscaping."

Turning her gaze on the white wood, she followed the lines of the building. "I feel a sense of coming home here. Something I've never felt before." She looked back at Keith. "Painting the house is important to me, even if it's a bit dangerous."

"I'm not so certain now that it's as dangerous for you as for your visitors."

"True," Debbie agreed, enjoying the camaraderie developing between them. "But besides the danger of possibly injuring you, I'm also out a bucket of expensive paint. This sort of action is not exactly what you would call beneficial for anyone."

"I guess not," Keith said as he looked at the empty pail lying on its side in the grass. "Not to mention what the paint might do to your lawn."

"My word, Keith, what have you done to yourself?" Cressie demanded as she opened the front door and came down the porch steps. Jenny, wearing a wide grin, followed close behind.

Keith's eyes lit with mischief. "I simply came by to invite Debbie to a party at Norma's next Saturday. She wants to introduce Debbie to the neighborhood."

"But the paint," Cressie said, her hands on her hips.

"He made Debbie mad and she threw paint on him," Jenny interjected.

"I did not! It was an accident."

"Isn't that great, Cressie?" Jenny's voice bubbled with admiration. "Maybe I could help you paint, Debbie, and maybe we could invite Michael over. Then I could 'accidentally' drop some paint on him—"

"It was an accident. Do you hear me, Jenny? *An accident!*" Debbie protested, wondering how she could convince the girl it was true.

"You shouldn't say such things, Jenny," Cressie warned.

"Why not?" Jenny asked abruptly. "You know he did something to my mother. Maybe he even killed her. And he wants to get rid of me, too." Tears glistened in her eyes as she stared defiantly at the adults.

Shocked, Debbie could only look at the girl, uncertain what she meant. Debbie recalled Norma saying on the telephone that Gloria was dead. Later, Cressie had said she'd been missing for six years. Was

Michael responsible, as Jenny suspected, and Norma aware of it?

"I knew it," Cressie wailed. Then, waving her hands through the air in a surrendering motion, she exclaimed, "I knew it was bound to be."

"You knew what?" Debbie asked, mesmerized.

"It's a sign of things to come. You've set the evil forces loose. There'll be more blood to pay before the past is happy. You be careful, Miss Debbie, that it's not your blood that spills out over the land, like that paint."

4

Cressie's pronouncement hung over them in the still, hot air. Somewhere in the distance a dog howled, a lonely, desolate sound. Debbie looked down at the earth. The pool of once white paint had mingled with the red clay and reflected an image of Cressie's prophesy.

Blood. It looked like blood puddling on the ground. Debbie shivered.

"That's enough, Cressie," Keith said. "You're scaring the girls." After a moment his expression relaxed. "Although Jenny probably needs to be shaken up a bit so she'll stop making such wild statements."

"That's not fair, and you know it," Jenny wailed.

Cressie stiffened. "Well, you mark my words—"

"Come on, Keith," Debbie interrupted. "Let's wash you off with the hose at the side of the house. Then if we throw your clothes in the washer before the paint has a chance to set, maybe we can get most of it out."

"That's fine for my clothes, but what about my body?" He fell in behind Debbie as she led the way around the house.

"Your what?" Debbie picked up the spray nozzle attached to the end of the hose. With the silver metal pointed at Keith, she turned on the faucet. A gushing spout of water pummeled into his chest, and he staggered backward.

"Hey, watch that. Turn it down," he complained, and used his hands to ward off the attacking stream.

Jenny giggled.

Relieved that the tension had dissolved with the water that now poured from Keith's dripping form, Debbie asked the teenager, "You want to cool off, too?" Teasingly she turned the water in Jenny's direction.

"No thanks—at least not that way!" Jenny stepped out of danger and laughed.

Keith frowned. "Just you wait, young lady."

Jenny giggled again. Keith's teasing had turned the whole eerie episode into something light and fun. And he had acted that way for the specific purpose of helping Jenny over a bad spell. Feeling a chink form in the cold wall she'd built around herself, Debbie met Keith's glance. A silent exchange passed between them.

"Get a towel, Jenny," she instructed, "and tell Cressie to put the teakettle on."

As Jenny scampered away, Keith scrubbed the shoulders of his shirt with his large hand, his long fingers probing and pulling to wipe the paint away. "I see you're falling into country ways already," he said as Debbie twisted the nozzle to spread the force of the water.

"How's that?" She moved so that the water would reach his back.

"Hot tea in a time of crisis."

"Well, if you'd rather, I might find some wine. I'm afraid I don't have anything stronger."

"Tea's fine, but I'm sure if you asked, Cressie could come up with some homemade wine that would carry more impact than anything you could buy at the liquor store."

"Are you serious?"

"Really. Cressie's famous for her wine. She also knows a lot about herbs and what to do with them, how to make home remedies and such." He shrugged. "It sort of goes with her predictions."

"She's like no one I've ever known, that's for certain."

"Or ever will meet again." Keith took the hose and directed the water on his head while raking his fingers through his hair. The sparkling water turned the white paint to streaks that gradually allowed the natural color to break through.

Debbie caught a glimpse of what he would look like when his hair started to gray. He would be as handsome then as he was now. The image wasn't at all unpleasant.

A spray of the cool water sprinkled her arm, and she stepped back. "What did Jenny mean when she accused her stepfather of having something to do with her mother's disappearance? I know you said Gloria left for Dallas and has been missing for six years, but surely someone knows more than that?"

"You mean the local gossip mill hasn't filled you in on those juicy morsels?" Keith pointed the water to the ground and shook his head, flinging water everywhere.

Debbie stepped back farther. "I guess I've been

too busy with my house and shipping my belongings. Anyway, no one has mentioned the Townsends except Cressie and you that first day when I looked at the house."

"I thought certainly Norma would have told you since she and Michael have become quite a two-some."

There was probably a great deal no one had mentioned to her about her neighbors. "No. She hasn't said anything. Mainly we discussed the sale, and I haven't seen her since I signed the papers. I wonder why Cressie never said anything."

Keith turned off the hose. "I imagine she knew you would learn more than you wanted to soon enough." His lips eased into a lopsided smile. "Besides, she probably didn't want to spoil your pleasure with your new toy."

"My new toy?"

He pointed at the house.

"Keith Douglas, I'll have you know this house is no toy!"

Reaching over to tap the end of her nose with his forefinger, Keith nodded. "My previous point exactly. This huge house is not a toy and not something you should be trying to paint by yourself."

Exasperated, Debbie cupped her hands on her hips. "I've already explained my views." When he continued to study her, she admitted reluctantly, "Besides, I can't afford a painter right now, and I don't want to wait."

Jenny walked up in time to hear Debbie's comment and said, "I'll be glad to help." She handed Keith a large blue towel. "That'll give me something to do after school and on weekends."

"I thought you were in the drill squad and practiced after school," Keith said through the folds of cloth covering his face while he dried himself.

"Well, that's not much fun." Looking over at Keith guiltily, she added, "I've been going. I've tried, just like I promised, but the girls aren't very friendly."

"Jenny, we've already had this discussion. You can't sit at home and mope about the past or what might have been. You need to make friends, get out and do things. You've known some of your classmates for years. They're not strangers. If you give them half a chance, they'll be friendly again."

"No, they won't. They look at me funny. They know my mother's gone, and they think I'm to blame. You just don't understand." Jenny's face crumpled as tears started slipping down her cheeks.

"Jenny, dear, surely no one blames you." Debbie brushed the hair back from the teenager's face, wishing there were more she could do to help.

"Yes, they do. You don't believe me because you haven't been here and seen how everybody acts. Keith only accepts what Michael and Teresa tell him. No one understands. It's terrible. I'm so alone," Jenny cried.

Her whole body shook with sobs, but when Debbie reached to hold her, Jenny pushed her away.

"No one really cares. I'm just in everyone's way. Only Nacho loves me." Jenny fled back around the house toward her beloved horse.

"Jenny!" Debbie called. "Jenny, come back here. Let's talk about this. I'll listen. I'll believe you. I promise." When only the pounding of racing hooves sounded in reply, she looked at Keith. She wanted him to explain. After all, despite her recent accusation, Jenny did seem to consider him her friend.

"She's taken her mother's disappearance hard," Keith replied. "It's not unusual in a divorce or even when one parent dies, for a child to feel responsible in some way and even rejected. Apparently Gloria kissed Jenny before she left, promised not to be long, and walked out of her life. Jenny's torn between the hurt of loss and the still nagging hope she'll come back. She's afraid she's done something to keep Gloria away."

The creases in his forehead and the lines beside his mouth denied the casual tone of his explanation.

"Hasn't there been any clue as to what happened? Surely the police must have theories."

"They can't even prove she ever arrived in Dallas. By now everyone assumes foul play, but since no body has been found, that's still up in the air. All anyone knows is what Jenny repeated and that Gloria drew a large sum of cash from her bank the last morning anyone here saw her."

"Jenny's been like this for six years? And no one has provided her with any professional counseling?"

Keith raised his hands in surrender. "I do the best I can as a family friend, but I've only been here since the beginning of summer. Jenny has refused to talk with anyone else, and Michael doesn't want to force her. He believes that would only build more resentment toward him."

"She talks to me."

"I think that's because you weren't here when Gloria disappeared and, ironically, your resemblance to Kate doesn't hurt. It seems to appeal to her imagination."

"And of course her talking has nothing to do with the simple fact that she may plain like me."

"Touché," he conceded.

"Are you qualified to counsel or simply doing your best?"

Keith shrugged. "I've earned a doctorate in psychology, but have never practiced. I prefer teaching and using the training for my books."

"So since her mother walked out six years ago and until this summer when you came along, Jenny has had no support? No wonder she has problems and seems immature for her age."

"She does act several years younger than she is, almost as though she hates to give up being Mommy's little girl. The best thing that could happen to her at this stage is to start mixing with people her own age and getting interested in clothes and boys, or whatever else high school girls dwell on. Maybe then she'll talk and let some of this out. It's going to take that for her to go forward with her life."

Debbie sighed. "Let's get you inside and see what we can find for you to put on while we wash and dry your clothes. Then you can tell me more about Jenny's mother over a cup of Cressie's tea."

Keith scowled. "Do you realize you're changing my whole approach to life?"

"How's that?"

"I'm not used to sitting around, gossiping with the girls and drinking tea." Looking down at her as he opened the back door, he added, "Although this time it might be fun."

Some of the guilt she had retained from Jenny's painful flight slipped away. Keith was right: an outsider could do only so much to help.

"Then why are you idling away your time so frivolously? You should be home at work," she challenged. She recalled Norma's warning that Keith would want firsthand information about the ghosts supposedly haunting the house. Was this his initial maneuver? she wondered.

"Why do you think?" he asked.

Since she didn't know what to think about anything at the moment, she raised and lowered her eyebrows in a poor imitation of Groucho Marx and out of the corner of her mouth said, "You want a little gossip? You want a nice cup of tea? Then strip, boy. The machine's in the utility room behind you."

"Now wait a minute," Keith protested when she started to walk away. "Lady, this is East Texas. Here, you never call a man a boy."

Debbie looked back over her shoulder. "Chauvinist."

"You can keep that wall in place by teasing me and calling me whatever, but never, ever, assume I'm anything less than a man."

She stopped then, seeing his expectant stance, but refused to comment. Instead she said, "I'll find you a blanket so you can play big chief and spread words of knowledge to your lowly captive audience. That's Cressie and me."

"Well, Cressie appreciates me whether you do or not."

Laughing softly at his disgruntled expression and seeing Cressie already preparing tea, she hurried through the kitchen.

At the entrance to the back parlor, she paused. What was she doing? Hadn't she learned anything from Charles? He too possessed charm galore, and look what a fool she'd made of herself. Picturing Keith standing in the laundry room, lifting his shirt over his head, she knew he could cause any woman trouble if she let him. No, she didn't need any more of that kind of pain. Not from anyone.

He had been nice over the paint episode, especially since his clothes were ruined. She couldn't be rude or nasty. She'd treat him the same as any other neighbor, but she would keep him in his place.

Her decision made, she opened the door to the back parlor. As she reached for the brightly patterned afghan on the back of the sofa, a cold draft sailed against her arms and face. Frowning, she looked around. The chilling air reeked with a pungent, musty odor. The afghan smelled worse. Suddenly a gust blew through the room and slammed the door shut. Debbie stood still, too astonished to move.

This can't be happening. I'm imagining this. She looked over her shoulder. The windows were closed. She was completely alone. The odor remained.

She drew a deep breath as she nonchalantly replaced the afghan on the sofa and walked over to open the door. She'd go upstairs and get a blanket from there.

Not wanting to explain to Cressie or Keith, Debbie slipped through the house, the strange events from the back parlor shadowing her steps. It had to be a figment of her imagination . . . maybe Cressie's earlier predictions influencing her mind. One thing for sure, she wasn't about to mention the episode to Cressie and get another sly smile.

She wouldn't mention it to Keith, either. He'd only laugh or start nosing into her affairs more than ever. He might want to spend time checking out the house. She couldn't think of anything she'd dislike more than to have him constantly underfoot. She'd prefer ghosts, if there were such things.

Debbie found a shockingly bright cotton quilt in the linen closet and grabbed a plastic bottle of shampoo from her own bathroom. She placed it beside a fresh towel in the large blue-and-silver bathroom near the back stairs.

There, she said to herself, looking to make sure he would have whatever he might need. That was the least she could do for a neighbor under the circumstances.

Turning, she carried the blanket down the stairs. Her breath caught when she opened the door from the kitchen to the utility room and saw Keith standing in nothing but a towel tied around his waist as his clothes swished in the washer. An odd-shaped brown mark beside his navel marred the perfection of the light tan that covered his chest and stomach.

Swallowing her discomfort, she handed him the blanket. "This should cover you. There's shampoo in the hall bath upstairs. If you need anything else, you can call down."

Keith's eyes narrowed at her crisp tone, but she didn't relent. She turned toward the kitchen.

Clutching the quilt around him with one hand, Keith stopped on the bottom step of the back stairs. He leaned against the flowered wallpaper and said, "I'm not quite sure what's happened, but I think it's important we clear the air about one point. Important for both of us."

Debbie grasped the back of a kitchen chair and looked over at him. "What's that?"

"You haven't acknowledged you consider me a man."

Warmth filled her cheeks as she recalled her joking instructions for the "boy" to strip. And from the silvery glint in his eyes, he was now a dangerous man, one not to tease unless you were willing to suffer the consequences. She wondered if he was teasing or if he somehow needed to hear her approval.

Debbie fought the attraction that seemed to pull her to him. But for some reason, he was demanding she face her feelings. She licked her dry lips. "You don't have to worry about that. I know what you are."

"Good." Keith nodded in satisfaction and turned to go up the stairs.

"What was that all about?" Cressie asked.

The thud of the teapot against the table jolted Debbie out of her reverie. She pulled out a chair and sat down gratefully. "Oh, you know how men are. They always have to prove their 'macho' image."

Cressie placed some lemon slices and a plate of cookies on the table. "Humph. I've never noticed that in Keith. He's always known his worth and at times even bent over backwards a mite toward lesser souls. No. He hasn't had to prove anythin'. Everyone just accepts he's a prime ring-tailed critter."

Debbie studied her folded hands.

"And I can guarantee there's not a female around who couldn't vouch for his masculine sex appeal."

"Even you, Cressie?"

"I may be gettin' on in years, but I'm not dead. Why, even Miss Sarah, when he was here a ways back, often claimed she might consider changin' her single status if she were a few years younger and if'n he showed an interest."

Debbie had her fill of discussing Keith's sex appeal. Pouring tea in her cup, she said, "Tell me about Jenny's mother and Michael Townsend."

"I figured that outburst of Jenny's would get you started." Cressie pursed her lips thoughtfully before continuing. "Young Gloria, as Miss Sarah used to call her, was a cheerful girl and full of mischief. Trouble daunted her footsteps, but she'd always laugh it off and wiggle her way out. She was a delightful child." Cressie paused, a half smile on her face. "She used to come over for Miss Sarah's hermits. My, how she loved those cookies. But even then Miss Sarah would shake her head and worry."

"Worry?" Debbie asked, intrigued.

Cressie nodded. "Miss Sarah said even then, when Gloria was a child, she would one day get herself into big trouble and laughter wouldn't get her out."

While nibbling on a cookie, Cressie seemed to drift back in time. Debbie pictured a young girl similar to Jenny, bouncing into the kitchen, munching on cookies and laughing as she tried to pick the tiny blue flowers from the wallpaper or peeking into one of the apothecary jars filled with wondrous-smelling herbs. "Didn't Miss Sarah ever warn her that she wouldn't always be able to joke her way out of mischief?" Debbie asked.

Cressie sniffed. "You can warn a body forever and tell 'em to be careful, but unless'n they've a mind to listen, you could just as easily save your breath."

The earlier warning Cressie had heralded on the front steps echoed silently in the room. Blood. Blood seeping into the ground like the white paint shaded red from the clay. Debbie sipped her tea, drawing comfort from the hot liquid. "So how did Teresa and Jenny come into the picture?"

"Gloria lived with her parents on the farm south of this land. They weren't poor, but they weren't rich, and the family had been in these parts almost as long as the Mullers. As soon as she graduated from high school—she was eighteen then—she went off to Dallas and met her a young man."

"Mr. Winthrope?" Debbie asked, reaching for a cookie.

"No, an Italian fellow . . . dark, good-lookin' he was, and he loved racin' them fast cars. Of course, Miss Gloria fell for him just like the rest of the girls did, but he married her. Then the trouble started. They followed the races, always movin', always aimin' for the big money. It wasn't long before Miss Teresa was born, and he had himself another woman. Didn't like kids . . . they got in his way."

Debbie studied the tea leaves in the bottom of her cup before refilling it. Teresa had inherited her outstanding dark looks from her father. That's why she and Jenny were so different. But what about her other traits? Was she more like him or her mother?

"So what did Gloria do then?"

Cressie shrugged. "What could she do? Gloria came home with her baby."

The shower turned off on the second floor, and Debbie looked up the stairway thoughtfully. Keith would be down shortly. But right now she was more interested in what Cressie had to say. "Then Teresa and Jenny are only half sisters?"

"Right," Cressie agreed, and brushed some crumbs from the table into her hand. She shed them in her saucer. "After the divorce Gloria stayed in these parts until she married the Winthrope boy. His family had a lot of money, and he loved horses. Somehow the young couple talked Gloria's folks into letting them use part of the land to raise and train horses. Then they bought more land." Cressie fell silent as she poured herself some tea.

"Sounds like things worked out for Gloria finally," Debbie said, urging Cressie to continue.

"True. There was no turnin' back for Gloria and her husband, Jim, at that point. It was like they found a gold mine; they were happy, and they had Jenny."

"And Gloria laughed with the good times?"

Cressie nodded. "Then one day they all planned to go to a horse race over in Louisiana, but Jenny took sick at the last minute and Gloria stayed home with her and Teresa. Gloria's parents and Jim were all killed in a wreck, along with the horse they were haulin' in the trailer."

Debbie picked up one of the cookies from the plate and nibbled the edge. "I don't see how Miss Sarah could blame Gloria for all of these tragedies. Maybe the early marriage and divorce, but certainly not the death of her family."

"Michael Townsend came to help with the horses and take care of the land. A year later he and Gloria married. Teresa was fifteen and Jenny three." Cressie ran her thumb along the saucer's edge. "We didn't see much of Gloria after that. We heard the stories, of course, of her busy life and shoppin' trips, but she didn't stop by to visit like she did before."

"Wasn't Miss Sarah happy everything was going so well for Gloria?"

Cressie looked up at the sound of footsteps above. "No, Miss Sarah could see the darkness. She worried, but whenever she tried to tell Gloria, whenever they met in town or such, Gloria just laughed. She didn't want to hear any more bad stuff. 'Negative thinkin',' she called it. Four years later Teresa married and left, and it almost seemed like Miss Sarah could be wrong . . . but I knew she weren't."

"And Jenny would have been seven or eight," Debbie added, and finished her cookie. "So what happened to Gloria then?"

"I see you didn't wait for me," Keith said from the foot of the stairs. The bright pink quilt was wrapped around him and draped over one shoulder.

"Cressie's filling me in on Gloria. I knew it would be old news to you."

"Come on, Mr. Keith. The tea's still hot, and I have some of your favorite cookies," Cressie said, pouring him a cup. She sat back and smiled when he grabbed three of the cookies and took a bite.

"Yes, please do help yourself," Debbie teased, amused by his eagerness.

"Mr. Keith likes my cookies." Cressie pushed the plate closer to him. "And I like a man who enjoys my cookin'."

"So what happened to Gloria after that?" Debbie prodded, more interested in Cressie's story than Keith's preferences.

"Rumors spread of fights between Gloria and Michael. They fought over the land, the horses, the money. Then, as though they'd reached an agreement, he stayed and ran things, and she started going on trips and shoppin' sprees."

Debbie frowned. "And I gather Jenny somehow got lost in the shuffle."

Cressie's lips tightened in disapproval, but she nodded. "Young Jenny used to come over here and have cookies with Miss Sarah, just like her mother did as a child. Miss Sarah would tell her to warn her mother to take care and mind what she was doing."

Debbie knew what Cressie left unsaid: no one listened.

"One day, Gloria left for Dallas to do some shoppin'. She never came home, and no one's heard from her since," Cressie finished.

"In reality," Keith said, joining in, "Jenny hasn't had her mother since she was ten. Now maybe you understand why she has some of these problems."

Debbie turned her gaze out the window. Leaves, small ones, big ones, orange, green, and yellow ones, skipped across the ground with the gentle breeze. It was September, high school had already begun, and she would start teaching at the college next week. Where had the summer gone? Where had Gloria gone? More important, how was Norma involved?

"Miss Sarah said Miss Gloria wouldn't be laughin' anymore," Cressie said quietly.

"Is there any truth to Jenny's statements concerning Michael?" Debbie asked Keith. "Could he be responsible for Gloria's disappearance?"

"Michael's a good guy. In his own way he cares about Jenny, but he understands horses. He claims to know nothing more about Gloria's whereabouts than the rest of us."

Cressie rose from the table and went into the utility room, where she began transferring Keith's clothes from the washer to the dryer.

"Did the paint come out?" Debbie asked when Cressie shut the door behind her.

"Mostly."

At Keith's mocking expression, Debbie raised her shoulders apologetically and said, "I guess I owe you some new clothes."

"Accidents happen."

"True, but I'll still replace your things."

"My, you do have a chip on your shoulder, don't you? Is it me, or are you distant with everyone?"

Debbie didn't like the challenge. She didn't have to explain herself, and she certainly didn't intend to tell Keith the gory details of her divorce. Taking a deep breath to calm herself, she responded, "Let's just say that I like to pay my own way. That way things aren't so apt to fly up and haunt me in the future."

Amusement glimmered in Keith's eyes. "You better not tell that to Kate. Cressie tells me she haunts here all the time." He whispered secretively, "She even talks to Cressie."

"Miss Debbie sure is the spittin' image of Miss Kate, isn't she, Mr. Keith?" Cressie asked.

At Cressie's words, Debbie felt a gentle stroking against her hair as though a hand brushed gently against the blond strands. She tensed and inhaled the sweet scent of jasmine floating around her. Her imagination was at work again. "A coincidence, I keep telling you. I've always heard people have doubles in the world. Mine happens to be from an earlier time."

"Well, if you encounter Miss Kate in person, let me know. Cressie keeps telling me the house is haunted, but so far I haven't found any signs of it." Keith squeezed the older woman's shoulder with affection, clearly attempting to soften his words. "Think how the discovery of actual ghosts would add to my new book and enlarge my education."

Cressie's eyes narrowed. "You just wait. You may be an authority on ghosts and the supernatural in other places, but you have a lot to learn about our ghosts in Nacogdoches."

Keith laughed. "Cressie, I would be delighted to meet your ghosts, anytime, anywhere. If you'll just tell me when."

Cressie stood and grabbed her cup and saucer. She

banged them against the kitchen counter. "Laugh all you want, Mr. Keith, but I'm thinkin' it'll be me who laughs last. The spirits are movin', and you best not get in their way." With that pronouncement Cressie picked up her purse. "I'll be goin' now."

Debbie struggled to keep the amusement from her face. "When will I see you again?"

"I'll be in Thursday, same as last week. Tuesdays, Thursdays, and addin' Saturdays now, what with you startin' teachin' next week." With a nod to both of them, Cressie walked out the door, her back straight.

"I think you upset her," Debbie said once she was certain Cressie was out of hearing.

"Don't tell me you believe all of this spiritual mumbo jumbo?"

Debbie shrugged, deliberately ignoring the strange events earlier in the kitchen and in the back parlor. There had to be an explanation. "I don't believe in ghosts, but Cressie is quite unusual."

"I know what you mean."

"How long have you known her?"

Leaning back on his chair and stretching his legs in front of him, Keith considered. "I first came to Nacogdoches when I was seventeen, before my senior year in high school. I met Cressie in the very beginning. She made quite an impression."

His eyebrows drew together in a frown as he idly turned his cup around on the table. "Teresa and I were swimming in the water hole. Cressie discovered us. Said she wouldn't have such 'goin's-on, 'specially on Miss Sarah's land.'"

Debbie pictured Cressie in all her indignity, looking at the young couple. Not much different, really, from her outraged stiffness a few moments ago when she walked out the back door. "What was wrong with your swimming on Muller land?"

"It wasn't our swimming on Muller land as much as that I was seventeen, Teresa was thirteen, and we didn't have many clothes on. I think Cressie was afraid of where the situation might lead."

Debbie couldn't keep from feeling somehow deflated at his words. "Four years might not be much now, but it's quite a difference at that age."

Keith seemed to read her mind. "Teresa acted way beyond her years even then," he said, "and since I had just met her, I didn't know she had lied about how old she was." Grinning sheepishly, he added, "We really were only swimming to cool off. I had no intention of doing something foolish. My future was planned, even back then."

"Norma mentioned Teresa, at one time, thought you and she might get married."

"Not likely. Maybe Teresa had some wild dreams, but we were both too young, and I had too much to do before considering settling down. Still do, for that matter."

"You haven't found anyone interesting enough, or are you simply against marriage?"

"Let's say so far I haven't met anyone I thought would be compatible with my goals or intriguing enough for me to consider a compromise."

He had handed her the perfect challenge, if she were interested enough in him. She wasn't. "You obviously made the right choice, considering your academic accomplishments . . . and your best-seller."

"Thank you."

Debbie refused to let Keith's smile intimidate her. "It's only the truth."

Finishing his tea, he asked, "What brings you here to Nacogdoches? Besides teaching at the college?"

"Teaching at the college is how I earn my living."

"But why choose Nacogdoches and Stephen F.?"

Picking up her empty cup, Debbie laughed. "Haven't you heard?" she asked, setting it on the counter beside Cressie's. "A beloved haunted house and a beguiling ghost. I'll check your clothes. They're probably dry, and I'm sure you have more important things to do today than sit and gossip over tea."

"Are you trying to get rid of me?"

Debbie glanced at Keith as he stood up with the bright quilt wrapped around him, a stubborn set to his chin. "I have to buy more paint before the store closes," she explained.

Keith shook his head. "I refuse to say another word."

Laughing, Debbie went out to the utility room and took his clothes from the dryer. They were warm and smelled of lemon fabric softener. Handing them to Keith, she asked, "Do you want to change out here or go upstairs?"

"I think it would be wiser if I went upstairs." After taking the clothes, he turned and climbed the steps. His feet made little sound against the oak flooring.

Debbie had washed and rinsed the dishes by the time he returned. "That didn't take long," she said.

"I didn't want to hold you up from your destiny at the paint store. After all, Miss Sarah's house needs a new gloss."

Debbie raised her hand. "Ms. Debbie's house."

"True," Keith agreed. "Speaking of which, I originally came by because Norma is having a get-acquainted barbecue at her house this Saturday in your honor. She said she would call you later herself, but I promised to stop and deliver the message. Besides, I wanted to make arrangements to pick you up."

"Won't you be bringing Teresa?"

Keith's expression cooled. "I make my own invitations, and I invited you to come with me. I thought you would find it much easier walking into a roomful of strangers with me to introduce you."

Color filled her face. He had certainly put her in her place, and having someone by her side to introduce her would be easier. "Thank you. I'd appreciate that."

Keith nodded and, walking to the doorway, said, "It's casual, and I'll pick you up about six-thirty. But we'll talk again before then."

"Oh?"

"I'll be over tomorrow to help you paint."

"But I'm sure you have other plans . . . your book . . . or whatever?"

"In small towns we help our neighbors, and I'll help with the second-floor painting and leave the first floor to you. That way I don't have to worry about you."

"I'm perfectly capable," she said slowly, ice dripping in her voice, "of painting the upstairs myself."

"Oh, I'm sure you are, but I'd rather be above you the next time you decide to spill the paint."

With a wave, he strolled out the door, whistling while he walked to his car.

Debbie was stunned. She didn't want or need his help painting. The work would get done faster with an extra pair of hands, but that meant he'd be around for several days. She'd have to be nice to him no matter how she felt. On top of that, he was a very attractive man, and that was the last thing she needed right now.

Big deal. She could handle Keith. He was merely a man.

5

"*You'd better get ready for* Norma's party now," Cressie called up from the foot of the ladder.

Debbie leaned back and looked at the gleaming white house. Sunlight sparkled on the windowpanes. Here and there colorful curtains peeked out and shared the inviting freshness. It had taken Keith's help the last three days, but only the back porch and the small portion she now worked on remained to be painted. She laughed with delight. She couldn't help it.

Wiping the perspiration from her face with the back of her hand, she called down, "Let me finish this last section. I'll be down in five minutes."

"See that you do. After all his work this week, you don't want to keep Mr. Keith waitin'," Cressie said.

Brush in hand, Debbie applied the thick white paint around the windowsill. From the corner of her eye she saw Cressie step back a few steps, hands on hips, and give the house a thorough scrutiny.

"It's lookin' good, almost like a new house. Miss Sarah would be pleased."

Miss Sarah indeed! Debbie glanced down, intending to remind Cressie who owned the property. Pride and admiration shone on Cressie's face. Her knot of hair had slipped as usual so that several strands blew about her face in the gentle breeze. Her flowered skirt brushed against her thin legs. Debbie shook her head, smiling.

"I should finish the painting tomorrow," Debbie said. "Then on Monday, not only will I begin my new job, but I can come home to a completely painted white house. A whole new beginning."

"You have a real feelin' for the place, don't you?"

"More than you can imagine."

"What you goin' to spend your time doin' next?"

Debbie looked at the fields of grass and the thick woods. "I'm going to explore my land, like I should have done in the first place."

She didn't explain that those first few days, nothing would have gotten her off in the woods alone. Not after that call at the motel. But now, since nothing further had happened, she'd come to believe the call was either a prank or Cressie's presence had frightened the caller from his threat.

"The house grabbed you and wouldn't let go," Cressie said, brushing at her skirt. "I knew when you came that would happen. You couldn't help yourself."

"Now, Cressie, there's no way you could have known such a thing. I was a complete stranger to you and these parts."

"I did know. Miss Kate told me it would happen."

Debbie opened her mouth to admonish Cressie, but the older woman spoke first.

"Besides, Miss Kate would be causin' problems if she weren't satisfied with the way things are goin'."

Debbie snapped her mouth closed. What was the use? Sometimes a person just had to accept another's idiosyncrasies.

"Sal's almost finished the flower beds on the other side. They'll be bloomin' somethin' fierce come spring. You goin' to plant anything on this side?" Cressie asked.

The dirt driveway wound from the paved street and split at the corner of the house, one branch ending at the front porch, the other continuing behind Debbie's ladder to disappear at the garage behind. "I want to get some gravel and have Sal level the drive before he does anything with the plants on this side. I'm tired of fighting the bumps and potholes every time I go in and out."

"That's a good idea. Once the rains come and winter starts to set in, it could be a problem." Cressie kicked at the rut near the back door. "I'll tell him so he can get the dirt and gravel delivered."

Debbie carefully applied paint to the final edge. She wasn't certain whether she sighed from the satisfaction at being almost finished with the painting or from frustration because the Slavanias continued to think she needed coddling. Deciding to take a stand, she called down, "I want to call around and get the best price."

"Sal'll know the proper place to buy. He won't let you get cheated, don't you worry about that. Wash up now. Mr. Keith'll be here in a little over an hour."

After climbing down the ladder, Debbie rinsed out the brush and closed up the paint can. She appreciated that Sal and Cressie had smoothed her entrance into the country community. It meant she could escape the wait-and-see attitude she had experienced in Vermont when she'd first married. But she wanted to run her own affairs, and somehow she would have to make the Slavanias understand.

A mouth-watering German chocolate cake sat on the kitchen table. "What's this for?" Debbie wiped her finger across some of the rich icing resting on the cake plate. After putting the creamy mixture in her mouth, she closed her eyes and rolled her tongue through the sweetness, savoring the taste. Cressie did know how to cook.

"Keep your hands off. That cake's for the party."

"Norma didn't tell me to bring anything." Debbie looked to see where she might scrape off another taste that wouldn't show.

"She knew I'd be sendin' my cake, and there wasn't any point in sayin' anythin' to you."

Debbie swirled another dab of the icing with her forefinger and stuck the mixture in her mouth. She looked back to see Cressie's twinkling blue eyes staring at her.

"Now you best run on up, Miss Debbie. You don't want to keep Mr. Keith waitin'."

The clock over the kitchen stove said five-fifteen. Cressie poured herself a cup of fresh coffee and sat down. Surprised, Debbie asked, "Isn't it about time for you to leave?"

"Sal's comin' over here this evening. We thought we'd watch your cable television since we don't have it. I didn't think you'd mind since you'd be goin' out."

"You know I don't mind, but—"

"I didn't think you would. Miss Sarah never did, either." Cressie sipped from her cup.

Miss Sarah again. If Cressie was ever to accept Debbie as the owner of this wonderful house, she would have to take a stronger stand. "As I said, it's fine this time, but in the future, please ask first. I might have some plans you don't know about."

Debbie's head jerked back suddenly as if someone had pulled her hair. She rubbed the back of her head in disbelief and, mad at herself for her wayward imagination, sped up the back stairs. Cressie couldn't make such things happen, and there were no such things as ghosts. It was the expression on Cressie's face, as if she wanted to discipline a mischievous child, plus her own reluctance to hurt Cressie's feelings, that made her head hurt.

The bedroom reeked of jasmine. She checked her cut-glass perfume bottle, sitting on her dresser. The lid felt tight, but memories floated back.

Not long after they were married and getting ready for an important faculty dinner, Charles had teased her about her love of the scent. He'd wrapped his arms around her and called her his southern belle.

Debbie set the bottle back on the dresser with a thump. At the end of their marriage, Charles had taunted her with the accusation that she had never grown up, had never accepted the world as it really was, had never accepted him. He'd blamed her immaturity for sending him elsewhere, saying his new love, even though younger than Debbie, favored a more sophisticated perfume.

Debbie walked across the hall to the yellow and white bedroom and looked out the side window. In the distance was a small stream weaving between trees and wild brush, but near the house she could see where Sal had worked so hard on the flower garden. The ground was a picture of turned earth, mulch, and trimmed plants. Yet he hadn't planted jasmine. It was only today that she had told him she wanted to plant some of the vines.

His face had blanked of all expression when she'd issued the instructions, but he'd only nodded and said, "I figured you would. Already talked with a friend about getting some."

After dropping the curtain back in place, Debbie hurried to turn on the bathwater. She added several drops of bath oil and watched the water begin to fill the tub. Probably all of her neighbors had heard about another similarity between Miss Kate and herself. They both enjoyed the fragrance of jasmine.

She removed her clothes and dropped them into the hamper before climbing into the tub to soak in the perfumed water. Small communities, she reflected, sighing deeply, were a fountain of shared information.

Still, that didn't explain why the scent of jasmine had been so strong in her bedroom. And it wasn't the first time she had come upon the aroma in the house. And not always just in her room.

There couldn't be any truth in all the rumors about Kate. There just couldn't. She shook her head and began to lather up. There really wasn't anything she could do but ignore the unexplained aroma.

A little over an hour later Debbie descended the wide front stairs. Letting her hand run down the scarred but polished wooden handrail, she imagined the delight of a young child sliding down gleefully to the entry below. The patterned red carpet on the staircase muffled the noise of her footsteps, but she could see thin places and carefully mended spots. It would be a shame to replace these relics that added so much character to the center of her house, but new carpet must be considered before long.

The doorbell rang as she reached the bottom. Glancing one final time at her flowered olive green skirt and matching cotton knit sweater, she hoped she had dressed properly for an East Texas informal barbecue. Impressions were important to any career, but particularly so in the academic field. People seemed to expect higher standards from teachers than from other professions.

Opening the door, she said, "Hi. You're right on time."

Keith, dressed in the now familiar plaid shirt, jeans, and boots, didn't at all resemble what she pictured as the normal college professor. His shirt, in shades of lavender and blue, accented his gray eyes and dark hair. The body-hugging jeans left little to the imagination. But then there was nothing typical about Keith. He was his own man. She had learned that while they'd painted the last few days.

"Don't forget the cake," Cressie said as she came up behind Debbie and handed her the carrier.

"Mmm, I can hardly wait," Keith commented, and looked longingly at the covered container. "I knew you wouldn't forget us."

Cressie smiled at his reaction before saying to Debbie, "Sal and I'll still be here when you get back, so don't you worry about a thing."

Debbie paused in the open doorway and counted slowly to ten. "There's no need for you to wait up for me. If you get tired and want to leave, simply lock the house."

"Miss Kate's been restless. There'll be a need for us to stay tonight," Cressie replied, and leaving a stunned pair watching her, she returned to the kitchen.

Debbie silently allowed Keith to help her into the passenger side of his Pathfinder. When he pulled onto the road, she asked, "What am I going to do about Cressie and Sal?"

After a quick glance in her direction, Keith turned his attention to his driving. "I think you should be thankful they care what happens to you. Believe me, their approval carries a lot of influence in this community."

"I know, and I appreciate what they do, but to invite themselves into my house to watch television and then tell me they'll wait up for me until I get home? I'm twenty-eight years old, Keith. I've been married and divorced. I'm not used to this. I don't like it, and yet I do care about them and don't want to hurt their feelings."

"You do have a problem," Keith said, accelerating around a pickup truck. "You might do what Miss Sarah did. When she was alive, they lived in the apartment over the garage. That kept them close in case of trouble but not under foot. It allows some privacy in case you want to do something you shouldn't." He winked at her meaningfully.

Debbie stared at him. "I didn't know the Slavanias used to live over the garage. Why didn't anyone tell me?"

"You didn't know about the apartment?"

Debbie's lips tightened at the disbelief in his voice. "Certainly I knew. Cressie took me through it the first day I saw the house."

"I didn't think you'd miss something so obvious before buying."

"Why is it men think they're so smart and women so naive? No matter what you may believe, I'm not a complete imbecile when it comes to business matters. I have done very well so far, even without your words of wisdom to guide me."

Keith shifted his hands on the steering wheel. "Cressie has strange ways that frighten some, and people tend to forget the Slavanias also have a great deal of pride."

"Why did they move out, then?"

"They had no choice when Miss Sarah died. Her nephew didn't like them or want them on the property. He thought they'd frighten away prospective buyers."

"They might have," Debbie agreed softly, remembering her own experience. "But I'm not sure Norma would have shown the house to just anybody, either."

Keith turned into a driveway partially filled with cars, the red-brick home typical of current building styles. She knew before entering that the house would contain three bedrooms, two baths, a living-dining area, and probably a den with a kitchen on the end. A large house for a single woman, but not particularly so for a family.

"It looks like some of the guests have already arrived," Keith commented as he helped Debbie from the car.

"How many are coming?"

"Norma said around twenty, but you've met most of them already."

The sun kissed the horizon, sending fingers of light up through the pines. Baby pink-and-mauve clouds mingled with the blue sky, and tantalizing smoke from the barbecue grille filled the air with a welcoming aroma. For the first time since Norma had mentioned having the get-acquainted party, Debbie looked forward to meeting her new neighbors. Maybe she was at last ready for the present, or maybe it was knowing that her own new home shone and glistened, ready to greet friends in return; whatever it was, she found herself anticipating the evening ahead. Keith tightened his grasp around her elbow and knocked on the door.

Norma, wearing deep pink slacks and a print blouse, greeted them warmly when she opened the door. Once Debbie had heard the story of Gloria, Norma's phone call that day in her office made more sense. Norma was not only a successful businesswoman and attractive to boot, she also owned property of her own and had an attachment with a man whose wife was presumed dead. Yet no one else spoke so authoritatively about Gloria. Debbie shook her head, banishing any unanswered questions from her mind for the evening.

Norma led them through a gray-and-pink living room that appeared to be a showplace for her business affairs. The soft nubby fabric and deeply cushioned sofa tempted with warmth and current fashion. The coffee and end tables picked up the natural wood of the trimmed soft pieces and added smooth flowing curves and a touch of glass. Plants of all sizes and shapes decorated the room, knickknacks of every description adorned the tables, and abstract paintings graced the walls. Furnishings told a lot about a person, and the room said Norma was modern, but with an undercurrent of clutter.

They passed through the imitation-leather-styled den and out a sliding glass door to the patio in back. Norma set the cake on a table already laden with bowls of different salads plus plates and silverware.

"Now let me see," Norma said, and looked around at the guests already present. Brightly colored candelabra lighted the edges of the cement patio and the settings of square tables.

Norma led Debbie to the nearest couple and introduced them. A few minutes later she took her over to another group. All three couples were in their forties, closer to Norma's age than Debbie's. All asked how she liked living in a haunted house and looked with disbelief when she stated firmly that there were no ghosts. Knowing this would be an impossible evening if it continued in this vein, she was relieved when Norma interrupted again.

"I'm going to drag the guest of honor away to meet Michael. You can talk more to Debbie later. Get yourselves another beer or more wine whenever you want. It's all in the kitchen."

Walking toward the man beside the two large barrel grilles, Debbie hid her surprise. Michael didn't look at all as she had imagined. Knowing he worked with and rode horses, she had pictured a small man dressed in the typical country garb of jeans and boots. Instead she faced a tall, slender man, almost aesthetic in appearance. He wore gray slacks and a black shirt that emphasized his dark good looks. Silver sprinkles distinguished his temples. Only his tanned skin laid claim to time spent working in the sun.

"I could use another pair of hands," Michael said, gesturing to the sizzling chicken, sausage, and hamburgers. To his side, smoke curled from a closed container and filled the air with the tantalizing odor of meat cooking over mesquite.

"Keith can help you," Norma said, tucking her arm through Michael's and drawing him close. "This is

Debbie Dillon, the lady who bought the Muller house."

Debbie smiled her greeting, observing that neither looked like a killer, merely two people who cared a great deal for each other. Still, Jenny claimed Michael had gotten rid of Gloria, and there was Norma's phone call.

Keith didn't seem to suffer any doubts, judging from his laughing interplay with Michael and Norma's enjoyment of the "hen-pecked male species" exchange. But then Keith had known both a long time and might not be objective.

Debbie looked around as two more couples bringing covered dishes came around the side of the house. When Norma went to meet them, Debbie asked Michael, "Are Jenny and Teresa coming?"

He frowned. "They should have been here by now, but Jenny sometimes tends to be difficult. Teresa may be having a problem."

"They'll be here, Debbie," Keith interjected. "Jenny likes you, and Teresa told me she was coming."

"Keith, why don't you come with me, and we'll find you and Debbie something to drink while she gets better acquainted with these people." Then, turning back to the four new people, Norma asked, "What can I get you?"

From that point on, Debbie lost track of time. After Keith handed her a beer, she lost him to Michael while they took turns over the grilles and visiting with the guests.

She waved at Eleanor when she arrived with a bowl of fruit salad but continued her conversation with the Nivers. She could talk with the banker later. Right now she was more interested in getting to know a couple nearer her own age. Besides, Carolyn Niver would also be teaching in the Business Department at the college.

Several more people arrived, including Mr. Johnson, the older man Debbie had met at the bank. Glancing at him from time to time, Debbie noticed that many of the guests appeared strained and a little ill at ease in his presence.

When he walked over and reminded her who he was, Debbie said, "I was surprised to see you here, especially after telling me what you did about Norma and Eleanor."

"Norma wouldn't dare not invite me. I'm your neighbor, and this is in your honor. Besides, she knew if she didn't, I'd squawk and either damage the respectable reputation she likes to claim or crash the party, were I inclined."

Debbie didn't know how to reply, so she sipped her beer.

"What say we stroll over there a ways. I'd like to have a private conversation with you before everyone gets here." Debbie was curious enough to agree.

Stopping several feet from anyone, Frank said, "You didn't take my advice, I see."

"Did you really expect me to?"

"Females tend to be contrary creatures."

"Funny, I would say it was the male sex who tended to be."

The harsh lines in his face indicated the years hadn't been easy, and with his cowboy clothes and light-colored mustache he would have made an ideal tough guy in an old western. Yet when he smiled, Debbie felt they might end up friends.

"I understand you and Miss Sarah liked to share a

nip of homemade wine occasionally. Is that why you told me not to buy her house?"

He stared at her in amazement for a moment before his almost silent laugh shook his husky frame and jiggled his protruding stomach. "Don't tell me you have the power as well?"

Debbie leaned closer and whispered, "Actually Cressie told me."

"Yeah, well, Miss Sarah and me were about the only ones in the area without an ax to grind."

The remark startled her until, looking at the firm jawline, she decided Mr. Johnson could probably be a stubborn and difficult man when he chose. That might explain why some of the neighbors acted the way they did around him. "You never did tell me what she actually said about me."

"Only that I'd have to deal with the new owner after she was gone. She was tired of my buggin' her, and you were up to handling the situation."

"Then she didn't say anything about me specifically?"

"Only that I wouldn't mistake you when I saw you, and I didn't."

Cressie had come out with some of the same crazy statements. Debbie knew she was getting used to them when Frank's statement didn't shake her clear down to her sandals. "So what did you want to talk with me about?"

"I wanted you to know that if you are ever of the mind to sell your place, or even part of your land, I would like to have the first option to buy."

"Sell my property? Despite your advice, I bought it. I've spent several weeks fixing it up to live there. Why would I want to sell it?"

"You haven't had any problems with the ghosts?"

"Ghosts? Mr. Johnson, since I first arrived in Nacogdoches, all I've heard is stories about ghosts, particularly about Miss Kate haunting my house. I'll tell you what I've told everyone else: Besides not believing in such things, I've seen no sign of ghosts. No, I'm sorry, but I have no intention of selling."

"Well, if the ghosts don't scare you away, the neighbors soon will."

"I don't understand."

"Just remember my offer when you change your mind."

"Problems?" Norma asked, joining them.

"No, Mr. Johnson just made an offer for my place should I decide to sell."

Norma shot Frank a look of disgust before taking Debbie by the arm. "We're going to start eating, and I want you to lead the food line."

"What about Jenny? She hasn't arrived yet."

"Teresa and Jenny will have to catch up when and if they get here." While they walked toward the table, Norma added, "I invited Frank because he is your neighbor, and I thought you should meet him. To be truthful, I was surprised he accepted, but then I guess he couldn't miss the opportunity."

"Opportunity?" Debbie picked up a plate and silverware from the long table filled with food.

"To make an offer. He's been wanting that land for the last ten years. He wants to put in some type of resort."

Debbie looked back as Keith fell in behind her, listening to their conversation. Other couples quickly joined the line as Norma urged her forward along the table, insisting she try a little of everything to avoid hurting anyone's feelings.

Debbie stopped to take a slice of the brisket that had been cooking on mesquite. "Oh, you mentioned that Frank wanted to build a resort, and also something about that being one of the reasons why Miss Sarah put that unusual condition in her will about the property not being sold to anyone living in Nacogdoches at the time of her death."

"Yes, well, I'm not quite certain that's why she had her will written the way she did, but even so, she wouldn't sell to Frank. Since you live here now and have met everyone, you understand that such a wild scheme would just about ruin all our properties, particularly with Frank heading up the operation."

"Why is that?"

"Frank has a vicious temper, and things have been known to get broken or damaged when he loses it."

"Well, I'm quite happy with my place. I've no intention of selling, so don't worry," Debbie said, smiling up at Norma.

Casting a quick look at Keith, Norma appeared to consider for a moment before plunging ahead in a quiet voice. "If something should ever make you change your mind—not that I want such a thing, you understand—please give Michael an opportunity to talk with you."

"He wants to buy my land, too?"

"Come on, let's find a place to sit," Keith said firmly. "Now's no time to discuss business, particularly this nonsense. You're under contract to teach, and you're not leaving any time soon."

Keith's clipped tones and the look of admonishment he sent Norma created a strange tension in Debbie. She was used to college intrigue, but this was different.

Keith and Debbie found seats at one of the card tables. Norma remained where they had left her, chewing on her bottom lip. Then, suddenly, she turned to urge more food and drinks on her other guests, engaging in laughter at their responses.

The uneasiness stayed with Debbie while she ate. She wondered why she had ever agreed to this party. She'd had enough deviousness in her life already. Life was so much better when everything was simple and straightforward. Maybe it would be best to cut off relations with her neighbors after this party. Then, hearing a burst of laughter from another table, Debbie realized how ridiculous that sounded. She couldn't cut herself off from people because of her past experiences. She simply had to manage the problems as they came along.

Finally, when she couldn't eat another bite, she eyed her half-full plate ruefully and broke the companionable silence she and Keith had shared. "I think I took too much."

"It happens. Maybe I can help you out." He reached over and took the piece of chicken still sitting at the side of her plate. Somehow the intimacy of the action reminded her of when she was married. Yet Charles, having been a member of a wealthy New England family, would never have allowed himself such an ill-mannered act. She smiled at Keith, then grinned when his eyebrows shot up quizzically.

"What did I do to deserve one of your brilliant smiles?" he asked.

Not wanting to tell him the truth, she evaded his eyes and watched Norma and Michael finish filling their plates and walk toward them.

"I can't imagine what's happened to Teresa and

Jenny," Norma said, setting down her plate and looking around the dimly lit patio at the other guests.

"They'll be here," Keith said.

Debbie, avoiding eye contact with the others, turned her gaze to the rosebushes that wound around the cement patio. Occasional late blooms decorated the thorny branches, their sweet fragrance contrasting with the more pungent aroma of cooked food.

"Sit down and eat," Michael instructed. "If they changed their minds and haven't any better manners than to call, I don't want you to let them spoil the evening for you."

Norma sighed and sat. "I tried to call a few minutes ago, but no one answered."

"Forget them. Those two spoiled girls can't think beyond their own interests." Michael popped an olive in his mouth.

Keith started to speak, then bit into the piece of chicken instead.

Debbie wanted to wander out the center walkway to the bubbling fountain or beyond to the thick carpet of grass. She knew she would enjoy the peace of the night and the moonlit beauty of the maples and oaks reaching to touch the star-filled sky. "Your place is lovely," she ventured a few minutes later when no one else had said a word.

Norma surveyed the area. "Thank you. I do quite a bit of entertaining out here. It saves wear on the house, although I do use the den for our annual Christmas party."

For lack of something to do with her hands, Debbie picked up a piece of celery and took a bite. She wasn't hungry, but the others were still eating. A cricket began to chirp in the soft darkness, and

Debbie sighed, letting the tension flow away.

"Michael? Norma? Are you back here?"

Teresa stood at the back door. The delicate pastel of her tailored purple ensemble heightened the impression of indignant royalty. When she stepped outside, the porch light shone on her blue-black hair and highlighted her exquisite features and the angry flush of her cheeks. "Michael!"

Debbie's pulse quickened. She had known something was wrong, but she hadn't known what. The other guests must have sensed it, too, because suddenly everyone stopped talking.

Norma rushed forward. "Where have you been? We've been worried."

"I had to run Jenny by the hospital."

Michael rose instantly. "Is she hurt? What happened?"

At that instant Jenny appeared behind Teresa and pushed her big sister aside. The teenager's right cheek bore a bad scrape, her right eye was swollen nearly shut, and her left arm hung in a sling. She stood with one fist clenched, her jeans-clad legs spread, and her booted feet planted firmly on the concrete. Defiance screamed from every pore. Her gaze fixed on her stepfather and her mouth opened and closed several times before she spoke. "No, I'm not hurt . . . not much, anyway. No thanks to you."

Norma reached Jenny's side and bent down. "Jenny, baby, what happened?"

Jenny ignored the older woman and stepped closer to Michael. Every line in her face and body strained with hatred. Sparks flew from her blue eyes. "You know what happened, don't you, Michael. You knew when I couldn't find my saddle, I would have used that old one. You knew the cinch would break on that dilapidated excuse for a piece of leather and that I'd fall."

"Don't be ridiculous."

"You hoped I'd be killed and you'd be rid of me, just like you got rid of my mother."

Michael jerked straight up. "That's enough, Jenny. You're in shock. You don't know what you're saying."

"Yes, I do. You want to inherit my money so you and Norma can buy your horses and make your trips. I know. I heard you talking about it!"

"Jenny, that's just hopes for the future, things we want to do later on," Norma protested, tears slipping down her cheeks. "You can't believe such a terrible thing of Michael . . . of me."

Jenny turned to Norma. "Like when I'm dead and gone?" Then, looking back at Michael, "Well, you didn't get away with it this time. I only got knocked out and sprained my wrist. You goofed, didn't you? A wasted effort. I'm still alive and here."

Her small frame curled up, and Jenny squatted on the floor. Her arm wrapped around herself. Sobs filled the stunned quiet, increasing as she rocked back and forth.

There was so much pain, so much fright and so much loneliness coming from that one small human being, that Debbie wanted to weep with her.

6

Michael's finely carved face twisted in anger when he looked at Teresa. "Why in the world did you bring her here when she's in this shape? Couldn't you have simply taken her home?" His voice whipped through the night air.

Surprise flickered through Teresa's violet eyes. She stepped back until she stood against the glass of the sliding door. Her nostrils quivered and flared. The fuchsia-tinted fullness of her lips thinned.

At the moment neither Teresa nor Michael seemed aware of the other numbed guests or the crying girl between them. Each silently battled the other, and the tension throbbed in the air.

Seeing the strength in Teresa and the tightly controlled Michael, Debbie felt a deep concern for Jenny. No one, especially a teenager with such bruised emotions, could thrive in this atmosphere.

Shrugging her shoulders with contempt, Teresa said sharply, "I promised Keith I would be here. Jenny promised Debbie. You've always told us it's important to keep our word. Don't you think you're being inconsistent?"

Teresa searched the area until she spotted Keith. She reached out beseechingly, and her husky voice broke when she called, "Keith, please come. See what you can do for Jenny. The child is beside herself, and my nerves are raw from her outrageous ravings."

Jenny looked at Teresa through swollen red eyes and tear-streaked cheeks. "I'm not a child! And my saddle was hidden!" She drooped forlornly. "You don't understand. You don't care. No one does."

The guests shifted to allow Keith to weave his way past the tables. Debbie followed in his wake.

"We don't need Keith's help to clean up our family affairs," Mike snapped at Teresa. "You should not have brought Jenny here when she was hurt and in this frame of mind."

Ignoring the obviously outraged Teresa, Michael bent down on one knee near the weeping girl. "This is not the way to act at a party, Jenny. You're making a spectacle of yourself and humiliating all of us. Now straighten up."

"Jenny, would you like to go in the house and talk about this?" Keith offered.

Jenny sobbed louder.

The pulse throbbed wildly at the side of Michael's neck, and Debbie cautiously stepped closer until she stood beside Keith.

Then, almost as though he couldn't restrain himself further, Michael grasped Jenny's shoulders and clipped, "We'll thrash this nonsense about the saddle out at home . . . privately. Now get hold of yourself."

"No! No! Stay away from me," Jenny cried, and scooted back, beyond Michael's reach.

Michael frowned. "You're making an exhibition of yourself! You claim you're not a child, but you're certainly acting like one. I won't have it, Jenny. Do you hear me? I won't tolerate any more of this."

His words shattered the silence.

"Jenny, honey, why don't you come inside and lie down," Norma suggested, her hand tenderly brushing the back of Jenny's golden-brown hair. "You'll feel much better after I wash your face with some cold water."

Looking at Keith, Debbie realized he was waiting to see the best way to defuse the exchange. But surely *he* didn't believe Jenny's accusations were outrageous. Debbie remembered Jenny's description of herself when they'd first met: "overly emotional . . . wild imagination . . . serious problems." Maybe Jenny was to some extent, but couldn't he understand that Jenny was frightened and screaming publicly for help?

Jenny's sobs pulled at Debbie's emotions, and she responded. Somehow, the grim Michael, dressed in black, fit easily into the role of villain. Yet she was unsure of what she could do to help Jenny that wouldn't cause more difficulties. There was nothing to do but wait for an appropriate opportunity and act.

"Come on, baby, let me help you up," Norma urged. Her arm encircled Jenny, and she tried to pull the young girl up.

Jenny looked at Debbie. Her blue eyes begged, and Debbie stepped around Michael to help Norma. Jenny's tears slowed when Debbie gently squeezed the hand of the uninjured arm.

Jenny hiccuped and wiped her free hand across her blotched face. "I came to your party," she said raggedly. "I promised I would, and I did."

"That you did, and I'm glad. It wouldn't have been the same without you," Debbie replied softly. "Do you hurt much?"

Jenny hiccuped again. "No, not really. We didn't need to go to the hospital, but Teresa insisted. She said she didn't want to take the responsibility. We would have been on time if we hadn't gone."

"But I'm glad she took you. This way we all know you're okay." Debbie glanced over at Michael's strained face. His brown eyes were as dark as pits of tar, his expression inscrutable. "Why don't we get one of these strong men to help you inside so you can lie down a few minutes?"

"I told you I'm okay. I don't know why I'm crying."

"But I'm not okay. I'm shaken, and I need to sit down quietly and maybe have a drink to calm my nerves. I thought you might join me and tell me how the accident happened. That's what friends are for, you know. To listen and help one another."

Jenny sniffed. "I didn't cry when I fell or when I was at the hospital. It was only when I got here and saw him."

It probably would have been better for everyone if Jenny had cried earlier and gotten over the shock before coming, but now was not the time for recriminations. Debbie ignored Jenny's confession and continued. "If you wash your face and hands, you'll feel better. And then after we talk, we can come back out and eat. I know you must be hungry, and I still haven't had my piece of Cressie's German chocolate cake."

Debbie heard Michael take a deep breath when Jenny nodded in acceptance, but his voice sounded perfectly natural when he added, "That's a good idea, and after you eat, I'll take you home. You don't want to spoil Norma's party for Debbie any more than you already have, do you, Jenny?"

Debbie wanted to hit him. Not giving Jenny a chance to respond, she coaxed instantly, "And I'll bet Keith would love to come with us and help you inside."

"Keith!" Teresa protested when Keith stepped forward and helped Jenny to her feet. With the girl leaning against him and his arm encircling her small body for support, he started walking toward the house.

"I won't be long, Teresa." Looking down at Jenny while Norma rushed to open the door, he said, "I remember when your mother fell off her horse one time."

Jenny's eyes widened. "She did? What happened?"

Something had to be done to defuse the turmoil of the past few minutes. So while Keith and Jenny followed Norma into the house, Debbie remained beside Michael. He stood rigid, staring at the doorway. Debbie offered, "I'll send Norma back out." She hoped that would help.

She swallowed the nervous knot lodged in her throat when he turned his gaze on her, his countenance grim. There didn't seem to be a breath of air stirring. When one of the other guests coughed softly, Debbie rubbed her arm and promised, "I'll talk with Jenny; she'll be all right."

"I didn't, you know. I didn't hide her saddle. One of the hands probably put it in the wrong place, or she did so herself the last time she used it. She's careless that way. If she had taken the time to search instead of being so impatient, I'm sure she would have found it. Then none of this would have happened."

Debbie didn't know what to say, she only knew what she felt. She couldn't agree that he was telling the truth any more than she could prove Jenny's version. "Well . . . let's just be thankful she wasn't badly hurt."

"I tell you, Michael, you need to have Jenny committed to some hospital. She gets worse all the time." Teresa's sudden interruption caused Debbie to jump.

"Committed? To what sort of hospital? Jenny may need help, but she's not crazy," Debbie protested.

"You're not around her all the time and don't have to listen to her wild stories," Teresa fired back immediately.

Debbie shook her head impatiently. While teaching the last few years, she had learned how to talk and manage young people, but now, watching Teresa brush a speck from the sleeve of her blouse, it was clear the other woman would refuse to listen to whatever Debbie might say. Still, she had to try. "No, but Jenny's been spending a great deal of time at my house the past couple of weeks, and I've come to care for her. Most teenagers tend to be overly emotional. Girls will be more dramatic when something upsets them, while boys often use mischief as a reaction. We need to understand and cope accordingly."

Teresa quirked an eyebrow. "You are an authority, aren't you? Since you're a newcomer to our community, I didn't realize . . . how . . . how knowledgeable you are. And apparently on so many . . . unexpected subjects. Are you teaching psychiatry at the college along with Keith?"

"No, business courses," Debbie answered firmly, and raised her chin. She was proud of her accomplishments and didn't intend to allow Teresa to diminish them or to patronize her in the process.

"Oh, for God's sake," Michael snapped. "Cut it out, Teresa. I've had enough for one night."

So had she. Glad to have an opportunity to escape, Debbie quipped, "I'll go check on Jenny."

"Don't forget to send Keith back out while you have your girl talk," Teresa called behind her.

Debbie stopped and turned. "Keith can do what he wants. He's already made it quite clear to me that he makes his own decisions." Without waiting for a response, she slipped into the house and followed the voices she heard from down the hall. In a pink-and-white bedroom, she found Jenny, Keith, and Norma.

Debbie knew she had to be careful to say the right words to comfort the teenager and prove she was her friend. At the same time she didn't want to play on Jenny's fears in case Michael was innocent. The evening was turning into a disaster, but maybe they'd all muddle through somehow.

Glancing at her watch, Debbie could scarcely believe that only an hour had passed since Jenny's dramatic entrance. It felt more like three. Still, once she had Jenny's full attention in the bedroom and they'd discussed the events of the accident, Jenny had been more than ready to come out and eat her dinner. Her stomach filled and the emotional tension passed, Jenny grew sleepy and was ready now to go home to bed.

Before leaving, she whispered to Debbie once again the promise she had made back in the bedroom: that she would look carefully for her own saddle the first thing in the morning, and if she found it, she would apologize to Michael for her behavior. Of course, the other part of the bargain was that if she didn't find the saddle, she would call and let Debbie know.

Debbie watched Michael and Jenny drive off, and as the car lights disappeared, she wondered what she would do if Jenny didn't find her saddle, especially since Michael was her guardian and Debbie simply a neighbor.

Teresa slammed her hand against her car, still complaining about her stepfather's instructions to follow closely behind so she could help Jenny to bed. She remained stubbornly straight beside her open car door, one hand on Keith's arm, and glared at Debbie.

"Shall we go back inside?" Norma suggested, and led the way.

The last thing Debbie heard before the door to Norma's house closed was Teresa saying to Keith, "I should have come to the party with you, and Jenny should have come with Michael. Then none of this would have happened. It has been a perfectly horrible evening. And no matter how hard I tried, nothing I did was right. It's not fair."

After a quick survey of the mulling guests in the backyard, Norma grimaced, poured herself some brandy, and tossed it down in one swallow. Setting the empty glass on the counter, she said, "I don't think I've ever been through such a terrible evening, and I hope to hell I don't ever again."

Debbie smiled reassuringly. "Now, Norma, the party has been delightful. In spite of the problem with Jenny, I've met a lot of nice people."

Norma shuddered. "You're a very nice person yourself, but then I knew you were when I sold you the Muller place. I guess we'd better join the others and try to make the best of what's left of the evening."

After glancing toward the living room and the closed front door, she added, "I assume Keith will be along shortly. Teresa doesn't like to be upstaged, and unfortunately, both you and Jenny did that this evening."

Debbie shrugged and, following Norma to the back door, said, "He apparently doesn't mind."

Norma paused. "Keith? Like you, he's a nice person, and is trying to smooth everyone's feelings. Believe me, if she wants, Teresa could be a real pain to Michael and Jenny when she gets home."

"I thought you mentioned earlier that when Teresa's divorce is final, Keith and Teresa might pick up where they left off several years ago."

Norma opened the door. "Maybe I did, but after watching you two this evening, I'd be more inclined to think Keith still likes playing the field."

"Have they gone?" Eleanor asked. She and Frank Johnson, along with two men whose names Debbie couldn't remember, were standing near the back door watching two women stacking dishes and straightening the table. The rest of the guests stood talking quietly in small groups.

Norma took a deep breath and smiled graciously. "Yes. That is, Michael and Jenny have. Teresa will be leaving shortly, as soon as she finishes talking with Keith."

"Teresa did that deliberately, you know," Eleanor said. Her calm arrogance sounded impressive under the circumstances.

"Did what?" Norma asked, obviously startled.

"She could have simply called and explained about the accident and said she and Jenny wouldn't be coming. Then your party wouldn't have turned into such a disaster," Eleanor explained sardonically.

"I wonder if Michael did have anything to do with Jenny's accident," one of the men suggested hesitantly.

The night air became taut with unspoken accusations as the others shuffled uneasily.

"Oh, I might have differences of opinion with Townsend, but I don't think he'd be dumb enough to try that sort of thing, not with Norma giving a party," Frank responded finally.

"You never know," said the first man. "That might be the perfect time, when no one would suspect. And then, too, that property's worth a bundle. If Gloria doesn't show up in the next year, Jenny will inherit the bulk, plus the money her Winthrope grandparents left her. She could wind up a mighty rich little girl."

"What does Gloria not returning in the next year have to do with the inheritance?" Debbie asked.

"In Texas, after a person's been missing seven years, the law presumes him dead, and Gloria's already been gone six," Frank explained.

Norma's hands trembled slightly when she grasped a stack of plates still remaining on the table. "Michael would never do anything to harm Jenny."

"You can't always tell what people will do if there's money involved," Eleanor threw in. "After all, Norma, you should be the first to realize that, after your fiasco of a marriage."

Color filled Norma's face. "My ex was a real bastard and got what he deserved. Michael is not like him at all." Then, struggling visibly to get a grip on herself, she said, "Michael had nothing to do with Gloria's disappearance, and he certainly isn't trying to harm Jenny."

"Once a woman attracts a certain type of man, she frequently will fall for another with the same character traits," Eleanor replied loftily, surveying Norma from head to toe.

After looking at Norma's distraught expression, Frank parried sharply, "I'd be careful what I said if I were you, Eleanor Farmsworth. You're not exactly in a position to cast stones."

Eleanor drew herself up to her full height. "Go back to tending your animals and fish. Your manners are more suitable for them."

Frank's silver-and-gold mustache quivered. "Well, I agree they are certainly more likable than some of the folks around here."

"Please . . . please," Norma whispered tearfully, barely maintaining control.

"See, Eleanor, you and your spiteful ways have caused more damage than anything young Jenny did," Frank snarled. "You're supposed to be Norma's friend. You're also supposed to be an adult."

"As usual, you have no idea what you're talking about," Eleanor replied coolly. "Norma knows I only have her best interests at heart. She doesn't need another man like her ex-husband."

Frank stiffened. "I don't know what I'm talking about, do I? Well, if you're so almighty smart about everything, then just explain why your own husband disappeared the day after Gloria did."

Blue ice seemed to fly through the air as Eleanor glared at her antagonist. "Don't you dare mention my husband's name in that vile manner. You know as well as I do, when the police found his car, there was blood inside."

"I know that his body has never been recovered and that he's still missing along with the bank's money he had with him."

"The police said robbery. . . ."

"And the police don't know if he was killed or if he stole the money and disappeared."

"There's not a word of truth in that, Frank Johnson, and you know it. You'd better be careful whom you malign. Herman was a good man and an honest one. He would never do such an outrageous thing. He's not like you." Eleanor's hands were clenched by her side.

"He was also a rich one and owned a bank. That's why you married him," Frank countered.

"I loved him. He was a better man than anyone else around here, and don't you forget it."

Frank's mouth tightened. His expression close to savage, he muttered a curse word softly and took several deep breaths of fresh air.

The other men in the group, averting their eyes, shuffled their feet.

When Frank's razor-sharp voice sliced out quietly, no one moved. "Well, I'm reminding you that you shouldn't be making accusations at what Townsend might inherit when you yourself have come out smelling like a rose."

Eleanor glared at him. "I'm warning you—"

"You did inherit the Farmsworth bank and all the prestige that goes with it. You can't deny that. And in another year it will be yours legally."

"I didn't need the bank or the prestige. I already had plenty."

Frank repeated, "You'll inherit everything Farmsworth owned, just like Jenny will inherit from her mother, and in either case, the sum is not to be sneezed at."

In the sudden silence, Debbie heard an engine

race and tires squeal, and for the first time she felt envious of Teresa.

Eleanor's gentle southern drawl became icily distinct. "And may I remind you that a man who passes out hot checks and is noted for featherbrained schemes is not exactly a reliable source of information. You're famous for your violent temper, and if you persist in this line of talk, I shall consult my lawyer. Before I'm through with you, you won't even have the land you now own."

"Hey, what's going on?"

Keith's voice cut through the tension, and Debbie could hear the universal sigh of relief. She turned and said, "Has Teresa gone?"

"Yes. What's wrong here?" Keith walked up beside Debbie, his gray eyes darting from the flushed and angry Frank, to the stiff, belligerent Eleanor, and finally settling on the silently crying Norma.

Frank smashed his empty beer can with one hand.

Eleanor stared at him a moment before looking at Norma. "I'm sorry about this. The party was a good idea, but you made a poor choice in some of the guests you invited."

"You certainly did," Frank agreed, and glared at Eleanor. He stalked to the side of the house, only to pause at the gate. "You know, Eleanor, have you ever thought that maybe if you found Gloria, you might discover Herman right beside her? She at least had something to offer a man."

Eleanor watched silently until Frank disappeared from view, then snapped, "That man should be outlawed from respectable society. I hope you remember that next time, Norma."

When Eleanor had walked over to the table to pick

up her empty salad bowl, Norma asked, "What do you suppose he meant by that?"

After tucking the bowl under her arm with all the grace and aplomb of silk sliding over steel, Eleanor turned to her friend. "You know very well the man has never recovered from my refusal of him or my marrying Herman. He's been an annoying burr ever since, always around at the most inconvenient times to stick in his treacherous spikes. He enjoys trying to hurt me. Unfortunately this time it's not only me he's attacking, but Gloria and Herman as well. I won't stand for anyone speaking ill of Herman."

With that the older woman marched out the same door Frank had used. Then, as though everyone wanted to escape, the other guests quickly gathered their things and said their good-byes until only Norma, Keith, and a relieved Debbie were left.

"I appreciate your giving me the party," Debbie said with genuine gratitude. "I'm sorry for the problems."

Norma grinned a humorless smile. "Thanks anyway for the kind words. Right now all I want is to curl up with a strong drink and wipe the whole damned thing from my mind."

"Then let's get everything put away so you can do exactly that," Keith said matter-of-factly, and began to fold the card tables and chairs before carrying them inside and setting them against the den wall.

Norma and Debbie cleaned up the debris and put away the remaining food. Within a few minutes little remained except the colored lights. When Keith began to unhook one, Norma said, "Leave them. I don't think it's going to rain, and right now I really could care less."

Debbie nodded at Keith's raised eyebrow. "If there

isn't anything else, Norma, then we'll go. Thanks again."

Norma nodded and followed them through the house, her shoulders drooping and her head lowered as she closed the front door behind them.

"How could a party with such a nice beginning wind up in such a complete shambles?" Debbie said quietly when Keith pulled out onto the street. The stars twinkled like polished silver in the velvet sky. A quarter moon peeked over the tops of the pines. The night was so quiet it seemed no one existed in the countryside but the two of them.

Debbie leaned her head back on the soft leather seat, and while enjoying the peace, another strange thought struck her. Despite the way she felt about men in general, Keith had somehow fallen into a slot all his own. At times while painting the house, he'd sensed her moods and acted accordingly. And tonight they had worked as a team to defuse a touchy situation without having to speak. Maybe it was because he was a psychologist and knew how to manipulate people, Debbie mused, but somehow it felt like more than that. There were times when she let down her guard that he seemed as familiar to her as if he were her other half, as though she had always known him. She'd never experienced such a thing with Charles, and she wasn't at all certain she was comfortable with the feeling now.

Keith would be leaving at the end of the college year for bigger and better things than she had planned for her life. What was more, she didn't have to prove her femininity or desirability, as some women did after a divorce. She knew who she was and what she wanted. And it wasn't a man to complicate her life. Maybe a friend, a companion to share thoughts with, but unfortunately she hadn't met a man yet who'd settle for that. And she doubted Keith was the exception.

"You realize that unless you want to get caught in the crossfire between Michael and Jenny, you're going to have to maintain your distance until this whole thing blows over," Keith stated.

Debbie instantly sat up straight. "Are you trying to tell me what to do again?"

He regarded her with hooded eyes. His mouth tightened and grooves appeared on either side. Turning back to his driving, he said, "No, I would never dream of doing such a thing, but since I've lived here longer than you, and know the people a little better, I was simply offering some friendly advice."

"How can you calmly sit there and give that advice when there's a possibility that Jenny could be killed in another accident?"

"Michael Townsend would never harm Jenny."

"That's not what she said this evening, nor, if you'll recall, earlier this week at my house."

"Jenny is an overly emotional teenage girl with a vivid imagination. Because she really has never had a mother, she's taking this means to attract attention."

"Are you saying that she's acting this way just so someone will notice her?"

"Yes."

"Well then, why doesn't Michael give her some love and attention?"

Keith drummed his fingers against the steering wheel. "Michael's first love is horses. His marriage to Gloria wasn't easy by any means, and Jenny is his stepdaughter. He was hurt by Gloria's defection, and unfortunately some of that probably comes through when he's dealing with Jenny. But he would never deliberately harm her."

Men and their damned inclination to stick by each other no matter who gets hurt. Debbie gathered her forces. "Then why doesn't Teresa do something to ease the situation and help Jenny?"

"Now don't start in on her. Teresa hasn't been here except the last two months. Besides, I doubt she knows how to handle Jenny any more than Michael does."

"And you know all the answers?"

Keith turned into Debbie's driveway. "I do have a doctorate in psychology."

"But you don't practice. You prefer hunting ghost stories," Debbie replied forcefully. All the anger that she had kept leashed through the evening seemed to be surfacing now.

Keith parked the car. "You don't get a degree in looking for the supernatural. You get educated in understanding people, their minds, how they think and react."

"You and Teresa seem to have all the answers tonight." Debbie opened the car door and climbed out. She kicked at a rut in her driveway; dirt and gravel scattered until some of the small stones bounced off the side of the porch.

Keith walked up beside her. "I don't know what you mean by that, but I do know you seem to have arrived in Nacogdoches with a chip on your shoulder. No person is an island. We all have problems, and we all need help at some time. I suggest you get your priorities in order."

Debbie shook from anger. "And perform while you pull the strings, is that right?"

"No, that isn't what I said."

"Why don't you take yourself off? Go find Teresa or whoever else catches your fancy and leave me alone. I'm tired of your constant bossiness and your sticking your nose in my affairs."

"You are, are you? It seems funny I didn't hear any complaints when I was working my tail off painting your damned house."

"And you can find some other house in which to hunt ghosts for your stupid book."

Keith gripped her arms so hard that she knew there would be bruise marks tomorrow from his fingers.

"You little blond hellcat."

They stood glaring at each other. Their bodies barely brushed, but Debbie was breathing much too rapidly. She struggled with her growing anger and reeling senses. He meant to intimidate her, bend her to his will, and she refused to allow it. Suddenly his mouth came down on hers with a fierce demand. And as the night closed in, he pushed her away and stalked angrily to his car.

"I'm quite capable of managing my own affairs, and don't you forget it," she called after him, fighting back the tears brimming in her eyes.

The car door slammed, the engine roared, and flying missiles of gravel and dirt stung her as Keith sped down the driveway.

She stood there watching until she could no longer see the red taillights. Biting her lip, she wiped her cheeks. She didn't want Cressie to see the tears. An owl hooted from the big oak, and the breeze blew against her face and cooled her trembling body.

Leaving Norma's house earlier, she'd had the sensation that she and Keith were the only two people in the world. Now she felt alone—all alone in a vacuum of viciously fighting neighbors, overemotional teenagers, and crazy psychic helpers who believed in ghosts and deadly prophecies. She didn't need this. Maybe she should stay uninvolved, as Keith suggested.

But his kiss had surfaced another problem she didn't want.

She shook her head and turned to climb the porch steps. She was alone, as she wanted to be, alone in her wonderful house, and beginning a new, exciting life. She had decided after Charles's betrayal that she would never again let any man get close and that there were other things in life.

But then why had Keith's kiss touched her so?

No, it hadn't. She was just suffering a reaction after the horrible evening. From now on she would tend to her own affairs and keep her emotions comfortably intact. Keith could tend to his career and whatever else took his interest.

Cressie opened the front door and stared at Debbie standing on the front porch. "I see you didn't have such a good time."

"No. It probably was one of the most grotesque evenings I've ever spent."

"Mr. Keith didn't stay?"

Debbie grimaced as she shut and locked the door behind her. "It's late. He had more important things to do."

"Mm. Well, come on in and sit a spell. I'll pour you some of my homemade wine. That'll make you feel better in no time."

Debbie nodded to Sal as she plopped down on the couch. She ran her fingers through her hair. Cressie handed her a glass half-filled with glowing red liquid, and immediately Debbie took a big swallow. Liquid fire coursed down her throat to her insides. She coughed, and her eyes watered as she gasped for cooling air. "My God, Keith said your wine was potent, but I didn't realize it had the punch of white lightning."

"I never tried white lightning myself. Never needed to," Cressie responded calmly, and began to rock in the chair across from Debbie. "Now why don't you tell me all about your party."

Debbie finished her wine about the same time she finished telling the events. Somehow by then the evening didn't appear as bad as it had, and she felt so light-headed that she seemed to be looking at the whole thing from a distance.

Cressie rose and nodded to her husband. "It's time we went home."

"Keith told me you used to stay in the apartment over the garage. We'll have to talk about that the next time you come, but not tonight." Debbie wondered if the room really was swinging slightly or if she might be a tiny bit intoxicated.

Cressie stopped in the doorway. "You'd better go on up to bed. Tomorrow will be better. The sun always helps."

Debbie shivered when a sudden cold draft swept over her and the smell of musty earth filled her nostrils. Shaking her head at the impossibility of such a thing in a house Cressie cleaned, she said thickly, "You couldn't believe the terrible accusations . . . and I'm worried about Jenny."

"Be gone, get away with you," Cressie suddenly called, and waved her hand erratically at the room.

Startled, Debbie sat up. "Cressie?"

"You go on up the stairs. I'll wait here until you get there. Then I'll lock up."

"What's the matter? What is it? Did you feel the draft, too?" Debbie asked while she obediently followed Cressie's instructions.

"It's the devil dad himself. He rides the wind and pounces on anyone in his way. You have to be careful, Miss Debbie, he sometimes strikes the innocent if they be in his path. He has terrible power."

"I don't see anything. Just feel a cold draft . . . smelly . . . like before in the back parlor," Debbie murmured to herself.

"Go on, away with you. I know what's here and what has to be done," Cressie said, her head upturned to the ceiling.

Debbie clung to the banister while she climbed the front stairs. It seemed a long way up, but finally she stood at the top and looked down. She watched Cressie nod and leave, locking the front door. Debbie was alone in her lovely house, in her domain, and there was no one to disturb her or tell her what to do. She was alone. She sighed and drifted into her bedroom.

She didn't remember getting ready for bed, but it wasn't long before she snuggled beneath the comforter and looked out through the window at the night sky. Suddenly the air filled with the scent of jasmine. It became stronger and stronger. Debbie sat up. There in the doorway to her bedroom she could see the outline of a woman . . . a misty, vague shape, almost like vapor. Surely she hadn't had that much to drink. She blinked rapidly, trying to focus her eyes. She could go over there and see if it was a hallucination, but she'd have to get out of bed.

Debbie shook her head to clear her senses. The room whirled and she hiccuped, but the shape remained.

"Oh, go away, Kate," she mumbled, and lay back down, pulling the covers under her chin. "I can't deal with you tonight. . . . Besides, I don't believe in ghosts."

7

The phone rang a second time and stopped. Debbie glanced at the kitchen clock. Who could be calling at eight on a Monday morning? Since she hadn't talked with anyone from the party besides Jenny, and hadn't really had a chance to get to know any of the other faculty members the first three weeks of the semester, the call had to be for one of the Slavanias. In one fell swoop Debbie finished her biscuit and coffee.

The hall door swung open behind her and Cressie said, "Your mother's on the line."

Debbie remained sitting for a moment, enjoying the sight of the sunlit field behind her house and the brightly colored autumn leaves that decorated the countryside. Reluctantly she walked over to the phone on the kitchen wall. "Hi, Mom. What's up?"

"Who answered the phone?"

Her mother's voice carried a nasal tone. She had to have been crying. "That was Cressie. She and her husband moved into the apartment above the garage this past weekend. Since there's an extension in their place, you're liable to reach any one of the three of us when you call."

"Yes . . . well, I hope I didn't disturb . . . but I'm glad you're not going to be living completely alone. It's not safe."

"Now, Mother, we've been through this before. I'm perfectly safe. And you didn't disturb them. They're early risers. Cressie even fixed breakfast for me this morning."

Her mother's voice was scratchy when she spoke again. "That's nice, dear, but mothers worry no matter how old or independent their children become. They can't help it. Someday you'll understand."

"I do understand. Now what's wrong? I doubt you called this early to discuss my household arrangements."

"I . . . I wanted to talk with you. . . . Is this a bad time?"

"I have a few minutes before I need to leave. What's the matter? Is Scottie giving you trouble again?"

The ragged breathing from the other end of the line indicated her mother was fighting for control. Her brother must have really pulled one this time.

"Oh, Debbie, I don't know what to do. He stayed out all night Saturday night. And I ask you, what could a sixteen-year-old boy do all night besides get into trouble?"

Debbie closed her eyes as she tried to remain calm. "When did Scottie get home?"

"He came in about two yesterday afternoon."

"What did he say he'd been doing all that time?"

"After the football game, he'd gone over to a

friend's house and simply stayed the night. They didn't wake up until late."

"And didn't he think he should have called and told you where he was so you wouldn't worry?"

"That's what I asked him, and he said he was old enough to take care of himself; that he wasn't a little boy tied to his mother's apron strings."

Debbie turned and leaned against the wall. She curled the cord around her hand while silently cursing the thoughtlessness of her younger brother. "You're going to have to cut off his allowance and restrict him from social activities for a while. And you're going to have to stand firm. If you don't, it's only going to get worse."

Debbie's mother broke into sobs. "I did . . . I did just that . . . Oh, Debbie, it's so awful. I'm so frightened. What if something dreadful has happened to him?"

"How could anything happen to him at home? Mom, quiet down, you're not making sense." Her mother began to cry harder. Debbie looked up when Cressie poured herself some coffee and sat at the table. Meeting the curious woman's eyes, Debbie shook her head and said, "Mom? What's happened? Why are you frightened?"

"I said all those things you said . . . and a few more . . ."

"Did Scottie know you meant them? That you were serious?"

"He said he'd do what he wanted. He was too old for me to give him orders or confine him to his room like a little kid, and no one would tell him how to live his life. After all, I did what I pleased. Then he stormed out of the house . . . I haven't seen or heard from him since."

She understood now why her mother was so upset. She would be, too. Debbie raked her fingers through her hair and rubbed her temples. Damn. Her head was pounding. "Well, I think in this instance no news is good news."

There was momentary silence on the other end of the line. "What do you mean?"

"I mean if you haven't heard anything from the police or a hospital by now, Scottie's probably fine. My guess is that he's staying with either the same friend he did Saturday night or maybe another one, hoping to wear you down, so that when he does decide to come home, you won't give him any more flak."

"Debbie, he couldn't be so cruel. Doesn't he know how worried I'd be?"

"I wish I could say he didn't."

Her mother cried softly in the phone, and Debbie thought about her own get-acquainted party and Jenny's actions. Could Michael be going through some of the same problems? Jenny seemed younger than Scottie, but really they were the same difficult age.

Keith and Norma had both insisted that Michael would never do anything to harm Jenny. And when Jenny had called the next day, she'd admitted she had found the saddle. The only thing she'd refused to admit was that she'd probably overlooked it in the first place. She'd remained steadfast in her claim that someone had returned it after the accident.

Debbie sighed. "Teenagers are frequently self-centered creatures. They haven't yet learned to consider other people's feelings. That comes with maturity. Your being upset and worrying is exactly

what Scottie wants you to do. It's his way of manipulating you."

"Oh, Debbie, what am I going to do? I need to go
to work, but I'm afraid to leave the house in case Scottie comes home or the police call or the hospital—"

"Scottie claims he's old enough to take care of
himself, so you'll have to assume that he is. If you
haven't heard from the police or the hospital by now,
I doubt that you will."

"I can't go on like nothing's happened, or pretend he
doesn't exist, and at the same time calmly do my work,"
her mother snapped back. "I'm not a computer."

"Then I suggest you call the school and talk to his
counselor. If Scottie's in class, I wouldn't disturb him,
but simply go on about my business. If he doesn't get
the reaction from you that he wants, he'll come home
himself given a little time. Then you'll have the upper
hand."

"But what if he stays with his friend?"

"Mom, get serious. The way Scottie eats no one
but no one, except family, is going to keep him
around for any length of time. They couldn't afford
to. Besides, sooner or later even Scottie is going to
want a change of clothes."

For the first time since her mother called, Debbie
heard a small laugh. "You're right. It does take moun-
tains of food to fill him up. I'll do it. I'll do what you
suggest. And Debbie . . . thanks."

"It'll all work out. Wait and see. Scottie is going
through a difficult period now—"

"Has he said anything to you?"

Debbie paused. "No, I haven't talked with him,
but we all face situations at some time or other that
we aren't sure how to handle. Maybe he's having girl-

friend problems. You never know. You and Dad have given him a good foundation. He'll make it."

"You never did these things."

"No, but girls are different. Listen, Mom, I have to run or I'll be late for class. Will you be okay?"

"I'll be fine. Thanks, for listening, Debbie. I'll call you if I hear from Scottie."

Debbie gave a big sigh as she hung up the phone. "I hope I'm right," she said to Cressie, who had been listening attentively to her side of the conversation.

"Families can bring a bucketful of pain or a pot full of gold," Cressie said. "Now you'd best be off. You don't want to be late."

While Debbie hurried upstairs for her purse and briefcase, she muttered, "And this is only Monday morning. I hope this isn't any indication of things to come."

Had her mother been holding back something, or had she just imagined it? She could always call tonight and press the question. On the other hand, her mother had never been the secretive type. Sooner or later she'd hear about it if it was something serious.

Later that afternoon Debbie sat grading papers in her cubbyhole of an office on the college campus. Tapping the eraser of her pencil against her front tooth, she considered a student's answer.

A throat cleared from her doorway, and a male voice said, "You're going to be late for the meeting."

She glanced up to see Keith leaning against the doorjamb. "What meeting?" she asked, trying to hide her pleasure at seeing him again. She'd told him to keep his distance but never dreamed he would take her so literally.

Straightening, he sauntered in and considered the picture hanging on her wall. "I like this. A majestic old oak, an enchanting swimming hole, a solid rock . . . they give a sense of endurance."

"I found it in a shop not far from the campus and couldn't resist buying it. From the first instant the scene appealed to me." She shrugged. "It may sound foolish, but I feel like I know that place . . . that I've been there."

"I know what you mean. It looks familiar to me, too."

A thoughtful expression formed lines in his forehead and between his dark brows as he assessed her. He turned and began to browse.

His intense inspection while he moved from item to item made her uncomfortable. "Are you looking for something? Or just curious?"

Ignoring her question, Keith picked up the small ceramic clown sitting on top of the file cabinet and touched the patch featured on the pants. "I see you've settled in. Have you had any problems?"

"No. I've spent most of my time fixing up my office and familiarizing myself with classes and students."

"Ah yes, the tunnel vision again. A typical initial reaction to hurt and frustration."

Debbie snapped her mouth shut as anger flashed through her. Damn him. "Jenny tells me you've been over at their house more than usual lately. Are you giving her more of your worldly wisdom because of what happened at the party, or are your visits for personal reasons?"

Keith carefully replaced the figurine. "Funny. I was under the impression that you weren't interested in my activities."

"I'm not." When he cocked one eyebrow and waited, she said recklessly, "I'm concerned about Jenny and thought perhaps you might be, too."

"Be careful or you might find yourself embroiled in the local intrigue. That would never do."

"Explain that uncalled-for remark."

"Since I first met you, you've made it clear your interests are your house and your job. I've received the impression you weren't anxious to become particularly friendly with anyone."

"Well, you're wrong. I like the people I've met and want to be friends. Settling in has been important to me because I want to start off right."

"And make certain you don't get your fingers burned again? I repeat, a typical initial reaction to hurt and frustration."

Debbie ignored his remark. "Jenny told me she apologized to Michael for her outburst at Norma's."

"I think Michael can thank you for that."

Debbie shifted nervously on her chair. "I care about her, and I'm worried there may be some truth to her accusations."

"There's none, although Jenny's a puzzle, and I'm never quite certain how she's going to react. I thought maybe if she could talk about some of the things troubling her and receive a little unofficial counseling by a family friend, it might help."

"You've done it before. Talked to her, I mean."

"True, but how did you know?"

"She told me the first day I met her. She said you spent time with her occasionally when someone thinks her imagination is running rampant."

"I didn't realize she knew."

"I think all of you underestimate Jenny, and that's

part of the problem. You're not really hearing what she's saying . . . but then I'm not an authority."

"That doesn't stop you from saying what you think, though, does it?"

"Should it?"

"Maybe if you're right and someone does want Jenny dead, you could be putting yourself in danger by sticking your nose where it doesn't belong. Have you considered that?"

"You can't be serious. Who?"

"No, I'm not serious. I think Jenny is suffering delusions because she wants love and attention, but it doesn't pay to be so outspoken that you offend people. Maybe staying clear of involvement is the best thing you can do."

Debbie played with her pencil, trying to think of a tactful way out of the conversation. She cleared her throat. "Do you think you're helping her overcome her problems?"

"I don't really know." Keith frowned. "One minute everything seems to be going just fine. Then the next, Jenny will pop up with some other out-of-the-blue notion. In many ways, however, she acts perfectly normal. . . ."

When he paused and stared at her pointedly, Debbie was afraid he might be speaking ambiguously and quickly countered, "Jenny is a normal teenager, immature maybe because she's not yet dating or interested in boys and clothes, emotional maybe because of the loss of her mother, but there's nothing wrong with her mind. Michael should be thankful she's not into drugs or alcohol."

Ignoring her interruption, Keith continued, "What disturbs me most is that I can't break through this fixation of hers that Michael has done something with her mother and that he wants her dead, too."

Thinking back to some of her own conversations with the young girl, Debbie said, "I know what you mean."

Keith ran his finger over the clown again. "It's like trying to get past the paint that's colored the surface in order to reach what's underneath." Suddenly he dropped his hand to his side. "If we could learn what happened to Gloria, of course, that would make all the difference. But I don't suppose anyone will ever be able to answer that one. Certainly the police haven't."

Debbie met Keith's eyes. "What does Teresa say about the whole matter?" she asked.

"She's tired of Jenny's outbursts and says she's glad Jenny is getting my professional help." His lips twitched slightly. "Although Teresa's not really convinced I can help Jenny."

Debbie smiled. "Does Teresa have any opinion as to what happened to her mother?"

"She doesn't know, but she doesn't negate the possibility that Michael might be responsible in some way. She thinks Michael's not the type to let opportunity slip through his fingers."

"That could mean almost anything."

Keith nodded and began to examine the papers on her desk.

Debbie set down her pencil and gathered the tests together. She wasn't in the mood to correct any more of them today. "So what meeting were you referring to earlier?"

"The dean's coordination meeting." Looking at the digital clock on the small radio sitting on the corner of her desk, he added, "It starts in three minutes."

Debbie stopped arranging files. "That's tomorrow. And how would you know? You're not in the Business Department."

"Ah," Keith said wisely, "but business students are required to take one of my classes, and the dean thought I needed to be at the meeting."

Debbie pointed to the page on her calendar. "The meeting's tomorrow. I marked it when I picked up the notice from my box."

Keith shook his head. "You must have misread the date. Aren't you ready for it? That would be a bad start."

Debbie frowned. She must have misread the notice or marked the wrong day. That had never happened to her before, and it was hard to believe she'd make such a mistake when she knew how important it was. She'd look at the notice again later.

Sighing, she grabbed her purse and briefcase. "I guess I'm lucky I worked up my plans this weekend."

She didn't like the amusement in Keith's eyes but decided to let it pass while she locked her door and fell into step beside him. She wished she had worn the straight-lined black suit she had been saving for this first important coordination meeting. The style promoted a businesslike appearance, and right now she could use the added confidence it always gave her. This was the first time she had ever begun completely on her own, without the knowledge that Charles, as dean of English, stood behind her. But nothing could be done about it; she would have to go in her clinging green knit. At least it was comfortable, and judging from Keith's admiring glance, it had another value.

Keith broke their silence on the way down the

stairs. "I know you've been totally absorbed with your house, but Dean Carrington is touchy about the staff making these meetings."

Anger heated Debbie's cheeks. She concentrated on looking straight ahead and keeping up with Keith.

Carolyn Niver, the teacher from Norma's party, surprised Debbie when she stopped to wait for them outside the meeting room door. Since the party, Carolyn had been distantly polite, even though Debbie had made several attempts to get better acquainted.

"Are you and Teresa coming tomorrow night?" Carolyn asked Keith.

"Plan to," he replied, and opened the door so Carolyn could enter first.

Carolyn smiled at his answer before making her way to a chair. Debbie had been neatly snubbed. "Are Carolyn and Teresa friends?" she whispered even though the dean was glaring at her impatiently.

"They went through school together," Keith whispered back, and pulled out a chair for her.

"If you're ready . . ." Dean Carrington's silky voice cut through the room, his blue eyes glittering behind the big round horn-rimmed glasses. He was living up to his no-nonsense reputation of "the stern lion."

Debbie, ignoring the looks cast in her direction, opened her briefcase and took out her papers. From the side pocket she saw the notice. The voice of the first teacher giving his report faded away while she stared at the date. The two had been neatly penned to a three. Someone had changed the date.

When the teacher finished his report and the dean began to question him, Debbie felt a small lump form in the pit of her stomach. What if she had waited until the last minute to write up her report? In the past she often had. She would have attended totally unprepared, if she had come at all. And that would have been disastrous to her credibility.

Suddenly she realized what a timely coincidence it was that Keith had stopped by for her. She definitely owed him a grateful thank-you, especially since she had been so rude after the party.

When it was her turn, Debbie smiled confidently around the table and began to read her notes. She knew she was presenting some innovative ideas for teaching the humdrum basics to students, but the techniques had worked in Vermont. She wanted her plans to work even better here and had prepared detailed reports to demonstrate how successful the approach could be.

At the beginning of the year she had even told Dean Carrington how well the program worked in conjunction with the English Department. At his prompting she had promised to search through her papers to find the written portion of Charles's contribution and share it with the dean of English here. Perhaps it could be initiated the following semester. She had been delighted at Dean Carrington's attitude. Whatever else one could say, he was for progress, and she was happy to be working under him.

When she sat down, she saw a smile of congratulations on Keith's face. In spite of the altered notice, she had come out well. For some reason, the threatening phone call in the motel came to her mind. She had since chalked it up to a prank, but it seemed the culprit was finally making a move.

This wasn't life threatening, but not showing up for a meeting or being unprepared could be career damaging, a different kind of death. If she pressed the dean's secretary for an explanation, the lady would certainly take offense. On the other hand, if this was deliberate and she did nothing, there was no telling what step the caller might take next. She had to ask. She couldn't afford to take the risk.

Debbie dropped her briefcase on the hall table and ran up the stairs. After quickly slipping into jeans and a cotton shirt, she made her way down the back steps to the kitchen. Cressie was slicing vegetables at the counter. "I'm home," Debbie announced.

"Who would have guessed," Cressie replied calmly, and dropped some sliced squash in the small pot. "I thought it must be at least an elephant that came flyin' through the house, what with all the noise and slammin' doors."

For the first time since discovering she had almost missed the dean's meeting because of someone else's actions, Debbie laughed. "Oh, Cressie, what would I ever do without you?"

Cressie slanted her a sharp glance. "Trouble?"

"Not really. I thought it might be nice to take a walk, get some fresh air and sunshine before dinner." Despite her intentions to keep her troubles to herself, Debbie began to tell Cressie what had happened that afternoon.

When she finished, Cressie started tearing pieces of lettuce into a bowl. "Did you tell anyone about it?"

"After the meeting I showed the note to the dean's secretary. She didn't know anything about the change, but said she'd talk to the student who helps out in her office." Debbie gave a forced laugh. "Do you know I even suspected the motel caller might be finally carrying out his threat by trying to damage my reputation at the college?"

"It might not hurt for you to start double-checkin' the schedule with the other teachers," Cressie said matter-of-factly.

About to eat a piece of carrot she'd just snitched from the salad, Debbie paused. "You think it was done intentionally . . . specifically for my benefit?"

Cressie stared out the window. "People do crazy things sometimes, for no apparent reason. You have an enemy here. I can feel fear and anger." She paused. "The colors are mixed. Somethin' isn't quite right. I don't know what it is, but you'd best be careful."

Another of Cressie's warnings. The carrot scraped down the sides of Debbie's throat as she swallowed. "You're always giving me warnings, Cressie, and they make me nervous. I wish you wouldn't."

Cressie cut the large ripe tomato into pieces and dropped them into the bowl. Setting down her knife, she turned. "I promised both Miss Sarah and Miss Kate I'd look out for you. I mean to do just that."

Debbie wanted to scream in frustration. "You mentioned something about that the first day I came and looked over the house. What do you mean, exactly?"

"They told me that whoever Miss Kate had been waitin' for would come. I was to take care of her the same as I did Miss Sarah. I knew who they meant the minute I saw you."

"Because I look like Miss Kate. . . ." When Cressie nodded, Debbie walked over to stare out the window at the Muller graveyard up on the hill. "Was Sarah Miss Kate's daughter?"

"Miss Sarah was her niece, Kate's brother's child."

"And Miss Sarah never married or had children either?"

"Nope. They was alike in many ways, from hear tell."

"What about the heir, then? The one who inherited this place?"

"Miss Sarah's nephew. Her brother's son. He ain't at all like Miss Sarah."

Debbie turned and watched as Cressie wiped her hands on her apron. "Tell me what you know about Sarah and Kate."

Cressie filled her cup from a freshly brewed pot of coffee. "Kyle Muller was Miss Kate's father. He was a young man during the Civil War. He didn't fight, but there was enough trouble around these parts to turn him bitter. He lost his first wife and two sons, and part of the house and all of the outbuildings was burnt."

"Part of this house was burned?"

Cressie nodded. "It weren't exactly like this before. Kyle added to it, made it a bigger, fancier place. He claimed that was his way of rubbin' the Yankees' noses in it when they was a-doin' all they could to take what he had away."

"So what happened then?"

"He married again, rebuilt, and had another son, Kate's older brother. Kyle always hated Yankees, from the burnin' and the killin' on. And it didn't help none when after the war durin' the Reconstruction, the Yankees located their headquarters in the old Nacogdoches University building, right on the square. They made things tough on old Kyle, and that heaped more coals on his hate." Cressie took the plates from the cupboard to set the table.

"I didn't know there was a university back then."

She took out the silverware and set it alongside the plates. "A man named John Cato built it before the Civil War, but the Confederates used it as a hospital. Many around here took it as a personal insult when the Yankees turned the building into their headquarters while a-doin' their dirty work."

Debbie smiled. She wondered if the antagonism from the Civil War would ever truly end in the South. "What about Kate?"

"When Miss Kate was just a young girl, her mother died of a fever, and it fell to Kate to run the house. She had some hard times, partly 'cause she was so young, partly 'cause her father was such a mean ole cuss, but she did later inherit the whole estate from her pa."

Debbie handed Cressie the napkin holder filled with flowered paper napkins. "What about the older brother? I would have thought he'd have inherited the property, particularly since men are the so-called superior beings in these parts."

"He weren't here. After a big fight, the old man disinherited him, and the boy went on out farther west. There was only Miss Kate and her pa."

"How do you know all this?" Debbie poured herself a cup of coffee and sat down at the table to listen.

"Miss Sarah told me some, and my family the rest. There's a journal in the library that belonged to Kyle. It's still there if'n you want to read it some time, and if'n you can make heads or tails out of his scratches."

"I'll probably do just that," Debbie said thoughtfully, although she knew it wouldn't be this evening. She still had to finish grading the tests.

"Miss Kate's buried up on the hill. You can find her gravestone if you look, as well as her pa's."

Debbie sipped her coffee. "So how did Miss Sarah inherit?"

"Miss Sarah was the granddaughter of Kate's brother, the one Kyle disinherited. See'n as how Miss Sarah never married, when Miss Kate died, she made Miss Sarah her heir. I guess there was a sort of knowin' between the two. At least Miss Sarah always said that even though Miss Kate was dead, she could still talk to her, same as I could."

Debbie didn't want to delve into that line of thought. She finished her coffee and pushed back her cup. "Why didn't Miss Sarah ever get married?"

Cressie ran her fingers around the flowers decorating the china. "I don't know if I should tell you that part. Miss Sarah told me confidential like."

Debbie wasn't about to let her tell only part of the story, especially not now that she was so thoroughly hooked into the family and the events. "Don't you trust me?" she pressed.

Cressie refilled her cup. When Debbie shook her head in response to Cressie's silent offer, Cressie sat back down. "When Miss Sarah was a young girl, some friend of the family got drunk one night and raped her. Her dad and brothers beat the boy within an inch of his life, but that didn't help Miss Sarah none. She would never have anythin' to do with men after that . . . other than her family, of course."

Debbie shook her head. "I hear about things like that today, but somehow I never think about it happening back then."

"Times change, but people don't. Anyway, when Miss Kate died, Miss Sarah was still a relatively young woman . . . in her thirties . . . and she came here to live out the rest of her life." Cressie idly turned her cup around before continuing. "She once said to me that no matter how hard it was at times, she never regretted leaving her family. Every time one of them looked at her she could feel their rememberin'. Like an itch that wouldn't go away. When she came here, no one knew the story, and she could just go on about her business."

"Miss Sarah lived a long time?"

"Both Kate and Sarah enjoyed full lives."

Debbie rose and returned to the back window. "Is Miss Sarah buried up on the hill, too?"

"All the Mullers are there, and a lot of the Slavanias."

"I went by the cemetery in town one day. There was a plaque that said the oldest dated grave was 1837."

"Oak Grove Cemetery," Cressie said placidly. "That's hardly surprisin' when you consider Nacogdoches is the oldest town in Texas. Have you seen the fort yet?"

"I haven't gone inside."

"Nacogdoches has a lot of historical places. When you get the time, you'll have to look around and see some. You'll have a better idea what you're part of when you do."

Debbie stared out the window for several minutes. The late afternoon sun caught the branches of the big oak standing imposingly at the top of the hill. The limbs seemed to reach up to touch the heavens while the leaves danced in the gentle breeze. Nearby, tombstones, like sentinels, guarded their secrets. Suddenly Debbie felt compelled to see the graves for herself. "I think I'll walk up to the cemetery before dinner."

Debbie stopped halfway up the hillside to watch a

covey of birds fly overhead. Looking back down the hill, she saw Sal climb out of his old Ford pickup and make his way to the apartment. He had been working at another place today, but the day before he'd told her he planned to plow the garden on Tuesday. Tomorrow.

As they had discussed the matter, Debbie had realized that while she might be buying more groceries in order to feed three people, other things like vegetables, beef, and chickens would be raised on her own land. Bending down, she grabbed a handful of the soft earth and let it slip between her fingers. She liked the idea of producing her own food. She raised her face to the setting sun and laughed. In reality Sal would be doing the work, but as owner of the land, she would be a necessary part of it as well.

Slowly she finished climbing to the graveyard. Starting under the big oak, she went from one gravestone to another until at the end of one row she came to a gray marble monument with a tangle of jasmine. The flowers were gone now, but spring would bring back their fragrant beauty. This was Kate's grave. She didn't have to read the inscription any more than she questioned that Sal tended to the foliage, as his forebears had.

Kate had been born in 1866 and died in 1943. She was seventy-seven and had lived a full life, if not necessarily a happy one.

From there, Debbie discovered the grave of Kyle Muller. Beside it was a stone bearing the name *Mary Muller* and the dates 1844–1872. This had to be Kate's mother. Down the slope a bit were three markers, one woman and two boys, all Mullers, and all died in 1862. This would be Kyle's first wife and two sons. At the end she found Sarah's grave. The monument shone as though someone polished it regularly, and the grass was meticulously trimmed.

Debbie stooped to pick up a leaf that marred the grave's perfection. Poor, sad Sarah, she thought, looking around at the house and land. Sarah, who seemed to have so much but who had been afraid to live, afraid to love, afraid to take a chance.

Debbie started to walk over to the other side to see the Slavania graves when the slamming of a car door drew her attention to the side drive. Keith ran up the back steps and knocked on the door. He had changed into his jeans and knit shirt. Because she had wanted to talk with the dean's secretary, they had separated, and he had left after the meeting. She wondered what he was doing here now.

Cressie stepped outside the door and pointed. Keith turned and looked up at Debbie. Her pulse quickened with anticipation while she watched him climb the hill.

Determined not to let him know how pleased she was to see him, she again studied Sarah's grave. The older woman must have suffered a terrible crisis as a young person, a problem that remained with her the rest of her life. It affected her viewpoint and actions until, at the end, she had died alone except for the friendship of the Slavanias and Kate's ghost. Could the bitterness have turned her mind so that she'd imagined things and even talked to invisible beings?

Debbie thought about her own experience of the vision the night after Norma's party. She had tried to shake it off as a result of drinking Cressie's wine.

"Hi," Keith said when he came up beside her. "Problems?"

"Hi yourself. What brings you this way?"

"I wanted to find out how you came out with the dean's secretary and if you'd been ground to hamburger."

Debbie gave a mock shudder. "If looks could kill . . . but as you can see, I'm whole and none the worse for wear."

"I'm glad. I know you think you can handle anything, but I sometimes shake at your lack of fear."

She heard tenderness in his voice and saw a twinkle in his gray eyes. She looked down at Sarah's grave. Sarah had spent a lifetime alone and had died without knowing the vital fulfillment of motherhood.

Debbie looked back at her own life, her marriage to Charles, which had been good in the beginning but had turned her bitter and against the idea of any future relationship. In that instant she realized she didn't want to wind up like Sarah, alone.

Looking up at Keith, she smiled. She had been wrong to turn aside his friendship. They might never be more than good neighbors, fellow teachers, and friends, but it was a beginning.

She said, "In answer to your question, the dean's secretary knew nothing about the note change but promised to check into the matter. I really don't expect anything to come from it, but at least she's aware that it happened."

"Good. That should take care of future mistakes." He placed her hand between his. "I'm glad you finally remembered I was standing here. For a minute there I thought you had taken off without me."

Debbie smiled. "Believe me, you are never overlooked."

"And don't you forget it." Turning, they started

down the hill. "Cressie invited me to stay for dinner, but I thought I'd best ask if you had any objections."

Beginning to feel free of the heavy weight that had burdened her for almost a year, Debbie laughed. Peeking up at him, she said, "So you came all the way up here for my endorsement?"

His deep, rich laugh seemed so familiar. The soothing sound healed her inner pain. His grin packed as much punch as the Prince's kiss when he woke Sleeping Beauty.

"You're damned right," Keith said, glancing down at her. "Cressie is the best cook in these parts. I'd do almost anything for one of her meals."

"You would, huh?" she taunted, drawn in by his wicked grin.

"What's your price, lady?"

Debbie jerked her hand free and raced down the hillside. Laughing back over her shoulder, she called, "I'll never tell, but the last one down has to wash the dishes!"

8

After dinner Debbie set the tray with coffee and whipped cream on the small walnut table and glanced around. This parlor at the back of the house had been her own special place from the beginning. Most of the contemporary furniture she brought from Vermont was here, the home entertainment center with her stereo, VCR, and television, a large russet velvet recliner, and the cushioned beige sofa. The glow from the fire in the small brick fireplace added a golden warmth.

From the portable liquor cabinet near the fish tanks, she took a bottle of amaretto, added a small amount to the two cups of coffee, and topped each with thick cream. Seeing Keith standing in the doorway and grinning like a boy discovering a hidden treasure increased her own delight even more.

"I haven't been in here," he said. "This is nice."

"Thanks. This room is special." Debbie handed him a cup.

Keith walked toward the sofa, but she blocked his

path. The corners of his mouth twitched with unspoken amusement. He turned and made himself comfortable on the recliner. "Am I the first to be invited into your inner sanctum?"

"You're the first." Debbie sat on the sofa and curled her leg up under her. "The Slavanias prefer the front parlor. Whenever they stay to watch cable, they sit in there. Sometimes I join them. But I read a lot and listen to the stereo. This room suits my needs better."

"Have you had many visitors yet?"

"Only Jenny and you."

"The others will come. They're giving you time to get settled." He tasted his drink again. "Are Cressie and Sal here much in the evenings?"

She couldn't tell if he was asking from idle curiosity or probing for specific information. "Not often, and it's mostly weekends. During the week they get up too early to stay up late."

"I gather you don't regret their moving into the apartment, or does Cressie cramp your life-style?"

"Not a bit," Debbie said, staring into the dancing flames of the fire. "They make life much easier, especially since school's started. You know how much work there is beginning in a new college, what with organizing your classes, meeting the students, and making certain your curriculum meets the dean's requirements."

"You're not sorry you moved to Nacogdoches?"

"Not at all." She laughed softly. When he glanced up quizzically, she added, "Despite your warnings about my neighbors and my neighbors' warnings about the ghosts."

"What about Cressie's strange predictions?"

"She's a wonderful housekeeper, but I doubt I'll ever be at ease with some of the weird things she says," Debbie admitted.

"Don't feel alone."

Keith tossed another log on the fire. "How do you get along with Sal's disconcerting solemnness?"

"Believe it or not, I find he bothers me more at times than Cressie. Maybe it's because he's not only tall and dark, but so eerily quiet, and the way he can look at you with those black eyes. It's as though he can see clear through you. He'd make a perfect handyman in a vampire movie." Knowing she was rambling, she paused. "Actually, he's kindness itself. He's helpful, industrious, and he lights a mean fire."

"A mean fire?"

"This room needs a good fire. It's frequently drafty." Debbie rubbed her cheek against the afghan resting on the back of the sofa. It sent out a sweet lemony odor. Cressie must have washed it since the day she'd spilled paint on Keith. Just thinking about that experience had her looking around cautiously.

Keith took a sip from his cup and licked his lips. He stretched out on the chair, the picture of contentment until she noticed the mockery in his gray eyes.

His low, rich voice melted into the atmosphere. "The fire, the beautiful surroundings, the closeness, are almost perfect."

She couldn't resist. "Almost?"

"Have you ever turned on the stereo to soft music, switched off the lights, and enjoyed the fire? The room could be extremely romantic."

"Frequently." She found a small extended nub on the sofa to twirl. It helped relieve the unwanted anticipation she felt. "And it's heavenly in here, except when there's the draft."

Keith frowned. "Does that happen much? I don't notice one now. In fact, the room's nice and warm. You might even say a cozy hideaway for one or two."

"No, not often, and I can't find any reason for the draft when it does appear. I mean, sometimes the weather is warm outside, or the sky can be stormy. Everything can seem perfect, and then there it is . . . popping out of nowhere. It makes no sense."

"Popping? Not a gradual seeping of cold air?"

"Popping. Suddenly. It's not there, then it is."

Keith straightened from his relaxed slouch. "Have you mentioned the draft to Sal or Cressie?"

"Yes, but they don't seem concerned. They simply say old houses are like that."

Keith looked around the room curiously, studying the corners and shadows.

"And don't mention ghosts in the house," she warned. "I don't believe in them, and I've heard enough of the subject."

"There usually is a logical explanation for so-called spiritual happenings. At least that's what I've always found."

"So I read." She didn't like the twinkle that suddenly appeared in his eyes.

His voice deepened suggestively. "Maybe if you sat side by side on the sofa with someone, you wouldn't notice any draft."

What he was suggesting was obvious, but she wasn't ready for their friendship to advance that fast—at least not yet, and maybe not ever. Actually she didn't know what she wanted, and that surprised her. A month ago she would have had no doubt. "I told you earlier, you're my first guest in here. What am I supposed to do when I'm alone?"

"Maybe you shouldn't spend so much time by yourself."

Debbie refused to discuss the subject further. "Tell me about your writing and your new book. Have you found any good stories since you've been in Texas?"

One side of Keith's mouth twisted upward while he shook his head. When he sat back more comfortably on the recliner, she relaxed: he had accepted her decision. A moment later she wondered at her own disappointment. She had neatly deflected his suggestions and yet a part of her wished he had been more persistent.

His head resting against the back of the chair, his eyes half-closed, Keith said, "I've heard a lot of ghost stories since I first began researching. Apparitions of tormented souls who cannot rest, spirits of pirates searching for treasure, slaves seeking atonement, murder victims wanting revenge . . . the stories are endless."

"But?"

"So far my investigations have proven them to be figments of someone's imagination, or a craving for notoriety." His eyes met hers. "That's why your attitude is so unusual. It makes me wonder what you're hiding, especially after all the gossip."

"Maybe I don't like notoriety, or maybe there's simply nothing to tell. Perhaps I'd prefer company who wants to be with me rather than someone whose prime interest is my house."

"No red-blooded male could ever not want to share your company, so rid yourself of that foolishness immediately." Keith sipped his coffee and continued agreeably. "If you've read my book, you know I spent a great deal of time checking out hauntings in the northeastern part of the country. With all the witch-hunts and present-day town promotions for tourists, Salem and its surrounding area were especially bountiful with tales."

"Why did you only write about events in that part of the country?" Debbie turned to face him, her arm resting on the back of the sofa.

"It's the seat of our country's history. People and records go back a long way there, so plenty of time has passed to allow a multitude of such things to happen." Keith shrugged. "I just decided I should start there." Finally, after a pause, he grinned and added, "Besides, I was teaching in that part of the country, which made my research easier."

Debbie laughed at the wicked sparkle in his eyes. The deep-seated history of the Northeast was the printed explanation used for publicity about the first book. She had suspected that he chose to start there because that was where he was teaching, and she liked this fresh honesty in Keith. "How did you ever get started in such a field?"

"Ironically enough, I think I first became interested in ghosts when I heard about Kate. The two summers I spent in Nacogdoches during and after high school, I never tired of hearing the local tales. And believe me, I listened to every story I heard."

"But you never saw any signs of Kate yourself?" She wondered what he would say if she told him her experience after Norma's party.

"No. Have you?"

Debbie watched the flame rise with a last-minute burst of defiance before dropping with the end of the log to mingle with the glowing embers. "Like you, I don't believe in ghosts, but I have encountered impressions, particularly after one of Cressie's wild predictions."

"What do you mean by impressions?"

"Oh, the sudden cold drafts, the scent of jasmine. Sometimes I feel like someone is watching me, but when I look, I don't find anyone."

Keith chuckled. "Drafts and odors can generally be explained if you know where to look. Usually some person is trying to put something over on you. Cressie is an expert at manipulation and could convince you spirits, both good and bad, roamed the house. If you believed everything she said, you'd spend all your time looking over your shoulder."

Since she didn't want to tell him about Kate's apparition, she dropped the subject. "Is your next book an extension of the first, covering a new part of the country, or are you going with a different slant?"

"So far I'm still researching."

"Did you know I was almost your neighbor?" When he shook his head, she explained. "The day I applied for the bank loan for my house, Eleanor offered to rent me one of her other houses if I would rather wait than buy so soon." Not able to resist a small jab, she added, "She also stressed that if I rented, I had to leave you to your privacy."

"Writers do need quiet, and some people can be nuisances. But I like company on occasion, especially attractive blondes with fascinating green eyes." When Debbie didn't respond he said, "I'm sure Eleanor didn't understand that you have an aversion to relationships with men right now."

Debbie took a big swallow of her coffee and

coughed as it burned her throat. When she'd regained control she inquired firmly, "So what are you researching now . . . for this new book of yours?"

"I'm working on ghost reportings in Navasota, Galveston, and around here, since Nacogdoches can be traced back as far as 1779. I was hoping with all the tales about Kate haunting this house, you might be able to contribute."

Irritated, Debbie steered the conversation into his camp. "Have you never thought of settling down and getting married, or is your career the only thing important to you?"

"I thought about it once, but Dad lost his money around that time, and I had to go to work to stay in school. When my girlfriend found someone else, I realized she wasn't that important, but my writing was."

"What about in the future?"

Keith gave her an appraising look. "Are you asking because you're interested or demonstrating typical female curiosity?"

Knowing he had put her in her place quite neatly, Debbie jumped up and grabbed their cups. "I'll get some more coffee. I know I could use another cup."

"You want more coffee or more amaretto?" Keith called laughingly behind her.

She refused to answer.

When she returned with their coffee to the back parlor doorway, soft music welcomed her. Keith was sitting on the sofa, his long legs stretched out in front. The flickering glow from the firelight cast patches of reflected color and contrasting shadows throughout the now darkened room and across Keith's satisfied expression while he soaked up the new atmosphere.

He had pressed for advancing their relationship after all. Debbie shook her head.

All at once the room turned cold, as though some-one had turned the air conditioner on full force and directed its entire barrage into the small space. Her nostrils filled with a pungent mustiness smelling of dormant dampness from the bowels of the earth. She shivered and looked for familiar items to fight the impression that she was entering an unknown cavern instead of her own private sanctuary.

A shadow invaded the room. It was formless at first but grew in size and shape while it struggled and twisted. Keith stiffened and bent forward, searching the corner near the fireplace. The glow of the coals faded while smoke saturated the room, spiraling toward the ceiling. Instinctively she fought the paraly-sis that threatened to consume her, wondering why Keith didn't say anything about it. This was nothing like the gentle apparition she had seen near her bed-room door.

Keith pushed at some bricks. "I see what you mean about the draft. It's like nothing I've felt before. Sud-den and downright smelly."

The form rose above Keith and took on a menac-ing, ugly air. Debbie struggled for her voice. "Keith . . . can't you see . . . ."

Keith frowned, a picture of concentrated puzzle-ment. "Have you ever considered that you might have a hidden space in this room?"

Debbie swallowed. "No. What kind of space? A secret room? A hidden passageway?"

"I definitely feel a draft, and it's damned cold . . . freezing almost, like a breeze off an iceberg."

"Possibly even a cavern with stalactites and stalagmites," Debbie managed hoarsely.

"Yeah, even the odor." He snapped his head around. "What's wrong?"

"Can't you see it? There over your head?"

Keith looked up, his eyes widened, and somehow Debbie broke free of her frozen state and flicked the light switch by the door. Her hands trembled, spilling coffee into the saucers, but the shadow disappeared with the brightness.

She set the cups down carefully and leaned against the wall. "Did you see it?"

Keith looked around, his mouth a white slash. "The draft must cause a pocket of smoke somehow when there's a fire. I don't think I've ever encountered anything quite like that before."

The phone rang. Debbie pushed her hair back from her face and drew a long, shaky breath. "That's the strangest smoke I've ever seen."

Keith regarded her, his face shuttered as though nothing had happened. "The phone's ringing. Don't you think you'd better answer it?"

Debbie shot him a furious glance and walked on rubbery legs back to the kitchen. She couldn't believe how calmly he was acting. Did he run into things like this all the time in his research? Maybe she should just brush it off, too. But it was frightening in its own peculiar way, and not at all like the shape of a woman in her bedroom doorway that night. Lord, she hoped it didn't come back. She wasn't sure what she'd do if it did and she was by herself.

Several minutes later Debbie set down the phone and gnawed at her lower lip. Teresa's words still rang in her ears, and she was torn between concern and irritation. Teresa hadn't bothered to mince her words: she wanted Keith. Jenny had fallen again.

"Who was it?" Keith asked, not giving her time to say anything.

"Teresa."

"What did she want?"

Debbie pressed her hand against her throat. She couldn't let this frightening, horrible knot gain control. She wondered if maybe some of Cressie's ravings had finally started to affect her mind. First the terrible smoky form just when Keith started making romantic advances, then Teresa's call, and now the most awful apprehension about Jenny. Pulling strength from deep within, she managed to instill a calmness in her voice that surprised her. "Jenny fell. She's hurt. Teresa wants you to come immediately."

"Is Jenny hurt bad?"

Debbie shook her head. "Teresa didn't say. She was crying, even screaming. I couldn't make much sense out of anything other than she was furious you were here, and she had wasted time trying to locate you."

"Where's Michael? Did she call an ambulance?"

"I don't know. She didn't say."

"We'd better go. How did Teresa know to call for me here?"

The music from the stereo stopped, and the room returned to normal. Yet it would never be quite the same for her. Keith grabbed her by the arm, urging her toward the door.

"Come on. Let's see how bad Jenny is."

"Not us. Teresa asked for you," Debbie emphasized bluntly.

"Us. If she called your house for help, that means both of us. Besides, if Teresa is as incoherent as you say, Jenny will need you. Teresa's never any good in an emergency."

"Wait, my purse," Debbie protested at the back door.

"You won't need it. I'll bring you home." He opened the car door so she could climb inside. "You didn't say how Teresa found me here."

"Eleanor told her she saw your car here on her way home from work."

"I wonder why she didn't ask Eleanor."

"I can understand. Eleanor doesn't encourage requests for help."

"Maybe not, but if Jenny's seriously injured, Eleanor has a cool head and would be quite capable in an emergency."

Keith gunned the engine, and gravel sprayed behind as they sped down the driveway. Debbie closed her eyes and prayed Jenny was all right and Teresa was simply overreacting.

Keith turned onto the paved roadway. Debbie couldn't shake the nagging suspicion that Jenny's earlier cries for help were bearing a nasty fruit.

The distance wasn't far by going directly through the woods and fields, but flying down the road through the darkness, Debbie thought it seemed to take forever. Every agonizing minute of the way, she couldn't escape the picture of Jenny as she had looked on the night of Norma's party, curled up and sobbing. How would they find her now?

Teresa ran out the front door of the two-story English-style house as they pulled to a stop in front. Cressie had once mentioned that Gloria and Jim Winthrope had spared little cost in the construction, wanting to present an affluent and prosperous impression to possible horse buyers.

"Oh, Keith," Teresa wailed. "I'm so glad you came. I thought I would never find you. I'm so worried. There's so much blood."

Keith caught Teresa when she flew into his arms. "Where's Jenny? How did it happen?" His dark brows drew together in concern. He turned Teresa around, encircled her shoulders with his arm, and hurried toward the house.

"Jenny's out back. I was afraid to move her."

Debbie was left behind, closing the car door and feeling like a fifth wheel. Other than tear stains, Teresa appeared as immaculately groomed and beautiful as always. Even the droop of her shoulders and her wet lashes added to her appeal, Debbie decided, irritated by Keith's response.

"Come on, Debbie, don't dally," Keith urged, looking over his shoulder, his eyes intent on her face.

Debbie raised her chin defiantly and followed them up the front steps. After all, she was here only to help Jenny and because Keith had insisted.

While following the others through the house, she noticed the Queen Anne furnishings and gold-and-white brocades, an extension of noble English ideology. It struck her as odd that Gloria would leave all this behind and never return. Was Jenny right in thinking Michael had disposed of Gloria? And was he trying to get rid of Jenny as well?

Her fears for Jenny mounted.

"What happened? How did Jenny get hurt?" Keith snapped while they rushed down the hall. He was obviously growing agitated with the crying, clinging girl at his side.

"I don't know what happened," Teresa moaned. "I was watching television. I thought Jenny was upstairs, but when I went up to see if she wanted some cocoa, I couldn't find her." She broke into heavy sobs.

"Come on, Teresa. I need to know what happened to Jenny." Keith's tone seethed with suppressed irritation.

Teresa explained while they went out the back door. "Jenny goes out every night to tell Nacho good night. . . . I couldn't find her anywhere in the house, so I . . . I decided to check to see if she was at the stables . . . and then I found her. Oh, God, I think she's dead."

"Where's Michael?" Keith snarled as he rushed down the back stairs to the girl lying at the bottom.

The moon shed little light on Jenny's pale face and closed eyes. She resembled a large discarded doll. One jeans-covered leg was curled beneath the other, and the sneaker on the foot of the straight leg rested against the last step. One arm rose over her head while the other rested at her side.

Debbie blinked, fighting her own panic. Jenny looked dead.

"My God," Keith whispered after a brief, heart-stopping moment. He bent to check for a pulse.

Jenny's very stillness hit Debbie hard. She wished desperately that the teenager would move, cry, anything to show she wasn't dead.

"Why in hell didn't you call an ambulance?" Keith groaned, and straightened up.

"I did, but they haven't come."

"Then she's alive," Debbie said, and moved around to the side. Where the shirt pulled up, torn and scraped skin marred Jenny's stomach. But worst was all the blood puddling on the concrete walkway around Jenny's head, mingling in her short golden-brown hair and streaking her skin.

Teresa wrung her hands. "I called you because I didn't want to go to the hospital alone. I'm so scared. Do you think she'll die?"

"I don't know," Keith replied. "She doesn't look good."

"What if she dies?" Teresa wailed hysterically.

"She won't die. We won't let her."

The certainty in his voice reassured Debbie as well as Teresa.

Shaking his head as though to clear his thoughts, Keith said, "We need to put a blanket over her."

"I'll go. Where will I find one?" Debbie offered.

Teresa's mouth opened and closed, but no sound came out.

Debbie gritted her teeth to keep from saying anything and turned to reenter the house. Not everyone responded well to a crisis. Perhaps Teresa couldn't help herself.

Climbing the stairs to the second floor, Debbie struggled with her own guilt feelings that she had let Jenny down in some way, that there was something she could have done to prevent this. She couldn't shed the suspicion that something wasn't right about the accident.

The first bedroom Debbie found at the top of the back stairs obviously belonged to Jenny. Clothes lay scattered on the blue carpet, on the flowered chair and on top of the thick comforter. Over a desk, a bulletin board was filled with newspaper clippings and ribbons. But hanging over the bed in prime prominence was a large picture of Jenny's horse, Nacho, with a laughing woman who closely resembled Jenny.

In the hall bath Debbie located the linen closet

and grabbed the first blanket she found. After considering a moment, she took a washcloth and held it under the cold water. She set the rag on top of a towel and carried everything down the stairs.

Handing the blanket to Keith, she asked, "How is she? Any change?"

Covering Jenny with the blanket, Keith said grimly, "No change. Thankfully she's still alive." He took the rag and, crouching down, wiped Jenny's face gingerly, then refolded it to a clean area and pressed the cloth against the cut in her head. "She's unconscious, but she's breathing. I guess that's something."

"She hasn't moved," Teresa sobbed.

"Where's Michael?" Keith asked.

"He went to Dallas, to meet with someone. He wasn't certain whether he would get back tonight or not," Teresa replied after a long struggle to regain control.

"What's taking that damned ambulance so long?" He lifted the rag to examine the cut again.

At that moment Keith seemed to age right before Debbie's eyes. She wanted to comfort him, but that might distract him, and Jenny needed all his attention.

"I couldn't find you. It took me forever to locate you," Teresa complained peevishly.

"Why didn't you ask Eleanor for help if you couldn't do something for Jenny yourself?" he parried sharply.

"I called the ambulance, but all that blood, I was afraid to touch her in case I did something wrong. I didn't know what to do."

From the distance the wail of a siren broke the stillness of the night. Debbie sighed with relief.

"It's about time," Keith muttered. He rearranged the

blanket over Jenny and applied pressure to the wound.

Debbie looked around at the four wooden steps leading down from the house. Partially buried bricks, turned on end, walled the concrete sidewalk that led through the grassy backyard to the brick fence beyond. Bushes and shrubs grew around the back of the house, and square and rectangular flower gardens with the same brick outline spotted the lawn. Everything appeared trimmed and edged, and nothing seemed out of place. "Can you tell what happened? Why she fell?"

Keith looked around. "Not really. It's dark. She must have tripped coming down the stairs."

"But she's come out here at night hundreds of times," Teresa protested. "Why should she trip now?"

"Who knows? Accidents happen," Keith replied somberly, and studied Jenny's still form.

"Oh, Jenny . . . Jenny . . . what have you done?" Teresa cried, and wrapped her arms around herself.

"Go and bring the paramedics back here," Keith said at the sound of the ambulance pulling up out front.

When Teresa continued to stand still, Debbie nodded and ran back through the house. On her way out the front door, she ran into the medics and directed them back through the house.

A short time later, after they'd placed Jenny safely in the ambulance, Keith said, "Teresa, do you want to ride with her?"

"Oh, Keith, do you think she'll be all right?" Teresa sobbed.

Debbie glanced at Keith's tight mouth and grim expression as he tried to comfort the clinging girl. "I'll ride with Jenny," she offered. "That way if she should regain consciousness, she won't be frightened at being with strangers. You bring Teresa with you."

"Come on, make up your minds," the medic prodded. "We need to get rolling."

"Thanks, Debbie. We'll be right behind," Keith
said.

After making certain Jenny was settled safely, the
medic turned his attention to the front. Debbie made
herself as comfortable as possible in the confined
space. When Jenny gave a low groan, Debbie picked
up her hand and squeezed gently. "You're going to be
okay, Jenny. We'll have you at the hospital in a few
minutes. Just hang on a little longer."

Jenny's eyes fluttered open. "Debbie?"

"I'm here." When Jenny's glance drifted around
the enclosed space, Debbie said, "You're in an ambulance. Teresa and Keith are following behind. It won't
be long. How do you feel?"

"My head hurts."

Thinking of all the blood she had seen, Debbie
wasn't surprised, but at least Jenny had regained consciousness. "The doctor will take care of you. You just
take it easy now."

Jenny's glazed eyes remained on her. Worried,
Debbie looked up at the medic.

"The fact she woke up is a good sign," he said.

"There was something on the step . . . long . . .
round . . . like a broom handle," Jenny whispered. "I
saw it, but I was rushing and couldn't stop in time. I
fell."

There hadn't been any broom handle lying around
that Debbie could see. But perhaps it had fallen over
the side into the bushes. She squeezed Jenny's hand.
"Don't worry about that now."

Jenny's eyes closed, and she slipped back into a

world of her own.

"Most accidents happen around the home," the medic commented. "I don't know why, but they do. And generally they're caused by someone's carelessness."

Debbie refused to look at him. She was afraid he might see the horror she was feeling. This could be another accident, like the last time, but everything around the house, with the exception of Jenny's room, was neat and in its place. Why would a broom handle be left haphazardly on the step? And where was it now?

Debbie clung to Jenny's hand. She wanted to reassure herself and at the same time comfort Jenny, but her mind raced with possibilities. The only two people in the house had been Jenny and Teresa, and as much as Debbie disliked Teresa, she couldn't think of any reason why she'd want to hurt her own sister . . . half sister.

Debbie bit her lip and considered the facts as she knew them. She hadn't seen any sign of a broom handle. Still . . . if there had been something on the step, if the accident had been rigged to look like one, as before with the saddle . . . "No," Debbie muttered. The whole idea was too farfetched. People in real life didn't do such things. At least none of her acquaintances did.

Yet she couldn't quiet the small voice inside her head that kept asking: Could Jenny's head injury make her imagine things, or was the girl right? Was someone trying to harm her?

Debbie recalled the day she'd spilled paint on Keith, the same day Jenny had first said Michael wanted to get rid of her, as he had her mother. Debbie closed her eyes. She wanted to deny the whole picture, forbid the mistrust that wove into her thoughts. But Cressie's warning refused to be held at bay: "You've set the forces loose. There'll be more blood to pay before the past is happy. You be careful, Miss Debbie, that it's not your blood that spills out over the land."

The ambulance drew up to the emergency entrance. The vehicle's back door opened, and Debbie slipped out so that Jenny could be wheeled inside. She began to shiver as she followed the stretcher through the hospital door. She felt so cold, but not as cold as Jenny must feel. For it hadn't been Debbie's blood that had spilled out on the land.

When the medical personnel wheeled Jenny into a room, Debbie stared after her. She must do whatever she could to keep anything like this from happening again. A third attempt might succeed.

9

Debbie crunched down on a worn vinyl chair in the ER waiting room. Ever since their arrival all Teresa had done was cry and cling to Keith until he now wore a white line around his lips. Muttering under her breath, Debbie kept her distance from the young woman.

Taking advantage of the nurse's appearance with a glass of water and a pill for Teresa that the doctor had prescribed, Debbie asked about Jenny.

"She's down in X-ray. The doctor should be here shortly to let you know what he finds. Now we need to get some forms filled out." Turning to Teresa, the nurse said, "As you're her closest relative, why don't you go to admittance and take care of that. Maybe by the time you finish the doctor can answer any questions you may have."

"I want to talk to the doctor first," Teresa insisted. "I have to know if Jenny will be all right."

The nurse shrugged and left. A few minutes later two ambulances arrived with three victims from a car wreck. At the sight of the badly injured people, Teresa again lost control.

Keith tried to stop her crying. He reassured her that Jenny would recover and insisted Michael would have been there to handle matters if he'd been in town. Debbie admitted to herself that he certainly knew the right buttons to punch with his low, confident voice. By the time the injured from the wreck were whisked out of sight, Teresa's eyes were glazed but she was quiet.

"Do you mind waiting here while Teresa and I go to the admitting office?" Keith asked Debbie. "She might find another part of the hospital more pleasant, and filling out the forms will help pass the time. I'd like to make a couple of phone calls, too."

Thankful to be rid of Teresa's emotional outbursts for a while, Debbie agreed. Once they were out of sight, she leaned her head against the ivory wall behind her chair and closed her eyes.

"Are you Jenny's friend, Debbie?"

The doctor stood in front of her, his hands in the pockets of his white jacket. She straightened and said, "Yes, I'm Debbie Dillon. How is she?"

"Jenny has a slight concussion and a gash on the side of her head. She has a broken finger, some pulled muscles in her back, and numerous scrapes and bruises. I want to sew up the cut, but she insists she wants to talk with you first. I think she might rest better afterward."

Debbie stood up. "Her sister is here. They just went down to admittance. . . ."

"Jenny asked for you specifically, and frankly, considering her sister's temperament and lack of control, I'd rather keep them separated. I don't want Jenny upset. Head injuries can be touchy."

"Will she be all right?"

"With time and rest, she should recover nicely."

Reassured by the confidence he radiated, Debbie followed him into a small emergency care room. The blood had been washed away from Jenny's face and hair, and she looked much better than when Debbie had last seen her.

"Head wounds generally bleed extensively and consequently appear worse than they are. Still, concussions are serious business," the doctor explained. Looking down at Jenny, he said, "I'll be back in a minute. Then, young lady, I expect your full cooperation."

Debbie stepped closer and smiled at the teenager. "You certainly gave us a fright, but the doctor says you're going to be fine."

Jenny bit her lower lip and moaned.

Debbie continued, "Teresa and Keith went to the office. They'll want to see you."

Jenny opened and closed her mouth twice before the low, ragged words came out. "You came when I needed you. I knew you would."

"Hey, we're friends, aren't we?"

Jenny grabbed Debbie's hand. "I heard . . . I heard the nurse tell . . . the doctor that Michael is out of town . . . that's why he isn't here."

Debbie brushed back a strand of hair from Jenny's cheek. "That's right, sweetheart, but we'll see that you're taken good care of, don't worry."

Jenny shook her head and winced. "No . . . you don't understand."

Debbie bent closer to hear the barely audible words. "What don't I understand?"

"Michael was at the house . . . earlier this evening. . . . I saw him . . . and Norma, too."

"But Teresa said—"

"Teresa might not know. She was watching a movie, but I saw them out my window. Michael went out the back door. . . . Norma was in the barn. Then they drove off. I wondered . . . that's when I decided I'd go see if Nacho was all right."

"Why wouldn't Nacho be okay?"

"Michael wants to sell Nacho. He says he's old and costly . . . that I should have a better mount."

Debbie frowned. "I doubt if he'd take him in the middle of the night."

"You don't understand. Nacho's mine. He was my mother's horse. I don't want another one." Jenny squeezed Debbie's hand. "Don't let them take Nacho while I'm in the hospital . . . don't let them take him."

"Maybe you should tell Teresa."

"She doesn't care. She won't help. Promise me. Promise you won't let them take Nacho."

"There now, young lady, it's time to sew up that head," the doctor said firmly as he entered. He shot Debbie a hard glare when he saw Jenny was upset.

Debbie refused to let the doctor rush her away. "I'll do my best. Maybe Keith can talk to Teresa."

"Teresa says Nacho's too old. He's no good anymore. She thinks I should let Michael get me a better horse. Please, Debbie, promise."

"I really need to finish this and move on to another patient," the doctor pressed. "Nurse? Do you have the tray ready?"

Debbie kissed Jenny's cheek. "I won't let anything happen to Nacho while you're in the hospital, I promise. But you have to promise to do what the doctor says, and get well."

"A deal." Jenny sighed, but her eyes widened at the sight of the hypodermic needle.

Debbie slipped out of the room.

As she reached the waiting room she saw Keith and Teresa walking down the corridor. At the sight of Teresa's hostile expression, Debbie rubbed her pounding temples.

"You saw Jenny?" Teresa asked, coming to a halt in front of Debbie.

"Yes, she's going to be fine."

"You have to keep butting in, don't you? Jenny's my sister, I should have seen her first."

"Can we see her?" Keith interjected smoothly.

After explaining the extent of Jenny's injuries, Debbie bent the truth to preserve harmony. "Jenny wanted to talk with someone before the doctor began suturing her gash. She was worried about her horse and wanted to make certain Nacho would be all right while she's in the hospital. Since the doctor is busy and I was the only one here, I went in."

"Do you know how upset and worried I've been?" Teresa asked, her voice rising. "I want to see Jenny myself. If you had refused, the doctor would have waited until I got back."

"I did what I thought best," Debbie said, knowing full well Teresa wouldn't get to see Jenny until the doctor approved. "Jenny did say she saw Michael at the house before her accident. He's in town somewhere."

"Michael's in town?" Teresa asked.

"Apparently so."

"You mean he was there when Jenny was hurt and went off, leaving me to take care of her?"

"No, I think he and Norma had left before the accident."

Turning on Keith, Teresa demanded, "You talked with Norma. Did she tell you Michael was here?"

"You were too busy complaining about all the forms to listen. She said Michael wasn't there. He had already gone home, but she promised to get him to the hospital as soon as possible."

Teresa opened and closed her mouth, her eyes glittering with anger. She turned on Debbie. "Why is it that ever since you arrived in town, there's been nothing but problems? Everyone used to get along just fine. What's more, Jenny didn't have all these accidents before you arrived, either."

Debbie was too stunned to say a word.

Nostrils quivering in suppressed anger, Teresa stepped closer to Debbie. "What did you really come to Nacogdoches for? What are you after?"

Unable to believe that Teresa actually felt she was to blame for Jenny's difficulties, Debbie stepped back. "Jenny had problems long before I arrived. The only thing I've done is try to be her friend."

"Her friend? Since she started spending so much time with you, she's either crying or yelling or saying the craziest things I've ever heard."

"That's hard to believe."

"Is it? She says way-out things like Michael wants to take Nacho away from her or Michael's trying to kill her."

Debbie blinked with discomfort.

Teresa moved closer until she was only inches from Debbie's face. "Or she says I don't care about her, Norma wants her out of the way. She even goes so far as to say Keith's playing with her mind." Teresa stomped her foot. "She's my sister, and I won't have any more of this."

"I've only been trying to help."

"Some help. You've got her convinced you're the only one who believes her or cares about her. Well, let me tell you one thing, I agree with Michael and Norma. You're not good for Jenny, and you better watch out."

Debbie grasped at the only thing she could. "Watch out for what?"

"People in these parts don't like outsiders stirring up trouble. We take care of our own."

"I'm only showing Jenny I care."

"You care so much you're trying to get her locked up in some mental institution. What is it with you . . . a way to get your kicks now that you don't have a man?"

With the strange incident in the parlor, Jenny's frightening accident, and now Teresa's accusing outburst, the whole evening suddenly became too much. Ignoring Keith's stunned expression and his attempt to pull Teresa back, Debbie set her hands on her hips and spat back, "Well, according to Cressie, I'm here because of Kate . . . and my purpose is to act as a catalyst to correct some wrongs from the past. So if you have any deep, dark secrets, I suggest you stay away from me and take care how *you* proceed in the future. Something terrible could befall *you* as well."

With that prophetic announcement, she brushed past the startled two and headed for the restroom.

From behind her Teresa called out, "Well, you don't have to worry about me. You're as crazy as that old witch, and I want no part of either of you. But you stay away from Jenny, do you hear me? Stay away from her!"

For once Debbie agreed with Teresa. She had

sounded as weird as Cressie, but she couldn't take back the words now. She could apologize and try to smooth things over. That certainly would be the mature thing to do. But it would also feel like groveling, and at the moment she didn't care if she ever saw Teresa or her family again—except for Jenny. No, she'd have to suffer the consequences of her outburst and go from here.

As for Keith . . . there was no telling what he thought about the exchange. But judging from his frown when she stalked off, he probably agreed with Teresa.

After washing her face and hands, Debbie wandered around the hospital hallways. Finally, when she felt enough time had passed for Michael to arrive, she headed back to the waiting room. Looking up at the big round clock on the wall, she saw it was almost morning. She had to go to work in a few short hours and needed to get home. If Keith wasn't ready to leave, she'd call a cab.

"Where have you been?" Keith asked tightly when she reappeared.

Debbie remained prudently quiet.

He grabbed her arm and said, "Come on, we're leaving. After I drop Teresa off, I'll take you home."

"Has Michael arrived?" Debbie asked bravely in spite of the killing look Teresa gave her and the harsh expression on Keith's face.

"Jenny's been taken to a room. Michael and Norma are staying with her for a while," Keith replied icily.

When Keith opened the passenger door, Debbie let Teresa slide in while she unlocked the door to the backseat and climbed inside. Keith slammed both doors, and the car shuddered with the impact. After settling in on the driver's side, he drove down the narrow city streets without saying a word. Even Teresa remained quiet.

Debbie looked out the window at the passing business buildings, the shops, dark restaurants, and the college. She kept replaying the trip to the hospital with Jenny in the ambulance. Had there really been something on the step to make Jenny fall? From what Teresa said, Debbie would never be invited back to find out.

She uttered a sigh of relief when they pulled into Teresa's driveway.

"I won't be long," Keith promised quietly when he opened the door for Teresa to get out.

Debbie nodded, but as soon as the two disappeared through the front door, she opened her car door and flew around the side of the house to the scene of Jenny's accident. She wasn't about to let Teresa's threat stop her from doing what she felt was right. But it had to be done now.

Debbie pushed around in the shrubs and bushes near the steps, looking for the broomsticklike object Jenny claimed made her fall. The dim light didn't help. She prodded and searched harder. Nothing. The object wasn't there.

Surely no one would have removed the round pole after Jenny fell, leaving the girl lying there injured. But if Jenny's accident wasn't an accident …

Debbie glanced toward the barn where Jenny had seen Norma and Michael. Biting her lip, she debated. Keith would be looking for her soon. Still, she didn't want to leave until she'd seen inside the barn. She might not get another chance.

And Keith . . . his cold anger on the drive from the hospital would have frozen the ears off Nacho if the horse had been in the car. There was no way she could appeal to Keith for help.

Further delay would be wasted time. She knew what she had to do. She ran to the barn door and, after turning on the light, went inside.

Nacho was safe in his stall, as were the other horses. Nothing appeared out of place. Everything was neat and orderly. The aroma of leather and stored hay fought for prominence with the pungent odors of horses.

Knowing she had to get back to the car, Debbie made her way through the barn to the door. She paused. Pitchforks and shovels hung on the wall, and several pieces of long pipe rested on the floor below. She studied each closely, trying to determine if there were any unusual markings that might indicate they had been the source of Jenny's accident.

"What in the hell are you doing in here? I thought I told you to wait in the car."

Debbie jumped at Keith's bark. "I wanted to check on Nacho." When Keith continued to stare at her, disbelief written across his face, she asked, "Why would there be pipe in the barn?"

After a tenuous moment he said, "Michael is putting in another water line. Now would you mind explaining why you want to know?"

Debbie couldn't think of a single plausible excuse with Keith leaning against the doorjamb, his arms crossed and effectively blocking her exit. Finally she gave up and told him what Jenny had said.

The rustle of shuffling straw permeated the air in the next few excruciating minutes. Debbie brushed back her hair with a trembling hand, but she refused to be the first to break eye contact.

Keith sighed, his shoulders slumped. "Come on, I'll take you home."

They walked side by side. The hoot of an owl disturbed the stillness of the night, and Debbie wrapped her arms around herself. She tried to locate the night predator, but he was as evasive as everything else that evening.

As she slid in the passenger side of the car, Keith stood holding the door. Anger darkened his gray eyes, and the grooves at the edge of his mouth deepened. She empathized with the mouse the owl might be hunting for his nightly meal.

"By God, I think Teresa may be right. You go out of your way to stir up trouble." Keith slammed her door.

His words stung. Debbie ignored him and stubbornly blinked back tears. Twice on the drive to her house he spoke her name, wanting her attention. She concentrated on the passing scenery.

"Oh, don't act so damned childish," he finally accused when he stopped the car. "Talk about temper tantrums."

"Childish? Temper tantrums? Maybe so, but I'm not such a blind pompous ass that I can't hear a teenager crying for help." She jumped out of the car, her chin held high, and refused to answer when he called her.

Keith's car sped off as she entered her house. Angrily she wiped away a tear that had somehow managed to slip free. It had taken her a long time to trust Keith enough to let their relationship progress a step further.

Now she felt even worse. It was as though she'd suffered a greater loss than she had after Norma's party when he drove away angry. But she wasn't going to back down and apologize. Maybe it was a mistake to relent her stand, even if dinner that evening had been fun. She'd survive.

And she refused to let Keith or Teresa make her feel guilty for being concerned about Jenny. The teenager needed help and depended on her friendship.

Furthermore, she wasn't stirring up trouble. Trouble haunted her.

After she turned off the lights and crawled into bed, the scent of jasmine enveloped her. Debbie refused to open her eyes. Between gritted teeth, she muttered, "Not tonight, Kate, not tonight." Pulling the covers over her head, she fell asleep.

It wasn't until she was dressing for work the next morning that she recalled her words to Kate and shook her head. The traumatic events of the night had her calmly talking to ghosts when she knew ghosts didn't exist. Then she recalled the smoky form in the back parlor. Well, she didn't think they existed.

Maybe there was some truth in Teresa's accusation at the hospital. Maybe being around Cressie was affecting her. But she'd take Cressie and Kate any day of the week over Teresa and Keith!

Two days later Debbie sat staring at the silent telephone on her office desk, wishing she hadn't cut Keith off quite so drastically the night of Jenny's accident. Maybe she had overreacted a bit, but he could have been as understanding with her as he'd been with Teresa.

Pushing her thoughts aside, she determinedly created new lesson plans, prepared pop quizzes for her classes, and even volunteered to help with a homecoming tea at the college.

Since the one time she had called Jenny at the hospital, and Teresa had answered saying Jenny was fine and then hung up, Debbie hadn't tried again. She'd simply made her inquiries directly to the nurses' station. Now she was through with that nonsense. She put away her papers and left the college.

Jenny was watching television when Debbie walked into the hospital room. "Hi, how's it going? You're certainly looking better."

"I'm fine except for headaches, and my back hurts when I move too quickly. The doctor says I need lots of bed rest."

"You sound bored. That's a good sign."

"I guess. At least I've had plenty of visitors, even some of the girls from school. And Keith says Nacho is missing me, so I have to do what the doctor says and get well fast."

Debbie was glad to hear that no matter how he felt about her, Keith was at least still concerned about Jenny. Leaning over to smell the largest of the bouquets of flowers that filled the room, Debbie said, "These are nice."

"They're from Michael and Norma." Jenny folded and unfolded the sheet edge. "Michael felt bad because he wasn't there when I was hurt. He's been here a lot. So has Norma."

Debbie sat on the chair next to the bed. "Can you tell me more about your accident?" When Jenny didn't respond but kept playing with the sheet, she said, "You told me in the ambulance that you tripped on your way down the stairs when you were going out to see Nacho."

Tears filled Jenny's eyes and slipped down her face. "I don't remember. I don't remember anything about that night. . . . And everyone keeps asking."

Sensing the teenager's confusion and pain, Debbie kept her face perfectly blank and her tone as unemotional as possible. "Did the doctor say why you couldn't remember?"

"He said not to worry. People forget things all the time when they've had a concussion."

Debbie hated to press when Jenny was so obviously already upset, but she needed to know. "Does he say you may remember later on?"

"Maybe. Maybe not."

"Oh, Debbie, I'm glad to find you here," Norma called jubilantly as she breezed into the room. Her striking maroon suit and frivolous pink blouse decorated with lace and a bow radiated more good cheer.

"And how do you feel today, sweetie?" Norma bent over and kissed Jenny's cheek. "Upset are we? Well, we'll just have to get over that. The doctor says you'll probably be able to go home Saturday. Won't that be nice?"

Norma paced around the room, rambling on about the flowers, the hospital food, and Jenny's visitors. Clearly any serious conversation would not be allowed. Glancing at her watch, Debbie rose. "I need to go. As usual I have lessons to prepare."

"You'll come back?" Jenny asked eagerly.

"You couldn't keep me away," Debbie promised before opening the door. "After all, you're one of my best friends in Nacogdoches."

"I'll be right back, Jenny dear. I want a few words

with Debbie," Norma said, and followed Debbie out into the hall. "Michael and I want to thank you for all your help and concern," Norma said, smiling. "I understand Teresa went to pieces at the sight of all the blood."

"Some people have difficulty responding in a crisis, particularly if it's someone they care about."

Norma gazed at the woman in uniform who was mopping the corridor a short distance away. Then, as though pulling her thoughts back, she asked, "Did Teresa happen to mention why she didn't call me when she couldn't find Keith at home?"

Debbie hesitated, not knowing what to answer.

"I mean," Norma continued, "Michael and I have been close friends for some time now. I would have thought . . . at least hoped she would have contacted me before bothering you."

"I think Teresa mainly wanted Keith, but if she had called you, would she have been able to find Michael as well as you?"

Giving a half smile, Norma said, "Not being certain exactly what time Jenny had her accident, I can't say, but Michael did spend a couple of hours with me before he went home."

Aware that either Norma was lying or Jenny was mistaken, Debbie said, "After Keith called you from the hospital, he said you told him that Michael had just left your house. He must have gone straight there when he returned from his trip to Dallas."

Once the words were spoken, Debbie couldn't take them back. They sounded presumptuous on her part, and she held her breath, hoping Norma wouldn't be angry.

"Oh, you know how these men are," Norma said

with a nervous little laugh. "If things don't go their way, they need a sympathetic ear." Then, not giving Debbie time to say any more, she said, "I'd best get back to Jenny. She'll think we're not telling her everything if I don't. Thanks again." Norma whirled around and disappeared inside Jenny's room.

It was useless to try to learn any more, so Debbie walked away. She had stepped outside the bounds of good manners, unless one knew the reason for her questions, and after Keith's reaction, Debbie wasn't sure it was wise to explain. Fortunately Norma hadn't taken offense.

When she saw the doctor at the nurses' station farther down the hall, she stopped there and greeted him. He smiled cordially, stated the same diagnosis Debbie had heard earlier, and even duplicated Jenny's explanation about her loss of memory. Still, Debbie wasn't satisfied. "That night in the ambulance and in the emergency room, Jenny told me a few things about her accident. Why can't she remember them now?"

A puzzled expression crossed his face. "You know, you're the third person who hasn't been satisfied with my explanation that people sometimes forget things when they have a concussion. Jenny is no exception. As to why she told you at first and can't remember now, I can only say the mind is a delicate instrument. It's quite capable of blocking out unpleasant memories or problems it doesn't want to deal with."

"But will she ever recall?"

"Who can say? But you're the first to mention that Jenny did actually remember after the accident. The others seemed only worried that she had forgotten and curious as to whether she would remember in the future." Glancing at a nearby nurse obviously waiting for him, he said, "I really must go. Don't worry. Jenny's young and healthy. She'll be fine."

He walked off, leaving Debbie staring at his back and speculating about who else had been asking questions and why. She could of course follow him and ask, but that might cause more complications. Jenny's family seemed to want her to stay out of their affairs. The smartest thing would be to say nothing. The only thing she knew for certain was that she wasn't dropping the matter completely. Her decision made, Debbie left the hospital.

For the next few days she spent the evenings in her small parlor and prepared lessons or graded papers while listening to music. Whenever it seemed as though there were something lacking in her life, she busied her thoughts on her work or a book. She consoled herself with the idea that at least Keith wasn't around saying "I told you so" or accusing her again of stirring up trouble.

She was thankful that at least the cold, musty draft or the gyrating smoke didn't return and spoil her pleasure in the back parlor. She wondered if maybe the experience was growing in her memory with time. Surely it couldn't have been as grotesque as she thought.

By the following Monday Jenny had gone home from the hospital, and Debbie admitted she didn't like being at odds with Keith. She wanted them to at least remain friends. Dragging her wayward thoughts back to the papers she was grading in her campus office, Debbie glanced at the clock on her desk. She had only one more hour to go before her posted office hours ended and she could go home.

When the phone rang, she was glad of the reprieve and grabbed the receiver. She was surprised to hear Eleanor on the other end.

Debbie set down her red marker. "Say that again. I don't believe I heard you correctly."

After a brief pause Eleanor spoke again. "You've missed two payments on your house loan, or, to be more exact: you haven't made any payments besides the initial down. If you miss any more, I'll have to commence foreclosure proceedings."

"But I mailed them. There's plenty of money in my account. You know that," Debbie protested, and brushed her hair back from her face.

"True, but you still have to make your monthly payments within the ten-day grace period."

"I did send them each month and exactly on the first. I remember distinctly putting them in the mailbox in front of my house."

"Has anything else you've mailed not arrived?"

Debbie's stomach tightened. She had been so upset over Jenny, she'd forgotten about the caller and the meeting notice. Could this be another coincidence, or had he taken her check from the box? The first payment would have gone missing before the changed meeting date, the second afterward.

Hearing Eleanor's voice calling her name, Debbie quickly said, "I haven't heard of anything else missing, but then I didn't know about the loan payments until you called."

"You mean you haven't reconciled your bank statement? That's foolish of you, and not at all good business."

"With Charles's last big cash settlement, I had no reason to worry. Other things seemed more pressing."

Eleanor's long silence grated on Debbie's nerves. She refused to explain what took priority.

Finally the banker said, "We normally have excellent postal service, but I assume there could be a first time. Still, it's hard to believe it happened two months in a row and only to your mortgage payments."

"But only one bank statement. Tell me, is it possible to make arrangements for you to deduct the payment each month directly from my account so this can't happen again?"

When Eleanor agreed, Debbie set up an appointment to go in and sign the necessary forms. She also promised to make up the back payments.

"You know, Debbie, financial responsibility is important. The lack of it will cause you problems in Nacogdoches and cost you friends. More important, if word gets around that you're irresponsible, you could lose your job at the college."

Debbie's insides churned faster and faster. "I'm aware of that, but this wasn't my fault, and unfortunately, I can't explain what's happened. I can only promise to take steps to prevent it from happening again."

"Well, I, of course, won't mention anything as long as you take care of the problem, but you had best make certain it isn't happening to other creditors as well. If it is, you could find living in Nacogdoches very uncomfortable. Small towns do have a few drawbacks that way."

"I'll take care of it . . . and thanks, Eleanor." Debbie set down the phone. She had to agree with the banker that two different checks going astray seemed highly unlikely.

Debbie placed the papers she had been grading

into two stacks, one finished and one to work on later. Taking her check register from her purse, and the phone book from her desk drawer, she began to call people she had mailed checks to since settling into her home.

An hour later, her calls completed, Debbie was on her way home. She had promised to make three more payments for checks not received, but the situation could be worse. Apparently the missing mail happened only on two specific days. One helpful clerk suggested a prank by some children, but because her mortgage payment was involved both times, Debbie felt there was more to it.

What she couldn't decide was if the missing mail was connected to the notice change and whether the events had been the work of her motel caller. Maybe there was no connection at all.

If they were connected, the caller wasn't going after her life, but her career and her reputation.

In the end she resolved that all she could do was not leave her mail in the box for pickup, contact the post office to alert them of her problem, and hope for the best.

When she approached the driveway to Jenny's house, she noticed Michael Townsend stop his pickup and climb out rather than drive onto the road. He waved at her, and she stopped.

His jeans and shirt were dirty, as were his hands when he wrapped them around the top of the lowered window glass. Bending so that he would be on her eye level, he said, "I've been busy, but I wanted to thank you for your help with Jenny."

"I'm glad she's better and not seriously hurt. I was worried for a while. I imagine she's glad to be home."

Nodding soberly, he continued, "Teresa tells me you rode in the ambulance with Jenny and might have been able to have a private talk with her before she spoke to anyone else."

He made her actions seem almost sinister. Teresa must have disclosed her own feelings about Debbie's part in Jenny's accident. Forcing a calmness she didn't feel, Debbie said, "That's right."

"Jenny tells me she doesn't remember what happened. Teresa says the only thing she knows is that she found Jenny lying at the foot of the steps and called for help. Keith suggested I talk with you."

Thanks a lot, Debbie said silently to the absent Keith. Then, as matter-of-factly as possible, she related Jenny's story. She had to pause several times when Michael's black eyes seemed to bore through her and restrained violence radiated from his white-knuckled hands.

When she finished, the silence that followed seemed impregnated with the odor of man and horse and the struggle for a man's control.

Time inched by, and Debbie wished bitterly that she had been a little more tactful in her approach rather than blurting out the incriminating statements.

"I'm not sure I want you around Jenny anymore. In fact, I'm not sure I even want you in this neighborhood."

Shocked, she said, "I'm afraid I'm not following your reasoning."

"Jenny has had problems ever since Gloria's disappearance. Things have been difficult enough. Now, since you came, she has become obsessed with the idea I'm responsible for Gloria's vanishing, and that I mean to harm her as well."

"I had nothing to do with her beliefs but have simply been trying to help a disturbed girl get through a difficult time. If you're upset because you don't like what I repeated about the ambulance trip and her worry about Nacho, remember you asked me what happened. I didn't come to you."

"How do I know you're telling the truth?"

"Why should I lie? Of course, you should keep in mind that because Jenny had a concussion, and I could find no proof that anything was on the step to make her fall, I've not mentioned the matter to anyone other than Keith."

The lines deepened at the sides of his mouth, and Michael's eyes narrowed momentarily to slits. "You're right. I did wave you down." He watched a car slow down to pass before he spoke again. "I did come back to the house that night to get out of my suit and into more comfortable clothes. I wanted to go over to Norma's and talk to her about the trip. Teresa was absorbed in the television. She didn't see me. I saw no sign of Jenny. I had nothing to do with Jenny's accident."

His explanation reminded her that she had left out the part of Jenny's seeing Norma there as well. "You hadn't been to Norma's before you came home to change?"

He slammed the top of the window with his hand. "What are you . . . Miss Inquisition? I just told you what happened."

Even though she knew it was foolish, Debbie braced her hands around the steering wheel and deliberately burst his bubble. "Jenny said Norma was with you, although she stayed outside, in the barn, while you were up at the house."

Behind Michael's shoulder Debbie saw Teresa walk onto the front porch of the house and look at them. The late afternoon sun caught the red of her dress, making her appear like an avenging fire goddess. She glared in their direction.

Michael, with his dark good looks, seemed the perfect extension of fire and brimstone. Despite the warm afternoon, Debbie shivered and spoke with an icy calm, a miracle considering Michael's savage expression. "I really need to go now. Cressie will be waiting dinner."

"Ms. Dillon, I know Norma told you I was interested in buying your property. Now I'm making it official. Just name your price."

"I don't want to sell."

"You will. Given time, you will. I promise." Stepping back from the car, he added before she could drive off, "Jenny recalls nothing about the night of the accident. If any of your wild stories are spread around, I'll suggest you've been influenced by Cressie's weird ways. The folks around here are nervous of Cressie. They don't think she's quite right. Nervous folks can react violently on occasion, if you get my meaning."

"Are you threatening me?"

"Just offering advice because Keith thinks highly of you."

Debbie stared at him for a few seconds.

"I'll only say this one more time. I would never hurt Jenny. Keep that in mind." With those final words, Michael nodded his head and turned to climb back in his truck.

Breathing deeply, Debbie stepped on the accelerator. There was the chance Michael was telling the truth. But would he spread gossip to turn the neighbors against her? She should probably be more tactful in championing Jenny. After all, she already had enough problems.

Turning into her driveway, she wondered if Michael could be behind the motel phone call or any of the other irregularities. More likely she was grasping at possibilities because of Jenny's influencing comments, and she'd best be careful if Michael meant what he said.

Cressie stood by the kitchen stove when Debbie walked in and offered her a cup of coffee.

"No," Debbie replied grimly, and pulled out a chair. "This evening I want a glass of your homemade wine."

Pursing her lips, Cressie took the wine from the cabinet and poured a full glass. She set it in front of Debbie, poured herself one, and sat across the table. "What are we celebratin'?"

Debbie took several swallows and closed her eyes, enjoying the warmth that followed the liquid to the fluttering in her stomach. "We are not celebrating. We are commiserating on the duplicity of men."

Cressie's eyebrows shot up. "You want to tell me about it?"

Debbie couldn't resist. She told Cressie all about Jenny's accident, the suspicions she hadn't told anyone but Keith. Then Debbie related her conversations with Eleanor and Michael. By the time she finished, so was her wine. She held out her glass for more.

"I don't mind gettin' you another glass, but how about a bowl of chicken and dumplin's, too." Not waiting for a reply, Cressie placed both the food and wine in front of Debbie, then sat down to watch her eat a spoonful of the chicken gravy. "You're not worried about Sal and me, are you?"

"I know you'll be fine. And no one's going to run me out, either."

"What's got you most riled is Mr. Keith's absence and his tellin' Mr. Michael."

"Wouldn't you be mad? Keith accused me of stirring up trouble and then he's the one who dumps me in the hot sauce."

"And 'specially since he wasn't there to share it."

Debbie's eyes narrowed. "What I'd really like to know is what he's up to. One minute he acts like my friend, the next he treats me like I'm a leper."

"Have you ever considered that maybe he has a problem of his own he's not quite sure how to handle?"

The spoon clicked as Debbie set it against the china. "Keith? Have a problem he couldn't solve? Never. He knows all the answers and isn't afraid to express them."

"Maybe he's never felt the first painful pangs of love before. . . ."

"Keith in love? Never happen." Debbie sipped her wine. "Besides, if he cares about anybody, it's Teresa."

Cressie rose as Sal came in the back door.

"The only interest Keith has in me," Debbie continued, "is to provide fodder for his ghost book. He thinks I'll tell him some goodies about this place, and he'll get another best-seller."

"Well, I'm sure you know best," Cressie replied soothingly, and dipped up two more bowls of food and set them on the table.

Debbie slammed down her glass. "I had enough of being used by Charles. No man is going to do that to me again."

"Sounds to me like Charles is a real pitiful creature." Cressie passed a basket of hot rolls.

Agreeing with her and happy he was history, Debbie pulled her roll apart and slapped butter on it. She dug into her dinner with enthusiasm as Cressie gazed out the kitchen window.

"Now Keith's another sort," Cressie commented thoughtfully. "He's smart enough to figure the best way to catch a honeybee is to snag the suspicious creature when it's unaware, and he's clever enough to see the best bee around."

"Honeybee? Suspicious creature?"

"Like when the bee's busy searching for pollen hidden 'mongst the different plants in all sorts of places, and doesn't realize there's someone with a net just waitin' to pounce."

Debbie finished her roll. "I'm not certain whether you're referring to the someone with the net as Keith or whoever is doing all of these crazy things around here."

Cressie nodded. "That's what makes life interestin'. The waitin', the watchin', the not knowin'."

"Cressie," Debbie said warningly.

"Mr. Keith won't hurt you, and you might even come to like havin' him around, but that doesn't mean another hand won't squash you if you give him half a chance. Whatever happens, you be careful."

10

Debbie's office pressed in around her and wrapped her with discontent. Outside, the sunshine beat down on the rush between classes, the students' voices ringing back and forth gaily. Yet neither of these was the reason she sat and stared at the ungraded papers in front of her. Concentration was impossible because she couldn't do anything but replay last night's dinner conversation with the Slavanias after her encounter with Michael. She couldn't forget Cressie's crazy comments.

Debbie disagreed with everything Cressie said about Keith, but that altered nothing. The possibility that Keith liked her more than she realized continued to buzz around in her thoughts. She considered her own feelings for him and whether her foolish actions might have lost her something significant.

Somehow, despite her affirmed intentions, Keith had become quite important to her. That being the case, it was up to her to take the next step, to call and apologize. After all, he'd made the first step after the first disagreement.

Playing idly with her marker, she anticipated his reaction. If he told her to shove off, she'd at least know how he felt and that Cressie was wrong. On the other hand, he could admit he shouldn't have accused her of stirring up trouble, and they could be friends again. He could do neither if she didn't make the call.

Tightening her mouth firmly, Debbie called information for Keith's phone number. When he didn't answer, she checked the teachers directory and called his college office. By the third ring, her shoulders slumped. Having made up her mind to take action, she was more disappointed than she'd anticipated. She wondered if she would have the courage to try again later.

"Hello," Keith answered in a brisk tone.

For a moment she couldn't think of a thing to say. "This is Debbie. I . . . I wanted to apologize. . . ."

"Where are you?"

"In my office."

"Let me call you back. I have someone with me now."

The sound of the disconnecting line left her staring at the black instrument with the same compelling disappointment a high-strung racehorse must feel, left standing at the starting gate while all the other horses speed around the track. Slowly she set the phone back in its cradle.

The chair became uncomfortable. She picked up her blue marker and attempted to correct more papers. Her mind refused to concentrate. Her mouth felt dry. She wanted a drink of water. She pushed back the chair and went out into the hall to the water fountain. After her drink, she returned to shut her office door. Up and down she paced in the four-by-nine-foot area in front of her desk.

The room shrank. Debbie flicked away dust from objects she picked up. The sunlight flowing through the window annoyed her. The sound of footsteps in the hall irritated her. She checked to make certain the damned electric clock still ran.

When the phone finally rang, she took a deep breath and sat down before answering. She didn't want Keith to think she had been sitting on top of the stupid thing, especially since he'd kept her waiting so long.

The voice on the other end wasn't Keith's. It belonged to the dean's secretary, informing her that Dean Carrington wished to see her. Immediately. He had to fit her in between appointments. Debbie was given no choice but to comply.

Her heart pumping furiously from her fast pace, she was there in minutes. Dean Carrington's blue eyes didn't twinkle behind the horn-rimmed glasses, and his large hand wasn't offered in greeting. He displayed all the characteristics of "the stern lion" she had first seen the day she'd almost missed the staff meeting. Nowhere did she find the friendly mentor she had come to know from private discussions.

The dean didn't ask her to sit down but left her standing in front of his desk. Leaning back on his chair, he asked politely, "You have been with us a little over a month now, haven't you, Ms. Dillon?" Not giving her time to respond, he said, "You came with very good recommendations, as I recall, but you left Vermont because of a divorce."

Confused, Debbie could only say, "Yes, that's correct."

"I know that sometimes such experiences can affect a person's behavior." He straightened and folded his hands on the desk. "My secretary informed me that you almost missed the staff meeting because the date on your notice slip had been changed. The dean of English now tells me that you haven't given him the details of the program you used in Vermont—the same program we discussed instigating here. You promised to send him an outline. Is there some problem you've failed to mention?"

Debbie wondered if his unblinking blue eyes could see her shock. "But I mailed them, Dean Carrington. I sent them the same week we discussed the matter."

"A good education is important in order to succeed in life, and it is almost too late now to use your ideas next semester. I also believe that accepting responsibility and meeting obligations in a timely fashion are as important as proper dress in the modern world. All make impressions. I expect my staff to set a good example."

Her association with the college seemed to be hanging by a thread. The dean couldn't have made it any clearer without saying the precise words.

Licking her dry lips so that she could speak naturally, Debbie said, "I've had trouble with mail I've put in my box at home. Some has gone astray. Other things, besides the details of the program for the dean of English, haven't been received, either. I'm sorry about this. I'll get him another copy immediately and hand-deliver it this time. Believe me, nothing like this will happen again."

Dean Carrington studied her closely for several

moments. "See that it doesn't. I'd hate to lose you. You're doing a fine job. The students like and respect you. That's important. Now run along and get the program details over to him today."

Hesitant to let him see how truly upset she was, Debbie let our her breath slowly. "I'll go right now."

His words stopped her at the door. "I hope there won't be any more changes on the notices. Most of my staff have been with me for a long time. I cannot imagine any of them changing the date to an incorrect one."

Debbie turned. "I hope you're not suggesting I changed the notice myself?"

"Ms. Dillon, I don't know what happened, and since you were prepared for the meeting, it doesn't matter at this point. I just wanted you to know you do have my attention."

Debbie bit her lower lip. He sounded like Keith, explaining Jenny's actions, how her wild imagination and tales were prompted by her need for love and affection. It was her way of seeking attention. Although this wasn't true in Debbie's case, it would still be a mistake for her to take exception to her superior's remarks. "Thank you, Dean Carrington. I appreciate your concern."

"Besides, you can always look on the bulletin board if you have any questions. The notices are posted."

"Thank you. I'll remember that." Clamping her mouth shut, she nodded and left quickly.

Debbie spared no time getting back to her office and grabbing the folder where she kept the program details. She went immediately to the copy machine. When everything was nicely placed in another folder, she dropped it off with the secretary to the dean of

English, explained what had happened, and extended her apologies for any trouble caused.

She knew Dean Carrington had simply reacted to his own embarrassment, but Debbie didn't like being called on the carpet like a wayward student. She didn't intend to put the dean or herself in such a predicament again.

It was more than an hour before she collapsed on her office chair, her head resting in her hands, the door shut to the outside world. She was so frustrated she wanted to throw something. After Eleanor's call she had stopped by the bank, filled out the monthly deduction form, and paid the past due payments; she'd also dropped off the other three missing payments. This time the consequences were more serious: now she had Dean Carrington's attention, and she could expect her job to be closely scrutinized.

The worst part was that all she could do was sit there and stew. Why? Who? What next? It was like hitting at smoke. Debbie massaged her pounding temples. Of course, she could start asking questions. But what could she say that wouldn't make her appear as crazy as Cressie, and whom should she ask? No, she could only wait and see what happened next and hope she could handle the difficulties as well as she had so far. Damn, but she hated to be at someone else's mercy this way. It was like life with Charles all over again.

The ringing of the phone broke into her thoughts. She didn't want to talk with anyone, but hiding wouldn't change what was to come. Reluctantly she picked up the receiver.

"I told you I'd call right back," Keith said icily. "Why didn't you stay by the phone?"

Debbie remained silent. Her head hurt like blazes; she wasn't in the mood for this. Finally, in a voice laced with sarcasm, she said, "Hard as it may seem, other people exist in my life besides you." Realizing she was again reacting unfairly, she relented. "Dean Carrington called. I had to go see him." She went on to explain what had happened with her missing mail.

"It could be some kids pulling a prank and might not happen again," Keith offered reassuringly.

It sounded good even if she didn't believe it. "I didn't call to tell you my hard luck story. I wanted to apologize for losing my temper and refusing to talk to you in the car. Sometimes I tend to say too much, like after Norma's party. Unfortunately, after Jenny's accident I overreacted the other way and said nothing."

Keith remained silent.

Having already decided on the importance of reestablishing their relationship, if possible, she decided to give him his pound of flesh. "Apparently my divorce left me with a few hang-ups. I shouldn't take them out on you. I would like us to be friends."

"I was beginning to think that might not be possible."

"I understand. It took me a long time to call, but I am sorry. Will you forgive me and come for supper?"

"Tonight? I can't. I already have plans."

Debbie heard the regret in his voice. Her response would affect their future. She gave a halfhearted laugh. "That's probably best, anyway. The way I'm feeling right now, it might turn into another disaster. We could make it another night, if you're free."

If he refused, there was nothing more she could do but accept the inevitable.

"How about tomorrow evening?"

"Perfect. I'll see you then."

She purposely didn't mention a time. She didn't want to give him a chance to reconsider. Whenever he arrived was fine with her.

Debbie placed the ungraded papers in her briefcase to finish at home. Satisfied that the office looked tidy, she locked the door and headed for her last class of the day. She might arrive a little early, but she enjoyed walking across the thick grass under the pines and watching people hurry about their affairs. The red-brick campus buildings lent an air of continuity; the carefree students, who had yet to face the trials of the outside world, bubbled with an air of great things to come. She liked this college. She wanted to stay.

Three hours later Debbie pulled up in her driveway beside a strange pickup. Wondering who was visiting, she gathered her things and stepped out of her car just as Frank Johnson stomped out the back door of her house. He called to Cressie, who stood in the doorway watching. "I'll talk to Debbie out here. You can go on about your business."

She hadn't seen Frank since his confrontation with Eleanor at Norma's party and wondered what prompted this unexpected visit. Cressie, she noticed, wore a frown and pursed lips as she watched through the screen. She didn't take kindly to being ignored, but from the set of Frank's shoulders and his quivering mustache, it was obvious he didn't care. Both looked ridiculous, and Debbie struggled to keep from laughing. She set down her purse and briefcase and waited for him by her car.

"I don't know how you can stand to live with that crazy woman. She would drive me up the wall, the way she carries on about Miss Kate or Miss Sarah or talks about evil spreading across the land."

Debbie smiled. "I won't ask if you'd like to go inside and have a drink while we talk."

"I've been inside, and I've had a drink. Now I just want to get my business over and get on my way." He turned around and glared at the woman still standing in the doorway.

Debbie leaned against the fender and folded her arms. "What can I do for you, Mr. Johnson?"

"You can sell me your land."

"We've had this discussion. I don't want to sell. I'm just getting settled, meeting new friends. Besides, I like my job."

He waved his hand, dismissing her words. "You can keep the house and front acre. That will leave you all you can manage, anyway. Think of the benefits. You won't have those weird Slavanias hanging on your every movement, bedeviling you with their eerie talk." Frank stuck his thumbs in the back pockets of his jeans. "What I'm interested in is the rest of the land."

"I told you at Norma's party I didn't intend to sell. What made you think I might change my mind?"

"Several things. You've been here a spell. You've had a chance to get to know the people, and you've had some time to live around that old woman."

"Is that all?"

Frank dug a line in the dirt with the edge of his boot before he met her unwavering gaze. "I heard you've had a few problems. . . . I heard Norma talking in the grocery store, telling someone Michael made an offer for your land. He don't need more land for his dang horses. If he does, he can go the other way. Both of them are mighty upset with you."

There are no secrets in a small town, but Debbie

was surprised at how fast news traveled. Did anyone know Michael had threatened her as well?

"What would you do with the land?" she asked.

"That's my business."

"Ah, but it's my land and my surroundings that would be affected if I sold to you."

Frank rocked up on the toes of his boots and back down. "You sound just like Miss Sarah. I want to put in a small resort with cabins that aren't stacked in each other's back pockets. Guests could fish in the pond. I might even put in a small restaurant and have horses for riding."

"There isn't much to draw people to Nacogdoches besides the college. You could lose your shirt, and the repercussions could affect the rest of us."

"There's good hunting close by and Sam Rayburn Lake for boat fishing. There's historical sights all around the area. It's peaceful and quiet in these parts. People like to escape from the rat race occasionally. Besides, in the beginning, because this area hasn't developed yet, I'd keep prices low. People could afford to stay."

"The neighbors would be against your commercializing and ruining their residential value."

"Neighbors don't bother me." He laughed slightly, displaying a trace of bitterness. "It might be kind of nice to have them sit up and take notice for a change."

The neighbors or Eleanor? she wondered. "I'm not interested in selling, Frank." She raised her hand to stop his interruption. "I know Michael made me an offer. You've made me one. I'm turning you both down. I like everything as it is now."

Looking back at the house, Frank grumbled, "That's hard to believe."

"No one is perfect. Cressie and Sal have good points, too. She's a fabulous cook, keeps the house immaculate, and Sal takes care of the land."

Frank dug another line in the dirt, his own expression shadowed and brooding. "I hear tell you've been having some problems with your mail."

"Do you know anything about that?"

His head snapped up. "Not me. I don't do that kind of shenanigans. But I reckon that once mischief starts, it tends to go on and grow. It can get wearisome and even dangerous."

"That almost sounds like a threat," Debbie said softly, recalling meeting Frank the morning after her first threat in Nacogdoches.

"I'm just offering a little neighborly advice since you're new to these parts. I know how people's minds work around here. I've been on the receiving end."

Debbie straightened. "Suddenly I seem to be having a problem getting along with my neighbors. Maybe I should just follow Miss Sarah's tactics and stick to my own affairs and let others tend to theirs."

"If it's not too late."

Debbie looked out across the yard to the stand of trees. Most of them had already shed a large part of their orange, yellow, and bronze foliage, so that the ground looked like a playground for squirrels and other small animals. Yet the branches still carried a token of leaves. Winter peeked around the corner, but fall still retained possession.

Sighing, Debbie retrieved her purse and briefcase from the car seat and looked back at Frank. "I can only do the best I can. I came to Nacogdoches to live, make it my home. I don't intend to let anyone run me out."

He nodded. "I sort of figured you might take that attitude. Still, I had to try."

"Come back, Mr. Johnson, when you have time for a cup of coffee or some of Cressie's wine."

"You called me Frank before. I kind of liked it."

Debbie nodded. "Frank. Come back and visit. I want to hear about your animals, and I'd like us to be friendly neighbors."

Frank, his head cocked to one side, curled the end of his mustache between his thumb and forefinger. "I think I might like that." He walked to his pickup, but before opening the door he said, "You know, if you don't feel like selling outright, you might consider us going into a partnership in a resort."

Startled at the unexpected idea, Debbie stood still.

"Then again, I don't reckon you'll be here long enough. I don't think folks want you around anymore. I think you may find your problems have just begun."

"What do you mean?"

He shifted his position. "Newcomers are outsiders. They don't always fathom our ways, and they tend to tread on seasoned toes. I don't think you're the type to step cautiously. Some might call you headstrong. In either case, you can pull a whole packet of trouble around your head if you're not careful."

He climbed in the truck and started the ignition. Debbie didn't move. She couldn't.

"Of course, that crazy old woman with her ghosts and ramblings could finish you off just as well . . . drive you clean up the wall. I don't know how you stand it." Frank drove off, leaving a spray of gravel behind.

At that moment Debbie considered Cressie the least of her worries. Maybe she should become a recluse. There was certainly something to be said for it. But that type of life didn't appeal as it had when she'd first come, she realized suddenly. She'd stirred things up since she'd arrived in Nacogdoches, but life had also taken on new meaning for her. She didn't want to go back to the old Debbie.

Cressie called out from the back doorway, "Telephone. It's Eleanor Farmsworth."

Debbie walked toward the house. She was in no hurry to learn what the banker wanted now. Still, it never paid to be rude.

Eleanor's unexpected tirade about hearing Debbie was considering selling and hadn't said a word to her was irritating in the extreme. When the woman actually accused her of being secretive and sneaky when the bank held the mortgage, Debbie leaned against the wall for support. Almost overnight, it seemed, everything had changed.

Her briefcase suddenly seemed much heavier. She set it on the floor, along with her purse, and used her free hand to massage her throbbing temples. "Listen, Eleanor, I don't know where you heard the news, but I'm not planning to sell . . . to Michael, to Frank Johnson . . . or to anyone. You don't need to worry about there being more smelly horses or a resort in the neighborhood ruining our property values."

"If you change your mind for any reason . . . any reason at all, I want you to let me know immediately. Before I'll let Frank have his way, I'll buy the damned placed myself," Eleanor snapped.

Debbie gathered the full measure of the banker's state of mind by the single curse word. Normally she played the Southern lady completely; bad language was crass. "There's really no need to worry. . . ."

Barely pausing for breath, Eleanor continued to

rage about Frank's violent and unsavory behavior and his lack of social graces and finished with, "He can't be trusted. He'll act so nice and then sneak around behind your back and pull some low-down stunt. Ask anyone—he can be a dangerous man. A very dangerous man."

Rolling her eyes gratefully at Cressie, who was pouring a glass of wine, Debbie managed to break in and say, "If I should change my mind about selling, I'll call you first thing. I promise. But believe me, there's no truth at all to the rumors. I like Nacogdoches and plan to stay."

When Eleanor paused and seemed to be considering her words, Debbie quickly said, "Good-bye," and hung up. She sank onto a kitchen chair and thankfully sipped her drink. Charles had frequently teased her about being a near teetotaler. That too had changed since her arrival in Texas. Academic life in Vermont and the life she'd found since buying the Muller house were worlds apart.

It was the not knowing that curdled her insides. Not knowing who or why or what would pop up next. Cold drafts, the aroma of jasmine, or the musty smell could possibly be explained. The eerie feeling of being watched, of sensing someone close when she knew she was alone, could not. Debbie set down her glass. Frank was right: Cressie's continuous rambling probably didn't help matters. But there was no way she could survive all this without Cressie's ever-present support.

The phone rang again. "No," Debbie groaned, and laid her head between her hands to hide the noise. Elbows propped on the table, she shook her head at Cressie. "I'm not home."

"It's your mother," Cressie insisted loudly as she held the phone out. "She's upset."

"No," Debbie groaned again as she reluctantly took the receiver. Cressie, the kitchen, her previous problems, all faded away. Only her mother's words drummed on and consumed her. Why now? she pleaded silently. The words droned on. Debbie kept shaking her head. Valiantly she fought the over-whelming impression that life had cheerfully dropped her into a deep well and was getting great pleasure in heaping manure on top of her.

But that didn't change the reason for her mother's hysterical call. Finally, drawing a deep breath and forcing a calmness she didn't feel into her voice, Debbie resigned herself. "Get Scottie's school records, pack up his belongings, and ship him up here on the bus. I'll enter him in school in Nacogdoches."

Mrs. Dillon paused. "Oh, Debbie, do you think that would work?"

"It'll work. Scottie won't dare pull any of this non-sense on me. I've had enough of this."

After a few more minutes, she hung up and looked at Cressie's amused expression. "Scottie was suspended from school. Mother blames the crowd he runs with since they also got suspended. But that doesn't allevi-ate the problem. If he stays there and continues to walk all over her, he'll wind up in worse trouble. It might be too late to help him then."

"Teenagers can be troublesome."

"Scottie won't be lectured: He's stubborn. Mother can't take anymore."

A strange smile touched Cressie's mouth. "When will he arrive?"

"She'll call and let us know, but probably sometime

tomorrow. If I'm not here, could you call the school to let me know so that either Sal or I can meet the bus?"

Cressie began to set the table. "He'll be good company for you, although a man your own age would be better."

Debbie shot her a glare of reproach.

"Of course, since he's about the same age as Jenny, that might work out even better." Cressie began dishing up the pot roast and vegetables.

Debbie asked, "Why would you think that?"

"Just a feelin' I have. I wouldn't be at all surprised if Scottie isn't the other link we've been waitin' for."

When Cressie didn't explain further, Debbie couldn't stand the suspense. "Do you want to tell me what you mean by that?"

"Well, when you came the spirits got restless. Evil slipped out and poked its way around. The past demands restitution. Now you've stirred things up so that everyone is jumpin' and spittin'. There's danger out there, Miss Debbie, and don't you forget it. With Mr. Scottie comin' to live here, I think the pot will really begin to boil."

Debbie closed her eyes and counted slowly to ten. "I'm not interested in the past or the boiling pot. Why should Scottie help Jenny's problem?"

"'Cause she'll know he couldn't be a part of any of the things that have been happenin' to her. He hasn't been around. Now eat your dinner. You're goin' to need to build up your strength."

Debbie didn't say another word. Once she started eating, she found she was hungry. Food quieted her revolving stomach. Little time had passed before she'd cleaned her plate. She set her dishes on the counter, picked up her briefcase and purse, and walked to the back stairs.

When she remembered her call to Keith, she stopped. After this dreadful day, it was almost anticlimactic, but earlier it had seemed important. "I invited Keith for dinner tomorrow evening." She couldn't contain her bitterness when she added, "It ought to be quite a party."

Climbing the stairs, she refused to think of anything except what projects she would start next in the house. She would let Scottie fix up his room the way he wanted once he was settled and in school. Maybe she would look for some new drapes for the living room or buy herself a new dress for the homecoming events. And there was always the new carpet she needed for the hall and staircase.

She dropped her things on the bed and walked to the window. Looking out at the darkened sky, she thought of her problems with her neighbors, and the eerie happenings in the house. She still planned on reading the journal that belonged to Kate's father. Cressie had said it was in the library. She could do with leaving the present for a while and spending time with a little ancient history.

After soaking in a hot tub, she donned her nightgown and finished grading the papers. But when she turned off the light and slipped into bed, sleep didn't come. Her lovely house didn't bring the usual respite. The mounting problems filled her with depression. She cuddled the extra pillow against her. Maybe she should sell. It might make life much easier.

She hated to be run out of what was hers. She'd run once and refused to do it again. And this house was more of a home than she'd ever had. If she could just sleep, everything would look better tomorrow. Debbie's eyes closed wearily.

She didn't know where she was in her dream, but she was walking through a garden filled with jasmine. The bushes grew to gigantic size. She fought the pulling vines. The sweet perfume was stifling. Fear became overpowering, and gasping for breath, she sat up, wide awake. Her bedroom reeked of jasmine. Tangled bedclothes were wrapped around her body. Her heart raced.

A glimmer of moonlight trickled through the curtains, but otherwise the room was in darkness, the furnishings black shadows. Uneasy, she looked around. The room appeared empty, yet her senses screamed. "Who's there?" she called.

Her voice sounded weak and wouldn't be heard beyond the walls of her room. She gathered her wits, realizing yelling was foolish. If someone had broken in, she didn't want them to know she was awake.

From a distance, almost in answer to her call, the beautiful tones of wind chimes filled the air. The volume increased and increased, as though the wind grew stronger or the chimes came closer.

Debbie pulled the blankets to her chin and hung on to the soft fabric for dear life. She dared not take her eyes from the dim outline of the open doorway to her bedroom. Louder and louder the eerie melody played, raking at the raw edges of her nerves.

Breathing was like sucking in pure jasmine flowers, smothering, painful. Debbie tightened her hold on the blanket and stared at the doorway. Fear prevented her from reaching out to turn on the bedside lamp. Terror paralyzed all but her hammering heart.

The noise of shattering glass filled the house. The

chimes stopped instantly. Then came silence . . . long and penetrating, with the force of slippery vines winding and choking everything standing in the way. Debbie wanted to scream, to let the world know the horror consuming her. Her voice refused to make a sound.

The scent of jasmine faded away with the passing of time. She was all alone, alone to discover who or what had been in her house. Alone to search for wind chimes, jasmine, and broken glass.

Several more minutes elapsed before she gathered sufficient courage to turn on the light. The room was the same as when she'd gone to bed. Not a single indication remained to bear witness to the event.

She would never fall asleep again until she looked through the house, and if she didn't do it soon, she'd cower the rest of the night in bed. Debbie rose and made herself put on her bathrobe and slippers.

Drawing a deep breath for courage and to quiet her racing heart, she began her search. She turned on the light switches and entered each room by turn on the second floor. All the while she put off the inevitable. The crash had come from below. Finally she tiptoed down the stairs.

Starting with the kitchen in the back, she searched each room, not sure what she'd do if she found someone. The longer she searched, the more certain she became: there was no evidence of any intrusion, and no one else was in her house.

No one . . . nothing is here. I don't believe in ghosts. I'm letting my imagination run away with me, she repeated again and again every trembling step of the way. Fear that she would find someone tortured her. Terror that she wouldn't became even worse.

Always at the back of her mind was the knowledge

that two days ago she had been over every inch of her house and had seen no wind chimes.

Debbie saved the living room for last. Maybe because it turned out that way; maybe because subconsciously she knew that if anything were to be found, it would be there. Finally, drawing another deep breath, she turned on the lights and entered.

Nothing. Nothing except the breeze blowing the front drapes into the room, making it appear as though some nebulous figure hovered tauntingly behind. But when she looked, she saw no feet below the flowered fabric, only pieces of broken glass. Someone had broken her front window.

Debbie pulled aside the curtain. Moonlight danced on the dark, velvetlike grass. Stars twinkled in the night sky. The trees raised their almost empty branches like grotesque watchmen standing guard against all invaders. The driveway and road wound through the countryside like black ribbons. Nothing stirred. No one moved.

Turning back to the room, Debbie looked around. Under the edge of a chair she saw a piece of paper secured by a rubber band around a large rock. Slowly she bent down and picked it up. Someone had thrown the rock through the front window. That was what had made the crashing sound. Someone had sent her a message. Unwrapping the plain white paper, she read: *LEAVE NACOGDOCHES OR ELSE!*

11

Debbie's hand trembled. She wanted to throw the rock so far that she would never see it again. A childish reaction, and it wouldn't alleviate the threat that hung over her. She had to face it and go from there. The message and the broken glass were real. For whatever reason, someone in Nacogdoches was aiming all sorts of ugliness at her.

Cressie had warned her, several times. It wasn't until Jenny lay with blood puddled around her head that she began to think Cressie wasn't as crazy as she sounded. She had also said Debbie was in danger. Something about the colors were mixed. Fear and hate, but that something wasn't right.

Looking down at the rock and the message, she understood the fear. Hers was certainly real. But she couldn't understand how someone could hate her before he knew her. The motel call had come the evening of her first day. It made no sense.

Someone was behind the threats, but that didn't explain the scent of jasmine and the sound of wind chimes. They were real. Because of the fragrance, she associated them with Kate. But Debbie couldn't admit the existence of ghosts when everything she had ever learned denied such nonsense. Still, something had awakened her and warned her. And she had found no signs of anyone else in the house. No one would believe her except Cressie.

Someone was doing a damned good job of manipulating her, trying to frighten her away. Yet for some reason she doubted that even Keith, with all his knowledge, could explain the happenings in the Muller place.

After turning off the lights, she went back upstairs. She set the rock and note on her dresser, crawled into bed, and pulled the covers up to ward off the chill she felt.

Looking around to make certain she didn't see the wispy outline of Kate, she thought about her conversation with Cressie after seeing the menacing apparition in the back parlor. The housekeeper had been no help, simply saying Debbie was being protected and not to worry.

Debbie hadn't believed her ears. She'd dropped her reticence and told the housekeeper about smelling the scent of jasmine, having the sensation of being watched, and seeing the faint figure of a woman. Cressie had smiled in that knowing way Debbie detested and started discussing the needed groceries. Debbie was left with frustrations, but no doubts that Cressie believed there were ghosts in the house.

Debbie turned out the light beside her bed and snuggled under the covers. A cold gyrating form . . . the soft apparition of a woman . . . the sense of menace . . . the sense of being watched . . . a musty aroma . . . the sweetness of jasmine . . . and now wind chimes. She couldn't deny it any longer. More and more she was accepting the existence of ghosts. And because of the variance, there had to be more than one, as Cressie had said that first day.

The worst part was not being able to tell anyone of the bizarre happenings. Cressie didn't count; she was part of them. Since everyone kept asking Debbie how she liked living in the Muller house, one complaint, one innuendo, and the story would grow like wildfire and her credibility and professional reputation in Nacogdoches would be ruined. Someone was already doing a good job of that now without her help.

Things could get worse. With this note, there didn't seem any indication of an end in sight. Although one thing had come from this warning. The act was no coincidence: it was a definite threat.

Debbie stared at the dark ceiling streaked by moonlight and considered each event that had occurred since her arrival in Nacogdoches. Whoever it was must be desperate to go so far.

She wondered what Keith would say, and if he cared at all what happened to her. After her "hands off" signals, she couldn't expect more than an objective viewpoint. Right now she needed that.

Twisting to find relief from the snarled bedcovers, Debbie thought of her mother's phone call. Having Scottie in the house might be a blessing in disguise. It would prevent sexual entanglements from occurring before Debbie was ready, and she could broadcast her refusal to be driven from her home by having her brother with her and enrolled in the high school.

Comforted with the probability that Scottie's

arrival might give someone else a few sleepless moments, Debbie drifted into a restful doze.

Dressed and drinking coffee, Debbie greeted Cressie the next morning when she walked in the back door. At the older woman's surprised exclamation on finding her in the kitchen, Debbie explained the events of the previous night.

Cressie narrowed her eyes and said, "Miss Kate protected you, that's for sure." She shook her head. "But what are the people around here comin' to? It's bad . . . bad . . . evil things are swirlin' and mixin'. I told you the colors were mixed. Fear and anger. Somethin's not right, and there's no tellin' where it's goin' to end. You be careful, Miss Debbie. Be very careful."

Cressie hummed a strange tune and took a package of bacon from the refrigerator. She dropped strips into an iron skillet. When Debbie asked the title to the song, Cressie paused, her face blank. She stared off into space for a moment, then turned on the fire under the skillet and replied, "Just a little ditty I know . . . to keep away the evil forces."

Despite the lecture she gave herself, Debbie shivered. She couldn't help it. But she'd be damned if she'd let Cressie know. She sipped her coffee and refused to say one more word about Cressie's strange actions.

Sal came in, and the three of them ate breakfast in silence.

Debbie was ready to leave for the college when Sal said, "I'll fix the window, so don't you worry about that none. It's a good thing Kate was a-watchin'."

Debbie stopped in the doorway, her heart beating erratically. Sal always came directly to the kitchen from their apartment. Not once since he'd entered to eat had she or Cressie mentioned the warnings or the shattered window. Not only that, Cressie didn't appear surprised at what he'd said. Debbie studied them. The two communicated without words; there was no other explanation.

The idea made her even more uneasy. She felt alone in the web of intrigue tightening around her, and worse, she was an outsider in her own home.

Early that afternoon Debbie received a phone call from her mother. Without giving Debbie time for more than a greeting, her mother announced the time of Scottie's arrival and said the school would forward the necessary papers to the high school in Nacogdoches. Because Scottie was underage, Mrs. Dillon had also obtained and sent along with him Debbie's power of guardianship.

Stunned momentarily at her mother's rapid efficiency, which seemed so out of character, Debbie didn't speak. Then in robot fashion she repeated the time Scottie would arrive and asked, "How did you manage all of this so fast?"

Mrs. Dillon issued a sigh of relief. "A friend advised me."

I should have known, Debbie thought. Mother relied on Dad too many years to take such quick initiative on her own. "Your friend, is she anyone I know?"

"She? Ah, no . . . it's someone from work." Quickly, almost as though she were afraid Debbie might change her mind, Mrs. Dillon rushed one final, unsettling proclamation: "For the time being, Scottie is your responsibility, but you know how much I appreciate your help." Then she hung up the phone.

Debbie shook her head. Scottie had indeed pushed her mother's back to the wall. Well, he needn't think he could try his shenanigans on his older sister. She would tie him up in little knots. Besides, she had all the problems she could manage, and Scottie would have to understand that. If she could get him on her side . . . Debbie shrugged. Action time was when he arrived. Right now she had to call Keith, tell him about Scottie, and get to her class.

Late afternoon found Debbie leaning against the bus station wall, waiting for the Greyhound to ease to a stop. She hadn't decided how to approach him on the reason for his sudden relocation, but she looked forward to the sight of his big frame filling the bus doorway. He might be only sixteen, but six feet four inches and two hundred and twenty pounds had to be taken seriously no matter what the age.

Scottie remained on the backseat until everyone else left. Dressed in faded jeans, rumpled knit shirt, and battered sneakers, he slowly descended the vehicle's steps. His longish red hair was tousled, as though he had raked his fingers through it numerous times. His mouth turned down at the corners in a sullen expression, but his square chin jutted forward with determination and his green eyes stared back defiantly.

He stuck his hands in his back pockets and walked toward Debbie. The freckles sprinkled across his nose stood out like signposts in his pale face. Normally they didn't. This was a good indication that despite his assured manner, he was anxious. She knew then exactly what she must do.

Grinning with the pleasure she truly felt, Debbie rushed over and wrapped her arms around his neck. "Hi, little brother. Glad you could come."

He sighed as he hugged her. His ragged breathing told her he found the meeting as emotional as she did.

Stepping back, he said, "Yeah, the bad penny has turned up after all. I hope it's not going to cramp your style too much."

Scottie had clearly been hurt, she realized, when she hadn't let him visit during the summer as originally planned. She knew then that their ability to live amicably together depended crucially on the next few minutes.

Debbie tucked her hand under his arm. "No. In fact, you couldn't have come at a more opportune time. Let's get your things, and I'll explain on the way home."

Scottie sucked in his breath, squeezed her arm against his side, and in a choked voice said, "A guy couldn't have a better sister. You just don't know. . . ."

Debbie fought the tears that welled in her eyes. Now was not the time to break down. "Thank you, but don't be too hasty. I want you to understand from the beginning, I don't intend to let you turn my life upside down like you did Mom's. You're going to have to pull your weight."

"It's not all my fault. Mom's not herself. She's acting real radical right now."

"But you have no right to turn her life into a nightmare. After all, things haven't been easy for her, either, since Dad died."

"That's just the problem. No one can replace Dad, and Mom has to understand a guy's father is special."

Peeking up at him as they walked back to the luggage hold, she decided to take a firm stand. "We'll discuss that another time. Right now, I need your help."

Scottie looked down at her intently. He straightened his shoulders and seemed to mature before her eyes. "You got it. Anything you want."

She couldn't stop the flood of pride and gratitude that filled her. They would help each other. "I've invited a friend for dinner this evening. I want you to meet him. His name is Keith Douglas. He's a teacher at the college, and he hunts ghost stories for his books."

Picking up his bags, Scottie asked, "Is this jerk giving you trouble? Do you want me to break his arm or simply show him the door?"

Debbie laughed. "No, he's a friend. I like him."

"Are you serious about each other? Are you afraid I'll be in the way? I know how to make myself scarce when need be."

"No, it's nothing like that," Debbie replied quickly, and wondered if he detected her wariness. "So far, we're nothing more than friends. After Charles I'm not too keen on getting involved with anyone again."

"Charles was a nerd. A rich nerd, maybe. You're better off without him."

Debbie recalled that the two had never gotten along well, even though Charles had allowed Scottie to visit several times. Maybe that was the key. Charles had "allowed" . . . he hadn't really wanted.

While they walked to her car, Scottie glanced around at the narrow streets and the ancient buildings.

"It's a nice town, really," she said mildly. "I've grown to like it very much."

"The town's okay, I guess." He glanced at her. "If this Keith isn't trying to make time with you, then it must be the fact he hunts ghosts that's giving you the problem."

Debbie unlocked the trunk of her car. "Actually, it's rumored my house is haunted."

"Cool! Any truth to it?" Scottie climbed into the passenger side of the car. "Have you seen a ghost?"

Debbie hesitated. "There are some strange things happening there. Very strange. So prepare yourself."

Making certain she had Scottie's total attention once they were on their way, she said, "I've also invited a young friend who's about your age for dinner this evening. Her name's Jenny. I'm hoping your timely arrival can benefit her as well." Debbie didn't explain that Keith had suggested including Jenny.

Rolling down the window so that he could rest his elbow on the edge, Scottie said, "I'm more than ready to meet a good-looking babe. It perks the situation up some." Frowning, he added, "I hope you're not intending to ask me to help with some dog. It would sure make it tough to refuse."

Debbie shook her head and passed the car in front. "Jenny's not a 'dog,' as you say, but a sweet, attractive sixteen-year-old. She hasn't socialized much with people her own age, so I'm counting on you to be nice to her."

"Are you trying to tell me in a polite way that she's a geek and doesn't usually associate with boys?"

Glancing at Scottie, she grinned at his scowl. "No, she doesn't date, or run with the girls to the movies and parties, but not for the reason you think. Actually, she believes her stepfather is trying to kill her."

Scottie straightened. He had taken the bait. The same sense of curiosity that ran through her had caught him. "Tell me more," he coaxed.

Turning onto the road that passed in front of her house, Debbie smiled at her younger brother. Carefully she related the events that had happened since her arrival in Nacogdoches.

Scottie didn't interrupt once. By the time she'd parked in her driveway, she was satisfied his stay with her would work out well.

After the first introductions, Keith won Scottie over without a struggle by offering to put in a good word for him with the high school coach. Scottie hoped someday to obtain a scholarship for college, and Keith's offer would counteract some of the dubious circumstances under which he'd arrived.

At first Jenny appeared shy and somewhat resistant to conversation, which seemed to have a similar effect on Scottie where she was concerned. Then Debbie, with Keith's assistance, brought up Scottie's athletic accomplishments. Judging from Jenny's reaction and the gleam in Scottie's eye, Debbie felt certain it was only a matter of time.

Debbie hid her smile when Scottie settled himself beside Jenny on the living room sofa and began asking about the high school. He clearly didn't consider her a "dog" by any stretch of the imagination. By the time dinner was ready, the two younger people appeared quite at ease.

Cressie had applied her keen knowledge of teenagers and men by making a large dish of lasagna and hot homemade bread sprinkled with butter and garlic. The meal was a success. After finishing the Dutch apple pie and ice cream, Debbie suggested, "Let's clear the table, load the dishwasher, and have coffee in the living room."

Scottie glanced at Jenny and asked, "We'll help with the dishes, but since we don't drink coffee, do you mind if we look around the house for the wind chimes?"

"What wind chimes?" Jenny asked immediately, her eyes growing round. "Oh, Debbie, has something exciting happened? Have you seen the ghost?"

Evading the subject for the moment, Debbie replied, "Actually, I had a visitor of a more earthly nature last night. Someone threw a rock through my living room window with a note warning me to get out of Nacogdoches."

"Do you still have it?" Keith asked.

The light-hearted atmosphere vanished, but Debbie insisted they clean up the dishes before she showed them the message. As they worked, she began to explain what had happened. She refused to admit to the existence of something supernatural, even though the younger people pressed the point. She was surprised that Keith didn't make any comments or ask any questions.

Half an hour later she placed the rock and note on the coffee table in front of Keith. After glancing at the note, Scottie grabbed Jenny by the hand, and the two ran out of the room for their hunt. The mysterious wind chimes beckoned with far more urgency.

Once the two disappeared down the hall, their voices eager with anticipation, Keith considered the newspaper cutouts on the plain white sheet of paper. Mounting anger darkened his gray eyes.

Debbie told him about the threatening call in the motel, and since he already knew about the changed notice and missing mail, she went on to relate her conversations with Michael, Frank, and Eleanor. When she finished Keith stared absently at the ceiling and rubbed the back of his neck.

"Wow." Humor tugged at his lips. "Without the rock and threat to you, the rest of it could almost be funny."

"I'm afraid I don't see it that way."

Shifting forward on the chair, he explained, "I know Michael is quite concerned about Jenny. That's why he wants me to talk with her. For what it's worth, and despite what he may have said to you, it's because he genuinely cares about her welfare that he agreed to let her come with me this evening."

"I was a little surprised," Debbie admitted, "but with so many other things happening, I didn't give it more than a passing thought."

"I told Michael that since Scottie was new to the area and would be going to the same high school, he might get Jenny's mind on boys and away from Michael. Frankly, he wouldn't be opposed to the idea. He knows how to handle boys."

"What about his threats to me?"

"My guess is that he didn't make them until you mentioned Norma might be responsible in some way for Jenny's accident. I wouldn't be surprised to see Michael and Norma get married eventually, and I believe he simply tried to protect her."

"But—"

"I don't doubt at all that if you shared a similar relationship, your man would say or do whatever was necessary to keep you from harm, whether from physical threats or from gossip."

"What do you think of Frank's offer?" she countered to keep from showing her pleasure at his explanation.

Keith glanced over his shoulder. "Are you cold?"

Puzzled, Debbie frowned. "No, I'm fine."

"I felt a draft. Maybe the kids opened a window or door. As to Frank's offer, I'd give it some serious thought and look into the plan a little more."

"But I don't want to sell."

"I didn't mean to sell. You might give some consideration to his suggestion of a partnership in a resort. You may not want to teach forever, or you may find somewhere down the road you'd like more than one source of income. Never close your mind to possible opportunities until you've considered all the facts."

"Eleanor would be furious."

"That's Eleanor's problem." Keith stood up and looked around the room. "There is a draft in here. What do you think those kids are into?"

"I'm quite comfortable. You're welcome to share the sofa with me." Debbie smiled and met Keith's penetrating stare.

"I see you're finally letting down your guard. That's good. You are a desirable woman, you know, no matter what your ex-husband had you believing."

Debbie sat up straight. "I didn't ask you to sit next to me to be psychoanalyzed, doctor. I suggested it because you felt a draft."

"And I will." Sitting beside her, he circled his arm around her shoulders. "You're going to be in a vulnerable stage for a period of time, you know. You're feeling again and may make mistakes where men and your emotions are concerned."

"Keith, drop it. I can take care of myself."

"I like you and don't want to see you hurt again."

"You may be the one who winds up injured if you pursue this conversation any further."

His lips twitched. "That sounds reasonable. Now tell me, you said you'd never heard the wind chimes before, but had you ever before noticed the aroma of jasmine?"

"You never give up, do you?"

"The subject of the supernatural seems a safe topic at the moment."

"You would think that."

"Well, have you?"

The scent of soap and spicy after-shave filled her nostrils, making her realize just how long it had been since a man had been this close to her, and all Keith wanted to do was talk about her house. Sighing, she said, "A few times, but I use a perfume with the fragrance. I thought maybe Cressie might have sampled some at various times."

"Damn, it's getting cold. And that smell. It's like it was in the back parlor that night." Keith straightened and looked around. His gaze focused on the fireplace. "Do you have just the two fireplaces?"

"Four, actually. The two downstairs and two directly above. My room's over this one, and Kate's old room is over the back parlor," she said as she stared at him.

"Maybe that explains the draft and the smell." Settling back again, he asked, "Would you mind if I came over some time and looked through your house? I'd like to see what I could find myself."

"You won't discover a thing, but come ahead." Debbie shifted, her body snug next to his.

"Did you look for the wind chimes yourself?"

"Yes. Both before and after."

"I don't understand."

"I've been through everything in this house since I've moved in. There were no wind chimes. I looked again today." Debbie lifted her face expectantly, hoping he would sense her waiting lips.

"Of course you could have dreamed it all. Sometimes dreams are so real you think you're awake."

"It's not me who doesn't know when her eyes are open. You're the one with the problem."

Keith cleared his throat. "You're a special person, Debbie. I realize that."

"Then stop talking about my house and kiss me."

He gazed thoughtfully into her eyes. His hands held her arms and he bent his head. Debbie wanted to scream. She wanted the man to kiss her, really kiss her, not taste to see if she was sweet or sour. She wanted to know what his lips felt like and discover if this was more than a passing attraction. She wanted to believe she was a woman again. She reached up and pulled him closer.

Keith tightened the embrace, and she lost herself in the wild sensations rushing through her.

"Oh, Debbie, I hope this isn't a mistake," he murmured, dropping kisses down the side of her face and on her neck before taking her mouth once more.

She murmured a protest when Keith pushed her away. Then, hearing Scottie and Jenny coming down the front stairs in the hallway, Debbie jerked back.

Keith clearly hadn't lost his senses. Damn the man! Was he always so in control of his emotions? Then, seeing his flushed skin, she smiled. He wasn't as cool and collected as he liked to appear.

By the time Scottie and Jenny entered the living room, Debbie and Keith were seated comfortably next to each other. "We didn't find them," Scottie grumbled, slumping down on a chair while Jenny wandered over to another. "And we looked everywhere."

"Maybe they're in that hidden space off your back parlor," Keith suggested.

Instantly Scottie sat up. "What space?"

Keith told of the draft he felt in the back room and explained that such an old house probably had a hidden space somewhere. Then he stopped, frowning. "The cold draft and the smell . . . were the same as in here tonight. Surely the Mullers wouldn't have hidden spaces in several places. Have you ever noticed the draft and odor upstairs?"

Irritated, Debbie shrugged. "Unlike you, I didn't notice anything in here."

"The only thing we noticed," Jenny said, "was the scent of jasmine. That was great."

"I use it all the time," Debbie replied, and looked pointedly at the clock on the mantel. "It's getting late."

Keith took the hint and stood up. "We'd better be running. Jenny has school tomorrow."

"I'll give you a call," Scottie promised Jenny as she followed Keith out the front door.

"I enjoyed myself," Keith added from the front porch.

His polite words hurt. "Thanks for the psychoanalysis. I'm sure it helped." She hoped he wouldn't see how false her smile really was.

"Don't mention it. Any time."

"And thanks for bringing Jenny. I'm sure it made Scottie's first night here more fun."

When both Jenny and Keith sat on the front seat

of Keith's car, he looked across at Scottie. "I'll call the coach tomorrow and have him keep an eye out for you."

"I really don't think he'll miss Scottie," Debbie replied. "Hardly anyone does."

Studying the big frame, Keith nodded. "Yeah, the football coach is going to love you."

Keith and Jenny drove off, and Debbie looped her arm through Scottie's and walked back inside the house. "What did you think of them?"

"I like Keith. Is it serious?"

Debbie began turning off the lights. "We're simply friends. He plans to move on in a year to do research in another area of the country for his next book. I have the impression he doesn't want any strong commitments."

"And how do you feel about that?"

Debbie considered. "I'm not sure if I want to prove to myself I'm still a desirable woman or if there could be more. I do know I'm finding Keith an interesting man. How about Jenny? What did you think of her?"

Scottie placed one foot on the bottom stair and dug his toe into the carpet. "You don't believe she's in danger, do you?"

"I don't honestly know. I think Jenny believes it. And that last accident she had could have been fatal."

"Jenny's a good kid. I think she's getting a raw deal. I might check the whole situation out," Scottie announced, and started up the stairs.

"That's not a bad idea," Debbie said, following. "She could use a friend her own age."

A faint floral scent reached her nose. "This must be where Jenny noticed the jasmine."

Scottie frowned. "No, actually, it was in that back bedroom where the picture is that looks so much like you."

"That's Miss Kate. She's the one who's supposed to haunt the house."

"It's strange the two of you look so much alike."

"Several people have said that."

Scottie reached the top of the stairs and stopped. Curious, Debbie hesitated and looked ahead of him.

"Debbie . . ."

The aroma of jasmine hung heavy in the air, almost sickeningly sweet.

Scottie cleared his throat. "Do you smell anything strange?"

Debbie remembered her first experience and smiled. "Strange? You could say that. Aren't you going to bed? We have to get up early in the morning."

"Debbie, this is really weird."

"I know. But living in this house, you'll have to get used to it."

"Ghosts?"

"I've never believed in ghosts. I've been a skeptic like Keith and thought such claims were people trying to get attention or wanting to cause a sensation."

"But, Debbie . . ."

"I'm a college professor, Scottie. I'm new in my job, and no one knows me very well yet. If I want to continue teaching, I have to consider my reputation as a rational and businesslike adult. If I want people to take me seriously, I have to be firm when I say there are no such things as ghosts. Now go to bed."

"Aren't you afraid?"

Debbie considered her experiences to date, particularly the one from the night before. "No. I can't explain these things, and I don't understand them, but I've never been harmed in any way. If there are ghosts, they mean me no harm. That's more than I can say for some live, walking-around person in this town."

Nodding, he walked reluctantly toward his own room next door, then paused in his doorway. "Uh, Debbie, if anything frightens you, just call out." Without waiting for her reply, he stepped inside his bedroom and shut the door.

Chuckling softly to herself, Debbie closed her door. She'd bet there weren't many things that made Scottie cautious. Maybe living with ghosts had its good points after all.

She hoped by letting him stay, she wasn't putting him in danger from a living person. She'd never forgive herself if she were. Of course, if it became too bad, she could send him back to Houston. If he would go. She'd leave that for another day, she decided, and prepared for bed.

12

Taking time out on Thursday to register Scottie at the high school proved simple compared to managing all the minor, everyday adjustments in her schedule. Although Scottie could ride the school bus in the mornings, Debbie needed to pick him up in the afternoons after football practice. It was tight, but after a week they had both settled into the routine.

Scottie seemed to be adjusting. Despite her fears that he would act up, he continued to be on his best behavior. Debbie began to feel optimistic about their arrangement.

Tuesday afternoon brought her first conflict. She had a staff meeting at the college at the same time she needed to pick up Scottie after football practice. Feeling constrained with the change in her life-style, she called him up and explained. When he didn't respond at first, she snapped, "If I'm late, don't go looking for trouble."

"What do you mean?" he fired back.

"Don't go painting any school statues or defaming

school property. I don't have time to do any more than I already am, and I might leave you locked up in jail for the night."

A short, poignant silence followed before Scottie growled, "Don't be an ass. I'm not about to do anything like that again. Besides, Jenny would be furious."

Debbie immediately regretted her words and the fact she had thrown up his past so cruelly. She *had* acted like an ass. "I'm sorry," she said softly. "I know you wouldn't pull such a stupid stunt. Not just because of Jenny, but because you wouldn't do it to yourself or to me."

Scottie cleared his throat several times. "I'll be here waiting, whenever you can make it."

For the first time, Debbie fully understood her mother's complaint that she never had time for a life of her own. It was much simpler to stand back from a problem and be objective in your advice than to know what was best when you barely had time to turn around.

Walking to her meeting, Debbie admitted that although she didn't regret letting Scottie come to live with her, it was certainly more difficult to guide a maturing teenager in the right way when you were fully responsible for him. She wondered if she was up to it.

She thought about what her own life might be like if she had a child of her own. Her thoughts drifted to Keith, and she wondered if he ever considered marrying and having children. Judging by his patience and tactful dealing with Scottie and Jenny, she knew he would make an excellent father and wondered how much his training had to do with it. Of course, he wasn't the expert when it came to her own state of emotional development since the divorce. He might think he understood her, but when a man didn't know a woman wanted him to kiss her, he had something to learn himself.

Her week dragged by with one irritating circumstance after another. Now that she admitted to herself she wanted to know Keith better, spend more time with him, maybe even share a few embraces, the hours she spent each evening preparing classwork or grading papers became drearier. Even watching Scottie and Jenny study together or hunt through the house searching for the wind chimes and the hidden space Keith thought existed didn't pick up her spirits any. She considered calling him, then decided against it. He'd only want to come over to investigate her house for his book. She wanted him missing her company.

Scottie's wariness of the upstairs hall and his reticence on speaking about the smell of jasmine were the brightest spots. For the first time she wasn't the only one with the sense of being watched, looking over a shoulder to find no one there. The disturbing part was the frequency with which this was happening since Scottie's arrival.

Keith finally called Wednesday evening. After a brief explanation that he'd been busy writing in order to meet his deadline, he hung up. Debbie cradled the receiver with regret. Now that she was finally interested in a man again, he didn't seem to have time for her.

She squared her shoulders to rid herself of her disparaging thoughts. She enjoyed Keith's companionship, but she also liked her new life-style. She liked being her own woman, handling her own affairs, and owning her lovely house. A man might not fit into these arrangements, especially one who didn't know when a woman would like to hear from him more or wanted him to kiss her.

Keith called her the next morning at her office and asked her to meet him for lunch in the school cafeteria. She was surprised but agreed.

She joined him at noon, and after they'd located an empty table in the noisy room, Debbie unloaded her tray. Her nose wrinkled as she set the daily special in front of her. At the time she'd chosen the casserole, the name "Happy Surprise" had appealed to her. Now, glancing at Keith's hamburger, fries, and iced tea, she wasn't so eager.

"Want to trade?" she asked.

Keith's lips twitched. "No, but I'm sure the food tastes better than it looks."

Debbie shook her head. "It doesn't look bad, especially the green salad. I'm wondering what's in the casserole."

"You've been spoiled."

Debbie watched him take a big bite of his hamburger, then raised the fork of mixed vegetables and meat to her mouth.

"How is it?"

She chewed, swallowed, and grinned. "Not bad, not bad at all."

"That's the way things usually turn out. The anticipation is worse than the actuality."

"Ah, yes, O learned one," she said, making a rolling motion with one hand and bowing her head. "I hear and I believe."

Keith joined her in laughter, and her irritation with his neglect vanished.

"How's the book coming?" she asked a few minutes later.

"I'm almost finished with the first draft."

"What's the holdup?"

Keith carefully considered a french fry before placing it in his mouth. "Kate is notorious in these parts. My book wouldn't be complete without relating several events from the Muller house."

"The Dillon house," Debbie corrected automatically as she set her fork on her plate. "And you want me to provide you with some specifics. You want me to be like one of those people you call 'sensation seekers.'"

"I hope you know me well enough by now to know I wouldn't put anything in that sounded derogatory about you," he challenged. "That's why I'm talking with you about it first. But there are stories there. I know it, and I'd like to use them."

After a moment of silence, he went on temptingly. "Imagine your name in a best-seller. Everyone reading about your experiences. You and the house could both become famous."

Debbie considered dumping the remainder of her casserole on his head.

Another voice intruded. "Debbie, Keith. I hope we're not interrupting?"

As Keith rose, Debbie regarded the two women standing next to their table. Teresa, dressed in a powder blue dress and dark blue boots, smiled back. Carolyn, the teacher from Debbie's department, looked uneasily down at her tray of food.

"As a matter of fact, you probably arrived at an opportune time," Debbie said, a tight smile on her lips.

Teresa laughed, her musical ripple drawing the attention of several nearby students. "Well, we don't want to join you. I just wanted to speak to you for a minute." Waving her hand at Keith, she instructed, "Sit down. Finish your meal."

Debbie looked up at Teresa. She'd straighten out this book business with Keith later, after she'd had more time to think about it. "What did you need, Teresa?"

"I want to apologize."

Debbie blinked several times.

Again Teresa's laugh made heads turn. "I'm afraid that I've been rude to you since we met. Keith pointed that out to me the other evening, and I wanted to tell you I'm sorry." She shrugged. "I'm having a difficult time with my husband over the divorce, but I shouldn't take it out on you."

Debbie didn't miss Teresa's comment about seeing Keith and wondered how he had managed to squeeze her into his schedule. This was again another matter for future thought. Now, since Teresa had extended a tentative olive branch, the least Debbie could do was reciprocate. "I understand. I finished with one of those myself before I came here."

"Men can be such dreadful creatures at times," Teresa offered confidentially.

"I couldn't agree with you more," Debbie agreed with a pointed look at Keith.

Teresa laughed again, and Carolyn broke in. "I need to eat and get on. I've things to finish before the president's tea this afternoon."

"Oh, that's right. If I want to avoid the heavy traffic, I have to leave for Dallas myself as soon as we eat. I've another appointment with my lawyer bright and early in the morning. My husband's ideas of a fit and proper alimony belong in the fifteenth century."

"You might have to settle for less," Carolyn replied.

"No way. Not after what I put up with." Teresa turned back to Debbie. "You were a big help with Jenny when she fell. I'm afraid with the terrible strain I've been under, and finding her with so much blood, I lost it that night. I do want to thank you." Teresa smiled at Keith, then strode off to another table a short distance away.

In the silence that followed, Debbie picked up her fork and began to eat. She was puzzled over Teresa's sudden change of behavior.

"A penny," Keith offered.

"I can't be bought."

"I beg your pardon?"

Sighing, Debbie set down her fork and pushed her plate away. "Just exactly what do you want from me, some juicy stories for your book, or something more?"

His gaze slid over the curves of her breasts, up over the texture of her skin, and fixed on the honey-colored hair. "Don't you know what I want?"

Debbie's breath quickened at the admiration she could see in his face, the darkening of his gray eyes. Her lips parted to utter an admonishment that never came as his scrutiny focused on her flushed cheeks. She could feel her body grow warm and begin to ache. A heartbeat of silence followed as she strove to maintain her anger. Finally she gave up. "Has anyone ever told you you're dangerous?"

"No. Most people consider me quite safe."

"You're about as safe as a carnivorous plant."

"Exactly. Quiet, determined, and efficient." He

took her hand in his. "I didn't mean to upset you by asking for your help with Miss Kate's ghost. If you seriously object, we'll forget the whole matter."

"Devious and smooth as silk. Deadly as a rapier."

Keith shook his head. "Does this mean we can't still be friends?"

Debbie looked at the big round clock on the wall. "I need to go. I have to pick up my briefcase before my next class."

"You're evading the issue."

She sighed at his persistence. "You know I want to remain friends, but I don't know if I want to discuss the ghosts in my house for your book." Pulling her hand free, she asked, "Satisfied?"

"Then you have noticed some things?"

Keith's eyes kept her from rising, so she watched the three students at the next table to keep from replying.

"If you'd rather I not write about your experiences, I'll have to accept your decision. I do want to keep seeing you."

Debbie didn't know what she wanted to do. She liked Keith and hoped a deeper relationship could grow between them. He clearly didn't feel as strongly about her as she did him, but for his sake, she still wanted his book to be a success. He believed she could help him accomplish this.

At the same time she didn't want to experience the nudges and sudden quiets she'd received in Vermont, nor did she like the idea of being considered a sensation seeker, as some would call her. Not to mention what her revelations might do to her career. Nothing was ever simple.

She grabbed her dirty dishes and piled them on

the tray. Picking up the tray and her purse, she said, "I have to go. I'll see you at the tea."

Debbie placed her tray on the conveyer belt, then hurried out the cafeteria door and across the lawn to her office building.

Several hours later, after her last class, Debbie finished applying lipstick and gave herself a once-over in the restroom mirror. Her appearance would have to do. If she didn't hurry, she'd be late for the tea, and no doubt Dean Carrington would notice. He managed to see everything.

She went out the building's side door, crossed the grass, and hurried to her parked car. Her right front tire was flat. Her heart dropped. "Damn! Damn! Double damn!"

She looked at her gold watch. There was no time to put on the spare now. She'd have to walk. The sad part was that even if she ran, she would still be late. Already feeling Dean Carrington's wrath, she closed her eyes in frustration.

"Trouble?" asked a familiar feminine voice.

Debbie looked up. "I have a flat."

"I'd say you have more than that."

Puzzled, Debbie looked back at her car. The back tire was flat also, but that wasn't where Carolyn was looking. Dreading what she might discover, Debbie walked between the parked cars, took a good look, and bit down on her lip. She had four flat tires.

"Do you want to ride with me to the tea? You can worry about this later," Carolyn offered.

Debbie accepted thankfully. "I'm lucky you came by at the right moment." She was even more lucky Carolyn had noticed her problem and stopped.

"My stopping isn't quite all coincidental. I've

noticed before that we both park in this same area. Today when I went to my car, I saw the flat tires. Then I saw you crossing the grass." Carolyn speeded up her car.

"It couldn't be something I ran over. Not with all four tires flat." Debbie rolled up the window.

"Have you given one of your students a hard time lately?"

"I'm strict, but I try to be fair. You don't think if one of them took such exception he'd go this far, do you?"

"What else could it be, other than some prankster picking a car at random." Leaving the red-brick buildings of the campus, Carolyn turned onto North Street.

"Yeah, this seems to be my lucky day all right."

Debbie watched the fall sunlight filter through the car windows and highlight Carolyn's skin and the red shades in her dark hair. Deciding to take advantage of the unexpected opportunity and Carolyn's new congeniality, Debbie asked, "Have you and Teresa been friends long?"

"Since grade school. At one time we were best friends. Then she married and left. I didn't see her again until this summer when she came home."

"She's been back only a month or so longer than I've been here," Debbie said. "Do you think she's changed much?"

"Some, but so have I. Teresa was sincere today when she apologized," Carolyn said, turning down the street that led to the president's home. "She knows you two didn't get off to a good start and regrets it."

Thinking back to the times she had seen Teresa, Debbie wondered if Carolyn knew everything. "A divorce can be quite unsettling."

Carolyn pulled into a parking place. "You have to

understand, Teresa has always been a beautiful girl, and her family spoiled her. She married a boy from a wealthy family in Dallas and thought her life would be full of the dreams she'd always imagined." Carolyn laughed softly. "Teresa married into what you might call a sort of Ewing family, like in the old television series 'Dallas.'"

Debbie nodded, wondering where all of this was leading.

"Then Daddy Wymans found out that Teresa, bored and with nothing to fill her time, had been doing a little gambling. He paid off her debts, but by then Teresa's husband had found someone else to play with. I don't think Teresa quite got over Keith, so it wasn't an easy marriage. The divorce is even a worse mess." Carolyn met Debbie's gaze. "I thought if you knew a little more about Teresa, you would understand better. She can be a good friend, and life hasn't been exactly easy for her."

Hoping she wouldn't appear too obvious as they made their way up the walkway, Debbie asked, "Do you know what Teresa plans to do once the divorce is final? I mean, will she live here or go back to Dallas?"

Carolyn didn't reply but fiddled with her scarf until they reached the door and the maid answered their ring.

Stepping inside, Debbie saw many small clusters of people in the large antique-filled room. The drone of the multiple conversations competed with the sounds of a string trio playing softly in the corner. She looked around for familiar faces.

"Oh, there's Jerri. I promised to meet her here," Carolyn said brightly, and began to walk away.

Debbie called after her, "Thanks for the ride."

Carolyn turned. "You're welcome." She hesitated. "You'll have to ask Teresa herself what she plans, but I don't think she'll stay in Nacogdoches any longer than she has to." She hurried toward her waiting friend. For the first time since meeting her colleague, Debbie felt they might also become friends.

After making a point of greeting the president and Dean Carrington, Debbie spoke briefly with several of the teachers she knew. Finally she made her way to the refreshment table. Hungry, she filled her plate, taking a sample from several dishes of meats, cheeses, and vegetable dips. After accepting a cup of tea, she wandered into a small alcove in the corner where she could eat quietly by herself and observe.

She saw Keith leaning against the mantel of the fireplace. His lips curved above the dimpled scar, and one dark eyebrow was cocked above the amusement in his gray eyes. A vivacious redhead held his attention. Debbie had seen her before; she worked in the Psychology Department with Keith.

Debbie nibbled on her food and watched. She wanted to tell him about her flat tires, but she didn't want to ask for help in front of the redhead.

Almost as though he felt her gaze, Keith looked over at her. Their eyes met, and his smile deepened. Ripples ran through her as the feminine part of her responded. He turned back to the redhead and after a few brief words started weaving his way across the room.

Debbie set her empty dishes on the edge of the serving table. She became conscious of body warmth and the scent of masculine cologne behind her. She turned. Keith narrowed his eyes, making the amber flecks glitter like drops of melted gold. In the heartbeat of the moment, he loomed very large, extremely intimidating and breathtakingly male.

"What's wrong?" he demanded.

She lifted her chin defiantly. "What makes you think something's wrong the minute you look at me?"

"I know you. Better than you think, and I can tell you're disturbed. Now what's happened?"

She fumed silently at his presumption.

"It apparently can't be too serious. You're still in there ready to fight."

Debbie brushed a piece of lint from the lapel of his blue-gray suit. "That depends on how little importance you place on four flat tires."

"All four?"

Debbie nodded, smiling sweetly. "Do you think you can give me a ride to the station so I can make arrangements to get them fixed or replaced?"

"Did someone let the air out or what?"

Debbie hated to admit she hadn't taken the time to look. "I didn't look. After Dean Carrington's lecture, I was more worried about being late for the tea. Fortunately Carolyn drove past, and I grabbed a ride with her. I decided to worry about the car later."

"I hope you're not going to accuse her of letting the air out of your tires?"

"I do not go around making wild accusations."

"Thank heaven for a few small favors."

Debbie glared at him. "Would you prefer I ask someone else to help me and let you get back to your redhead?"

"Don't be ridiculous." Taking her by the elbow, he headed for the door. "I assume you've said all your pretty speeches and paid suitable homage so you can leave."

Debbie tried to pull free. When she couldn't, she

stopped struggling and allowed herself to be escorted out the front door. "Well, if I haven't, it's a little late now."

"I have never met anyone who could find so much trouble in so little time," Keith said as he unlocked the car door so she could slide in.

"I hope you don't think any of this is my fault," she snapped as he started the car. "I came to Nacogdoches with perfectly good intentions. Can I help it if you people seem to be harboring some weird psycho who gets thrills out of tormenting newcomers?"

"Do you honestly believe that's what's behind these attacks?"

Debbie shrugged. "If I knew who or what was behind all of this, I would have long since turned the instigator into a quivering mass of jelly."

Hearing a choking sound, she looked at Keith. The damned man was laughing!

He patted her clenched hand. "I'm glad it's not me."

"This is not a laughing matter," she said, glaring.

"I know it's not, but when you first came, you would never have gone looking for a fight. That would have meant involvement. I'm glad you finally turned your emotions loose." He pulled into the faculty parking area and braked behind her car.

"Stop psychoanalyzing me. I hate it!"

He turned and pressed a finger to the end of her nose. "So you'll know, I was only filling time with that redhead until you arrived."

Before she could think of an appropriate response, Keith stepped out of the car and began looking at her flat tires. His expression grew grimmer at each stop until deep lines dug between his dark brows and his mouth appeared nothing more than a thin line.

"What did you find?" she asked when he returned.

"I doubt that the tires can be fixed. I'll take you to a station a friend of mine owns. He'll do whatever's best."

"The air wasn't just let out?"

"The tires each have a slit in the side, like someone stuck a knife in them." Turning the ignition key, Keith started the car and pulled out, maneuvering his way through the early evening traffic until the campus slipped from sight and nothing but businesses and restaurants took its place.

"How long do you think it'll take?" Debbie asked. "I have to pick up Scottie."

"We'll get him while my friend takes care of your car."

"Thank you," she said. She couldn't think of anything else to say. She leaned her head back and closed her eyes.

There had to be a way she could learn whether someone deliberately slashed her tires or had picked a random car. Maybe if she asked some of the students or other teachers, one of them might have noticed the culprit. And maybe she'd come up empty-handed, as she had in the past.

An hour and a half later Debbie drove down the road to her house with Scottie sitting beside her. She had invited Keith for dinner, but he had declined, saying he needed to return to his writing if he wanted to make his deadline. Since he had done so much already, she didn't argue.

As she passed the curve that wound in front of her house, she noticed something lying on the front step of her porch. Knowing the continuously hungry Scottie wanted to eat, she didn't say anything as she parked at the back. After he had scooted inside, she walked around to the front.

Debbie paused at the corner of the house. Her steps grew slower and slower as she neared the front porch.

Her stomach churned in protest at the sight of the smashed, bloody, dead cat. She turned away and stared at the flower garden Sal had prepared. A scattering of mums brightened the landscape, but the bright orange red of some resembled the sight on the porch far too much.

She didn't need this. Not this evening . . . not after her slashed tires.

Wondering if anyone was watching her reaction, she looked around. The manicured lawn fell softly to the passing road. A gentle breeze sighed in the branches of the trees. She saw nothing suspicious. The darkening sky, the single call of an owl, taunted her aloneness, her vulnerability. She shivered.

She made herself look at the porch, and anger took hold. Fierce, maddening rage swirled and tumbled like an East Texas tornado.

"Scottie . . . Scottie, come here!" she yelled at the top of her lungs.

Her hand trembled when she reached for the white sheet of paper beside the cat. A rock, similar to the one that had come through her window, held the paper down. She clenched her jaw.

The front door flew open and Scottie rushed out. "What's wrong?"

He stopped, his mouth open, his eyes widened, at the sight of the cat in front of Debbie.

"Oh, my sainted stars," Cressie muttered from the doorway. "The spirits didn't say . . . they didn't say. Yet I knew they was afoot and restless. I should have paid more attention."

"How did that get there?" Scottie asked, pointing to the dead animal.

"From the note, I'd say someone left us a little present," Debbie replied in a shaky voice. She wanted this cruel, elusive tormentor; she wanted her hands on him; she wanted to hear him beg for mercy. Not satisfied with just breaking windows, he was now killing helpless animals.

"Jeeze," Scottie growled. "He didn't kill the cat on purpose, did he? Whose cat is it?"

Debbie shook her head. "The cat's been run over. That's all I can say."

Moving closer for a better look, Cressie said, "It looks like one of Michael Townsend's, one of the cats they keep in the barn."

"Find a shovel, Scottie, and bury the poor thing," Debbie instructed, and pushed past the other two to enter the house. "When you finish, we'll eat dinner."

"Ah, sis, can't it wait until after I eat?"

"No. I want the cat buried immediately. I don't want to walk out and find a bird or some animal messing with it."

"I'll get Sal to take care of it. He won't mind. You two go on in and get some supper," Cressie said, following behind.

Debbie washed her hands while Scottie served up his food and began to eat. His face was white, and he kept peeking at her every few moments. He was clearly upset, but nothing, absolutely nothing, interfered with his appetite. She wished she were more like him.

She stubbornly remained silent. She'd never been so mad. She was even angrier than when she had learned that Charles was sleeping with one of his students. At least then she'd known where to vent her fury. She had no idea how to stop this.

There was always the police, but they wouldn't do

anything about a dead cat. They'd probably say it was another prank. And there was little hope of tracing either note.

No, she'd have to go on as she was. Sooner or later this culprit would make a mistake, and she'd be ready.

"It's all taken care of," Cressie said as she and Sal entered through the back door. "The poor creature's been put to rest."

Scottie swallowed a mouthful of roast. "What are you going to do, Debbie?"

Cressie and Sal glanced at each other uneasily before sitting down at the table.

"You didn't see or hear anyone?" Debbie asked the two.

"Sal spent the day in the back field. I've been can-nin' here in the kitchen. I didn't hear a thing," Cressie replied.

When the silence seemed to take over the house, Debbie asked, "How could someone do such a thing? That poor animal."

"What did the note say?" Scottie asked.

Debbie examined the paper, pressing out the wrin-kles from where she had scrunched it up in her fist.

"'When you don't pay attention, accidents hap-pen,'" she read out loud.

"Evil's a-walkin'. The cauldron's bubblin'."

"Evil's a-walking all right, and evil someone's going to get." Debbie slammed her hand down on the table with a bang.

"What you gonna do, Miss Debbie?"

"I'm not sure, but you can bet your last dollar I'll find out who's doing these terrible things. And when I do, he's going to know he took on the wrong person."

13

Debbie prowled restlessly through the house. She was so mad that grading papers was the last thing she wanted to do. Since she couldn't relieve her frustration, she needed something interesting enough to deflect her thoughts.

She gazed out the window at the graveyard atop the hill with its pale tombstones reaching toward the night sky. The Muller family with all their secrets lay up there. As if she were drawn to it, Debbie walked into the library in search of Kyle Muller's journal.

She took the old, battered volume from the shelf and returned to the kitchen. "Cressie, I've found Kyle's journal. Will it tell me why Kate haunts the house?"

"She's restless 'cause she can't find peace."

"That means nothing."

The housekeeper smiled and said, "You'll know everythin' when it's time."

Debbie refused to argue. It wouldn't do any good, anyway. She took the book into the back parlor, turned on the floor lamp by the large, comfortable chair, and propped her feet on the footstool. When she opened the cover, she saw faded ink that resembled chicken scratches more than handwriting.

"To my descendants, so you'll know how it all began," Kyle wrote first, then went on to relate a summary of the Muller family history back east. This was followed by their decision to move west, along with other families wanting to start a new life and make their fortune.

The original Slavanias, Gypsy outcasts from Europe, came to America but found few friends. The Mullers took them in hand, entering into various enterprises together. When the Mullers came west, so did Pierre Slavania.

Instead of the Mullers and Pierre working and sharing with the other new settlers, they set about life in their own way. Because of his psychic powers, Pierre influenced nearby Indians and even married one. Tale after tale followed, telling how the Mullers and Pierre acquired land, money, and other valuable assets. Possessions and power were always the chief goals, and the acquisition of more was a matter of pride. A special room was built to safeguard the Mullers' wealth.

Somewhere in the next generations, the Slavanias lost their wealth while the Mullers grew richer. Yet the Mullers always kept the Slavanias employed and saw that they never went without the necessities. Because of outlaws, the Mullers even stored the Slavanias' few remaining valuables in the hidden room with their own.

The Civil War changed many things. Kyle Muller sympathized with the South, but if the profit was high enough, he didn't mind transacting a little business with the North. Gold was the only acceptable form of exchange.

Then a Yankee set fire to the place when Kyle was away from home, a retaliation for Kyle's duplicity. Kyle returned to learn that his wife and two young sons had perished in the burning buildings.

Ink blots dotted the yellowed pages, and Debbie sensed the man's sorrow as he recorded the loss of his family.

Kyle quickly resumed his emotionless form, stating that assistance by neighbors and servants kept the house from being totally destroyed and no one had discovered the hidden room by the parlor or any of its treasures.

Debbie's breath quickened. The parlor had to be the room she was in, since it was part of the original house. But where could the hidden room be? She kept reading.

He repeatedly damned the Yankees and never forgave them what they had done. As an act of defiance, he rebuilt his house in southern mansion style.

Suddenly chilled, Debbie glanced around. The familiar musty odor was everywhere. Refusing to stop reading, she grabbed the afghan from the small sofa and wrapped it around her shoulders.

After rebuilding his house, Kyle married a local girl, and they had two children. Carl was born in 1863 and Kate in 1866, but by this time Kyle, apparently warped with bitterness, wrote harshly of his neighbors and business associates. He hated Yankees and felt no pity for the weak and suffering. Since he also faulted his dead wife for the loss of his two sons, his comments showed little respect for women and even less for his second wife.

"Damned chauvinist," Debbie muttered.

A gust of cold draft whipped the page over. Stubbornly Debbie tightened the afghan, turned back, and continued reading.

Kate's mother died, and at the age of six Kate fell heir to the housework, a job Kyle clearly believed fitted the female species. Her brother fared only slightly better. Totally unable to satisfy his father's demands, sixteen-year-old Carl fought one last argument with Kyle and then left home. Kyle disinherited his son, leaving Kate to bear her father's dictates and his wealth.

Several times Kyle mentioned aiding people wanted by the law or the military, hiding them in the secret room. All for a very good price. Three times he had hid there himself when visited by outlaws and twice from Yankees.

When Kyle wrote he had found the perfect son-in-law for Kate to marry, a boy named Henry Farmsworth and younger son of the local banker, Debbie caught her breath in surprise. But Kyle went on to mention the family assets and the excellent prospects of such a union. As soon as he stated that Henry could help him run his affairs as well as provide Kate with a husband, Debbie slammed the book shut in dismay at his apparent disregard for his daughter's feelings.

Yawning, she saw it was almost two in the morning. Her last waking thought after getting in bed was to remind herself to ask Eleanor if Henry was an ancestor of her missing husband, Herman.

Not wanting to distract Scottie from school, she didn't mention her discovery the next morning. She did stick the journal in her briefcase to take with her. She hoped to read between classes and discover the secret location of the room.

Later that morning Keith called to invite her to Scottie's first football game. Too excited to keep the news entirely to herself, she told Keith about the journal. Catching her enthusiasm, he suggested they look for the hidden room after the game, and Debbie readily agreed.

Scottie played an excellent game, and the Dragons won. As part of their celebration, Debbie placed big scoops of vanilla ice cream on plates containing slices of Cressie's homemade apple pie and set the dishes beside the coffee. When she carried the tray into the back parlor, she could barely suppress her eagerness.

Keith, struggling with the passages she had marked in the journal, looked up when she set the tray in front of him. He wore a ferocious frown. "I don't know how you managed to read as much as you did."

"Eat your pie before the ice cream melts. Then I'll read the instructions I found while you search."

"What time do you expect Scottie?" Keith asked.

Debbie smiled. He certainly didn't intend to waste any time. "Around twelve-thirty. Jenny has to be home right after the school dance."

"Jenny has changed since Scottie came. She doesn't seem like the same girl. Even Michael commented on it the other day."

"So Michael doesn't think I'm such a bad neighbor after all?" Debbie teased, making no effort to hide her light-heartedness. She licked some remaining ice cream from her fork. After all, it wasn't every day you were able to help three people badly in need, just by providing a home for a troubled brother. From an earlier phone call, she knew her mother was surprised at how well Scottie was behaving. And now praise from Michael about Jenny.

Keith set his empty plate on the table. "Okay, I'm ready. Read the part about the hidden opening."

After listening to her instructions, he bent down to press the bottom brick of the outside edge of the fireplace. The stone hugged the darkness of the corner. He pushed and tugged until a low click broke the silence.

The panel beside the fireplace slid open. Debbie stared into a black, beckoning cavern. The tantalizing temptation raised goose bumps along her arms.

While Keith checked how to reopen the door should it close when they were inside, she searched for a flashlight. After handing it to him, she followed his cautious steps down the stairs that led into the hidden basement room. With each step her breathing quickened with anticipation.

The light flicked across the dirt floor and over the walls. "I would say Cressie and Sal have known about this room all the time," Keith commented when the side of a glass jar caught and reflected the focused brightness.

Canned fruit, vegetables, and preserves sat on shelves and filled one side of the room. On another wall they found bottles of Cressie's homemade wine along with other vintages.

"I wonder why she never said anything," Debbie said, studying the jars closely. "And how many other things do you suppose she hasn't mentioned?"

"Maybe she thought you knew."

"I doubt that. She seems to have her own ideas

about what and when I should know things, and this
is just one more." She walked around the cold,
musty room, peeking closely at the shelves, trying to
discover if anything of importance lurked in the
darkness.

"The way she carries on about Miss Kate and Miss
Sarah, you might have not been paying attention."
Keith bent and picked up a small golden key lying in
the corner of the shelf next to a bottle of Cressie's
wine. "I wonder what this goes to."

Debbie took the key. After turning it over several
times, she slipped it into her pocket. "Tomorrow I'll
ask Cressie if she knows."

"There doesn't seem to be anything of importance."

"No, there doesn't," Debbie agreed, not letting
her disappointment show. "That's why I can't understand why Cressie didn't show me the room or tell
me how to get down here. I've complained about the
draft in the back parlor often enough. You'd think
she'd have said something then."

"This room could never create the draft. There's
no place for the air to come from. Besides, hot air
rises, not cold."

Keith flicked the light around the ceiling. Something gleamed near the corner.

Debbie caught his hand. "Look up there. What's
that?"

"Well, I'll be damned." Shining pieces of glass,
decorated with pictures of small jasmine flowers and
hanging from thin wires, glittered in the light.

"The wind chimes."

Keith brushed his fingers against the dangling
rectangles. A sweet tinkling responded.

"But if there's no wind, how can they ring by

themselves?" Debbie protested.

Keith lowered his voice and laced his words with a mysterious tone. "Maybe a ghost provided the wind and the draft. It's rumored the house is haunted, you know."

Debbie's lips tightened. Despite his attempt at humor, he didn't realize how accurate she believed his explanation to be. But she had to react rationally. "There's no way I would hear these wind chimes up in my room, even if there was a gust of wind to move them. There must be others in another part of the house."

"Hey, where is everybody?" Scottie's voice echoed from the first floor. A door slammed behind him.

Keith looked down at her, his eyes dancing with amusement. "I'd say Scottie's making sure we know he's arrived and roaming around."

"He's a real diplomat," Debbie agreed. After one final search to determine if she had missed anything, she went back up to the small parlor and left Keith investigating the names on the bottles of wine.

"Hey, what's that?" Scottie said through a mouthful of pie and ice cream. Excitement shone in his eyes.

"That's the hidden room, and it contains wind chimes."

Finishing his pie with one big bite, Scottie slapped his plate on the bar and ran down the stairs to join Keith.

Debbie sat on the couch and tried to analyze why this keen sense of disappointment should overwhelm her so. Exactly what had she expected to find in the room? Treasures or answers?

She would rather have answers. She wanted to know the truth about Kate. Cressie must have realized this, and knowing the room wouldn't provide them, she'd let Debbie search on her own. There was no other explanation for her secrecy.

From the corner of her eye, she caught a movement in the hallway and tightened her hold on the arm of the sofa. The revolting odor of mold wafted through the air and pressed in around her. Maybe what she felt was not disappointment at all. Maybe it was a sense of foreboding; maybe someone wasn't pleased they had discovered the hidden room.

The soft ringing of the wind chimes drifted up the open doorway, along with Scottie's laughter. Reassured, Debbie relaxed.

Almost as though someone mocked her trust, the air chilled instantly, making her shiver. Reluctantly she glanced toward the hallway. Nothing. A door closed from another part of the house. Her body went rigid. She held her breath, her whole being concentrating on listening. Scottie and Keith started up the stairs from the secret room, and she exhaled slowly.

Simultaneously with Scottie's reaching the top step, a distant door squeaked. Once more Debbie snapped around to stare at the hallway door. Nothing was there, but the waves of displeasure that vibrated through the air sent quivers of apprehension up her spine.

"Hey, sis, what's the matter? Whew, what's that smell?"

Debbie swallowed. "I thought I heard someone in the other part of the house."

"Maybe it's Cressie."

"No . . . no, I don't think so. She and Sal are in bed by now."

Keith joined them in the parlor and closed the

secret door. "Problem?"

"Debbie thinks she heard someone in the house."

"Don't mind me. I suffer from fear of attacks. Someone wants me to leave Nacogdoches and is willing to do almost anything." She tried to smile. "I guess, Dr. Douglas, you could diagnose the problem as a case of stressed-out nerves."

"I somehow never considered you as the nervous type."

"Hey, don't let these noises get to you now, sis. Last night you were all out for retaliation," Scottie teased. "I'll tell you what. Since you found the dead cat, I'll go check the house out. How's that?"

Scottie walked out into the hall nonchalantly, and Debbie looked up to find Keith still staring at her.

"Dead cat?" he asked.

Debbie raked her fingers through her hair and explained what she'd found after leaving him. When she finished she said, "I've thought about this, and I think the only way to stop whoever is doing these things is to come out in the open and let everyone know what's happening, and that I intend to prosecute."

Keith stuck his hands in his pockets, concern in his eyes. "A get-tough approach?"

"Something like that. Someone obviously considers me a softie. I need to let them know I will not be intimidated."

"That sounds plausible."

"I thought I'd start with the obvious list of people and make certain I talk to each one personally. Word will spread, and maybe these pranks will stop."

"Whom do you consider the obvious people?"

Debbie found and twirled a string on the sofa.

"Mostly the people from Norma's party."

After a moment Keith walked over to the hallway and called out, "Find anything?"

"Not so far," Scottie replied from the front staircase. "It's as quiet as a grave."

His laughter followed. He seemed to be treating the whole affair as if it were a carnival sideshow. Debbie broke off a loose string from the sofa. He certainly hadn't been so nonchalant the night of his arrival. His act must be for Keith's benefit, to prove he was a true man of the house.

Turning back to Debbie, Keith asked, "How would you like to have dinner with me tomorrow evening? We could go someplace nice, without the kids."

"What do you have in mind?"

Keith's mouth quirked. "I've already told you I think you're a special lady, but actually I thought I'd ask Norma and Michael to meet us at the restaurant. That way we could start on your plan."

"But I thought Michael and Norma were good friends of yours. You've always insisted that Michael couldn't do any of the things Jenny has accused him of doing."

Keith's level gaze locked with hers. "I haven't changed my mind, but I think in this case you have a different opinion. I'm willing to accept the possibility I could be wrong."

"Nothing except the stink of jasmine," Scottie said as he came striding into the room. "Hey, what's up? Did I miss something?"

Not taking her eyes from Keith's, Debbie said, "Scottie, you don't mind staying by yourself tomorrow evening, do you? Keith and I are going out to dinner with Norma and Michael."

"You can't!" Scottie cried, his fists clenching at his

sides.

"What do you mean, 'we can't'?" Keith asked.

"Sis, you can't go out and eat with that bastard. It's disloyal. Michael's trying to do away with Jenny. I thought you were on her side. She said no one ever believed her before you came."

"Don't talk to your sister like that," Keith said tightly.

Debbie put up her hand to stop him. Then, concentrating on Scottie, she said, "I have to find out who's playing these tricks—my mail, the rock, the threats, the cat—don't you understand? The best way is to take the attack into the opponent's camp. Hopefully he'll either back down or do something foolish, and we'll catch him."

"And you think Michael is behind these things?" Scottie straightened, and with a gleam of anticipation, he said, "I can always beat the shit out of him. That'd stop him from hurting you or Jenny."

"A mature adult tries to find a more peaceful way to solve his problems," Keith interjected.

"And if he can't?" Scottie challenged.

Keith shrugged, and after a moment he countered more gently, "Then he beats the shit out of him. But first the adult has to be absolutely certain he has the right man. You don't go around beating up everyone in sight simply because you suffer a difference of opinion."

"I'm going to bed," Scottie announced huffily. "Do what you think best." Then he stopped in the doorway and looked at Debbie. "But if you want me to beat the—"

"That's all right," Debbie replied. "I understand. And thanks, Scottie."

Scottie nodded and, after a last glance at Keith,

stuck his hands in his pockets and walked down the hallway.

"I didn't realize Scottie took Jenny's accusations so seriously," Keith commented thoughtfully.

"I didn't either." Debbie sighed. Standing, she walked over to Keith and placed her hands on his shoulders. "I appreciate your talking to him like you did. He hasn't had a male figure to look up to in a long time, and I was surprised he listened."

Keith wrapped his arms around her waist and pulled her close. "I'm beginning to have a particular liking for all the Dillons, but I'm especially partial to the honey blonde with green eyes."

Then his lips claimed hers. Debbie reeled in extreme pleasure and forgot everything but the sensations Keith produced in her body.

Both were flushed when he pulled away. "I'd better go while I still can."

He was right, but she hated to see him leave.

"Maybe tomorrow night after dinner with Norma and Michael, you might like to stop by my cottage and see how a professor cum writer lives?"

Tucking her arm under his, she walked beside him out into the hall, peeking up now and then to see his face. The scent of his after-shave filled her nostrils. His body warmth seared her own wherever they touched. He was coming out of his stand in a big way.

And suddenly she wasn't sure. To go to bed with Keith was a big step, another milestone since her divorce. She knew he wasn't offering anything more than an affair; also, he'd tried to warn that women frequently entered into relationships to prove their femininity. He hadn't wanted to hurt her or hear recriminations when he left Nacogdoches. Apparently he thought she was strong enough to handle an affair now.

At that moment she accepted that she cared about him, enjoyed his kisses, but she wasn't sure she wanted a light-hearted dalliance. It could end very painfully for her.

"Why don't we see how things go tomorrow evening," she suggested.

"Whatever you say." Standing in the outside doorway, he kissed her roughly one more time.

His lips softened, gentled, and Debbie felt desire licking through her.

She broke away. "Yep, it's a fact I'll swear to. You are indeed a provocative man, a very dangerous man for a poor working girl."

Laughing, she patted his cheek and let her fingers slide down to brush against the whiskers that broke the smoothness of his chin. She teasingly poked her forefinger into his dimpled scar in his chin. When he reached for her again, she quickly closed the door.

Leaning against the wooden barrier, she heard his footsteps fade toward his car. It had taken her so long to find this man, and soon, he would be gone from her life.

The next evening at the Western Corral, Keith located Norma and Michael across the wooden-paneled and red-carpeted room before Debbie saw them. While they wove their way around the other diners, Debbie wondered if the seated couple had any inkling that tonight a different Debbie joined them, one with a mission in mind.

"Don't you look smashing in your red dress,"

Norma greeted her.

Norma wore a delicate pastel print dress in shades of pink, mauve, and turquoise. Debbie couldn't imagine her throwing rocks or handling dead cats, and she almost gave up her plan. But then she tightened her resolve. How well did one person really know another in only a couple of months? Successful real estate salespeople had to possess guile, and from every indication, by Nacogdoches standards Norma was very successful.

Debbie didn't find Michael quite as handsomely sinister in the dark gray suit as he'd looked at Norma's party. The wide smile he gave her when she sat down helped to remove any lingering worries she had as to the success of the evening. Still, he was no match in appearance for Keith in his own gray suit. She spread the napkin across her lap and relaxed.

"I recommend the sirloin," Michael suggested after Debbie opened her menu.

"The zucchini-and-mushroom appetizer is out of this world, too," Norma added.

"And what do you suggest?" Debbie asked, looking at Keith beside her. He wore a tangy cologne this evening, and the fragrance threatened her determination to appear calm and cool.

"I like their chocolate mousse pie."

Debbie laughed. "Why don't I let the rest of you order for me, and I'll sit back and let my taste buds judge how you do."

The evening began merrily, and the gaiety continued throughout the meal. Debbie saw for herself why Keith believed Michael could never harm Jenny. While he discussed his horses and his plans for the future, he frequently touched Norma, showing a gentler side. He obviously kept much of himself hidden from other people.

"Jenny has become a different girl since Scottie came," Norma said, her pleasure lighting up her face. "She's interested in clothes, school dances, things she never cared about before. She's even neglecting Nacho, something we had given up hope of ever seeing. Michael might hesitate to tell you how pleased we are, but I won't."

Debbie blinked. Norma clearly didn't see Michael as Debbie did. Still, she had provided an opening. "Scottie has been a big help to me as well, especially the other evening when I found a dead cat on my doorstep and another threatening note."

Meeting Michael's expressionless gaze, she added, "Cressie mentioned she thought the cat might be yours. I hope you don't mind, but I had Sal bury it without calling you first."

"Another threatening note?" Norma asked abruptly, her eyes full of questions.

"Yes." Debbie set her fork on the side of her plate and went on to tell about the rock through her window.

"I heard you were having problems with the mail, but I had no idea . . ." Michael said, his voice trailing off.

When the others couldn't seem to find anything to say, Debbie added, "Jenny and I seem to have something in common. Someone doesn't like us."

"I told you before, I wouldn't harm Jenny. I hope you're not suggesting now that I've stooped to throwing rocks with notes at women and killing cats," Michael said with quiet anger.

Keith broke the strained silence. "Norma, I know

that even though you had the house listed since Sarah died, you showed the Muller house to very few people. What made you decide Debbie might be interested?"

"Because she looked so much like Miss Kate's picture and even resembled Sarah. It seemed right somehow that she at least consider the house. She could have refused." Norma laughed uneasily. "Maybe I couldn't forget Cressie's telling me not to worry, that Sarah told her the right person would come along and snatch up the place. When I first saw Debbie, it all seemed to fall into place."

"But you didn't show the Muller house to me at first," Debbie said. "We went all over Nacogdoches in the beginning, even up on the hill where the large new houses aren't even for sale."

"I know. I couldn't make myself actually believe that Cressie could be right. I did try to warn you that things might not be quite what they seemed at the Muller house."

"Because of the ghost stories?" Keith interjected.

"Actually, I don't believe in those tales," Norma said. "No, more because I knew Cressie would never let go of the house. If the new owner didn't turn out to be a tolerant person, I could see our whole neighborhood becoming embroiled in a real disaster with Cressie and Sal at the heart of the problem."

"Do you have any idea who might make these threats on Debbie?" Keith asked.

Michael straightened on his chair. "If Cressie's as fond of the house as you say, maybe she's behind these things. Maybe she thinks the house should be hers."

A haughty voice interrupted them. "I'm surprised

you dared showed yourselves in public, especially in this restaurant where you know I always eat on Saturday nights."

Startled, Debbie looked up to find Eleanor standing beside their table and glaring down at Norma and Michael.

Michael and Keith both stood politely. An angry Eleanor squared her shoulders. "How could you?" she asked through clenched teeth. "How could you do such a thing?"

"Do what?" Norma asked.

"And to think I considered you friends." Eleanor gave a sharp little sound as she bit her lower lip.

Norma looked beseechingly at Michael, who remained as grimly silent as a stone statue. Forcing a smile, she took hold of Eleanor's hand and said, "We are your friends. What do you think we've done?"

"That letter . . . that terrible letter you sent me."

"What letter?" Keith asked. "What did the letter say?"

Eleanor jerked her hand free from Norma's. "One of them wrote a letter, a love letter, and forged Herman's signature on the bottom."

"So . . . ?" Keith pressed.

"The letter was addressed to Gloria." Eleanor pointed her finger at Michael accusingly. "That man's wife. His Gloria. Where else would it come from, who else would send me such a terrible thing if not one of them?"

"If the letter was false and Herman's signature forged, it could have come from anyone," Keith explained carefully.

Eleanor's hand went flat on the table with an urgent slapping sound. She looked down at the nearby plate. The steak knife blade gleamed in the table's candelabra light. She seemed fascinated by the sight.

"Eleanor, honey, I know how you loved Herman. I didn't send the letter. I wouldn't do such a thing," Norma murmured gently.

Eleanor's nostrils quivered. "Michael could have sent it. He hated Herman because he wouldn't give him the loan he wanted."

"But he likes you," Norma pointed out. "He wouldn't send you such a letter. Look at him. Look at Michael, Eleanor. He's hurting as much as you are from this. After all, Gloria was . . . is his wife."

Eleanor's blue eyes narrowed. "Jenny thinks he's trying to kill her. She said so at your party. How do you know you can trust him? How do I know I can?"

The situation was getting out of hand. Everyone was looking at them. Yet Debbie hated to stop it. She needed answers. This might provide them.

Then she realized she didn't want to air their troubles for everyone to see and hear. This problem belonged to a close-knit group that lived on the same road. Despite what someone wanted her to believe, she was now a part of that group, and she'd have to find another way to learn who wanted her to leave.

She rose, wrapped her arm through Eleanor's, and walked the banker through the restaurant. "Have you heard what happened to me?" She explained about the rock, the cat, and the notes. "Maybe there's some nut loose in the neighborhood, someone wanting to hurt us both."

A strange smiled formed on Eleanor's face. "Cressie warned us, you know," she said, stopping by the cash register. "The devil's disciple is running loose. Judgment is upon us, and only the letting of blood will cure the ills of the past and bring peace."

Debbie didn't know how to respond.

Eleanor walked out the door with the hostess calling after her to pay her check.

Debbie raised her hand to catch the young woman's attention. "Don't worry about it. We'll take care of it with ours."

As she walked back to the table, Debbie wondered where this would all end.

No one wanted dessert; the atmosphere now was too strained. Michael requested the bill and, despite Keith's objections, paid the full amount, including Eleanor's.

After saying good night and watching the other two drive off, Debbie climbed into the car beside Keith. The bright neon sign displaying the restaurant's name sent eerie swatches of color over his face and across the dash. Red, the same as her dress, the same as the color of blood. She shivered.

Keith started the motor and after several moments switched on the heater. "You're cold. It may take a few minutes, but the car will warm up nicely."

"Who would have thought the evening would turn out like this?" She looked across the street at the yellow neon of another restaurant and the flashing headlights of passing cars. Up in the dark velvet sky, stars glittered. She searched for the normalcy that she knew existed, anything to quiet this terrible foreboding that made her question people's sanity. There was nothing she could do.

Keith sat hunched over the steering wheel. "Do you want me to take you home, or would you like to see where I live?"

She was thankful he hadn't simply driven home

without asking. She longed to run her fingers through his hair and kiss his dimpled chin. But tonight had made her realize she wasn't ready to commit herself to a lengthy affair. That wouldn't be wise for her or fair to Keith. When or if they came together, they both had to know exactly where they stood within themselves. Keith apparently did already, or at least he thought so. She didn't.

"I'm sorry. I can't play games. When I go to bed with someone, it means something. I like you, Keith, more than I thought I would ever like any man again, but I'm not ready yet to commit to more than companionship."

Keith started the car and drove out onto North Street. "Don't worry about it."

"You're not mad?"

Keith grinned. "Lady, with all the excitement you have in your life and everything you have going for you, you couldn't drive me away."

Debbie sighed with relief and relaxed. There were definitely certain advantages to dating a psychologist, and there was always tomorrow.

14

College homecoming fell on the following Saturday, and beginning early Monday morning, Debbie scurried from meeting to meeting, worked on reports, and gathered figures together to meet the dean's demands.

Dean Carrington was like the heads of college departments everywhere. This annual event provided him with an opportunity to remind alumni of the need for donations and to discuss special projects that would build his particular little kingdom into the most powerful in the state. In this instance, the Business Department would be the means to attain his goal.

Determined that Dean Carrington would find no fault with her reports and would accept her as a contributing member of the staff, Debbie rose early, went to bed late, and seemed in a continual fog of must do's and "Where is the time?" Stress became a natural part of all her endeavors.

Arriving home Friday after Scottie's football game, she collapsed into bed. She still hadn't seen Keith, but her last waking thoughts were of tomorrow. She, Keith, Scottie, and Jenny were going to the Lumberjacks big Homecoming Game, and then she and Keith would attend a party afterward. Tomorrow she finally had time to spend with Keith.

Able at last to put aside work and enjoy herself, Debbie slept late the next morning. After a leisurely brunch, she soaked in the tub, washed her hair, manicured her nails, and lazily prepared for Keith's arrival.

He was late, and it was close to one before he rang the doorbell. They needed to hurry. For once she enjoyed his masterful ways and the pampering he gave her while he took charge.

"Damn, it's hot," he grumbled, as they walked toward the stadium arm in arm.

"It's a beautiful day," she admonished him.

"Where did all these people come from? It's worse than the streets of New York during a parade."

"The week's finally over," Debbie countered. "No more reports, no more meetings, no more Dean Carrington. How can you complain?"

"I think every alum, student, and parent is here today," Keith said, leading her through a chattering circle of people and toward the ramp to the entrance.

"It's marvelous that everyone came. Oh, Keith, can't you feel the excitement? It's better than a carnival." Seeing Keith's twinkling eyes, she punched his arm. "I wondered why you were suddenly a grouch."

"Are you trying to tell me you think I'm even-tempered, or that you enjoy my company?"

"Why is it a man's ego constantly needs feeding?"

"At least you don't call me a boy anymore."

"I know what you are." Remembering her uncertainty and Keith's patience, she felt embarrassed. He was a generous, giving man. So why couldn't she make up her mind and go for it?

Calls of hucksters selling their souvenir programs or balloons greeted them at the gate. Penetrating aromas of grilling hot dogs and popcorn wafted through the crowd when Debbie and Keith, with Scottie and Jenny close behind, walked up the aisle in search of their seats.

"Hey, sis, how about a snack before the game starts?"

"But you had lunch just before we left the house."

"That's not the same," Keith chimed in immediately. "You have to join in the swing of things to fully appreciate the day."

Seeing Scottie's and Jenny's eager looks at the vendors, and Keith's equally excited face, Debbie said, "I might go for a box of popcorn and a Coke."

"Great!" Scottie exclaimed. "I'd like a couple of hot dogs myself."

"You girls save the seats. Scottie and I'll see what we can forage," Keith said.

Debbie watched the two make their way through the crowd and shook her head. Scottie was insatiable when it came to food. Then, hearing Jenny's giggle beside her, Debbie laughed. "I'm not sure which is more important to Scottie, food or football," she said.

"He has a craving for both," Jenny agreed.

Curious, Debbie looked around. Sororities and fraternities competed for attention, checkering the stands and end zones with signs and posters. Everywhere the charged air rang with hope for the day. People filled the seats while still more enthusiasts poured down the aisles.

"Here we go. One box of popcorn and one large Coke," Keith said.

As he handed her the treats, Debbie read a promise for later in his eyes, and her breath caught. Once more she faced the issue of whether she wanted to enter an affair.

The Lumberjacks controlled the playing field, a fact no one doubted from the first kick-off of the day. Debbie yelled and cheered at the top of her lungs along with the crowd. Despite the break at halftime, while the homecoming queen reigned and the band performed, when the victorious game ended, Debbie could barely speak.

Keith laughed. "Had a good time, did you?"

"I never cared for football, until I started going to Scottie's games. Somehow I've acquired a different attitude."

"It's like a virus. It can sneak up on you and take over importance in your life."

"A virus?"

"Yuck," Scottie growled from behind.

"If you can't beat it, you have to join the ranks of cheerleaders," Debbie said happily.

"Cheerleaders can be a lot of fun," Keith replied.

Seeing the shine of the scar in his dimple, she impulsively kissed the end of her finger and stuck the tip in the indentation. "I couldn't resist."

"I can't, either." Keith grabbed her fingers and kissed each one.

"Come on, you two. We'll never get home if we don't keep moving," Scottie complained.

"You have something special planned?" Debbie tucked her arm under Keith's as they started down the ramp.

"Since you and Keith are going to that party at Carolyn Niver's, Jenny and I planned to go horseback riding and have a picnic by the swimming hole this evening."

Debbie looked at the low-hanging afternoon sun. "You're not going to have much time before dark. Why don't you go tomorrow?"

"You can't go back on your word, Debbie. You already said we could, and Cressie's packed a food basket."

Debbie frowned. She didn't remember this conversation at all, but then she recalled little of their conversations during the past week. "I don't want you out late after dark."

"My God, you'd think we were kids instead of sixteen."

"Scottie . . ."

"We won't be. Just don't go back on your word."

When Keith unlocked the car, his speculative look held Scottie beside him while Jenny climbed inside. Debbie waited to listen.

Keith's firm voice remained low. "You do remember that Jenny didn't date before you arrived. I wouldn't want you to take advantage of her . . . her infatuation, or the romantic seclusion."

"Speaking from your own experience?" Scottie retaliated.

"You might say that. I'm also speaking as your friend and Jenny's. She has enough on her plate now. I don't want her to anchor on to you and then be hurt when you return home. I don't want you to suffer any guilt, knowing you caused her more pain."

Debbie nodded. "He speaks for me, too, Scottie. You're my brother, and I love you, but Jenny's my friend. I care about you both."

Scottie's mouth tightened momentarily before he shrugged. "I thought you both knew me better. I like Jenny, probably more than either of you do. I would never do anything to hurt her. You don't have to worry about my getting carried away, either."

Keith nodded, and Scottie joined Jenny on the backseat.

Another milestone, an important one, had been passed. This conversation with her brother would have been very difficult for her, although she had been considering it. Keith had dealt with the problem quite efficiently. She smiled at him gratefully.

It took almost an hour to pick up the food basket Cressie had left and then drop Jenny and Scottie at Jenny's house. Seeing the deserted grounds, Debbie had second thoughts. She'd known Teresa would be at Carolyn's since Keith and Teresa had been helping Carolyn with the plans, but she hadn't realized Michael had plans as well.

Scottie and Jenny made their way instantly to the stable without stopping at the house. Knowing her brother took his promises seriously, Debbie pushed away the uneasy qualms she felt. But with everything that had happened lately, she didn't want them out in the woods after dark. She almost called them back, but she didn't have the heart to stop them. She had to trust nothing would happen.

"Shall we?" Keith asked, and drove off when she nodded.

The party proved to be a delightful way to end the week. Debbie nibbled hungrily at the barbecued ribs and beef, ate far too much potato salad and beans, and swallowed it all down with the cold beer.

Whenever she looked across the room for Keith,

she continually locked eyes with him. Whenever they stood or sat side by side, his spicy after-shave drew her even closer to him. She knew he felt the same way, because he found constant opportunities to touch her face, or clasp her hand, or wrap his arm around her waist and hug her close.

The excitement of the day, the game, the good conversation with friends, left Debbie wanting to share something special with Keith. Yet later, when they drove away in his car and he asked her again if she was interested in seeing his cottage, she said, "It's close to ten. I need to get home and check on Scottie and Jenny."

"Don't, Debbie. If you don't want to go to bed with me, say so. But don't use the kids as an excuse."

Was that what she was doing?

She wanted him. Her body begged for the release she knew he could give her, and her senses cried for this man to take her. But the fear of making a mistake, doing something foolish that would bring more pain, controlled her more.

At the same time, she wasn't being fair to him.

"I'm sorry," she whispered. "It's not that I don't find you attractive. You know better."

"Damn!" He slammed his hand against the steering wheel. "Don't patronize me. I know what's going through your head. I know you want me as much as I want you. I also know you're afraid. You don't trust me not to hurt you, and you don't trust yourself enough to let go of the past."

She glanced over at Keith's profile. His concentration was on the road ahead, and she wondered what she could say that would bring back the joy of the earlier evening. "I missed seeing you this week. Today's been fun."

"I enjoyed today, too."

The night sky didn't seem so black now. Debbie settled against the cushioned back of the seat and drew pleasure from the quiet. Keith was a very understanding person, but she wasn't sure how long she could keep him hanging.

"Weren't Scottie and Jenny coming back here?" Keith asked as they turned into Debbie's driveway.

The moonlight flickered over the dark house, casting eerie shadows against the white paint. "That's what I understood." Concerned, Debbie chewed on her lower lip.

"Maybe they stayed at Jenny's when they took the horses back."

The Slavanias' apartment above the garage also stood silent and dark. "Cressie mentioned they were visiting friends this evening. They must not be back yet, either."

Keith stopped the car beside the back door but kept the motor idling. "Shall we both go in and see if they've been here, or do you want me to run over to Jenny's?"

Debbie's fingers played with the door handle. "Scottie promised. . . ."

"Teenage boys are famous for their hormones, and Jenny is crazy about him. Sometimes these things happen, despite the best intentions."

Keith was talking about Scottie and Jenny, but suddenly it seemed as though he could have been discussing their own roller-coaster relationship. She sighed from the weight of indecision and concentrated on what had to be done now. "I'll look here while you run over to Jenny's."

"I can see if the horses are back. That'll tell us something."

Debbie opened the car door. "They're probably both exhausted and fast asleep already. Scottie here and Jenny there." She slammed the door and walked up the back steps.

Keith called through his open window, "Don't be too disappointed if you don't find him. I'll be right back."

She watched the red of his car's taillights fade onto the main road before she entered the house. She wished she didn't feel this gnawing apprehension. Wandering through the empty house, she turned on the lights. There was no sign of either teenager, nor was there any indication that they had been back since they'd left with the picnic basket.

Debbie sat at the kitchen table and waited for Keith to return. The clock ticked with annoying loudness while the minute hand crawled past the numbers. Finally she walked to the front parlor to watch for Keith's car. Anger warred with anxiety, and she began to pace. If Scottie was sitting comfortably, totally unconcerned over at Jenny's while she was making herself sick worrying, she'd kill him when he got home.

But if he wasn't there? . . . Debbie stopped. What if this crazy person had carried out his threat in some way on Scottie and Jenny this time? Or there could have been another accident—what if one of them were dead? Or both? After all, someone had killed the cat and almost succeeded with Jenny.

Debbie raked her fingers through her hair. "Damn it. Why doesn't Keith come?"

When she looked out the window again, she saw the car's headlights and rushed to her back door. Her heart pounded while she waited until Keith pulled up and stopped. "Well?"

"No sign of them or the horses," he replied, and followed her back into the house.

"Something must have happened," Debbie said, tears welling in her eyes. "One of them must be hurt. I knew I shouldn't have let them go. I knew it."

"Now don't get yourself worked up. I doubt if anything serious has happened to them."

"You don't think this crazy person, or Michael—"

"No, I don't. I think your imagination is working overtime."

Keith wrapped his arms around her and drew her close. His thumping heart beat reassuringly beneath her ear.

"But Scottie promised. Besides, they wouldn't stay this late. They know we'd worry." She ran her own hand over his broad chest and up to the fluttering pulse just below his ear. She was so glad he was here.

"I'll get the flashlight from my car. Do you have another here in the house?"

Debbie drew a deep breath. "In the drawer over there."

"Grab a jacket, and you may want to put on some walking shoes. It's quite a ways to the swimming hole." Without waiting for her reply, Keith picked up the flashlight from the drawer and went out the back door.

Debbie hurried, stopping only for a moment to tie her shoes. She left the lights on in the house to act as a beacon for their return.

Since Keith thought the teenagers would probably return to Jenny's first to put the horses away, Keith and Debbie followed a path through the flower garden, emerging in a turf of earthy scents. This way, he explained, they would intercept them.

After weaving their way through the vines and tall grass, they finally reached the side of the gurgling stream. The night breeze chilled her skin, and Debbie was glad of her jacket. She clenched her hands to keep from shaking. "How long will it take to get to the swimming hole?"

"Tired already?"

"No, anxious."

"Fifteen or twenty minutes, if we hurry."

The rough mounds and holes in the ground were hidden as varying shades of shadow in the grove of pines. The needles and clumps of grass proved equally dangerous. Debbie tightened her grip on her flashlight and picked her way cautiously. Keith didn't seem to have the same problem and soon began to creep ahead.

The weaving branches of the trees created eerie, frightening shadows. A noise in the underbrush startled her, and she hurried to catch up. Keith seemed to know when she drew closer because his pace also increased.

Debbie's breathing was ragged before they finally broke through the trees and into a secluded clearing. A large pool shimmered with moonlight, and the tang of pine filled the air. Red and gold autumn leaves from dogwoods and sweet gums lay scattered through the grass. One large oak guarded the pool with majestic splendor on the other side. The swimming hole had a serene beauty, but she could only stare with despair at the deserted spot. As apprehension gave way to fear, her heart hammered furiously beneath her breast. There was no indication that Scottie or Jenny had even been there.

"They're not here," she said flatly.

Keith walked around a particularly thick area of

grass, kicking at the surrounding bushes, peeking between the vines. Finally he bent and picked up something beside a broken branch.

"What is it? What did you find?" Debbie's voice quivered. She was afraid, so afraid that something had happened. She hesitated to hope.

"A paper napkin and a chicken bone. I'd say they at least ate here." Keith searched the area further, stepping back into the trees, shining his light wherever possible. Several times the scampering of small feet through the undergrowth broke the endless quiet.

Debbie, gathering her courage, started around the pool to search in the other direction. "Scottie . . . Jenny . . ."

An owl hooted. She jumped, stumbling over a tuft of thick grass. She leaned and stepped precariously, trying to regain her balance and not fall on the slippery edge of the pool. Her foot squashed into the soft, wet mud. "Damn," she muttered, her heart racing. She was frightened they wouldn't find the kids, but she positively trembled at the thought of what condition they might be in if she and Keith *did* find them. "Scottie . . . Jenny . . ."

After looking everywhere feasible, Keith walked up beside her and brushed back a strand of hair from her face. "They've been here, but there's no sign of them now."

Debbie fought back her fear that they might discover the teenagers' smashed bodies hidden in this deserted place. "So what should we do now?"

The flashlight threw weird shadows across Keith's face, sharpening the creases, highlighting the planes. "We'll take the shortcut back to the house and call for a search party."

Debbie filled with a horror that eclipsed all her other thoughts. Then, because this was not the time to fall apart, she shut off her emotions and said flatly, "You think something's happened to them, don't you? You believe that terrible maniac has done what he promised . . . he's hurt them . . . like that cat. . . ."

Keith's hands gripped her arms. The sheer force of his will took control of hers. "I think nothing of the sort. I think we'll find them, and hopefully nothing will have happened."

"But—"

"Maybe one of the horses fell in a hole in the dark. Maybe one of the kids fell off. Who knows? Accidents happen, but I truly believe we'll find them alive. Do you hear me?"

Debbie nodded.

After an agonizing heartbeat, Keith pulled her to him and kissed her lips, hard, until the trembling came from a different source. Then he stepped back. "You going to be okay?"

Debbie nodded.

"Good. Let's start back. The faster we go, the quicker we can get help." Without giving her any time to react, he turned and led the way down another path and through the inky depths of the trees. The wind sighed around them, and a leaf fell into her hair. She stubbornly bit back a scream.

It was dark, a deep, velvet, heavy darkness that would have been terrifying if she hadn't known Keith was close. Debbie forced every thought but one from her mind: They must find Scottie and Jenny. Determinedly, she placed one foot in front of the other and stumbled after him.

Keith's steps quickened. Now she could only look

at the ground and his broad back. Her pulse pounded in her ears from the fast pace and the fright she held within.

Suddenly he stopped, causing her to ram into the back of him. He grabbed her arm to steady her, and looking up at him, she listened to distant voices.

"We've got to get back, Jenny. Debbie's going to be furious."

"Just finish this last one, please."

"We've already dug up two. You need to know more where to look. I can't keep digging up the whole stupid place."

"I know she's here. I just know it."

The sound of metal striking something solid ripped through the air, and Debbie drew a deep breath of relief. They were alive!

Stepping around Keith and past the small grove of trees, Debbie stared at the two teenagers in the distance. They were digging in the graveyard. Jenny held the flashlight toward the ground as Scottie shoveled dirt.

"I'll kill them. I'll kill them myself," she muttered between clenched teeth.

"Come on. Let's see what their story is." Keith took Debbie's arm.

Keith sounded calm and unemotional, but, glancing up at the set of his jaw and the glitter in his eyes, she knew retribution was at hand.

"Uh-oh . . ." Jenny's soft voice flicked through the air when her light turned from the dark earth to the approaching adults. "Ah, Scottie, we have company."

Scottie straightened. His body stiffened, and his hands clung to the shovel while he turned. Debbie couldn't decide whether to grab the shovel from his hand and hit him over the head with it or to hug him.

Brother and sister looked at each other until Scottie gave a half smile and said, "Hi, Debbie, Keith. What are you two doing out here?"

"Looking for injured or dead teenagers who should have been home hours ago," Keith clipped back.

Scottie looked sheepishly at the overturned dirt and elongated hole. He glanced at the other two gaping pits of darkness that broke the smooth line of the mowed grass in the graveyard. "I guess we are a little bit late."

"Little bit . . . little bit late!" Debbie's voice rose with disbelief. "Do you have any idea what time it is?"

Jenny rushed in immediately. "Ah, Debbie, don't be mad at Scottie. It's all my fault. I had to know. Really. He said we should wait, but I couldn't."

"Why couldn't you wait?" Keith's quiet voice restored calm.

Jenny glanced briefly at Scottie.

Shuffling uneasily, he began to explain. "Wednesday night Jenny overheard Norma and Michael talking in the den. They said Gloria hadn't run away. They said she was dead."

"Jenny?" Keith asked.

"Norma said Mama was dead, and no one would ever find her body," Jenny said softly. "She said Michael needed to start thinking ahead to when he inherited and what he planned to do. She said there would be plenty of money then . . . to maybe travel . . . to build new barns, buy horses, or—" Her voice broke.

"But, Jenny, you've known most of this before. You've told me," Debbie protested.

Jenny swallowed. "But they've never said no one

would find Mama's body. It was like they knew something no one else did. Scottie and I talked. You know
I've always thought Michael had something to do
with Mama's going. Now I know he killed her and
buried her body somewhere."

"Come on, Jenny," Keith cajoled. "I don't know
what you overheard, but obviously you didn't hear all
the conversation. Michael loved your mother. He's
told me so on several occasions."

"Then why does he date Norma?"

"Because your mother's been gone six years. A
man likes companionship. He has to get on with his
life, not live in the past," Keith explained.

"He was seeing her back then. I heard Mama and
him fighting about it once."

Seeing Keith stare thoughtfully at the young girl,
Debbie said, "But that doesn't explain why you two
are out here in the middle of the night digging in the
graveyard."

"Don't you see? If I had a body and had to hide it
somewhere, the best place would be the obvious—
with other bodies." Jenny glanced around at the
tombstones and grave markings that sprinkled the
area.

"But you have no idea where. You don't know for
certain if it's even here in this particular graveyard.
You're just guessing."

"Then you do agree, Jenny's mother is dead," Scottie interjected, obviously trying to drive his point
home.

Debbie raised her eyes skyward and counted slowly
to ten.

"She didn't say that at all," Keith replied.

"What I believe or don't believe is irrelevant,"

Debbie snapped. "What I want to know is, why you weren't long since home when you promised you would be? It's dark, almost midnight, and definitely not the time to be digging in graveyards. Do you have any idea how worried I've been? I thought that maniac who deposited that dead cat on our doorstep had gotten hold of you, and one or both of you were hurt or maybe dead."

"But, Debbie, that's ridiculous. I'm sorry you were worried, and we did think we'd be back before you were home, but no one is likely to hurt me. I mean, look at me, I'd make mincemeat of anyone who tried."

Scottie stood with his arms held out, one hand holding the handle as the metal shovel rested on the ground. In the moonlight and standing with the big oak a short space behind him, Debbie could understand his skepticism. That still didn't mean he should scare her to death because he and Jenny had developed a whim to dig up a graveyard.

"Your sister has been half out of her mind. Maybe you know you can take care of yourself, but you are still her little brother, and she is responsible for you. You pull a stunt like this again, and giant or not, I'll tear you apart. Do I make myself clear? I'll not let you put Debbie through this, especially after everything that's already happened to her."

Keith's coldly clipped words whipped through the air with the deadliness of a bullet, and Debbie felt the last of her fear and anxiety slip away.

"Come on, let's go home. I'm glad you're safe. You can fill in the holes tomorrow, and I don't want you to ever—*ever*, do you hear?—do such a thing again." Debbie started to the house, but after taking a few steps, she stopped and spoke to Jenny.

"I'm sorry about your mother, and you may be right. She is dead and buried somewhere. But under no circumstances are you to dig in the Muller graveyard again without my permission. This is my land, and unless you have more proof than some partially overheard conversation and wild imaginative ideas, I don't want the graveyard disturbed. The Mullers deserve to be left to rest in peace."

"I still think it's the best place to hide a body," Jenny said, as she untied the horses.

"And what would you do, young lady, if you did find your mother buried there? How would you feel? How do you think she'd look after all this time?" Keith cut in.

Jenny swallowed and mounted the horse. She sat there, her head lowered, while Scottie set down the shovel and climbed on his mare.

"Now you two walk those horses to the barn. I don't want to chance their tripping and one of you getting injured. When you arrive, unsaddle and take care of them. I'll follow shortly in the car and pick Scottie up and bring him home. Now, move it." Keith's stern voice set the two teenagers on their way.

Neither looked back, and both appeared quite chastised, with their bent heads and slumped shoulders. Debbie sighed, glad that everything had worked out all right. Maybe she had let her imagination run away with her, as Jenny had, but it told her how worried she really was, no matter how much of a bold front she put on. She didn't know what she would do, but she knew she needed to take some definite steps to clear the air or she would never find peace in her lovely home. And next time Keith might not be around.

15

Life settled into a routine. Scottie was on his best behavior, and Jenny was especially polite when she visited. Yet Debbie couldn't forget that night. It wasn't only the fear for the teenagers she had suffered, but the fields and groves of trees that covered her eighty acres that beckoned for her attention. She kept staring out at her land, wanting to explore it in the daylight, and she particularly wanted to visit the swimming hole.

Impatience made her edgy. Nothing seemed to go right, and she knew if she didn't want to cower forever, she had to push the threats aside and go on with her life. She asked Keith if he would accompany her around her property, and two weeks later, on a warm Saturday morning, he borrowed two horses from Michael.

Debbie handed Keith the picnic lunch and a blanket, and he tied them into place. They both mounted and began to wind their way across the nearby field.

Sunlight beat down from the blue sky and skipped

over the fields of browning grass. A soft breeze rippled through the almost bare branches of trees and brushed against her skin. It was a perfect day for a ride.

At one point it was necessary for her to fall behind and allow her horse to follow Keith's through a narrow path in the wild undergrowth. Now was the time to ask her question, when Keith couldn't see her expression. "Do you have plans for Thanksgiving?"

"Are you asking me to join you and Scottie? Won't you be going to your mom's in Houston?"

"Several of the people she works with are going on a short trip and have invited her to go along. I told her to go. Scottie and I will have our dinner here." She didn't want him to know how important his answer was to her, so rather than look at him when he stopped and waited for her horse to come alongside, she stared out at the field nearby.

"I'd like to have Thanksgiving with you. Tell me, is your mother turning over all responsibility of Scottie to you?"

Debbie hesitated. Her answer could be important to her relationship with Keith, and she wanted to be fair to everyone. "My father died five years ago when he suffered a second heart attack. He'd been ill from the first, but the doctors thought he was getting better."

"That must have been tough."

"It was. He was an accountant and always worked hard to provide us with a good life and so Mom wouldn't have to work. He even sent me to college back east. But when Dad became ill, there were medical bills, and he died without ever returning to work. The insurance paid a lot, but far from all of it. Charles and I helped some, but Charles wasn't into sharing much."

"I know what you mean. My dad had some pretty hefty bills at one time himself. He had an automobile agency back home, and when his friend stole from him, Dad wound up losing his business. I thought we'd lose him as well."

"But you didn't, did you?" Debbie shifted her reins.

"No, but he's never recovered. How's your mom doing now?"

"After Dad died, she was forced to go to work and has been supporting Scottie and herself ever since. Scottie's basically a good kid, but as you know, he's given her problems. That hasn't helped. She misses having Dad to take charge."

"But she's had you to fill in some of the gap."

"Since I'm not there, I can only do so much. Scottie has been a big expense when the money isn't there like it used to be. That's why now that she can finally take a vacation, I want her to enjoy herself."

Keith glanced at her with a big smile. "I imagine the food cost to feed Scottie alone could almost sink Fort Knox."

"That's an understatement. I'm glad Sal planted the garden and is raising chickens. He's even talking of getting a calf or two next spring."

Keith's low, rich laughter sent a hovering squirrel scampering for safety in a nearby tree. "At least something can get a rise out of that man, even if it's only Scottie's eating ability."

Debbie smiled. Sal was the silent, serious type. Creepy, almost, until you were used to his ways. "Mom's planning on Scottie returning to Houston at Christmas."

Keith remained silent for a few moments. "What does Scottie say about going back?"

"We haven't discussed it."

Keith nudged his horse so that they again fell into single file as they entered the thick woods. They were heading for the swimming hole, and from the scenery Debbie remembered, they had to be close.

Keith spoke back over his shoulder. "Scottie seems to have settled down here. He likes the school, and I know the coach is planning on his staying and playing next year. Jenny might not take too well to Scottie's going back to Houston, either."

Debbie didn't know what to say. Scottie did have only two more years of high school, but she wasn't sure she wanted that responsibility. She had her own life, and Scottie's presence definitely altered her life-style.

As they passed through thick bushes, they came upon the clearing: shimmering blue-green water, a scattering of ferns, the majestic oak, and the white rock that seemed almost a marker to note a place of extreme loveliness. "It's beautiful," Debbie whispered, her voice husky.

"I've always had a special feeling for this place."

Debbie let her horse walk over to the edge of the water. She sat patiently when he dipped his head for a drink beside Keith's horse. "Because of Teresa?"

Keith frowned. "No." He looked around, studying the area carefully before smiling at Debbie. "From the first time I saw this place, when I was still in high school, I've felt the place was special. I can't explain it. It's simply something that is."

"I feel the same way." After a short time she pointed to a small space free of brush and trees on the other side of the water. "If a painter sat here, she could paint the scene in the picture hanging in my office."

Keith considered. "You're right. Maybe that's why

I like that painting." He climbed down and led their horses to a bush, where he tied the reins. After grabbing her about the waist, he practically lifted her off the horse. "Are you ready for lunch?"

"Whenever you are."

He spread the blanket on the thickest grass. Bushes protected the area from any breeze, yet they would have a clear view of the water and the oak tree. Instead of taking the food from the bag, he set the sack nearby and turned to take her in his arms. "I couldn't leave here without taking another special memory with me."

Desire glimmered in his eyes, and her breath quickened. She wouldn't say no this time.

He ran his little finger gently down the side of her neck and around her mouth, caressing her lower lip and sending desire racing through her. He planted soft kisses on her cheek while his hands played provocatively across her skin. Her pulse hammered, and her whole body ached for more. Finally his lips pressed hard against hers, and she opened her mouth to the exploration of his tongue.

She vaguely knew when he raised her in his arms and lowered her to the blanket. She sighed with pleasure as his hands roamed under her sweatshirt. The smell of grass and the fragrance of pine mingled with the scent of his cologne. And when he moved so that his body squared over hers, his arousal hard against her, she fell into her own paradise, a memory that would always be engraved on her mind. She was glad she had waited.

His fingers found her nipples. She whimpered with pleasure and began her own necessary search, touching the soft hair that curled across his broad chest, the back of his neck. Her fingers entwined the smooth silkiness at the back of his head, and she drew him closer.

He pulled the sweatshirt over her head and flung it to one side. His lips followed his fingers over her breasts and made her ache with the sensations that rippled through her taut body. Slowly he loosened the belt on her jeans, unsnapped the clasp, and slid bikinis and blue denims together down her thighs. Heat soared through her, almost like a fever.

Keith uttered a frantic groan when he quickly unzipped his own pants and slid them down and out of the way. She ran her hand across his buttocks, felt them tense and tighten. He, too, burned with need, as desperately as she did.

He poised above her, his gray eyes demanding. "I want to ravage you so that you'll never forget this place, or me, so that our time together will be forever stamped into our memories."

She was a little unnerved by what he said. It was so close to her own thoughts. "Is that important?"

"Damned important. I don't want you to ever forget." Without waiting for either of them to say more, he thrust into her.

Debbie closed her eyes and followed where he led. Time was nothing. This man filled the longing of her heart and met every need her body demanded. She gasped as the rhythm grew, urgent, quick, fierce.

When the shudders became convulsive, the pleasure a contorted blur of frenzy, she cried out from the core of her being, vaguely aware of his own shuddering release.

He lay in her arms, and she lay in his, the two of them one. The savoring calm of the togetherness brought a pleasurable peace, compelling as the earlier fire. Debbie tightened her hold around him. No matter how he might feel, at that moment she knew: there would never be another man for her but Keith.

Finally he sighed and rolled off her. She lay looking at the blue sky, the puffy white clouds, the grove of crowding trees that protected them. This was a special place, this an extraordinary man. He needn't worry that she would ever forget, either.

A few minutes later he drew a deep sigh of regret. "I could stay here all day, and I would like nothing more than to make love to you over and over."

"Me too." At that moment her stomach uttered a protest of hunger.

He laughed. "Maybe we'd better eat our lunch."

They shared the food with their kisses and with tasting each other, tantalizing, tempting, until once more they united, slowly and completely, relishing each other in the beautiful spot.

Debbie had never spent a more wonderful day. She lay there replete, enjoying the sight of Keith surrounded by trees and plants against the backdrop of the shimmering of the pool, a sight as primitive as first man.

Finally Keith raised up on one elbow. "If we want to cover that area next to Johnson's land, we have to get moving."

"You're right, but I hate to leave." They had ridden out for a specific purpose, but she hated to have the interlude end. Somehow it seemed almost an omen, as though this might be the beginning and the end of her affair with Keith, that she might never see him again.

He rose and, after fastening his clothes, helped

pull her up. He walked over to stare at the water while she straightened herself and joined him. He took her hand in his and kissed the palm. "This will always be our place, no matter what the future brings or where we go."

"Yes," she agreed softly. Pulling her eyes from his, she looked around to embed the scene in her memory. "This will always be our special place."

When everything was packed Keith helped her mount. After climbing up on his own horse, he started down a path that wove between two trees on the other side of the pond. Debbie let her horse fall behind his and gave a final glance at the clearing they left behind.

After a few minutes he asked, "Are you giving serious thought to Frank's resort idea, or are we looking at the area out of curiosity?"

"I'm following some advice you gave me. I'm considering."

Keith looked back at her over his shoulder. "I can't believe you're actually not accusing me of interfering in your affairs, but giving serious thought to my worldly wisdom."

Debbie felt embarrassed and glanced down at her saddle. "I know you a little better now."

"And you're not going around with that chip on your shoulder anymore," he said softly.

"With all of the problems and threats I've had since I came, I decided I shouldn't completely ignore Frank's suggestion. I might need another income at some time in the future."

"Has anything else happened recently?" he asked quickly.

"Not since the cat, but Cressie keeps warning it's

the lull before the storm."

"Sometimes Cressie should keep her comments to herself," Keith snapped, and kicked his horse into a mild trot.

After a while they left the track and plunged through what appeared to be utter wilderness. At one place a fallen tree lay across the way, and at another their path took them through the stream of water. Always they traveled steadily, penetrating the maze of windy shadows, yet civilization was only a short distance away. Debbie saw a faint blur of movement in the distance about the size of a large deer and remembered Frank's comment about hunting in the area.

Looking tenderly at the back of Keith's dark blue windbreaker, she felt a warmth for this man that made the whole world brighter. He showed a gentleness and a caring she had never before experienced. But he also talked of his writing, his search for ghost stories, and trips he planned to make. He never mentioned a future together with her, and the thought of losing him now that she'd finally accepted how much she truly loved him brought a lump to her throat.

Keith brushed back a strand of his dark hair from his forehead, and Debbie smiled at the endearing gesture. She wanted so much to tell him of her love; she almost had, beside the pool. She didn't know if she'd regret not having done so. She still could later today.

No, she had made the right decision. No matter how close they became, how much lovemaking they shared, she would never be the first to admit her feelings. If he knew she loved him, he might break things off sooner and not wait until the natural separation of his leaving. She wanted whatever time there was left between them. She needed this memory for her lonely future.

A shocking, startling sound broke the quiet of the afternoon. Something whisked past her head. Chips from the nearby tree trunk bit into her hand, breaking the skin and spouting drops of blood. The horse reared. Debbie hung on for dear life as her mount gathered speed and whizzed through the trees, over logs, and around bushes.

"Hold on!" Keith called frantically.

The pounding of his horse's hooves followed close behind. Never an experienced rider, Debbie clung to the saddle horn with one hand, the reins with the other, and tightened her legs around the horse's sides. She bent low to avoid branches and narrowed her eyes against the whipping wind.

Still, the slap of vines against her face, the occasional sharp scrape of a branch against her leg, and the pull of the reins against her arms seemed minor compared to the frantic sound of the frightened horse and her own racing heart. The fear that she would fall or be knocked off grew, but she refused to give up without doing her best to stick on the beast to the bitter end.

Once they came to an open space, Keith moved his mount alongside and grabbed for the reins. He pulled. Using his horse for leverage, he forced hers to slow down until finally the animal stopped. Debbie sat there and shook. Even though Keith climbed down and, after fastening the reins, stood beside her, she couldn't make herself lift her leg over the horse and get down to the ground. It wouldn't do any good, anyway. She could never stand up by herself.

"Debbie, honey, are you all right? You're not hurt,

are you?"

Tears streamed down her cheeks. She shook her head, but she couldn't find the strength to utter a word.

Keith grabbed her arms and pulled her from the horse. Trembling, she leaned against him and absorbed the wonderful heat of his strong body. She sobbed quietly against his chest, then she simply stood and clung. She wallowed in the feel of his arms holding her close and making her feel safe.

"Better?" Keith asked.

Debbie nodded and snuggled closer. She wanted never to let go. Life had never seemed more precious or Keith more endearing.

"Am I interrupting?" asked a gruff voice.

Debbie tried to push out of Keith's arms but was secretly glad when he tightened them to prevent her.

"No, Frank. We had a scare. Someone fired a shot and spooked the horses. Debbie's not an experienced rider." Keith turned her so that she could look at Frank, but he kept holding her close, secure within the circle of his arm.

"Heard the shot myself. Thought I would investigate. I don't like people hunting my land unless I give permission. Accidents happen. People wind up dead."

Debbie stared at her neighbor, and an uneasiness filled her. His dirty clothes indicated he had spent a good bit of time in the woods. But then so had she and Keith. Perhaps it was the way the sunlight filtered through the trees and cast shadows across Frank's face and mustache, obscuring his eyes, that made something seem not quite right, that gave her this uneasiness. Or maybe it was the way he held the rifle under his arm that disturbed her.

"Did you shoot at us?" she asked impulsively.

Frank stepped forward, and his blue eyes blazed. "If I had shot at you, you'd be dead. I hit what I aim for," he barked.

"Did you fire the gun that frightened our horses?" Keith asked in a deadly calm.

Frank glared at Keith, indignation radiating from every muscle. Keith's body stiffened beside her. Then, slowly, as if he were preparing for combat, he loosened his arm from around her shoulders and stepped to the side.

Eleanor had said Frank could be dangerous, and Debbie had seen how others had reacted warily during the confrontation at Norma's party. Now he was like a powderkeg on a short fuse. Debbie bit her lip to keep from crying out.

Finally Frank spoke. "I already told you I heard a shot, figured it was an illegal hunter, and came to investigate."

"You brought a gun," Keith stated and asked at the same time.

Frank nodded. "You never know when you'll find a wounded animal that needs finishing."

Debbie wanted out of the woods, away from the whole frightening scene. "Let's go." She tugged at Keith's arm.

Keith looked at her closely. "Are you able to ride?"

She nodded. "I can ride. You might have to help me get up. My legs aren't very steady yet, but I can ride."

Keith hesitated before taking her arm and helping her to the side of her horse. He added his strength to hers when she lifted her foot and placed it in the stirrup, and she quickly sat in the saddle and looked down at the two men. "Let's go," she urged again.

She wanted away from the gun and the man she knew fully capable of using it if he so desired. She was afraid Keith intended to say something more to Frank if she didn't insist they leave. And that brought more fear.

Keith climbed on his horse and, after starting her off in the right direction, nodded for her to take the lead to keep himself between her and Frank's gun. She clamped her teeth together to hold back a protest. He wouldn't listen anyway. No, they had to get away, fast.

"Debbie," Frank called. "If you might consider selling your property any time soon, give me a call. I'm still interested."

She waved her hand in acknowledgment but didn't reply. Instead she kicked the sides of her horse, urging him faster. She wanted to get home. She wanted to sit in her house in front of a nice fire and drink some of Cressie's wine. The eerie happenings in her house were tame compared to the outside world.

It didn't take long to arrive back at Michael's and drop off the horses. Not wanting to see or talk with anyone, they quickly tended to the animals and drove in Keith's car back to her house.

"Are you all right?" Keith asked when she collapsed onto one of the kitchen chairs. "You've barely said a word since the gunshot."

At that moment Cressie walked into the kitchen. She stopped abruptly at Keith's words and asked, "Gunshot? What gunshot? You're not hurt, are you, Miss Debbie?" Her thin, worn hand fluttered over her heart.

"I could use a big glass of your wine, and I'm sure Keith could, too," Debbie said, wiping a tear from her face.

Keith explained to Cressie about the gunfire, Debbie's wild ride, and their meeting with Frank Johnson. Cressie poured them each a glass of her wine.

"Do you think he shot at us?" Debbie asked.

Keith studied the red liquid as he rolled his glass between his palms. "I don't know. Frank's an odd one. You can never be sure what he's likely to do when the mood strikes him."

"He's always seemed friendly to me," Debbie mused. "Strange, but friendly. Until today."

"He wants your land. I've heard others tell about another side of him. Eleanor is particularly vocal."

Cressie snorted. "She didn't do right by him no matter what she claims now. The man has good grounds for his grievance. They was all set to announce their engagement when along comes Herman Farmsworth back from his travelin' and sweeps Eleanor off her feet, before she knew what she was doin'. Or so she claims. Frank never had a chance, poor and strugglin' as he was."

"Somehow I have trouble picturing Eleanor ever not knowing what she's doing," Debbie said, and sipped her wine.

"She puts up a good front, I s'pose, but we all have times when things get to be too much and we lose control. She's no dif'runt than the rest," Cressie replied.

Keith broke the thoughtful quiet. "It could have been a hunter who fired the shot today. Unless Frank thought that might frighten you into selling your land, he wouldn't have any reason to shoot at us. And I've heard he's an excellent shot, so I believe him when he says he hits whatever he aims at."

"He's a good shot all right," Cressie agreed, "but don't underestimate him. He's capable of doin' any of these shenanigans that's been frightenin' Miss Debbie. He can be a mean cuss, if'n he's a mind."

"So with Michael and Frank both wanting my land and both capable of terrorizing me, we have two strong suspects," Debbie said, not bothering to hide her bitterness.

"Oh, there's more than that capable," Cressie said.

Keith banged his glass against the table. "Maybe we should go through the list and see who we can eliminate. Since we've agreed on Michael and Frank, let's consider Norma. She could have taken your mail, thrown the rock, punctured your tires, and even dropped off the dead cat. Everything except maybe take that shot at us today. But for what reason, other than to help Michael? And if that were the case, why sell you the property in the beginning?"

"I warned you things weren't quiet yet. The spirits been restless," Cressie muttered ominously. "There's no reason why Norma couldn't have taken another horse and followed you, lookin' for an opportunity to scare you. She's a good shot. She used to win awards when she was younger and married to that no-good husband of hers."

"Whatever happened there?" Debbie asked.

Cressie glanced at Keith before she answered. "Times got hard. Norma's husband lost his job and took to robbin'. He said a man had his pride, and he weren't lettin' no woman support him. He finally got killed while holding up some store in Oklahoma."

"The macho men of East Texas and their pride," Debbie said.

"Don't look at me when you use that tone of voice," Keith said, amusement in his eyes. "I believe in the liberation of women. I even enjoy it."

"Are we talking about the same thing?" she asked with false sweetness. Then, not wanting to give him time for a reply, she added, "You know, the first day I came to Nacogdoches and was in the real estate office, I overheard Norma on a phone conversation. It really sounded sinister because she said that Gloria was dead and whoever was on the other end needed to start accepting that fact and go ahead with life. I know now she must have been talking with Michael, and that he was probably having some difficulties handling Jenny. But the fact she was so definite in her statement that Gloria was dead has always stayed with me."

"You haven't mentioned this before, not even when we found Scottie and Jenny up at the grave-yard," Keith said.

"I know, but I'm wondering now if Gloria's disappearance could have any bearing on what's been happening to me."

"In what way?" Keith asked, watching closely.

Debbie shrugged. "I don't know. It's just an idea, a possibility. Maybe Norma sold me the house, and someone else doesn't like it. Maybe that person is trying to frighten me into leaving Nacogdoches."

"So you're saying maybe it's connected with Gloria's disappearance in some way." Keith frowned and became lost in his own thoughts.

Cressie got up to get the wine bottle from the counter and refilled Keith's and Debbie's glasses before she set a pot of coffee on to drip. Leaning against the cabinet, she said, "I think Miss Sarah knew somethin' about Gloria's disappearance."

"Why's that?" Keith asked.

"Because that's about the time she started stayin'

at home and not mixin' with anyone. She fretted and worried, claimin' to be sickly, until she finally said, as she was a-dyin', that the next owner would have to take care of the problem. Of course she knew Miss Kate would help."

Keith sipped his wine. "Since we don't know who's frightening Debbie or why, let's look at this from that angle. Who could be responsible for Gloria's demise?"

"You're assuming, then, that she is dead?" Debbie asked.

Keith nodded. "On that point, although I've never come right out and told her so, I think Jenny is right. I think someone would have seen or heard something from Gloria before now if she were alive."

"But you don't think anyone is trying to harm Jenny, right? You think all the accidents are her imagination?" Debbie pressed.

Keith twirled his glass. "I don't know what to believe there. I've always thought that while Michael may not love her as he might his own child, he genuinely cares about her welfare. It's possible I've been wrong."

"He could be afraid that if Gloria's body ever did turn up, Jenny's accusations might be accepted as fact," Debbie added thoughtfully.

"Something like that. So that puts us back where we were. Who had motives to get rid of Gloria, besides Michael for the obvious inheritance?"

Debbie suggested, "If Jenny's right and Michael and Norma were having an affair even before Gloria disappeared, Norma could be a suspect. She might know more than Michael, even."

"And she could easily have done all of those things to you, besides following us today and firing the gun," Keith agreed.

Frowning, Debbie looked at Keith and Cressie. "What about Teresa?"

"She weren't here at the time Gloria up and left," Cressie said. "But even with that fancy man she married and all his money, Teresa can always use more."

"But even if she would do some of those things to me, I can't see her hauling a dead cat around or following us into the woods and shooting at us," Debbie countered. "She might get dirty or muss her hair."

"Don't seem likely," Cressie agreed, "but then when she were little she used to hunt some with her stepdad. She hasn't always dressed and acted like she were Miss America."

"I didn't think Michael hunted," Keith said.

"He don't. Jim Winthrope did, though," Cressie explained.

"I keep forgetting she and Jenny are only half sisters, and that Teresa had two stepfathers," Keith said.

"What about Frank Johnson?" Debbie asked. "Would he have a motive?"

Cressie snorted. "Frank would have a good motive. He gave Gloria a hot check, a big one, and she was threatening to press charges. Maybe send him to jail. Frank could never have stood confinement in jail. What with Gloria missin' and the police findin' Herman's empty car with bloodstains, the whole check matter just sort of died down."

Remembering Eleanor's reference to Frank's bad checks, Debbie asked, "Did he ever make it good?"

"Must have. I'm sure Michael wouldn't let that pass otherwise," Cressie said. She poured herself a cup of coffee from the freshly dripped pot and sat back down at the table.

Debbie studied her glass. "You know, we're right

back where we were. We have the exact same suspects as before, with the exception of Eleanor."

"We can't even write her off," Keith countered. "If there's anything to that letter she claimed was forged . . . the one from Herman to Gloria, she might have found out six years ago and got rid of Gloria then."

Debbie gasped. "I can't believe she'd have harmed Herman, not the way she talks."

"Herman could have been killed by robbers, like the police decided," Keith explained.

"But there's no way Eleanor would soil her fingers with a dead cat or put on pants to ride horseback in the woods to shoot at us," Debbie said finally.

"You're right there," Keith agreed. "It sounds like we're back at the illegal hunter again, right where we started."

"Saints preserve us," Cressie exclaimed, "and the spirits protect us. We can't trust anyone."

"Cressie," Keith said warningly.

"Reprisal draws near, I can feel it in my bones. That's why the ghosts be so restless. They know. They know the past is about to claim justice."

"Cressie, please," Keith said. "Debbie doesn't need any more to frighten her today. Besides, we haven't discussed how you and Sal could be involved."

Cressie slammed down her cup and stiffened with indignation. "Me and Sal? You thinkin' we had somethin' to do with all of this?"

"I believe you know a hell of a lot you're not saying," Keith said firmly.

Cressie rose. "Maybe I do and maybe I don't. But you just be careful you don't get in the way when the time for justice comes. You be mighty careful."

"Cressie," Debbie pleaded, startled that this could all be happening in her kitchen and with these two people she had come to trust.

"And you be careful, too, Miss Debbie. Miss Kate has plans of her own for you. She won't take kindly to someone causin' her more grief." With that, Cressie stomped out the back door.

"I can't believe this. I can't believe this," Debbie said, rubbing her throbbing temples.

"I think you'd better," Keith replied with deadly seriousness. "I think we'd both better."

Keith was right, she thought. Maybe it was time to call in the police, though she didn't know what to tell them. She had no concrete proof against any single person, only suspicions. She'd have to wait and hope for the best.

16

The dishwasher swished the soapy water over its loaded contents. Thanksgiving was work; there was no getting around it. Having Cressie every day had spoiled her. Yet today she had enjoyed cooking on her own, and the Slavanias would be back tomorrow from visiting their daughter.

She wondered what Scottie had wanted to talk with Keith about privately. Although she hated cleaning up as much as anyone, it hadn't been difficult after the table was cleared to insist they watch television, and it gave Scottie the time he wanted.

Debbie prepared the coffee tray and walked to the back parlor. Keith and Scottie were thoroughly involved in the football game on television and barely glanced at her. She poured coffee for her and Keith and set his in front of him before curling up on the end of the sofa with her own cup.

Her attention fell to the fireplace. The hidden room didn't hold the mystery it once did, although the wind chimes still hung in its corner. And the room hadn't provided any answers as to why Kate and her father refused to rest, unless the golden key meant something. Debbie hadn't discovered anything the key fit.

She thought about the time she'd scolded Cressie for not telling her about the hidden room. The housekeeper had given her that sly smile and said, "Why, where else would I store the canned goods and my bottled wine but in a cool, dark room?"

Debbie hated that smile. Between gritted teeth she'd asked, "Why didn't you show me the room when I first looked at the house or at least after I moved in?"

Cressie had shrugged. "Miss Sarah told me never to show it. When the time was right for the new owner to know, she'd discover the room herself."

Debbie was stumped for a reply. Then, deciding she needed to express her ownership of the house and rightful authority, she'd said, "Are there any other little such surprises that I don't know about?"

"Like what?"

Futile anger filled her, but determined to stand up for herself, Debbie had said, "*I* own this house now, not Miss Sarah nor Miss Kate. They're dead. If there is anything else I should know, I want you to tell me."

Cressie's eyes had locked with hers. Hands on hips, she'd said, "I know you own the house. Don't I cook for you, and clean? I try and take care of you and Mr. Scottie the best I know how. Sal and I give you all the protection and carin' we can, despite what you might think sometimes. But there are times, Miss Debbie, when a person just has to learn about certain things for herself."

Debbie had dropped the subject. She knew if the older woman didn't want to explain, she couldn't force her to do so. And she had to admit that both Sal and Cressie did take good care of her, even to the point of driving her up the wall with foreboding warnings and eerie, silent watchfulness.

Later, when Debbie had talked the matter over with Keith, he'd laughed, kissed her, and said, "You have to accept Cressie and Sal for what they are—strange, different, even frightening at times. Everyone knows they take excellent care of the two of you, and for what it's worth, the people in Nacogdoches give the Slavanias a wide berth rather than cross words with either."

Aggravated though she was, Debbie had found comfort and reassurance in the knowledge. She'd also found tenderness in Keith's arms and readily dropped the topic.

Debbie looked around the room and smiled. She loved this old house. The place brought a peacefulness to her spirit, a sense of belonging. Maybe Kate had felt the same way, and that was why she didn't leave.

Debbie closed her eyes. She had changed so much since arriving in Nacogdoches. Here she sat, calmly accepting the existence of ghosts, whereas logically she had never believed in them.

Finally the game was over, and a jubilant Scottie turned off the television. "I'm going to call Jenny," he said, leaving the room.

"That must have been some game," Debbie said softly, and sipped her coffee.

Keith grinned. "It always brings a certain satisfaction when your team wins in spite of the odds. You can't help feeling that there's a certain amount of justice in this world after all."

"I know what you mean."

As though by silent consent, they drank coffee and stared into the fire. Perhaps it was their same seating arrangements, or the way the fire flickered its red-and-gold light across Keith's face, that reminded Debbie of the first evening they had sat in this room. It was the night of Jenny's accident and also the night Keith first suggested a hidden room.

"Keith," Debbie said, "have you ever considered that if there is space here for the stairwell down to the basement, there must be a similar area upstairs as well?"

His long, silent stare made her feel the need to defend her idea. "I mean, the room upstairs was Kate's bedroom, and as far as I can tell, the wall is in about the same place as down here. What happens to that space by the fireplace up there?"

Keith set down his cup with such deliberate slowness that Debbie wondered if he felt her question was ridiculous.

"You may have something there. Why didn't I think of that! Come on, let's go check."

Excitement filled her as they hurried up the front stairs. She heard Scottie talking on the phone when they passed his doorway, but neither paused. She was right on Keith's heels when they entered Kate's room. He stooped to investigate the small fireplace. Debbie began to hope that maybe they were going to learn something about Kate at long last.

There was a click, and a small panel in the wall slipped open. The pattern in the wallpaper easily hid the existence of the cubbyhole space. The area could not have been more than three feet by four, but that was about the same space needed for the stairwell below. In the concealed alcove sat two chests, one of cedar, the other resembling an old metal strongbox.

"What have we here?" Keith gasped excitedly, kneeling. He pulled the cedar chest out into the room, and while Debbie opened the lid, he dragged out the metal chest.

"Oh . . ." Debbie sighed, pulling out the dress shown in the picture. "It's Kate's." Standing, she held the delicate white muslin against her and was instantly assailed with the mixed scent of cedar and jasmine.

Keith uttered a strange sound. "I can't believe it," he said hoarsely. A muscle twitched in the side of his cheek as he stared from her to the picture. "I knew you resembled Kate, but if you put on that dress, no one could tell the difference."

Debbie laughed, her pleasure bubbling out. "Isn't this exciting? What else is in there?" She laid the dress on the bed and reached in the chest.

There was a pair of dainty white shoes that must have been worn with the dress, a petticoat, and finally the most beautiful green shawl Debbie had ever seen. The color exactly matched her eyes.

She also found an old torn blue shirt that had seen lots of wear and belonged to a big man with broad shoulders. At the bottom she discovered a knitted baby blanket in a delicate shade of pink and a sheer white baby dress, hand-stitched and decorated with yellow ribbons.

Holding up the dress, she asked, "What do you make of this?"

"Looks to me like it belongs to a baby."

"I know, but whose? Nowhere in Kyle's journal does he mention Kate having a baby. In fact, the only thing he does say regarding Kate's personal life is that she finally accepted the Farmsworth younger son for her husband, and later how Kyle was glad to be rid of the ungrateful, good-for-nothing upstart."

"Maybe it was Kate's as a baby," Keith suggested.

"Or maybe Kate had one of her own, and she died," Debbie added thoughtfully. The idea saddened her, and she was surprised to feel tears well in her eyes.

"What makes you think the baby was a girl?"

"Because the blanket is pink, and the trim on the dress is yellow." Carefully she replaced the items in the cedar chest, not daring to look up at Keith for fear he would notice how much the baby clothes had distressed her.

Breaking into her musings, Keith asked, "Where's that key we found in the basement?"

"In my room."

"Would you get it? This metal box is locked, and I think that key might fit."

Debbie stared at him for a moment. Why would someone leave a key in the hidden room that opened a box up here? Then, almost as though someone had answered her question, she knew. Anyone moving into the house would find the hidden room first. The key was a message that there was more to discover.

She rushed to her room and took the key from the side of her jewelry box. As she passed Scottie's room, she heard him still talking. She knew he would be disappointed not to be in on the discovery, but she could let him see everything later. Now she wanted to share only with Keith. This would be another special, intimate memory between the two of them, as was the beautiful interlude by the enchanting swimming hole.

The key fit, and when Keith opened the lid, Debbie saw several journals and a small wooden box with a hand-carved picture on top. The picture showed two hearts pierced with an arrow. One heart bore KM; the other, MD.

Debbie ran her fingers over the engravings. "I wonder who MD is?"

Keith shrugged. "Well, the only thing I can say for certain is that it's not an F for Farmsworth."

"Interesting," Debbie mumbled, and opened the lid. She found three gold coins certainly valuable in the 1880s but almost priceless now. She pushed them aside when she discovered a string of pearls a young woman might have worn, a small hank of dark hair, and a gold locket that set her heart pounding.

"What's inside?" Keith asked. He took the locket from her and opened the dainty catch.

The picture of Kate was clear, but the oil miniature of the young man opposite her was startling. He had dark hair, gray eyes, and was extremely handsome with his dark mustache. He was a man of his times, and by the firm jawline and curving mouth that disclosed a full lower lip, Debbie knew he was a man of determination and strength, a man of compassion.

"I wonder who this is," she said, rubbing her finger carefully over the locket and picture. She looked up. Keith, his eyes narrowed and two deep lines forming between his brows, had the strangest expression on his face.

"He must have been someone she cared about . . . maybe this MD that's on the box," he finally replied after several long minutes.

"Must be," Debbie said, and replaced the locket in the box with the other items. She began to look through the journals.

"Oh, look. These are Kate's. They start when she was a young girl and go through most of her lifetime."

"And I suppose you intend to read them all?"

"Certainly." After looking at the number of journals, she added, "But not all tonight. Let's see if we can find the one that covers the time she married."

Laughing, Keith helped her search until she picked out two she wanted.

"Let's go downstairs where we can be comfortable," she suggested, rising.

When they were once more settled in front of the fire, she opened the first journal and began to read.

> *I saw him again today, the man with the dark wavy hair. He's the most handsome fellow I've ever seen, not only in appearance, but in the way he looks at me from inside those gray eyes. He makes my heart flutter until I can scarcely catch my breath.*
>
> *He was outside the store, and he was with another man, a big burly fellow Pa calls Yatzee. Pa became furious when he saw Yatzee and said the interloper was a-trying to steal everything people in these parts have worked hard for. I laughed when Pa spat in front of the burly man and almost hit him with the tobacco. But I slipped inside the store when Yatzee roared cause I didn't want to hear the fighting when the interloper threatened Pa. He, the handsome one, followed me.*
>
> *I know I shouldn't have answered when he asked my name, but I knew he could find out anyway. Everyone knows Pa. He told me his name was Matthew Douglas. I don't think I've ever heard such a fine name or met a man I admire more.*

Debbie looked over at Keith. "Now we know the name that matches the initials on the wooden box. Matthew Douglas."

"Matthew Douglas," Keith repeated softly.

Debbie laughed when she saw him narrow his

eyes again in that strange expression. "Did you have any ancestors in Nacogdoches about that time?"

"My family's been in Illinois for generations and hadn't moved from the state until my uncle came to Nacogdoches ten years ago. I have a multitude of Douglas relatives back in Illinois."

"What brought your uncle here?"

"Times change things, and it's not unusual anymore for people to move around with jobs. He's a salesman, and his territory covers parts of Texas, Louisiana, and Oklahoma. This is centrally located for him, besides being a nice town to live in and not expensive."

"My grandparents moved from Dallas to Houston for the same reason, and I even lived in Vermont for a while." Debbie skipped several pages in the journal.

> *Henry Farmsworth came by again today. Pa wants me to marry him. He says if I marry a banker, it could open all kinds of doors for him. Of course, Henry's only the younger son and his older brother will probably inherit the bank. Still, Pa says there's always the possibility that Henry could wind up with the bank. People have been known to die in these hard times. Pa says people naturally trust bankers. What he didn't say was that they don't always trust Pa. I've heard some say he's too wily. Of course, no one's ever openly accused him of cheating, but then they wouldn't dare, knowing Pa.*
>
> *I don't like Henry. He is skinny and not very tall and he always tries to sneak a kiss when Pa isn't around. He's not a bit like Matthew. Matthew is always a gentleman and treats me like a lady, even when I slip down to the swimming hole to*

meet him. I know it's wrong and that I shouldn't,
but I can't seem to help myself. Matthew has a
way about him that can make me forget all my
good sense.

Debbie looked up at Keith. "I wonder if that's the
same swimming hole where we—"

"I don't know of any other around here," Keith said.

Debbie didn't appreciate the humor she saw in his
eyes or the way his lips twitched. How could she say
what she meant, that she wondered if it was the same
swimming hole where they'd made love the first
time, when she couldn't tell him she loved him?
Keith believed they were simply having an affair. She
skipped over a few more pages and read some more.

Today was the most wonderful and the most
awful day of my life. I met Matthew at our special
place, and he told me he had to leave Nacogdoches.
He was needed back home. I thought I would die.
Then he kissed me, and I was sure I was in heaven.

Matthew was determined to do the proper
thing, even though I told him not to. I knew Pa
wouldn't listen; Pa calls him a damned Yankee. But
my Matthew is proud, too, and honorable. That's why
I love him so much.

He called on Pa, proper like, and asked for
my hand in marriage. Pa had no right to grab the
gun and threaten him if he didn't get off his prop-
erty. Pa had no right to tell Matthew he'd sooner
see me dead than married to a damned no-good
Yankee. Pa had no right to tell him I was already
spoken for, and to keep away from me. I told Pa I
would never ever marry Henry Farmsworth, and

*he knows I mean it, no matter how he threatens
me or whips me. I love Matthew. I always will.*

Debbie choked as she read the last words. Kate's
pain when her father drove her love away resembled
her own suffering at the thought of Keith leaving her
life. Of course, there was one main difference. There
wasn't a man alive who would dare whip her. And one
main similarity. Although modern times had emanci-
pated females, nothing prevented broken hearts.

She cleared her throat. "I think we may have discovered the reason Cressie claims Kate haunts the
house."

"Searching for Matthew? Read some more, and
let's see."

> *Pa is having my picture painted by Ted Sla-
> vania. Pa says it's my engagement picture for
> Henry and sitting for it will keep me occupied
> when I'm not at my chores. Pa doesn't know I'm
> having Ted paint some smaller pictures for me and
> for Matthew as well and that Pa's paying for them,
> too. Somehow it just seems fair since I have to
> sneak out at night now to meet Matthew.*
>
> > *Matthew's delayed leaving. There's a big
> July 4 celebration coming up, and he thinks we
> can slip out of town in all the commotion. We'll get
> married and go live with his folks. I can hardly
> wait to become Matthew's wife.*

When Debbie paused, Keith asked, "Do you have
any more coffee?"

Surprised, she answered, "Sure. I'll just heat what's
left in the pot."

She took the pot into the kitchen and set it in the microwave to heat. Looking at the clock, she saw it was almost ten. Where had the evening gone?

Keith's jaw had tightened and he'd clenched his hand when she'd read the part about Kate being eager to be Matthew's wife. Maybe that part had affected him as much as it had her. Maybe it would make him begin to think about marriage . . . or maybe he was afraid it would give her ideas.

Taking the heated coffee, she returned to the back parlor where she filled their cups. She picked up the journal, turned several pages and read.

> *Today's the 4th and Pa kept me by his side the whole day. It was almost as if he knew. He claimed that there was a lot of rabble in town, and he didn't dare not protect me. He was saving me for my fiancé. Henry hung on me, too. I can't stand his touch. His hands are sweaty, but maybe I've been spoiled by the tender feel of Matthew's hands.*
>
> *I tried and tried to slip away, making all kinds of excuses until Pa asked me once what the matter was with me. Henry laughed, and I could have kicked him. I felt then that they knew something . . . something they weren't telling me. That's when my dreadful fear began. Fear for Matthew. Fear for Matthew and for me.*
>
> *I finally slipped down to the swimming hole, to our special place. It was late, but I couldn't get away sooner. I took my bag with my things and my three gold pieces I'd been saving. I waited and waited. Surely Matthew must have known I would come as soon as I could. Surely he wouldn't have gone off and left without me. He knows I love him;*

he is my life. He would come. Something must have happened. I waited until almost daylight. He never came. He couldn't have forgotten me. Surely, he'll let me know his new plan as soon as he can.

Debbie stopped to sip her coffee and fight back the tears that threatened while she read. The story seemed so sad. She could feel Kate's uncertainty and pain.

"I'd like to get my hands on that old reprobate of a father of hers," Keith snarled.

Debbie choked. "You think he was behind Matthew's not showing up?"

"Don't you?"

Debbie set down her cup. "Probably. Either he or Henry or both." She refused to look at Keith as she voiced another possibility. "Then, too, we could have it wrong. Sometimes men . . . enjoy women, their company, whatever, and then go on about their business. They never really consider all the circumstances they might leave behind."

Keith's brows shot up. "After reading what Kate says about Matthew, you actually think he could be that type of man?"

Debbie took a deep breath for courage. "Sometimes a woman falls in love with a man and weaves all kinds of impossible dreams. She thinks if she believes hard enough, loves enough, the man may change his plans. The man, on the other hand, sees an entirely different picture. Maybe he's told her he won't be staying long, and he doesn't realize how seriously she takes everything he says and does. Maybe he doesn't even know he causes pain and broken dreams when he leaves." Finally she met Keith's eyes. "When you don't know all the circumstances, you have to be fair to everyone."

The silence that followed seemed to go on endlessly. Then at long last Keith spoke. "You've become quite the psychologist yourself, haven't you?"

Debbie shrugged and ruffled the pages of the journal with her thumb. "I want to be fair to Matthew, too."

Keith sat back. "I don't believe Matthew was that kind of person. I think he was everything Kate believed, and I'm convinced her father had something to do with his not showing up."

"I guess we'll have to keep reading and see if we can find some answers."

"Skip over several pages and see what she's written," Keith said impatiently.

Debbie cleared her throat and began to read.

> A year has passed since I last saw Matthew. Tomorrow is July 4. Not in all this time have I heard from him. It's almost as though he never existed. I take out my box and look at my locket with the pictures, and kiss the hank of Matthew's hair. I rub Matthew's shirt against by face, but my heart breaks at the sight of the wasted gold coins. My heart cries for Matthew.
>
> For a whole year I've hoped and prayed. I've fought with Papa, I've taken his whippings, I've taken his abuse. I guess it really doesn't matter now. If I can't have Matthew, it doesn't matter who I marry. Henry Farmsworth will do as well as anyone, and Papa says I must marry. He wants someone to help him with the work.

Debbie closed the book. She couldn't read any more tonight. Kate's story was so depressing, she didn't blame her in the least for haunting the house, searching for a missed love. Everyone should find love in her life, and it was unfortunate Kate's lasted such a short time. She admired Kate for getting on with her life whatever the heartaches. And Kate did live on, until she was well into her seventies.

Scottie walked into the room and plopped down on the other end of the sofa. "Are you two still talking? It's close to midnight, not that I'm keeping track of the time, mind you. But what's so interesting?"

Debbie set the journal beside the unread one. "Have you been talking with Jenny all this time?"

Color seeped into Scottie's face. "Well, most of it."

"What did you talk about all this time that was so interesting?"

"Ah, Debbie, cut it out. I'm sorry if I seemed nosey."

Debbie relented. "We've been reading from Kate's journal. We found a secret cubbyhole in her room, and—"

"Where?"

Laughing, Keith answered, "In the same place as down here. Go on up and look. I left the door open."

After Scottie had raced from the room, Keith rose. "I think I'd better take the hint from the man of the house and amble on home."

Debbie stood up. "You don't have to go if you don't want to. Scottie doesn't run this house."

Keith drew her against him. "I've enjoyed today. You cook as beautifully as you look, and if I haven't told you lately, I'm particularly fond of blond-haired, green-eyed college professors."

His lips took hers, gently at first, then his tongue circled the edge of her lips until she whimpered and snuggled closer.

Her arms reached around his neck and she pressed so hard against him, she felt part of him. His tongue danced with hers, his scent filled her head, until she seemed to be a living, breathing part of him. She loved Keith just as Kate loved Matthew.

And she wanted to tell Keith she loved him. But she couldn't. Those very words might drive him away. She'd lose him soon enough, just as Kate lost Matthew. Kate had her memories. Debbie wanted hers.

Finally Keith drew away. Both were breathing heavily when he brushed back a curl of her hair.

"I have to go. It's late, and I have to get up early to work on my writing tomorrow."

"Ah, the magic life of a writer."

"Magic, hell. It's hard work." He wrapped his arm around her waist, and they walked together to the door.

Lifting her chin with his forefinger, he said, "Today has been special. It's the best Thanksgiving I can remember." His lips brushed hers. "Unfortunately it's over, and I'll have to work some long hours the rest of the weekend to make up."

Knowing she had to keep it light because Keith had never really committed himself, she asked, "What did Scottie want to talk with you about today while you were watching the game?"

"How did you know?"

"I know Scottie."

Keith broke contact and opened the door to leave. "I'm not certain I should say. After all, it was man-to-man talk and Scottie felt it was important."

Debbie's breath caught. "Jenny?"

Keith smiled. "No, Debbie. He threatened to beat the stuffing out of me if I ever hurt you like Charles did."

"Oh—" Debbie choked. There was really nothing else she could say.

Keith climbed in his car and drove off.

17

After Keith left, Debbie went upstairs to her bedroom and read from Kate's first journal. The book was filled with Kate's fears, anguish, and heartbreak while growing up under Kyle's domination.

"Poor Kate," Debbie murmured, closing the journal. "I'd want to escape from Kyle, too. No wonder Matthew was irresistible."

She turned out the light and quickly fell asleep.

Waking early she immediately picked up another journal. By the time she reached the journal and the part where Matthew failed to come, she also felt Kate's deep and sincere love for Matthew, and she suffered along with Kate the loss and pain of her shattered dreams. Kate was left with only a bitter, domineering father and an apathetic fiancé whose touch she could barely tolerate.

The tale was so compelling, Debbie picked up the phone to call Keith and share her thoughts with him. But she replaced the receiver before she made the connection. He had told her he needed to work on his book.

By Friday afternoon Debbie was plagued with restlessness and missed desperately the ability to share her findings with Keith. Refusing to continue feeling depressed, she picked up her purse and drove to town to shop. Something new always helped pull her from the doldrums.

When she stopped at the bank, she immediately saw Eleanor, engaged in serious conversation with an employee. The banker took time to smile a greeting. After Debbie turned from the teller, her cash in hand, she found Eleanor waiting for her.

"Did you have a pleasant Thanksgiving?" Eleanor asked.

"Yes, very nice. Keith and I discovered a hidden space in Kate's old bedroom and inside was a chest with her journals. Did you know Kate married a man named Henry Farmsworth?"

"You've got to be kidding," Norma interjected from behind Debbie. "Are you referring to the ghost Cressie talks about?"

Debbie turned. "Oh, hello, Norma. I didn't see you."

"Did I hear you correctly? I thought Kate was an old maid like Sarah. Did she actually marry a Farmsworth?" When Debbie nodded, Norma giggled. "Do you suppose that's why she's so restless and haunts the house?"

"What do you mean by that?" Eleanor asked, bristling.

"What do you suppose I mean?" Norma replied. "That Kate probably haunts the house because she misses the old boy."

Eleanor relaxed. "That's possible. If Kate did marry a Farmsworth, she naturally would have been happily married."

"Ah, come on, Eleanor, the Farmsworths haven't all walked on water."

"The Farmsworths are not only good, hardworking people, but come from excellent stock—" Eleanor broke off when Norma started laughing.

"Oh, Eleanor, I can't believe you said that. You could be talking about cattle and specialized breeding. You're supposed to marry for love," Norma said, chuckling.

"Like you married that young rapscallion who became a thief, or the gold digger you're associated with now?"

"Michael is not a gold digger," Norma defended. "He's a fine, considerate man. Just because he didn't grow up around here, none of you understand what he's been through. You always think the worst, and I don't think that's fair."

"If he's so fine, why did he send me that forged letter about Herman? My husband loved me, and I didn't appreciate receiving that poison. Why are you shaking your head?"

"Because neither Michael nor I know anything about that letter."

Seeing Eleanor's pursed lips and hostile glare at the equally angry and flushed Norma, Debbie interceded. "Did either of you know somebody shot at me while Keith and I were out riding?" Seeing she had the total attention of both women, she explained what had happened.

"You know, Frank could be trying to frighten you away," Norma said thoughtfully. "He could even be behind those other attacks on you. Frank's a strange man, spends a lot of time by himself, and he's been known to do some pretty frightening things at times."

"He beat up a man once because he didn't like something he said," Eleanor said. "Norma's right. He can be dangerous."

Norma nodded her head. "He might be obsessed with that resort scheme of his and see you as a threat to his plans. He may think by driving you off, he could get his hands on your property."

"And he's malicious enough to even have sent me that forged letter," Eleanor added thoughtfully.

Debbie didn't like their irate expressions. The two women seemed to be gathering their courage, possibly to rush out to Frank's and accuse him openly. "Frank claimed he didn't fire the shot," she said.

"He had a gun, didn't he?" Norma snapped.

"And there was that drunken vagrant the police found shot on his land several years ago," Eleanor said. "The police decided some unidentified hunter killed him. If the man was trespassing, Frank's quite capable of shooting him and claiming it was an accident."

"It was five or six years ago," Norma added. "At the time everyone thought good riddance to bad rubbish because he was always drunk and digging into garbage cans and such. He gave me the creeps, although I don't know that he actually ever did any harm. I wonder if Frank did shoot him."

Debbie, wishing she'd never brought up the subject, said, "Frank's not the only one capable of firing a gun, and any number of people could be responsible for these attacks on me."

"I suppose you're trying to put the blame on Michael again," Norma retorted, her eyes flashing. "Jenny started all this with her crazy tales this summer, of his wanting to get rid of her. Nothing's been right since."

Debbie frowned. "I thought Jenny felt that way about Michael ever since her mother first disappeared?"

Norma's laugh expressed no humor. "No, Jenny has been emotional and difficult to handle, but at first she believed Gloria would be back. Then she went through the stage of blaming herself, thinking she must have done something to make her mother go away and leave her. She resented the fact that Michael was there and Gloria wasn't. It wasn't until this summer, however, that she actually accused Michael of wanting her out of the way."

"I'm sure that's because the seven years is almost up and the estate will be probated," Eleanor inserted before smiling with false sweetness. "Jenny probably overheard you and Michael talking, and making plans. You never did know how to be discreet."

Debbie couldn't agree more, but now wasn't the time to add fuel to Norma's anger. "What we need to do is sit down together and discuss all of this. You know, clear the air. I'm not going to sell, and some innocent could get hurt if these tactics continue. I don't believe any of us want that any more than we want the police involved and asking questions."

"Are you thinking of going to the police?" Eleanor asked.

"I've considered it." Debbie didn't add she hadn't already done so because of lack of evidence.

"I hardly see what they can do," Eleanor said, frowning. "Most of the incidents have appeared more like pranks, and you've waited so long to call them, the police may place little value in your complaints."

"I disagree. When a situation deteriorates to the point where someone fires a gun at me, I think the police would take my complaints quite seriously."

"But you didn't report it immediately, and Frank claims it was an illegal hunter," Eleanor reminded her.

"I don't have to wait until someone is killed to talk with them," Debbie retaliated.

"You know what we should do? And it would solve everything." Norma radiated excitement as she smiled at Debbie expectantly. "We'd learn not only who's trying to frighten you, but we'd clear up Jenny's wild claims about Michael."

Debbie hesitated for a moment. She couldn't shake the sneaking suspicion that she wouldn't like Norma's idea at all.

"What do you have in mind?" Eleanor asked.

"Let's have a séance. Cressie claims she has special psychic powers and is able to talk with the spirits. Let's hold a séance and get Cressie to ask the ghosts what's going on."

Startled, Debbie said, "That's no way to find answers—"

"Sure it is. What's more, it would be the quickest," Norma fired back. "We could settle everything at one time. You would find out who's trying to frighten you, Eleanor would learn who sent her the forged letter, and Jenny could be reassured that Michael doesn't intend her any harm."

"I don't believe in séances," Debbie said.

"Why? Because you're the practical professor or because you're afraid to try a new way to come up with an answer?" Norma pressed.

"I simply don't think this is the way to go about finding out what's going on. Besides, I'm sure Cressie would never agree to such an outrageous scheme." She looked to Eleanor for confirmation of her stand.

The banker's eyes narrowed thoughtfully. "You know, it might not be such a bad idea after all."

Debbie was shocked. Had everyone suddenly gone nuts? "I thought neither of you believed in ghosts."

"Cressie said some terrible things when they found Herman's car. I wouldn't at all mind exposing her for the fraud she is."

The gleam in Eleanor's eyes and the smug expression on her face angered Debbie.

"And I'd try anything to clear up this mess," Norma said fervently. "It's settled, then."

"No, it's not settled," Debbie insisted.

Norma ignored her. "I'll talk to everyone and tell them what's planned. We'll have the séance at your house, Debbie, next Saturday. That's a week from tomorrow. You only have to get Cressie to agree."

"It's a ridiculous idea, and I doubt Cressie will have anything to do with it," Debbie protested.

"Either you ask her or I will. We can hold it at my house without you, but you won't get answers if you're not there." Norma smiled expectantly.

There was no way around it. Debbie disregarded the knot of apprehension forming in her stomach. "Okay," she said. "I'll talk to Cressie."

"I thought you would," Norma said.

Ignoring Norma's snide remark, Debbie asked calmly, "Who else are you planning to invite besides Michael and Jenny?"

Norma began to count on her fingers. "I'll have to ask Teresa because she wouldn't stay home anyway when she knows what we're planning."

"Keith will want to be there if for no other reason than research for his book," Eleanor added.

The knot in Debbie's stomach intensified. She

questioned why Eleanor would give that explanation for Keith's presence. Everyone must know by now the two of them were dating. Maybe Keith had already indicated in some way that he intended to sever their association. Hiding her doubts, she said, "And of course there's Scottie."

"I think we should ask Frank," Norma said.

Eleanor sucked in her breath, and Norma rushed on. "You may not like him personally and think he's dangerous, but you can't deny he's as good a suspect as there is. He has to be there."

"Unfortunately, I'm afraid you're right," Eleanor agreed. "My assistant is waving at me, I have to go. I'll see you both next Saturday, then. What time?"

"Seven-thirty?" Debbie suggested.

Eleanor nodded and walked back toward her office.

Norma squeezed Debbie's arm. "I can hardly wait. I hope this ends all these accusations, and Michael won't continue to feel like everyone is out to get him. Now I have to run, too. I'll call everyone, so you don't have to worry about a thing except Cressie."

Norma rushed from the bank, with Debbie following slowly. Her spirits didn't improve any while she drove home and contemplated how to approach Cressie with Norma's wild scheme. A séance was a crazy idea, and she knew it. She could cancel the whole affair. But she was as desperate as Norma at this point. She wanted answers and would try just about anything. By the time she walked into the kitchen, she was overcome with a sense of dread.

"That didn't take long," Cressie said. "What did you buy?"

Looking at the clock, Debbie saw she had been

gone only an hour. She slumped down on a kitchen chair and said, "I have something to discuss with you."

"You sound serious." Cressie poured two cups of coffee and sat opposite her at the table. "Has something else happened?"

"You might say that." Debbie rubbed her temples. She was getting a headache, and that didn't help. "I ran into Norma and Eleanor at the bank."

"Ah," Cressie said sagely. "Those two never bring you good news."

Debbie hadn't felt that way before, but she definitely agreed now. Every time she talked with one of them, her life turned upside down. She sipped her coffee, considering how to approach the question.

When several moments went by, Cressie pointed out, "With Eleanor, it's a money problem. She bulldozes anythin' else with dainty white gloves. With Norma and the dizzy trail she weaves through life, it could be anythin'. So what have they got you upset about this time?"

Debbie ran her finger around the rim of her cup. Clearing her throat, she spoke as calmly as she could, considering how ridiculous she felt. "Have you ever conducted a séance?"

Debbie shifted uneasily with Cressie's long scrutiny and concentrated on keeping her own expression blank.

"Can't say as I have."

"Do you know how it's done?"

"All Slavanias know about such things. However, we don't need such theatrical shows and fancy arrangements to talk with the spirits. We can do that any time."

"Do you remember when Keith and I were talking

to you after someone shot at me, and we considered all the possibilities for who might be behind these scares?"

Cressie nodded. "I remember, and I warned you justice was approachin' and told you and Mr. Keith to be careful."

Debbie licked her lips. "We discussed Gloria's disappearance and wondered if there could be a connection."

"I remember."

"When Gloria disappeared and everyone thought she was in Dallas shopping, did she drive her car or go with someone else?"

"Miss Gloria drove a Corvette. I don't know whether it was associatin' with that race driver husband of hers or what, but after her first marriage she always owned a fast car. The police found it wrecked and stripped down in Dallas a month after she left. That's what alerted everyone that she was missin'."

"A month after she left? And the alarm didn't go out until the police found the car? Didn't Michael worry when he didn't hear from her?"

"Apparently there were words between them about her goin', and he figured she didn't call for spite. He said he knew she'd come home when she was tired of playin'."

"That must have been some marriage. No wonder Jenny has so many problems."

"Jenny's better now that Scottie's come, and she'll be all right once things are settled about her mother. It's the not knowin' that tears at her."

Debbie sighed. "Well, I hope Scottie doesn't end up hurting her when he goes back to Houston to school."

Cressie cocked her head and gave Debbie that strange, sly smile. "I'm thinkin' you might be the one to be surprised."

"What do you mean by that?"

"Time will tell. Now what did Eleanor and Norma say that upset you so?"

Cressie obviously didn't intend to say more about Scottie, and she was right in a way. Scottie wasn't the important issue at the moment.

"Norma suggested we hold a séance and invite people wanting some answers. She says this would be the quickest way to find them. She mentioned you would make a good medium."

"Who did she have in mind to invite?"

"Besides you, Scottie, and me, there would be Michael, Teresa, Jenny, Norma, Eleanor, Frank, and Keith."

"And Sal," Cressie added softly. "That would make eleven, a magical number."

"Then you'll do it?"

Cressie didn't reply at first, merely sipped her coffee and stared off into space. Then, finally breaking the silence, she asked, "What exactly are they hopin' to learn?"

"Norma wants to prove to Jenny that Michael isn't trying to hurt her. She also said it might clear up who's pulling these scare tactics on me."

"Things might not turn out like she thinks."

After that comment, Debbie hesitated to say what Eleanor wanted. She peeked at Cressie through her lashes. Seeing that the older woman remained undisturbed she rushed to finish. "Norma suggested that you could tell Eleanor who sent her that forged love letter from Herman to Gloria, but Eleanor thinks you'll make a fool of yourself. She apparently harbors some resentment from remarks you made when Herman's car was found, and the police believed he was murdered for money."

"And I bet Teresa would like to know the winnin' horses at the next horse race she's plannin' to place a little money on," Cressie added caustically, "and Frank will want to learn how to get his resort scheme under way."

Debbie swallowed the lump her agitation created at the blatant exposure of everyone's vulnerable points. At least Cressie hadn't thrown a motive for Keith in the bubbling pot. She'd better mention it so Cressie would know exactly what she would be letting herself in for if she agreed. "Eleanor thought Keith could use the séance as a good resource experience for his book. You might be exposing yourself to his probing, if you agree."

"And if you add Scottie worryin' about his future, you have all of you wantin' answers of one sort or another," Cressie summarized.

"People always have unanswered questions they worry about in their lives. Things they want to know, circumstances they fear. But you're right. The idea of holding a séance to give them some solutions is ridiculous. I knew it from the beginning. That's not the way to resolve anything. Forget I even brought up the idea." Debbie relaxed now that the matter was settled to her satisfaction.

"People don't realize that when they break through to the spirit world, the channel isn't always smooth and it doesn't always flow the way it's 'spected."

"I don't understand." Debbie tensed with uneasiness.

"Norma and Eleanor think a séance is a game, something new and different to enjoy and fill them with excitement while at the same time bringin' them either an easy way out of their problems or a way to laugh them off. That may be true if you're dealin' with a fake, someone out for the money, but it's not the case with me."

"You don't have to do this. The only good part is that with everyone gathered together we could talk and maybe resolve some things."

"That won't work. Those folks have too many secrets and too little trust in one another. No, Norma is right. A séance will bring answers, but it won't bring what everyone 'spects."

"What do you mean?"

"The spirits don't discriminate. They tell it all. Your guests may uncover more than they can possibly imagine."

Debbie sighed as she considered Cressie's warning. If she was right, the ramifications might bring more trouble than anyone faced now. But if Cressie *could* talk to the spirits, it was better to get everything out in the open. Then people would know what they faced and what their choices were instead of enduring innuendos and intrigue.

Her lips curved wryly. Thanks to Cressie, she'd gone from disbelieving in séances to accepting the possibility that some good might come from one. At least it was worth a try.

"Let's go for it," Debbie said. "We'll let the chips fall where they may."

Cressie nodded and rose. After setting her cup in the dishwasher, she added, "You made the right decision, although you've opened a door to danger for yourself. Once you set the spirits free, the dark ones walk alongside the good ones. You best be careful."

"I'm always careful," Debbie said, forcing a laugh.

"Miss Kate will be here. She'll help you as she's been doin'." Cressie studied Debbie a long while before she added, "I think Miss Kate's about ready to let you know why she called you home."

Stunned, Debbie stared at Cressie. Her mouth opened once to ask Cressie what she meant, but before she could find her voice, Cressie slipped out the back door, heading for her apartment.

Debbie raced to the door after her. "Cressie, wait. What did you mean?"

Cressie paused. "You didn't think you came here and bought this house on your own, did you? The spirits have been guidin' you, helpin' you, just as they do all of us when we let them."

Debbie wanted to shout, "I don't believe in ghosts! I don't believe in spirits or all of this nonsense, you know that." But she didn't. She couldn't. It wouldn't be true. So she simply stood there, feeling helpless.

"Trust in Miss Kate," Cressie persisted before continuing on her way.

Standing in the doorway watching her, Debbie admitted that maybe she hadn't believed in ghosts or spirits when she'd come to Nacogdoches, but she had accepted a guiding hand in her affairs—whether from the spirits, God's hand, or whatever. Good or bad, for better or worse, her beliefs had changed as completely as an immature girl changes and grows into a woman when she marries.

She knew that sometimes experience could bring a new depth to life. Sometimes it could dump disaster, but it always allowed a person growth, a chance to expand or the opportunity to crumble with defeat. Life's rewards and life's tragedies were as necessary as love and death.

Debbie shut the door and called Norma to tell her Cressie would do the séance. Norma was delighted and promised to contact everyone as soon as possible.

Alone, Debbie roamed through the house restlessly. She ran her fingers lovingly over the patterned sofa in the living room and stared out the window at the big pecan tree. She touched the fireplace mantel. This fireplace sat below the one in her room, as the one in the back parlor sat below Kate's old room. It was almost a symbol of the new versus the old, since this room was part of the new addition Kyle had built and the other was part of the original. Debbie was the new owner; Kate, a former owner. Both were tenuous comparisons, but ones that came to mind. Suddenly the thought struck Debbie that she could wind up like Kate, dying alone and perhaps wandering the rooms of the old house as a ghost with Kate, both searching.

She started to leave the room but stopped beside the cherrywood table. The lingering aroma of lemon polish filled the air. The room shone with the care given it. She loved this old house, and she loved Keith. So much had happened that she wanted to tell him. Why didn't he call?

No sooner had she openly admitted the wanting than she shut her mind to it. Chin held high with determination, she marched into the back parlor and picked up the next volume of Kate's journal. No longer would she lament Keith's lack of attention. She would read about Kate and her marriage to Henry.

She settled into the corner of the sofa, turned on the lamp, and began.

I haven't written in my journal for a while. I've been too miserable to express my feelings. I hurt inside and feel dirty.

I'm Henry's wife now, and he uses me like a whore. He takes his pleasure, but cares nothing for me. I know now he married me for Pa's inheri-

tance. Henry is always telling me how he's going to spend Pa's wealth when Pa dies. Henry has grand plans, but I don't think he includes me in them. I don't care. As long as Henry leaves.

It's almost funny how Henry looks when Pa gives him orders and fills his days with chores. Henry hasn't realized yet that Pa considers him the same as he does me, a free pair of hands.

Oh, how I miss Matthew. When things become too bad, I pull out all the beautiful memories of the times shared with Matthew and dream of how it might have been. I wonder where he is and if he ever thinks of me.

Debbie wiped the tears from her eyes. "Damn men," she muttered.

The writing went on to tell of hard work and increasing arguments between Henry and Kyle. It described the horror Kate felt at the touch of Henry's cold, clammy hands when they shared a bed at night and how much she hated Henry's smooth, unblemished, hairless body covering hers. It described Kate's loneliness and her treasured escapes to the comfort of the swimming hole.

The entries became farther and farther apart while Kate struggled with her pain and the mounting disagreements between the two men in her life. Frequently she became the outlet each used to vent frustrations. Kate's despair was almost unbearable, her depression complete.

When Scottie came home, Debbie quit reading and heated leftovers for supper. Afterward she made popcorn and spent the evening watching television with her younger brother. She found that even the gunfighting and terror of wounded bystanders when the police chased criminals was better than being alone with her own thoughts.

Somehow Saturday flowed into Sunday with Scottie disappearing after lunch to go to Jenny's, and Debbie left in the quiet solitude of her house reading the journals. She'd heard nothing from Keith and wondered if her brother, guessing of her love, had told Keith during their private talk. As a result, he might be wanting to break free of their affair before he left Nacogdoches. She might be losing Keith . . . as Kate lost Matthew.

She couldn't let this worry consume her so. She had to control her own life. Angrily she picked up Kate's journal to read. Later, deep into the diary, her anger faded as she read:

> *I'm going to have a baby. Henry and I have been married two years now, and both he and Pa had given up. I didn't care, because a child wouldn't be Matthew's, but I couldn't tell them. Still, the thought of a baby, someone I can love and care for and who'll love me back, brings a ray of joy to my life that's been missing. I want this child and look forward to having her. I say her because I want a girl. Pa and Henry talk about a son, the all-important male descendant, but I know she'll be a girl, and she'll be mine to care for and to love.*

While Debbie prepared supper Sunday evening, her thoughts turned to Kyle's journal. He had disclosed a big argument between him and Henry. Kyle had been glad to be rid of the no-good, money-hungry upstart. He'd been almost as bad as the damned Yankee. Anxious to learn what Kate had to say about the split and what had happened to her baby, Debbie hurriedly warmed the leftovers from the refrigerator.

When they sat down, Scottie stared pointedly at the food. Debbie smiled sweetly and said, "You can always fix yourself a sandwich if you're still hungry afterward."

"How about two?" Scottie muttered, and began to eat.

When the phone rang, Debbie jumped. It hadn't rung all weekend. Now she wasn't sure what she would say.

"You want me to answer it?" Scottie asked.

"No. Eat your dinner," she said, and picked up the receiver.

A strange male voice came on the other end. "Is this Debbie Dillon? Is Pamela Dillon of Houston your mother?"

"She's my mother. What is it? What's happened?" Debbie asked, leaning against the wall. As she listened she noticed that Scottie, after looking at her, set down his fork, his food forgotten. When his face paled beneath his freckles, she knew he had to be seeing some of the horror she was feeling. As she continued to remain silent, listening, his hand clenched beside his plate.

Finally Debbie shut her eyes and replied with such calm that she surprised herself. "We'll be there as soon as possible."

"What is it? What's happened to Mom?" Scottie asked when Debbie set down the receiver.

"She was in a car accident. She's in the hospital. That was a friend of hers, an Alec Lindsey. He doesn't know how serious it is other than she was cut pretty badly and unconscious when they put her in the ambulance."

"Yeah, I know Alec," Scottie said with a frown. "If he saw her loaded in the ambulance, he must have been with her. He was probably driving. If he's hurt her, I'll make him sorry he was ever born."

"It was an accident. The other driver ran a red light and hit the passenger side of the car." Debbie massaged her pounding head. She needed to contact the dean and tell him she would be out of town and unable to teach her classes. "Go pack some things. We may be there a few days."

Scottie rose, most of his dinner still sitting on his plate. "I'll need to tell Jenny I'm going."

"You get ready while I make some calls. Then you can call her while I pack."

Debbie quickly called the dean and explained the situation, after which she rang through to Cressie. The older woman listened a few moments and promised to take care of everything, including calling the school for Scottie. She ended with telling Debbie to call Norma before leaving town just in case they'd have to postpone the séance.

Debbie called Norma and explained what had happened. It didn't help at all when Norma told her before hanging up that Keith had just been offered a job teaching in Virginia next year.

Debbie bit her lip as she set down the phone. Now she knew why she hadn't heard anything from him all weekend. He had acquired the position he'd been hoping to get in order to research the next book. She thought about calling him, but what could she say? Congratulations, it's been fun. Or she could act as if it didn't matter at all to her.

"Are you off yet?" Scottie yelled through the house.

Debbie took a deep breath to ease the pain that circled her heart. Her mother must come first. She'd deal with Keith later.

18

Debbie and Scottie arrived in Houston close to midnight and drove straight to the hospital. They met Alec Lindsey in the waiting room, and he filled them in on details of the accident and their mother's condition, including the fact that a plastic surgeon had already made repairs to prevent scarring.

Debbie gathered immediately from Scottie's belligerent manner that he did not like Alec. On the other hand, the tall lean man with kind blue eyes and straight brown hair made it equally clear his interest in their mother was more than casual, and he wouldn't tolerate Scottie's hostile attitude. Since Alec seemed somewhat entrenched in her mother's life, Debbie wondered why neither her mother nor Scottie had mentioned him other than by implication. She would definitely bring up the matter tomorrow. Tonight she was too tired.

Alec led them through the hospital and past the nurses' station to Pamela Dillon's room. Debbie glanced uneasily at Alec, and he said, "Relax, they've seen me before, and you'll have a moment with your mother before they run us out."

Scottie sniffed, letting them know he wasn't happy with the circumstances, but Debbie ignored him.

At first the extensive bandages on their mother's face and around her head startled Debbie. Pamela's arm also lay in a cast at her side, but she was conscious and her groggy blue eyes smiled a welcome.

Reassured, Debbie laid her hand in her mother's. "No, don't try to speak. We'll be back tomorrow to visit, but we couldn't rest without seeing you first."

Before another word could be uttered, the room door swung open, and a bristling nurse said, "Who allowed you in? Visiting hours are over."

"We're her children. We were notified of the accident, and just arrived from out of town. We wanted to see her."

"Humph. Well, get along with you now. She needs her rest. You can visit tomorrow."

As they crossed the hospital lobby, Debbie thanked Alec for taking care of Pamela, and then she and Scottie went to their mother's house and to bed.

Debbie wanted to learn more about Alec and see if she could discover why Scottie was so hostile toward him. So the next morning over breakfast, she asked her brother about the man.

"I don't like the creep, that's all."

"Why not? He seems all right to me, and he and Mom seem on pretty good terms."

"He's not going to take Dad's place."

"Is he trying? How did they meet?"

Scottie stuffed his mouth with toast. "He's an engineer and works at the same firm as Mom. Since she's the bookkeeper, and he's in charge of one of the projects, they started talking or something."

"It's odd Mom never mentioned him by name. How long has he been there?"

"Since the first of the year. He and Mom started going out a couple of months later. I don't like him. He's a jerk."

Seeing Scottie's belligerent expression, Debbie probed gently, "Why do you think that?"

"He's always sticking his nose into our family business and trying to tell me what to do. I'd thought if I could visit you in Vermont this summer, it would be over by the time I came home. But I didn't get to go."

Debbie ignored his attempt at manipulation. "You know Mom has been lonely since Dad died. She's not the type to stand on her own. She wants someone to lean on and help take care of her. Is Alec divorced or what?"

"Yeah, he's divorced."

"He's probably wanting companionship, too, and this might be a good thing for both of them."

Scottie's chin jutted out. "Alec's not my father."

Giving up, Debbie suggested they go see their mother.

When they arrived at the hospital, Pamela greeted them with a smile and claimed she felt better, but as they talked she appeared nervous and on edge. When a nurse stuck her head around the door to see if she needed anything, Pamela jumped and looked guilty until she realized who it was.

It was time to bring Alec out into the open. Debbie said, "We met Alec. He seems to think a lot of you."

Pamela smiled briefly before glancing uneasily at her son. "I like him, too."

Scottie snorted. "I'm going to see if there are any Cokes around." He walked out the door.

Debbie sat on a chair next to the bed and, taking her mother's frail hand between her own, asked, "Can you tell me about it?"

Tears streamed down Pamela's cheeks as she explained how she and Alec had been attracted from the beginning, but Scottie had been difficult and opposed their dating. Whenever Alec had tried to reason with Scottie, there'd been an argument and Scottie usually went out with friends and created problems.

Listening, Debbie could understand the torment and fear both suffered. Pamela wanted to fill the void in her life but didn't want to lose her son in the process. Scottie resented anyone trying to take his father's place and feared that if Alec should succeed, changes would follow.

Finally Debbie asked, "Why didn't you tell me about Alec before? It would have explained some of Scottie's actions."

Pamela wadded the edge of the sheet. "You were having such a bad time yourself with your divorce and moving. I didn't want to burden you with my problems. And I was afraid you might feel the same as Scottie, and I didn't want to lose you, too."

Debbie shook her head at the complexity of the situation. Plain old-fashioned fear on everyone's part. Fear of looking for answers, of forcing issues until solutions were found. But she couldn't condemn her mother when she too had suffered fear of losing her reputation, her job, even Keith, and hadn't faced issues herself.

Debbie left her mother resting and went out into

the hall to search for Scottie. She found him in a heated discussion with Alec. She didn't interrupt but stood by and listened.

Alec nodded at her and continued. "Your mother will be going home in a few days. When she does, she's going to need someone around at least part of the time to help her fix meals and such. If I talk to the school about letting you reenter, will you come back and take care of her?"

Scottie's eyes widened, and Debbie realized he hadn't considered what his mother would do when she left the hospital.

His toe dug at the tile floor. Sighing, he said, "I guess I could."

"After all she's done for you, I would think you'd be anxious to repay her now that you have the chance," Alec said, his tone curt with displeasure.

"I said I would," Scottie said sullenly.

"You're the most likely candidate, since your sister has her job and home in Nacogdoches," Alec pressed, clearly wanting something more than he was getting.

Debbie understood her brother's dilemma and ached for him as he struggled within herself. Scottie had finally settled in Nacogdoches. He had made new friends he enjoyed, and most of all, he had found Jenny. Now he was being asked to forfeit this to help his mother, whom he loved in spite of their past difficulties. And there were no guarantees that if he did come back to Houston, the same problems wouldn't arise when their mother was better.

"If you'd rather stay with Debbie the rest of the semester, I'm willing to take care of your mother in your place. But if I do, you must understand, I won't relinquish this responsibility when you return. You will have to accept that I'm a part of your mother's life as much as you are and that I won't allow you to pull all-night escapades to upset her. I won't tolerate that behavior. I won't have your mother go through that again," Alec said in a firm voice.

Scottie stared at the tile floor. He was being asked to let go of the past, not forget it, but to put it in its proper place and accept the present.

After several long minutes, Scottie inhaled and met Alec's gaze. "I think Mom would like to have you with her."

"You're sure?" Alec pressed.

Scottie nodded.

"Okay, then. I'll make arrangements to take some time off so I can stay with her starting Thursday. I believe they intend to release her then." Almost as an afterthought, he asked Debbie, "Is that arrangement all right with you?"

"I think Mom's a lucky woman."

When Alec had left, Debbie said, "I know that was tough for you, but I'm very proud of you."

Scottie grimaced. "Yeah, tougher than you realize, but I knew whether I liked Alec or not didn't really matter. I'll be going to college in a couple of years, and after watching you, I don't want Mom to be alone the rest of her life. Besides, I can't leave Nacogdoches now. With all of these threats, you need me in the house, and Jenny needs to know I won't let anyone harm her. She feels safe knowing I'll be there if she calls."

Debbie spoke past the emotion that tightened her throat. "I appreciate your concern for me, but just how serious are things between you and Jenny?"

Scottie frowned. "She's my best friend, and I like

her a lot. Right now she needs me, really needs me, like no one ever has before. Can you understand that?"

When Debbie nodded, Scottie grinned. "And I don't want to miss the séance, either. After the things I've seen and smelled since I arrived, I want to know why Kate haunts the house."

Debbie laughed. "Don't tell me you're letting Kate manipulate you, too?"

When Scottie nodded sheepishly, Debbie laughed louder and tucked her arm in his. "Come on, let's go home. You can call some of your friends while we're here, and I'll get the house ready for Mom's return."

"When do you think we'll go back?" Scottie asked as they walked through the corridors.

"We'll visit with Mom tomorrow and make sure she's still getting better. If everything's okay, we'll go back Wednesday. That way Alec can move the things he needs into the house before Mom comes home without our being in the way."

"Have I told you lately what a great sister I have?" Scottie asked.

Debbie squeezed his arm. "I told Mom not to worry. Having her and Dad for parents, you were bound to turn out fine."

Scottie blushed. "I guess I did make things kind of tough on her for a while."

"We all have bad patches in our life, Scottie. It's what we do afterward and what we learn from them that counts."

"Like you have?"

"I hope so," Debbie replied softly.

Monday evening, after a brief visit with their mother, Scottie left to go out with some of his friends while Debbie sat and told her mother more about the events in Nacogdoches. She was careful not to mention the threats or the gunshot, but told her a little about Cressie and Keith.

"You care for him a lot, don't you?" her mother asked after listening to Debbie talk.

Determined to put on a good front, Debbie said, "I like him, but I don't expect anything to come from it. He's been offered a job teaching in Virginia next year."

"That doesn't mean he couldn't take you with him."

"I don't think Keith is the settling-down kind. At least not yet. He still has big plans for what he wants to do with his life, and he's never short of company."

Her mother was quiet for a moment. "I hope you find someone someday. A big house can get awfully lonely at times, no matter how much you do to keep yourself busy."

Debbie leaned down and kissed her mother's forehead. "I hope so too." Then, straightening, she told Pamela what she had read in the journals about Kate's life.

When she was finished, Pamela lay quietly. "You know, I'd forgotten about it, but there's an old footlocker in the attic that used to belong to your grandmother. She has old family pictures, papers, and small mementos in there. When you go back to Nacogdoches, why don't you take it along with you? In your spare time, you can look through the thing."

"That might be fun, but do you have something specific in mind to suggest it now?"

"Since you say you resemble Kate so much in appearance, maybe you'll find something in the locker that indicates a family relationship. There is that possibility, since the Mullers and the Dillons have both been in Texas for so many years."

"That would explain more than simply saying it's a coincidence. Maybe I'll do just that." Excitement quickened Debbie's pulse. There was no telling what she could learn.

Wednesday morning, after a final visit with their mother, Debbie and Scottie drove back to Nacogdoches. Reassured that her mother would be fine and that Alec would take good care of her, Debbie turned eagerly to thoughts of her own home and Keith. She wondered if he knew she'd been gone or if he even cared. And she was worried whether she could hide her hurt from him. At times, life was really difficult.

Keith reminded her so much of Matthew, or at least what she had read about him in Kate's diary. Her thoughts drifted to a possible connection between Matthew and Keith. Her solution felt right, but her mind protested at the coincidence of the farfetched idea. Yet she traveled many miles dreaming up explanations her grandmother's footlocker might reveal.

"Are we still having the séance Saturday?" Scottie asked, breaking into the silence that had lasted for most of the three-hour trip.

"I'm afraid so," Debbie replied. She was ready for some answers and hoped this could provide them. It was one thing to fight a known enemy, to stand up and defend oneself, but something else when the enemy was faceless and offered nothing tangible to fight against. This gathering would at least bring everyone together.

"Radical," Scottie said laughingly. "I can hardly wait."

＊　＊　＊

Keith was the first to arrive Saturday evening. The instant Debbie let him in, he said, "Why didn't you call and tell me about your mother's accident?"

Averting her eyes, Debbie shut the door. "You were busy writing all weekend. I assumed you wouldn't want to be interrupted."

Keith grabbed her shoulders and with his fingers raised her chin, forcing her to look at him. "I was busy fighting a deadline, but I'm never too busy if you need me. Remember that."

He bent his head, and his lips covered hers. Debbie leaned against him. She'd missed him so. What was she going to do when he left for Virginia? She pulled back, but he refused to let her draw completely away from him.

They went into the living room, which had been arranged so that a circle of eleven chairs covered the front part of the room. They sat on the sofa, which had been pushed back along with the coffee table and a chair and faced the small fire that glowed in the fireplace across the room. Debbie told Keith about her mother's accident and the problems between Alec and Scottie.

"Scottie is going through some of the same crises as Jenny is right now," Keith observed.

"I don't see that. He certainly doesn't think anyone's trying to harm him."

"No, but he doesn't feel the same sense of security with his mother he had before, and while he likes living here, he knows it's unlikely he can stay here until he goes to college. Jenny also lacks security in her home, but for a different reason."

"I never thought of that," Debbie said thoughtfully, but before she could continue, the doorbell rang. "Sounds like more guests have arrived."

"Whatever made you agree to this crazy scheme?"

Debbie tugged free from his grasp. "I'm tired of not knowing who's trying to frighten me away. We've tried everything else—"

"You didn't go to the police."

"Do you think they could have done more than we did? I think people would be more apt to talk to you than the police."

"You're probably right. People automatically clam up when the police start asking questions. Even innocent people are afraid they might find themselves in trouble."

"When Norma suggested a séance and Cressie agreed, I went along with it. Reluctantly, but I did agree." She let him see her amusement when she added, "Besides, think of how the experience can add to your book."

Keith followed her to the door. "Cressie thought it was a good idea?"

"She said we would find answers. Maybe not the ones we want, exactly, and some of us may not like what we hear, but we'll learn more than we know now."

Debbie opened the door to greet Michael, Norma, Jenny, and Teresa. "Why don't you get Scottie from the back parlor," she suggested to Jenny. "There's coffee, tea, or soft drinks and some cake on the dining room table if you want anything while we wait for the others."

"Eleanor's car was right behind us, and Frank is generally on time," Norma spoke, glancing at her watch. Her face was flushed with excitement, and her brown eyes danced. "I can hardly wait. This has been the longest week," she confided.

The doorbell rang again, and Debbie found Eleanor at the door, with Frank walking up the steps.

Everyone had arrived, and they all wanted to wait on refreshments. Debbie had only to get the Slavanias and they could begin.

Cressie and Sal came immediately when she called. "If you will please all find your place in the circle, Sal can turn out the light," Cressie said. "The spirits are sensitive and react best to semidarkness."

Debbie thought back to her previous experiences with the apparitions. Both Kate's image and the bizarre form had appeared only after dark, but she had frequently sensed their presence in the daylight.

She sat with Keith on one side and Scottie on the other. Jenny sat beyond Scottie and next to where Sal would sit. Teresa took a chair on the other side of Keith, with Norma and Michael beyond. Eleanor sat next to Michael and Frank between her and Cressie. Debbie's heart raced with anticipation.

"Please hold hands so the circle will be complete," Cressie instructed and scanned the circle with her piercing blue eyes, taking in every detail. They contradicted her air of repose as she sat quietly with a bland smile on her lips. When she nodded, Sal flipped off the switch.

Debbie found Keith's hand warm, his grasp firm. Scottie's hand was sweaty, and she could feel a nervous twitching he tried to hide with his blasé attitude at Jenny's giggling. Sal joined the circle and took Jenny's other hand.

The glow from the fireplace made it possible to

see. Looking around at the participants, Debbie sensed none of them were as calm as they pretended. She knew she wasn't.

Cressie bowed her head. "May the spirits of light come and protect this gatherin' from the devils of darkness."

A long silence followed. Cressie's breathing deepened and slowed until she appeared to be in a trance-like state.

Ever so faintly, Debbie heard the sound of wind chimes. Louder and louder they grew, and the scent of jasmine filled the air.

Jenny gasped. Michael cleared his throat. The air hovered as it did with the coming of a tornado, the pressure, the tempo, rising until finally Cressie spoke. Her accent and tone had changed. Her voice carried a soft southern drawl. "Good evening."

"Good evenin', Kate," Sal responded. "It's been a while. How are you doin'?"

"I'm tiring with my search, but my goal grows closer. Soon I may find peace. How may I help you this evening?"

"We have some folks gathered here tonight who have some questions. They're wonderin' if you can give them answers."

Debbie peeked at Sal. This was the most she had ever heard him say at one time, but there was nothing reserved about him now.

"I'll try, but they may not hear what they want. Several among you may wish you had never called me forth."

Sal looked around the circle. "Do any of you wish to stop the séance at this point?" When no one responded he said, "Then on your own heads be it."

The icy pronouncement of his words sent a quiver of apprehension through Debbie. She wanted to stand, to stop this eerie event. She felt afraid, as though life as she had known it would never be the same. Several others shifted, making rustling sounds on the chairs. They, too, felt the poignant pronouncement. But no one spoke.

"My young friend, Scottie, has come to stay in this house for a period of time. I 'spect you've seen him about. He's wonderin' about his future," Sal began.

"The young man wonders about a home, but he will find boundless love from three houses. He should put away his fears. All will be well."

Scottie's hand trembled in Debbie's, and she felt a sense of relief. He clearly had heard the reassurance he needed to firm up his foundations—even more so because it came from an outside source and not from her or their mother.

"Jenny also has many questions," Sal continued. "She doesn't know where to turn."

"The young girl searches for her mother. Rest assured, she will be found, and sooner than any of you think. Her finding will bring great upheaval. Evil lurks close behind. So beware."

There was an audible gasp from someone in the circle, but the voice, through Cressie, droned on.

"The young girl is in much danger and should be very careful. Attempts to send her to the spirit world have already been made. Blood flowed upon the ground, almost sending her into the darkness forever. One amongst you is filled with a desperate drive."

Jenny whimpered as Scottie straightened on his chair and glared at the participants in the circle. His gaze settled on Norma and Michael before Debbie tugged his hand and nodded for him to sit back. He obliged her, but from the set of his jaw and the stiffness in his body, it was clear the matter had only been postponed.

The silence that followed sucked the air from the room, and Debbie took a deep breath.

Then Frank asked, "What about my resort?"

Debbie smiled wryly. Nothing seemed to deter Frank from his own plans, and she wondered if Kate would expose him.

"You were a good friend to Sarah. She hasn't forgotten. Your life will be changing, and so will your wants."

"What the hell does that mean?" Frank grumbled.

"Patience is a virtue and so rewarded. Impatience can call forth the devil's workings."

Eleanor didn't give him an opportunity to pursue the matter. "Who sent me that terrible letter and signed Herman's name?"

"The hand of justice cast down a ripple upon the water. Righteousness will prevail. Answers will pour forth revealing all, and the devil's hole of darkness shall be fed."

Debbie didn't understand that answer. While she was contemplating all the implications, Norma spoke.

"Can you tell me if the clouds of suspicion will be raised from Michael?"

"Blood has been shed. Bones will rise and seek vengeance. He shall suffer much with the bands of steel."

"This is all a fake. I don't believe any of this," Norma cried out, rising from her chair.

A gust of cold wind instantly swept through the room. A loud, bizarre laugh filled the air. Norma sat down. Silence encased the circle of people with the effectiveness of a casket sealed.

The waiting ate at her, and Debbie asked, "Can you tell me who has been trying to frighten me away?"

"Ah," the soft voice drawled. "I've been waiting for you, waiting so long."

The scent of jasmine thickened in the air, and the faint ringing of wind chimes sounded. On and on the mixture continued, growing, until Debbie wanted to scream. Her nerves were raw with the strain. The others in the circle didn't appear much better.

The soft voice spoke. "It has been such a long search, so hard, so difficult. I'd about given up hope." The voice paused. "I was afraid I might walk the halls of nothingness forever."

"What is it, Kate?" Sal asked. "What have you been searchin' for?"

Debbie felt a tug at her hair, a brush against her neck, before the cold wind wafted through the room and wiped away the sweetness. The smell of musty earth remained in its place, reeking in Debbie's nostrils and causing her eyes to water. The faint melody of the reassuring wind chimes suddenly stilled, and a sense of foreboding pressed around her. She shivered at someone's frightened moan.

"No, go away. You won't stop me now," Kate's voice rang out. "I won't let you, do you hear me? I won't let you."

A growing grotesque form rose from behind Sal. Debbie had felt its menace the night of Jenny's accident, but now, in the midst of fearful whimpers from the circled group, the form reeked of hate and evil. Keith's hand tightened around hers, and she knew he saw the ominous shape, too. Somehow that comforted her.

"Get home, girl. Get back where you belong and stop this nonsense," a loud, boisterous voice boomed from Sal.

"Never. I'll never go there, not until I find what I seek."

"What's done is done."

"It's all your fault. You wouldn't listen to me, you wouldn't even try to understand."

"I heard you, but I'll have no damned Yankee in my family. Do you hear? They're nothing but a bunch of thieving rascals out to do a poor hardworking man in and take all his savings."

"Matthew wasn't like that. He loved me. We were meant for each other . . . forever." Sobs filled the still air.

"Hell and damnation on the Yankee and his descendants. I'll not have this, do you hear? It will stop now."

"Matthew, oh, Matthew, where are you? Why didn't you come? Why did you leave me? I was so lonely."

"You married, didn't you? You had me, didn't you? I kept you busy, kept your hands occupied. How could you be lonely?"

"You stole her, you stole her from me, just like you stole my Matthew!" Loud, hysterical laughter mixed with sobs bounced through the room with the force of a ringing bell in a small tower, and it echoed and echoed.

Stunned and frightened with the sudden force of violence that seemed all around her, Debbie clung tightly to Keith's hand. She was afraid to move, afraid to breathe, and saw from the wide eyes of the other participants that they felt the same way.

"Oh, Matthew, why didn't you come? And my poor, poor Georgette. I'll never rest until I know."

"Damn the Yankee. He's the cause of all this trouble all these years. I should have shot him the first time I laid eyes on him."

"You stole the loves of my life. I'll never forgive you. The scales of justice must be balanced."

"The devil's wrath on the Yankee and his kin. As for Georgette, it was for your own good. You never cared for that no-good Farmsworth scoundrel anyway."

The people in the circle gasped as a unit. Debbie understood that although most of them weren't following the conversation now since they hadn't read the journals, they did at least recognize the banker's name.

"But Georgette—"

"I'll have no mention of Farmsworth ever again, do you hear me? He was a yellow, money-hungry upstart."

"Then remove the Farmsworth from the graveyard. Remove the taint of the other outsider from the Muller graveyard. Even the scent of jasmine can't disguise the evil it brings. Do whatever you will, but you'll not stop me from finding what I seek. You'll not."

The room vibrated, almost as though a battle of wills struggled through eternity and fell into Debbie's front parlor to shake the walls and everyone in it.

A scream ripped through the air.

Debbie looked at Cressie and Sal, who sat slumped on their chairs. They resembled rag dolls, limp and silent.

Keith jumped up and ran to turn on the switch.

Several seconds passed before Debbie's eyes adjusted to the light, but she saw everyone else still sitting, frozen in place. Only the heartrending sobs coming from Jenny broke the quiet.

"Jenny, what is it?" Scottie asked, looking helpless and frightened at the girl's complete breakdown.

Jenny flung herself at Scottie and wrapped her arms around his neck. She buried her face in his broad chest.

"It's over, Jenny. The séance is over," Debbie said softly, trying to reassure the girl. "I'm sorry it upset you so, but they're gone now. Only your friends are here."

"I knew it, I just knew it!" Jenny sobbed.

Scottie looked at Debbie, his eyes pleading for help.

Keith walked over behind Scottie and lifted Jenny's head up with one hand while brushing the hair back from her face with the other. "You knew what, Jenny?" he asked.

"Didn't you hear her? Didn't you hear what she said?" Jenny answered brokenly.

"You mean Kate? Of course we did."

"How could we help it?" Teresa interjected scathingly.

Debbie noticed Teresa's hand shook when she held on to the chair and stood up. She wasn't as unaffected as she pretended.

"My God, that was terrible," Norma moaned. "I had no idea, and what in the world were they talking about—Matthew, Georgette, damned Yankee?"

"But there was an accurate description of a Farmsworth." Frank half chuckled, then ducked when Eleanor, for once losing her control, reached over and slapped him.

"You have your nerve," she snapped. "You, a no-good nothing, saying things like that about a Farmsworth."

"Stop it. Stop it!" Jenny screamed. "Didn't you hear? Don't you know what she said? Kate said to remove the taint of the other outsider from the Muller graveyard. She meant my mother."

"Jenny, honey," Debbie began.

"No. You won't stop me from looking this time. Kate said someone was buried in the graveyard, and earlier she said we'd find my mother sooner than we thought. We have to look. We have to. I know she's there . . . just like I told you before. You'll help me, won't you, Scottie? You'll help me like you promised?"

Scottie locked eyes momentarily with Debbie. "I'll help you look, just like I promised."

In that instant Debbie understood what Cressie had meant when she'd said that the séance might bring more than anyone anticipated, and that some might regret the event.

"I'll help, too," Keith said.

"When? When are we going to look?" Jenny demanded.

Keith rubbed the back of his neck and looked out the window. Debbie, following his gaze, saw the night sky, a velvet blackness dimly lit by a half-moon and scattered stars. Her breath caught as she awaited his decision.

"What better time than now? I don't think any of us will sleep anyway until we at least see if Gloria's there."

19

Sal went to get the shovels and a lantern while Debbie sent Cressie to the kitchen for a flashlight.

With Jenny's impatient urging, she and Scottie rushed from the room, planning to obtain a second flashlight from Debbie's car. From the determined expression on Scottie's face, and Jenny's sad blue eyes, Debbie saw how intent they were on finding answers. If Gloria's body was discovered, tragedy would strike more than one life, Jenny's included.

Norma, clutching Michael's right arm, had pasted a confident smile on her face that was clearly at odds with the fear in her brown eyes. Because her poise was admirable under the circumstances, Debbie smiled back.

Michael remained his usual stoic self, appearing undisturbed by the tension in the room or the furtive glances cast in his direction. Only the whitened knuckles of his hand as he covered Norma's indicated any inner turmoil.

Since the two walked over to stand beside Keith,

Debbie assumed they intended to be among the first in the search. This could be from fear of missing an important discovery that might affect their lives, or perhaps a precaution in order to determine how to defend their position should Gloria's body be located. Perhaps they were simply relieved that the suspicions and uncertainty might finally end. Debbie couldn't tell which was more accurate.

Looking at Eleanor's and Teresa's more elegant attire, Debbie offered, "If anyone would prefer to remain in the house with Cressie, there's cake and coffee in the dining room."

"These old things," Teresa replied, and studied her heels and hose and the slim-fitting purple designer dress she wore. "I wouldn't miss this grave digging for the world, and especially not for these clothes. I can always buy more."

Norma looked at Teresa, lowered her eyes, and slowly moved her head from side to side.

Debbie felt a similar reaction to Teresa's attitude, but she said nothing, turning instead to Eleanor. Teresa was totally self-centered, but her flippant attitude could be her way of hiding her true feelings at the possibility of solving the mystery around her mother's disappearance.

Eleanor drew herself up straight, the ever-present matriarch in her gray silk suit, and replied, "I intend to go also." She moved to stand beside Teresa.

That left Debbie and Frank to bring up the rear of the procession. Yet when he stepped beside her, she wasn't sure she liked the idea. Seeing his narrowed eyes scrutinizing those around him reminded her of the day she and Keith had met him with the gun. Because of his casual country ways, Frank was deceptive. But the knowledge that Frank was quite capable of shooting to kill made Debbie uncomfortable.

Maybe she was letting her imagination run away with her, she thought. Still, in a short span of time six or seven years ago, there had been three unexplained missing or dead individuals. A surprising number for a town of thirty-five thousand people.

Cressie came back and handed Keith a large flashlight. After nodding his head reassuringly at Debbie, he led the group out the door.

Even though Frank stayed by her side, Debbie stopped a moment to leave instructions as Cressie handed her a smaller light. "Keep your eyes open. If you think it's necessary, call the police."

"I reckon the police will be comin', but I'll give you a few minutes before I call them."

Hardly able to accept Cressie's bold statement, Debbie stared at her until the silence forced her to ask, "What will we find?"

"I reckon you'll find what you're lookin' for. Just be careful, Miss Debbie. Things are not always what they seem, and the black cloud of the devil spreads easily, lookin' to prey on the innocent who thwart him."

"Shut up, you crazy old woman," Frank snarled. "If you knew Gloria was buried out there, why didn't you tell the police instead of doing all of this hokey pokey nonsense?" He took Debbie's arm and urged her after the others. "If I had to listen to that babble every day, I'd go stark, raving mad."

They hurried behind, trying to catch up with the others. "I thought you and Sarah were good friends," Debbie said. "You must have seen Cressie often."

"Sarah knew how I felt. She kept Cressie out of my way."

Debbie reassured herself with the thought that Sarah must have liked and trusted Frank to accommodate him in such a way. Therefore there really was no reason to feel this insane quivering inside of her that grew as they climbed the hill to the graveyard. "Do you think Cressie actually knows that Gloria's buried here?"

"If she does, then the police should be asking her and Sal some very pointed questions," Frank replied. "It's more than likely, though, that she likes to use those weird ways of hers to keep people off balance. It gives her a sense of power."

"I don't understand."

"She says crazy things because she and Sal are different. It's her way of protecting them against being lumped with the other poor, uneducated people in these parts."

Debbie thought back to Cressie's predictions, the apparitions in her house, and the recent vicious attacks directed against her. "I don't agree. Whether it's good or bad, I don't know, but I think Cressie and Sal have a special ability that's uncanny at times."

Debbie and Frank joined the spectators already grouped together in a half circle near a grave. Keith had passed his flashlight to Jenny and held the lantern high while Sal and Scottie dug. Reacting to Kate's comment during the séance, they turned the earth next to her grave by the jasmine climbing her tombstone.

Flashes of light and darkness intermingled and flickered across the faces of Scottie and Sal as they rose and bent with each shovel of dirt. Their shadows, like hovering spirits, cast grotesque figures across the graveyard, while the sound of scraping metal against the earth filled the dark night with cries of protest.

The breeze blew against the loosened soil, carrying the odor of decay to Debbie's nostrils. Specks of dirt scattered across her loafers and against the bottoms of her black slacks. The scene of anxious companions with all the intent of robbing the dark graveyard of its secrets could have come straight from a horror movie, and she was right in the middle of it.

Suddenly an inane satisfaction filled her because, like Norma and Jenny, she had dressed casually for the séance. She didn't have to worry about her clothes while digging up corpses. Debbie momentarily covered her mouth to hide the unwarranted laugh that threatened. She was as bad as Teresa for thinking about her clothes at a time like this, but it was the best defense she had against the quivering jelly filling her insides.

Like a sinister omen, the howl of a dog in the distance lent an eeriness to the already baleful night. A black cloud crossed the half-moon, and Debbie shivered with a strange foreboding.

Hoping to keep her imagination from flying completely out of control, she studied Keith. Lines of strain furrowed deeper in the sides of his mouth while he stood beside the tombstone. As though he could feel her eyes on him and sense her need for comfort, he looked up and met her gaze. For an instant the two of them were alone together, a pair of isolated observers to the raw emotions of the people around them. Then he turned his attention back to Scottie and Sal as they continued to dig.

The time stretched into forever, but the hole

wasn't more than two feet deep when Scottie called, "Wait a minute."

Sal stopped digging. Frank pressed against Debbie, shoving her closer to Eleanor, who stepped toward Teresa. Frank, despite his disclaimers, was no different from the rest. They all wanted to see. No one wanted to miss anything.

"I've hit something." Scottie knelt and gently pushed the dirt aside.

When he raised the skeleton bones of a hand, Debbie's gasp merged with the identical mass reaction. Two rings slid off the end of a finger bone and fell into the dirt. Scottie gingerly picked them up and handed them to Keith before rising and leaning against his shovel.

Dirt filled the grooves of the rings and dulled their shine, but the large diamond in one and the ring of diamonds on the other still caught the lantern's light and flashed defiantly against the darkness of the night.

When Keith showed the rings to Michael, he paled and appeared on the verge of fainting. He didn't say a word or take the rings. Instead he stuck his hands behind his back.

Jenny grabbed at Keith's hand and pulled it so she could see the contents.

"Those are Mama's! That's her buried down there, just like Kate said. I knew it! I knew she was here." Jenny's voice broke while tears rolled down her face. Scottie immediately stepped out of the hole and drew her against his chest while he stroked the back of her head.

Keith said, "We'd better not disturb the area any more than we already have. The police will want to search for clues."

No one responded. Debbie, finally breaking free of the shocked state she had fallen into at the sight of the bones, suggested, "Shall we all go back to the house to wait? I could use a strong cup of hot coffee myself."

"I could use something a little more potent," Frank retorted.

Using her flashlight, Debbie led the procession back down the hill. Teresa and Eleanor stumbled behind her as though they found coming down more difficult than climbing up. Perhaps it was the shock. If Frank's hand hadn't been at Debbie's elbow occasionally, she might be having more trouble herself.

Wondering if the others were reminded of Jenny's accusations that Michael had killed his wife and buried her there, Debbie wished she could see the faces behind her. She had become quite involved with them all in only a matter of months, yet she knew so little about any of them.

The dog howled again, raising goose bumps on her arms. Such a lonely and depressing sound. The dark shadows only increased the eeriness of the night.

As they entered the house, Cressie greeted Debbie with the news that she had already called the police. Debbie nodded, and getting a bottle of Cressie's wine and some glasses from the cabinet, she walked into the dining room. When each guest entered quietly, shock and fear engraved in his face, Debbie asked what he or she preferred to drink and handed each his choice. To Scottie and Jenny she automatically handed Cokes.

Keith and Sal brought up the rear, and while Sal remained by Cressie's side, Debbie asked Keith, "What can I pour you?"

Keith nodded at the coffeepot and joined her. "I left the lantern beside the hole," he explained, and took his cup. "I was watching everyone while they came down, and I think they were all pretty shook up."

"I never dreamed the séance would end like this," Debbie said, looking at her guests from the doorway between the dining room and living room. "Look where everyone's sitting. In the same places they sat before. It's uncanny."

She felt a waft of warm air on her neck and looked at Keith standing beside her. He was drinking his coffee and staring at Michael, who was in such shock he appeared almost corpselike himself. Then Debbie caught the faint aroma of jasmine. She could sense excitement and pleasure in the air.

A siren shrilled in the distance, coming closer. The sound seemed ridiculous in the circumstances. Why were the police in such a rush when the body had been in the same spot for years? Still, it wasn't every day strange bodies were dug up from graveyards. Or maybe the police were afraid some of the diggers might flee before they could be questioned. This was big news, finding Gloria's body after six years, and the police would want to make the most of it. Debbie studied the circle of guests and noted their unrest.

Norma, frowning and clearly worried, spoke a few soft words to Michael. He remained deathly pale, cheeks almost sunken in his finely boned face, lips pressed together.

Jenny, on the other hand, did nothing to control her emotions. Sobbing, she sought Scottie's arms for comfort. He handed her his handkerchief after wiping her face when the tears slowed.

Teresa sat tragically pale, the picture of discreet

mourning. Yet she needed both trembling hands to drink her wine.

Frank and Eleanor sat side by side, neither speaking. Yet Frank, his mustache quivering, kept casting speculative glances at the rigid woman beside him. Debbie hadn't been surprised when he took wine, but she had been when Eleanor had asked for it, saying she was chilled.

The approaching siren grated against already raw nerves.

Finally Eleanor broke the deathly quiet in the room. "I hope you're satisfied, Norma."

"Satisfied? About what?" Norma asked, looking up from Michael.

"It's all your fault we're mixed up in this dreadful matter, the police, the scandal. It won't help my bank one bit. If you hadn't wanted the séance—"

Jenny straightened up from Scottie. "It's Kate who told us where we could find Mama. If she hadn't told us tonight, we might have gone on wondering forever. I'm glad we held the séance! I'm glad we finally know!"

"I must admit, since the police discovered Mother's car in Dallas, I never expected we'd find her body here," Teresa chimed in.

"But you've told me you agree with me." Jenny sniffled and wiped her face before continuing. "You said you thought Michael had something to do with Mama's disappearance. And when I had my accidents a couple of months ago, you agreed that Michael could be responsible and said you and I both should be very careful. Scottie's been protecting me . . ."

"I wondered why he was either always underfoot or on the phone," Teresa chided. "You were barely recovered from your fall when he seemed to annex himself to you. I thought you might be finally growing up and getting interested in boys like a normal girl of sixteen instead of moaning over Nacho and Mother and what Michael's doing next."

Norma jumped up, anger in her eyes. "I'm sick and tired of both of you accusing Michael of these things. How can you believe them, what's more repeat them, after all the things he's done for you?"

"Norma, you're upset," Debbie said, not wanting another fight.

Norma ignored her. "Especially you, Teresa, when Michael supports you without any cost whatsoever to yourself while you get your divorce. He even paid your gambling debts."

Teresa remained quiet, but her eyes glittered in response and color filled her face.

Norma directed her gaze to Jenny. "And you . . . always moaning around about your mother. What I want to know is, what did she ever do for you besides give you birth?"

"Don't you say anything against my mother," Jenny raged, tears completely forgotten in her anger.

"Your precious mother, who made Michael's life hell by leaving him to do all the work at the stables and raise you kids while she played around. She taunted him with her boyfriends, and spent the money he worked hard for like it was water. Sure she was sweet to you, when she had time for you. Sure she brought you lovely presents when she returned from all those damned trips. But when did she ever take time to really love and care for you like a mother should and like you deserve?"

Norma stopped a moment when tears welled up

and trickled down Jenny's tightly drawn face. "When Michael made that business trip to Dallas, he also stopped by to see a friend who had a beautiful horse for sale. Since all you seemed to care about was horses, he wanted to buy you that animal, one you could be proud of and maybe jump in shows. But you couldn't act like any other normal teenager. You wouldn't have her because you wanted your mother's horse, Nacho. Always your mother."

Norma's voice rose as she spoke, and she paused to take several calming breaths. "That night after Michael had been to see the horse and we went to the barn to plan the surprise . . . we were both so excited. We thought you'd be thrilled. And what did you do?"

Norma turned on Debbie. "You accused Michael and me of having caused Jenny's fall down the back stairs. You thought we would deliberately harm her when all we wanted was to surprise her with a beautiful horse."

"Oh, Norma, I'm sorry. Why didn't you or Michael explain?" Debbie asked, sincerely regretting her suspicion.

"Neither Michael nor I need to explain our actions to you."

"I didn't notice a new horse," Keith said.

"I didn't get it because Jenny didn't want it," Michael spoke up.

"But knowing what Jenny saw, you could have told us and stopped the speculation," Keith said.

"I knew we had done nothing wrong, and I'm tired of all the accusations every time I turn around. I don't need to defend myself to you, to Debbie, or to anyone," Michael asserted as the siren came screaming up the driveway to halt in front of the house.

"I hope you're right," Keith said softly. "I truly hope you're right."

Debbie went to answer the doorbell. She already felt drained, and the night wasn't over. She wished she could undo all the hurtful words slung out this evening and repair the damage to friendships. At the same time she knew it was best to get all the information, hurt, and accusations in the open. This was what she had hoped to accomplish, by getting everyone together. But she had wanted answers for herself, not pain for someone else.

Opening the door, she knew there was no going back. Cressie was right: the séance had brought far more than anyone dreamed.

Two hours later a defeated-looking Michael left with the police. They were holding him in custody until they could examine the gravesite in daylight. Because he had the most to gain from Gloria's death, the police wanted him close at hand for further questioning.

The investigating officer warned before he left Debbie's that a guard would remain at the graveyard to make certain no one disturbed anything.

"I'll hire a lawyer, and we'll be down as soon as possible," Norma pledged. As Michael walked out with the officers and the door closed behind them, she turned to the remaining guests. "I hope you're pleased with yourselves," she accused.

"I'm sorry about Michael," Debbie said, "but we had to tell the police everything we knew. How else can they clear this matter up?"

"And you had to tell them everything, didn't you, even the mail being stolen out of your box, the rock through your window, the punctured tires. You even insinuated that Michael left that dead cat on your doorstep."

"Now wait a minute," Debbie countered defensively. "I told them Cressie identified the cat as belonging to Michael."

"How could you possibly think any of those things had anything to do with Gloria's death or with Michael?" Norma raged, hands clenched at her sides.

"Someone did take a shot at Debbie," Keith said. "And Gloria's body was found on her land. We don't know that there isn't a connection to all of this."

"I wished I'd never sold you this place, never laid eyes on you." Norma stared at Debbie for a moment, then turned to Teresa. "It looks like you have the responsibility of Jenny for the time being. Let's hope she doesn't start accusing you of all sorts of things or you might find yourself in the cell next to Michael."

Jenny reached for Scottie's hand.

"And you, Jenny," Norma cried. "I hope you find the satisfaction you've hoped for once your mother was found, and Michael—"

Her voice broke, but she gathered herself together quickly. "Michael's gone because of your wild imagination and lies to the police."

"That's enough," Keith snapped.

"Is it, Keith? Is it? Michael and I thought you were a friend, someone to help Teresa in her trauma with the divorce, and to talk with Jenny . . . but you sold us out, didn't you? You sold us like Judas for a few pieces of silver."

"Wait a minute, Norma, I know you're upset. That's understandable, and I've tried to be lenient, but you're going too far," Keith objected.

"You sold us out for exciting firsthand stories about Kate's ghost, so your book would hit the best-seller list, like the last one. Well, I hope you choke on it, every last word. I hope Debbie sees that you're just using her and will forget all about her once you get what you want and go to Virginia next year."

Norma looked at Debbie. "I hope you suffer all the agonies of loneliness while you sit in this dreadful house all by yourself once Keith's gone, suffer like I'm going to if they blame Michael for something he didn't do and lock him away because of your accusations." She choked back a harsh laugh. "Three dreadful old women in a row, Kate, Sarah, and now you."

Finally breaking into heartrending sobs, Norma turned and ran out the front door, slamming it behind her.

Debbie was torn between going after Norma and remaining where she was, locked in her own pain from Norma's verbal lashes. She had blasted them all on Michael's behalf, but her charges had caused shattering results.

Debbie looked at Keith, wanting to get some reassurance that he wasn't just using her for his own gain, as Norma had suggested. His lips were pressed together and his body was rigid. When he returned her gaze, Debbie could read nothing in his eyes. He brushed his fingers against her chin and whispered, "We'll talk later."

The sound of the racing engine faded into the distance before Eleanor spoke. "Norma always was the emotional type. That's how she got mixed up with that first husband of hers. She felt sorry for him and thought she could help. He almost destroyed her. From the looks of things, Michael might accomplish what he didn't."

"At least she has feelings, which is more than I can say for some folks I know," Frank commented, and walked to the dining room with his empty glass.

"I don't care what Norma says," Jenny wailed. "I'm glad we know the truth about Mama. I'm glad Kate told us where to find her."

"Kate nothing," Teresa sniffed. "Like I told the police, Cressie's trying to scare everyone. Those words came out of her mouth. She uses this ghost business to manipulate people. She could even teach my father-in-law, the rich and conniving Papa Wymans, a thing or two."

"The police didn't seem interested when you told them they should ask Cressie how she knew the body was buried there," Frank said, sitting back down, his glass once more filled. "It was almost as though they considered us all loonies anyway to even participate in a séance and Cressie a lucky nut to have guessed right."

"That's all a pack of lies and you know it, Frank Johnson." Cressie stormed into the room, hands on her hips. "People know I can communicate with the spirits, and they know Kate walks the floors of this house. And knowin' neither Sal nor I have anythin' to gain from Gloria's death, they used good sense and didn't pay no heed to Miss Teresa's accusations." Cressie glared at Teresa. "A word of wisdom to you, my girl. You're up against more than you reckon. Miss Kate protects Debbie 'cause she has plans for her."

"I can't believe this insane nonsense," Teresa said, rising. "Come on, Jenny, let's go home."

The teenager didn't move but with wide eyes asked her sister, "What's going to happen to me if they lock Michael up?"

"You should have thought of that before you began this whole thing," Teresa taunted. "You'll be my responsibility, as Norma said."

"You don't want me. I'll just be in your way."

"I'll be here. I'm your friend," Scottie interjected.

"That's not the same thing." Jenny pleaded with Cressie, "Ask Kate what's going to happen to me."

"Oh, for heaven's sake. Stop it, Jenny, do you hear me? Cressie can't ask Kate anything. Kate is dead." Teresa's raised voice wobbled.

Debbie felt a tug on the back of her head, and the scent of jasmine swirled around her. The very air she breathed vibrated with anticipation. The next tug hurt.

Knowing she was about to throw away her credibility, Debbie cleared her throat and said, "You're wrong, Teresa. I live here and I know. Kate very much exists in this house. I've smelled her jasmine scent, felt her presence, and even on occasion seen her ghostlike form. The night someone threw the rock through my window, threatening me, she warned me with wind chimes, so don't ever take her ghost lightly."

"Debbie, why didn't you ever tell me you'd seen her?" Keith exclaimed, his face lighting up with eagerness.

"Come on, Jenny." Teresa grabbed Jenny's hand and pulled her up. "We're getting out of here." Pushing Jenny's reluctant form ahead of her, Teresa said, "I wish I could say the evening's been fun, but it hasn't."

"I'll see you tomorrow," Scottie promised Jenny when she looked back over her shoulder at him. "Call if you need me."

"Let me know if there's anything I can do to help," Debbie said, following close behind.

Teresa's eyes narrowed, and she laughed bitterly. "Get serious. Haven't you created enough havoc since you arrived in Nacogdoches?"

"I'll see you tomorrow," Keith called as he joined Debbie at the front door.

Teresa barely spared them a glance when she climbed in her car and drove off.

"I think I'll be off, too," Frank said, and waited until Keith moved so he could get through. "I'm still interested in buying your place, Debbie. Just let me know when and how much." He waved as he strolled down to his pickup.

"I knew this was a mistake," Eleanor whispered as she walked through the front door. "Never in my life could I imagine such a night. How's it all going to end?" She shook her head and opened the door to her Cadillac.

Debbie and Keith stood in the doorway, watching the red taillights fade into the darkness. At last Debbie closed the front door and leaned thankfully against the strong wooden support.

Scottie walked up to Keith. "What do you think's going to happen to Michael?"

Keith rubbed the back of his neck and studied the teenager. "I think Michael's in for a rough time of it, but just because they found Gloria's body doesn't mean Michael killed her. The police have to be able to come up with a case, and with what we know now, a good lawyer could probably get him off."

"And Jenny?" Scottie pressed.

"I think she may find life a little difficult at first, but with good friends, she'll be better off in the long run. She knows at last she's in no way responsible for her mother's disappearance."

"It's been quite a night," Scottie said. "I'm going to bed. I need to get up early so I can go to Jenny's."

"Good night," Debbie called, watching him mount the front stairs to his room.

"Now for our little talk," Keith said, taking her hand and leading her into the living room.

"Sal and I are going to bed, too," Cressie said from the dining room doorway. "I've put away ev'rythin' that needs it, and I'll clean the rest up in the mornin'."

"I'll see you in the morning," Debbie agreed. Feeling completely drained, she collapsed on the sofa.

"There's just one thing, Miss Debbie," Cressie said, blue veins at her temples standing out like marked roadways.

Debbie caught her breath with dread. "What's that?"

"You be careful. All is not what it seems."

"Meaning?" Keith charged when Debbie didn't speak.

Cressie's blue eyes glowed like crystals when she spoke to Debbie. "The black cloud of danger hovers all around you. The forces be mixed. Fear and hate. Listen to Miss Kate." Cressie turned, and joining Sal, the two went out the back.

"Can I get you anything?" Keith asked. "You look like you can't take on much more."

Debbie shook her head, hoping she didn't look as bad as she felt at that moment. "No thanks."

Keith sat beside her and pulled her into his arms. She delighted in the pleasure and warmth his body provided and in the security his encircling arms furnished. She sank into the tenderness his butterfly kisses created while his lips caressed her temple, her eyelids, her cheek, her neck, and finally her eager, wanting mouth. She drowned in the desire he ignited within her, knowing nothing could wash away her fears like the charms of the man she loved so dearly.

A short time later Keith drew away and helped her straighten her clothes. He kissed the tip of her nose. "I should get on home. With Scottie in the house, you should be safe from anyone but Kate."

Debbie smiled tiredly. "Are you making fun of me?"

He kissed her eyelids. "No. We need to talk, though, and I intend for you to tell me all about her. But not tonight. You need to get some sleep. This evening has been difficult."

"I noticed."

Keith flicked her lightly with his finger. "Naughty, naughty."

She laughed as he pulled her to her feet. He wrapped his arm around her shoulders, and they walked to the front door.

"I'll see you tomorrow, and we'll have that talk."

Her happiness faded as she recalled Norma's accusations. "What about that teaching position you've been offered in Virginia next year?"

Keith brushed her lips with his. "That's part of what I want to discuss. But not tonight. You need sleep."

Her short respite of happiness ended. "There's something that's been bothering me."

"Tomorrow, Debbie, tomorrow. You're tired and at the end of your rope."

"Something Cressie said made me start wondering. Can you think of any reason why Teresa might want to drive me out of Nacogdoches?"

His brows drew together. "No. Teresa would never live in a small town. There's not enough excitement for her. And whether you live here or not would be immaterial to her."

"Then do you think Michael is responsible?"

Keith frowned. "It's funny, but even after all that has happened tonight, I still have no idea."

"Do you think it could be Frank? They did find that dead vagrant on his land a few months after Gloria disappeared."

Keith's eyes narrowed. "Maybe you'd better tell me about that one. I don't think I've heard about any dead vagrant."

When Debbie finished, Keith drew her close to him and hugged her tightly. "We're both tired and not able to think straight. We're jumping to all kinds of conclusions. We'll talk again tomorrow. Go to bed now and sleep."

He kissed her, and once more she succumbed to the desire he could so easily bring. He pulled back, and not giving her time to delay him again, he walked down the front steps to his car. "I'll call you tomorrow."

Debbie watched his car drive away and, recalling Cressie's warning, whispered to the soft murmur of the breeze in the leaves of the majestic oak, "What if there is no tomorrow?"

20

Debbie turned off the lights and slowly climbed the stairs. The evening's events had left her totally exhausted.

Why wouldn't Keith explain about his teaching offer in Virginia? Was he afraid she'd make a scene? She could, but she wouldn't. Like Kate, she'd live with her memories.

She left her clothes where they fell, pulled on her nightgown, and crawled into bed. Sleep claimed her almost instantly. . . .

Debbie was cold. Half-awake, she reached for another blanket. The dark room felt like a cavern, musty and chilly. The very thought shocked her awake. She lay listening, her eyes piercing the blackness, wondering how long she'd slept.

The aroma of jasmine gradually overcame the coldness and mustiness. As the scent increased, the low tingling of wind chimes began. The noise grew louder and louder. When the sweetness of jasmine was so thick she could barely breathe, and the chimes so loud she held her hands over her ears, Debbie saw the gauzy apparition of a woman in her bedroom doorway.

Startled, she stared. Kate had brought the wind chimes to warn her, the same as she had the night someone had thrown the rock through her window. This time, however, the danger must be greater.

Scottie would help her. Debbie pushed aside the covers—and stopped. If someone were in the house, that person wanted her. If her brother continued to sleep, maybe he would be safe. She couldn't risk Scottie's life to save her own.

Quietly she reached for the phone by her bedside. It was hard to see, the room was so dark, but when a breeze from out of nowhere brushed the drape forward enough so she could make out the buttons on her phone, she called Keith.

He wouldn't believe her, but she had to try. After two rings, his sleepy voice answered. "Someone's in the house. Kate's in the doorway, and the wind chimes are ringing," Debbie whispered hurriedly.

"Go to Scottie's room. I'll be right there."

He hung up before she could explain she wouldn't endanger her brother.

She listened carefully. Footsteps thudded against the worn carpet of the front stairs. She couldn't lie here cowering, waiting for the intruder to reach her room. No, it would be best to meet the person on the stairs, where she would have the advantage of height.

As Debbie slipped across her room, she searched for some sort of weapon. Nothing. Everything was neat and orderly. But the aroma of jasmine gave her an idea. She picked up her aerosol can of hairspray. If she could get close enough, it might work—since such a bold, arrogant action would be unexpected and might give her an opportunity to act.

As she stepped into the hall, a waft of warm air fanned across her cheek. A few short months ago she would have laughed at the idea that the ghost of Kate stood nearby, but tonight the conviction brought comfort and steadied her.

Debbie reached the stairs and saw a form halfway up. She flicked the switch. Looking up at her, gun in hand, was Eleanor Farmsworth. Eleanor blinked, trying to adjust to the sudden intrusion of light, but despite her discomfort the gun never wavered. It was pointed directly at Debbie.

As the shock of finding Eleanor raced through her body, Debbie remained poised, the can hidden in her hand.

The odor of jasmine circled and swirled down the stairway. Eleanor cleared her throat. "I see you heard me."

"Kate woke me. She knew someone was in the house." Debbie couldn't believe her eyes. Gone was the perfectly groomed and attired banker, replaced by a shabbily dressed woman in a torn, stained sweatsuit. Her pale face lacked makeup, there was a streak of dirt across one cheek, and her hair flew in every direction. Eleanor gave a laugh that sent chills up Debbie's spine.

"Why? Eleanor, why?"

"It's you. You're evil. Since you came to this town, nothing has been the same. Our peaceful place has turned into a den of ugliness, of vile intrigue, a cauldron for wicked spirits." The banker slowly took another step up the stairs.

Eleanor sounded like Cressie. Her heart pounding, Debbie said, "I haven't done anything but try to be friends with everyone while getting on with my own life."

Eleanor's eyes narrowed. "You've brought dishonor to the Farmsworth name. You told people Herman's ancestor married that hideous Kate. You even laughed and joked about it in the bank. And tonight you had that crazy woman and her husband tell everyone at the séance that Farmsworth was a no-good scoundrel. He wasn't. He was a good man, a loving husband."

"That wasn't Herman, Eleanor. That was Henry, someone who lived long ago." The jasmine scent steadily grew stronger. Kate's presence gave Debbie strength.

Eleanor stepped closer and coughed. "She said to remove 'the Farmsworth' from the graveyard. I heard her. It's you that's brought this disaster down on us. It's you that's brought destruction."

"Kate meant Henry. He must be buried out there."

Eleanor's lips curved into a sly smile, and a look of cunning flooded her blue eyes. "Herman's buried there with Gloria. I know. That old vagrant and I put him there."

Debbie's mouth opened, but she didn't know what to say. Eleanor took another step. Debbie wanted to turn and run, but if she did, Eleanor was certain to fire. And there was Scottie. He would run into the hallway at the noise, and this deranged woman would shoot him as well. No, she had to stay with her plan, weak as it seemed.

"It was all Gloria's fault," Eleanor continued. "She never was happy with what she had but used her looks and her grasping ways to take from everyone around her. She had Frank once, a long time ago when she was but a girl. That's when I knew he wasn't good enough for me and I married Herman."

"I've always heard you say how much you and Herman loved each other."

Jasmine seemed to replace the oxygen in the air.

Eleanor's eyes started to water. "When she was tired of all the available men, she turned her greedy little hands on my Herman. He didn't know what he was doing. He loved me, but he stole and spent the bank's money . . . on her! I covered for him, but when I went home unexpectedly one afternoon and found them in my bed together, I had enough. I shot them both."

"You killed both of them?" Debbie's heart raced as she stared at the older woman.

"I knew their habits. It was easy to cover up. I had that vagrant help me bury them in the closest graveyard. I thought if anyone ever discovered their bones, they wouldn't question them. You expect to find bodies in graves. We planted the jasmine vine, knowing the Slavanias and Sarah would believe someone planted a homage for Kate. And it worked, although Sarah asked a few questions for a while. Then she didn't talk to anyone."

Hoping to trick Eleanor into complacency so she wouldn't be expecting anything, Debbie said, "That was clever of you."

"We carried the bodies in Herman's car. That's how his blood got there. The next day I told everyone Herman had taken some money for a business loan. Then I drove his car out in the woods and left it for someone to find."

Eleanor stopped, and Debbie asked, "Why are you telling me all of this?" She had to keep Eleanor talking.

"Everyone believed me. Why not? I'm Eleanor Farmsworth. Herman missing with money also explained the discrepancy from the bank. As to Gloria, with her wicked ways, all I had to do was call her house and ask Jenny when she expected her mother back from Dallas, and Jenny automatically assumed her mother had already gone on her trip."

"But Gloria's car?"

"I drove the car myself to Dallas and left it in a slum area. I knew a sports car wouldn't stay there long."

"Did you kill the vagrant on Frank's land?"

"His demands grew completely out of hand."

"These tricks on me, why did you do those?"

Eleanor coughed again, her eyes watering more. The jasmine was as thick as fog now. "I intended to drive you away. I made that phone call to the motel the day you saw the property, but I never had the chance to do more. Someone else seemed determined to do the job for me. I waited to see what would happen."

"But you have a good idea who, don't you?"

Eleanor gasped, struggling to breathe as she stepped closer. "My guess would be Teresa. She's like her mother. Grasping hands, wanting whatever she sees no matter who gets hurt."

"But her sister?"

"With Jenny dead and Michael blamed, Teresa would get it all, but you kept getting in her way, making people believe Jenny and not what Teresa wanted them to think. Now it's your turn. When they dig Gloria's body out tomorrow, they'll find Herman's as well, and they'll know. It'll all be over."

"But why shoot me? You'll never get away with it."

Eleanor gave an eerie, wild laugh. "I'm not. Kate's ghost is going to frighten you so much, you'll trip and fall down the stairs. That seems only fair. After all, it's your fault everything's spoiled now. You need to be punished. Just like Gloria and Herman, you must pay for your evil ways."

There was a tug on her hair, and Debbie knew then what she must do. "Don't you understand, I was serious earlier. Kate's here now. She'll protect me. Can't you see her? She's behind me. Her jasmine is everywhere. Can't you smell it?"

Eleanor grasped her throat. "I . . . I can't breathe."

Debbie stepped closer. Only a couple of steps separated them. She whispered menacingly, "Look up. Look up behind me. See Kate? Can you see her there watching you, waiting for you?"

Eleanor coughed. "No. You're not fooling me."

"I'm not lying. Kate's there, protecting me. She won't let you harm me. Look. Look behind me."

Eleanor looked up, and her eyes widened. She screamed, a high, piercing shrill that sent nerve-racking ripples of fear through Debbie. But she wouldn't get a better chance. She sprayed the hairspray straight into Eleanor's eyes and at the same time grabbed for the gun.

Eleanor let go of the weapon without a struggle and, still screaming, turned to flee down the stairs. Then Eleanor was falling, rolling faster and faster. She reached the bottom and stopped, a broken and discarded toy.

"Debbie!" Scottie exclaimed.

Debbie turned, expecting to see her brother at the top of the stairs. Instead she saw the wispy outline of a woman fade away and heard the dying sound of the wind chimes. She had been taunting Eleanor, playing on the earlier conversations. She had not expected Kate actually to appear, but the ghost had followed Debbie's instructions to the letter.

"Scottie, get out of bed and come down here."
Debbie descended the stairs slowly, keeping a close
watch on Eleanor.

"What's going on? Was it you who gave that gosh-
awful scream?" Scottie said, running down the stairs
behind her.

"No. It was Eleanor. Quick, I want you to phone to
see if Keith's left yet and then call the police." Debbie
held the gun on Eleanor in case the woman stirred.
She wanted no more trouble.

Cautiously she knelt down and checked Eleanor for
a pulse. Finding one, she sighed with relief. At least
she wouldn't have Eleanor's death on her conscience.
"She's alive. I'll watch her. You go make those phone
calls, and tell the police to send an ambulance."

Scottie disappeared down the hall.

Debbie's hand began to shake. Reaction was setting in, and she walked over to sit on the steps where
she could rest her elbows on her knees and hold the
gun with her hands.

First Michael and now Eleanor had their lives
twisted forever. Was that the fear and hate Cressie
mentioned, or was there more? Debbie's shoulders
sagged with relief when she heard Keith call her
name as he raced through the front door. At least now
there would be a today and a tomorrow.

When Debbie woke, it was afternoon. Sunlight slipped
through the drapes and cast a golden glow throughout
her room. The world seemed a much better place.

She relived her conversation with Eleanor as the
banker left in the ambulance under police custody.
Eleanor had regained consciousness soon after the

police arrived, and she'd murmured, "Why didn't you listen? Why didn't you heed my warning?"

"At the motel?" Debbie had asked.

"Norma told me you were coming into the bank. She said you were the image of Kate. I had a terrible premonition and I called, trying to talk you out of buying. You wouldn't listen."

Debbie hadn't wanted to tell Eleanor how close she'd come to succeeding.

Eleanor had pointed a finger at Debbie. "You're evil. You work with that devil Kate. You should be dead, but the black wickedness protected you. Everything would have gone on as before, and I would have been safe, if it weren't for you and Kate." Eleanor had closed her eyes then and drifted into her own world of silence as the police and ambulance took her away.

Debbie had related the events to Keith and the police when they'd first arrived, while Eleanor was still unconscious. As he'd held her and comforted her, she'd also told them about her suspicions of Teresa and Eleanor's confirmation. Neither the police nor Keith had said much, but Keith had kissed her, telling her it was all over now. She was safe.

He had gone with the police, leaving her and Scottie to have an early breakfast with Cressie and Sal. "The color of fear is gone," Cressie had said, "and the evil from the recent past rests. The color of hate still hovers, and the evil must be corrected. Be prepared."

Exhausted, Debbie had shaken her head in protest and gone to bed. Now she was awake again, the day bright and sunny, and she was eager to hear what was happening.

Downstairs she found Cressie popping black-eyed peas for dinner. "Where's Scottie?"

"He's gone to see Jenny."

Debbie poured herself a cup of coffee. "Has Keith called?"

Cressie nodded. "He said he'd call back this evenin'."

Disappointment filled her. She knew this meant Keith didn't intend to see her today. She sat at the table and watched Cressie. "Have you heard anything?"

"Keith said they've released Michael, but Eleanor's still in the hospital. The police found Herman's body. They took the remains and left a short while ago."

Debbie looked out the window at the graveyard. The dark earth spotted the recently disturbed graves, but all signs of activity were gone. The sentinel oak stood alone, guarding the dead and reaching toward the blue sky. The jasmine vine, its roots destroyed, wilted on Kate's stone.

Debbie turned back to the kitchen. "I wonder who sent Eleanor that love letter from Herman to Gloria. She starting breaking up at the restaurant that evening."

"I did."

Debbie's brows shot up in surprise. "*You* did?"

Cressie nodded. "Miss Sarah knew before they disappeared that they were sneakin' around together, but when she tackled Gloria, that young lady laughed and taunted her with the letter. That's when Miss Sarah warned her. Miss Gloria laughed at her spookiness. We never saw her again."

"But how did Miss Sarah get the letter, and why did you wait to send it to Eleanor?"

Cressie seasoned the peas and put them on to cook. "Gloria left the letter here the last time she came, although if the truth were known, I imagine Miss Sarah slipped it in her pocket without tellin'.

Not long after, she had a slight stroke and didn't mix much anymore with folks. When she knew she was dyin', she told me you'd be comin' and would remedy matters she was too old and sick to take care of. She gave me the envelope addressed to Eleanor and told me to mail it when I knew the time was right. I wasn't to say anythin' about it."

"But when did you know to mail it?"

"Miss Sarah told me when." Cressie gave Debbie her sly smile.

Cressie's smile didn't bother Debbie this time. She was getting used to her strange ways. The more she considered it, the more she realized the house wouldn't be the same if Cressie and Sal weren't here. Actually, the fact that Cressie said Sarah told her when to mail the envelope seemed perfectly acceptable.

"If Miss Sarah thought Eleanor had done something to Gloria and Herman, why didn't she notify the police?"

"I didn't say she thought Eleanor had done somethin'. She was suspicious and didn't feel right 'bout the whole mess, but Miss Sarah couldn't prove anythin'. There were no bodies found. But she knew if anyone were blamed, it would be Michael." Cressie winked. "She were right, weren't she?"

"I thought she didn't care much for Michael?"

"She didn't, but that didn't mean she thought he killed Gloria. No, the fact is she wasn't sure Gloria was dead. She thought maybe they run off together."

"How come none of you were suspicious about the sudden planting of jasmine by Kate's grave?"

"Sal worked other places as he does now. We thought Miss Sarah must have planted it. She must have thought Sal did. And of course, Miss Kate could have put it there herself, for all we knew. She has her ways, she does."

Eleanor had been smart, and knowing everyone's habits had made it easy for her to get away with the crime. That was the way it was in small towns; people really knew their neighbors.

For the first time the truth of Eleanor's statement that no one would suspect her thoroughly sank home. She was a pillar of the community, the matriarch of the social set, a true southern lady with white gloves and steel beneath.

But except for the call, she'd denied pulling any of the tricks on Debbie. Someone else had done them first. Teresa had the time, the self-centeredness, and the gumption. She'd come back to Nacogdoches at the beginning of summer. According to Norma, that was about the time Jenny had started expressing her extreme fears about Michael. Debbie's arrival and strong defense of Jenny must have created serious problems for Teresa. For her plan to work, she had to stop Debbie.

Debbie massaged her forehead. She hated to think Teresa would try to kill her own sister, but she was the one nearest Jenny when both accidents occurred. Furthermore, Teresa had quite capably tried to discredit Debbie in the hospital by claiming the accidents hadn't started until after Debbie arrived.

Debbie began to pace. Teresa wanted Michael accused of killing Jenny and arrested. That way Teresa could become the administrator of the estate. Once Gloria was declared legally dead and with Jenny dead, Teresa could sell the property and start over elsewhere with a great deal of money. She'd have ready funds to feed her gambling habit.

She'd probably want Keith for the same reason.

Besides being handsome, considerate, and caring, he also had nationwide recognition and the ability to earn a great deal of money from his books. She could have pulled all the tricks, including shooting at Debbie. And if she'd followed Keith when he had picked up the horses, and watched Keith's and Debbie's interlude at the swimming hole, the shooting could have been an act of retaliation.

Unfortunately, as Keith and the police both had pointed out this morning, there was no proof Teresa had done any of the acts.

Debbie reached for the phone. She had promised herself if she ever found out, she would take action. Now was the time.

"Hello, Teresa? This is Debbie. I'd like you to come over. We have a few things to settle between us."

"You've got to be kidding."

"No, I'm perfectly serious. In fact, if you don't come, I won't hesitate to contact your ex-husband and tell him what you've been doing here in Nacogdoches. That might affect your divorce settlement."

Teresa hesitated, so Debbie turned the screw tighter. "Having recently been through a divorce, I'm sure he would welcome learning you've broken a few laws."

"You have no proof of that."

"Don't I? Why don't you come over and we'll talk." Debbie could almost hear Teresa's mind turn over as she considered ways to avoid the confrontation.

"Okay, but it'd better be quick."

Debbie smiled as she set down the phone.

Cressie shook her head, her hands on her hips. "I reckon you got to do it, but be careful. And mind, Sal and I'll be in the kitchen here if you need us." She went to the back door and yelled for Sal.

Debbie considered her strategy carefully. By the time the front doorbell rang, she was ready. She opened the door, and the two women stared at each other. Then Teresa shrugged.

"Keith's at the house. I can't stay long."

Debbie led the way to the back parlor and motioned for Teresa to sit. "This shouldn't take long. You know about Eleanor, since I understand Michael's been released, but do you know that she accused you of being the one who played all of those nasty tricks on me, trying to drive me away?"

Teresa relaxed on the sofa, obviously intending to enjoy herself. "Eleanor's stark, raving nuts. Her mind's gone. They're taking her to the loony bin. Whatever she may have told you, no one will believe it now."

This wasn't going at all like Debbie had hoped. She would have to try a stronger approach. "I know you changed the time on my notice at school that day, probably when you were visiting Carolyn at the college."

"So?"

"You're also the one who took my mail, and that's a federal offense."

"Prove it."

"You punctured my tires the day you had lunch with Carolyn at the college and later left that cat and note on my doorstep."

"If this is all you have to say, I'm leaving." Teresa rose.

"Why did you shoot at me?"

Teresa smiled. "Keith's mine."

"Then you're admitting—"

"Nothing. I'm just telling you I intend to marry Keith."

Debbie felt a strong tug on the back of her hair.

Kate was ready, as she had been when Eleanor came. "The night you threw the note through my window, did you know Kate warned me you were here?"

Teresa laughed. "Not ghosts again. I thought we finished with that nonsense at the séance. You're starting to sound as loony as Eleanor and Cressie."

Debbie walked to the fireplace, near the hidden brick opener. "Did you know that Kate appeared last night when Eleanor came here to kill me? She frightened Eleanor so badly, she fell down the stairs trying to escape."

"You don't really expect me to believe that, do you?"

"You said Eleanor had lost her mind. Haven't you heard what she said when she regained consciousness?"

Teresa's hand twitched at her side. "You're trying to say a ghost had something to do with her losing her mind?"

"Haven't you heard?"

Teresa bit her lower lip and looked down at the rug. "Keith did tell me that when Eleanor regained consciousness, she ranted and raved about the evil spirits corrupting the world, even her poor Herman." She looked directly at Debbie. "She can't tell anyone anything. You're wasting your time. Now I need to get back."

Debbie pressed the brick, and the door to the hidden room slid open. "Kate's father hid people in this room. No one could ever find them. A person could stay there forever with no one for company except the ghosts."

Teresa stepped away, a wary expression on her face. "You're as crazy as Eleanor."

"Kate's waiting for you. She protects me."

"You're stark, raving nuts, too." Teresa edged farther away.

A cold draft blew through the room, and Teresa glanced around uneasily. The aroma of jasmine mingled with a musty odor and swirled like a small whirlwind encircling the women. Fear shone from Teresa's eyes when she stared at Debbie.

Debbie walked closer to Teresa, speaking softly, menacingly, all the way. "The ghosts are here. Kyle and Kate are waiting for you . . . waiting for you to join them in the room below. They protect me, and they know what you've done. You can't escape."

"I don't believe you. You're making this up."

Suddenly the sound of wind chimes, ringing from below, filtered into the room, louder and louder.

Teresa turned, fear evident in every strained muscle of her body. "I'm going. I'm not going to stand for this."

The rug slipped out from under her feet and she fell to the floor. She scooted backward on her butt, using her feet and hands to claw herself away from Debbie and the opened doorway to the basement. She was frantic to reach the hall and escape.

"I told you the ghosts protect me. You can't harm me ever again." Debbie stepped closer. "And what's more, I'll protect Jenny from you, any way I can."

Teresa's violet eyes were wide with terror when she finally managed to scramble to her feet.

"Remember, Teresa, Eleanor may have snapped at the strain, but people know about you, about your tricks. Kate knows—"

"Stay away from me!" Teresa turned and ran down the hall. Moments later the front door slammed behind her.

Debbie looked up to see Cressie standing in the kitchen doorway watching her.

The housekeeper smiled. "I guess you took care of

her without any problem. I see the color of hate is gone."

"Not me, Cressie. It was Kate."

The two women laughed.

Cressie left to return to Sal in the kitchen, and Debbie walked over to push the brick that closed the hidden room. Teresa wouldn't be playing any more vicious tricks on her.

Recalling all her worries and anxieties the past few months, she was surprised at how quickly the end had come. She wondered what she could have done differently so that things wouldn't have gone so far, but it seemed as if the whole situation had been destined to happen.

A short time later Debbie dragged out the footlocker she had brought from her mother's and searched its contents. She lost herself in her own family history until Cressie called her for dinner. She could barely restrain her excitement at what she had discovered, but she wanted Keith to be the first to know.

At the table Scottie was full of the events at the Winthrope-Townsend house and mentioned Jenny had decided to let Michael buy her the new horse. Nacho was getting old and deserved an easier life.

He also told them Keith had spent most of the afternoon talking with Michael, Norma, and Teresa and was having dinner there. Scottie seemed completely unaware of Debbie's pain at his revelations, and that her appetite had suddenly vanished.

Between mouthfuls he said, "I'm going to Jenny's from school tomorrow. I'll have dinner over there."

Scottie didn't mention Teresa's visit with Debbie, and she wondered if Teresa had told anyone where she had gone. If not, Debbie didn't intend to say anything for the time being.

An hour later Scottie was studying upstairs and Debbie sat reading the next volume of Kate's journals. The phone rang, and she answered. Keith's voice was on the other end.

"I'm sorry I didn't get back to you sooner."

Debbie wrapped the cord around her finger. "I understand you've been busy at Jenny's."

"Yes, and I think I'm making headway. I'm still here, so I can't talk long. I'm wondering if we can have dinner together tomorrow evening."

Debbie couldn't decide what she should do.

"Since Scottie's going to be over here, we'll be alone. We have a lot to talk about," Keith coaxed.

"You're interested in hearing more about Kate's ghost?"

Keith laughed. "That and a few other things. I had my parents mail me something I want to show you."

Debbie couldn't resist. She wanted to see him; she wanted to be with him no matter what his reasons. "Dinner sounds fine. I'll tell Cressie. I heard about Eleanor going to the mental hospital. Funny as it may sound, I feel sorry for her."

"Don't. She brought it on herself. After all, she not only tried to kill you, but actually did kill three people, not to mention the untold suffering she caused Jenny and Michael over the years. She deserves much worse than she's going to get."

Debbie sighed. "I guess you're right."

"By the way, Norma wanted me to tell you she was sorry for the things she said and hopes you understand she wasn't herself at the time. She plans to call you tomorrow."

"That's okay. I understand."

"Did the police have anything else to say?"

"The police?"

"Isn't that where you heard about Eleanor?"

"No, from Teresa. She and I had a little talk this afternoon. I don't think she enjoyed it much."

"So that's where she went. Did you learn anything?"

"She won't be playing any more vicious tricks on me, and I doubt if Jenny will have any more mysterious accidents."

Keith was quiet a moment. "I see. I have to go now. Sleep tight and dream of me."

Debbie set down the receiver. Keith's words left a world of longing. At that moment she accepted that for whatever time he remained in Nacogdoches she would find happiness in his company and build up a treasure of memories. When he left, although the pain would be great, she would wish him well. She loved him enough for that. And if by some chance he should ask her to go with him, she would do so gladly, even at the price of selling her beloved house.

When Debbie arrived home from the college the next evening, she found the dining room set for two with her best china and crystal. Red candles and poinsettias decorated the center of the white lace cloth, denoting the approach of the Christmas season and the festive occasion of the evening.

The appetizing smells from the kitchen brought growls from her stomach, and she laughed happily when Cressie instructed her to change clothes. Debbie was more than ready for a romantic evening with Keith. She had so much to tell him, and she longed to be in his arms again.

Keith's eyes glittered with appreciation when she

let him in the front door. His mouth curved, the dimpled scar in his chin catching the light. Her arms slid over his shoulders, and she clasped her hands behind his neck. Rising up on tiptoes, she brushed her parted lips across his. "I've missed you."

"It's been too long since we've had time for only the two of us," Keith murmured.

She tilted her head to one side and, cupping the back of his, drew his head down. Her fingers curled through his hair, and when she circled the edge of his lips with the tip of her tongue, she felt his muscles tense. Their mouths met, his kiss everything she could have wanted.

"Dinner's on the table. Sal and I will be going now." Cressie's voice broke them apart.

"Cressie, your timing is terrible," Keith complained.

"Yeah, well, I reckon you both need some nourishment at the moment. You'll have time to discuss other matters later."

Catching her breath, Debbie laughed. Leave it to Cressie to keep priorities in order. Taking Keith's hand, she led him into the dining room.

Cressie hovered in the doorway, checking everything on the table. Satisfied, she nodded. As Keith pulled out Debbie's chair, Cressie asked, "What's goin' to happen to Teresa?"

Keith's face changed, his expression becoming harsh. "Michael's made arrangements for her to enter a hospital where she'll receive psychiatric treatment. He's making the Wymans family pay the expenses, claiming they drove her over the edge with worries about her debts. Since Papa Wymans doesn't want a lawsuit and the resulting publicity, he's agreed. Besides, I think he feels in the long run Teresa may wind up easier to handle in the divorce if he goes along with this now."

"How does Jenny feel about everything?" Debbie asked. "After all, it was Teresa who tried to kill her."

"Teresa is all the blood family Jenny has left, even if she's only a half sister. Jenny doesn't want to lose her, too, no matter what's she done. Now that Jenny knows what's happened to Gloria, it's settled her own insecurities about herself. She understands Michael's not the most diplomatic person in the world, but he does have her interests at heart. She should settle down and become a perfectly normal teenager whose prime interest is one big redheaded boy."

"Does that mean Teresa's been arrested?" Cressie demanded.

"No one pressed charges, so the police can't do anything. They're happy having these other unsolved cases finally cleared up and quite willing to let Michael take care of his family problems. Teresa will have to stay in the hospital until the doctor releases her."

"She's such a pretty woman," Debbie said, not knowing what else to say.

"She has her father's looks and her mother's ways," Cressie explained. Preparing to leave, she added, "Sal built a nice fire in the back parlor. We'll go now. You think over what I said earlier, Miss Debbie. You can let me know tomorrow."

"All right. Good night," Debbie called. Cressie would never cease to amaze her with the things she said, and her suggestion this afternoon had been one of the most surprising.

"What was that all about?" Keith asked.

"I'll tell you later, after our talk."

Keith's eyes met Debbie's. She could see his desire

and knew it matched her own. But first things first.

While they ate, they discussed the college, the holiday activities and parties, and finally Keith's book. He asked her about Kate, and she told him all about her various experiences since moving into the house. While she spoke, she noticed his questions were those of an interested loved one wanting to share, not those of a writer digging for research.

Finally she had to ask, "That evening when Jenny fell down the back stairs, I saw one of the ghosts in the back parlor. You never said anything, but I wondered if you saw it, too."

Keith grimaced. "I saw. But you didn't say anything about the gyrating form, so I certainly wasn't going to bring up the subject. Every time I tried to ask you about ghosts after that, you clammed up because you thought I was curious for my book."

"I'm sorry."

"Don't be. I didn't exactly push my seeing the damned thing, and I could have. You may have noticed I did keep looking for an explanation. After all, that's what I'm noted for, disproving ghost claims, not supporting them."

Both laughed. When they finished they left everything on the table, and after Keith took out an envelope from his jacket pocket, they wandered into the back parlor. Keith stoked the fire, then sat beside Debbie on the sofa, drawing her into his arms. This time their kiss was soft and gentle, full of tender caring.

Debbie sighed and touched Keith's dimple with her finger. She loved the feel of his body next to hers, and the scent of his after-shave became more potent all the time. She wanted him, but first she had things to tell him.

"How did you get this scar?" she asked.

Keith glanced at Debbie out of the corner of his eyes. "That first summer I was here in Nacogdoches when I was a teenager, I was down at the swimming hole with Teresa. Things were getting a little out of hand when I slipped on some grass. I fell against a tree trunk. Blood gushed everywhere. Needless to say, that was the end of our dalliance. We never came that close again."

Delighted, Debbie laughed. Then, unbuttoning the bottom button on his shirt, she pointed to the small birthmark by his navel, the small pinecone-shaped one she'd first noticed after dropping paint on him. "Have I mentioned I like your birthmark?"

Keith looked down. He brought her hand to his lips, where he kissed her palm. "That's a family birthmark. All the men in my family have had one like that for generations."

"Did you know that Kate's Matthew had one, too? I read about it in this last journal. I also know why she's so unhappy and refuses to rest."

"I'm not surprised Matthew had one, but first tell me about Kate."

"Almost two years after she was married, Kate had a baby girl. By then Kate's father and her husband were at total odds. When the baby turned out to be a girl, Kyle ran Henry off. I gather neither Kyle nor Kate was sorry to see the last of him."

"That must be her baby's dress we found in the cedar chest."

"I'm sure it is. Anyway, Kate became ill and almost died. Kyle was angry. He blamed Kate's illness and the fact that the baby was a girl on Henry's weaknesses. He blamed Kate's failure to make her marriage work on her ridiculous infatuation for a damned Yankee.

When a certain family left the area heading for Dallas during this time, he gave them Kate's baby, together with some money."

Keith quirked his eyebrow. "Kyle gave her baby away when she was too sick to fight back?"

"It seems so. Anyway, when she recovered, she told him she'd never forgive him. She swore she'd never rest until she found her baby. He drove Matthew from her, but he wasn't going to deprive her of the baby, Georgette, as well."

Keith's thumb idly circled her palm as he stared into the fire. She could feel his anger.

"Did Kate ever find her?"

"Not that I discovered, although she did learn a family named Hudson took her baby. She swore never to rest until she put right the wrongs her father did to her."

"He really was a sorry bastard, wasn't he?" Keith said.

Immediately a chilling draft blew through the room. A musty odor invaded the aroma of burning oak. Keith threw another log on the fire while Debbie picked up a paper from the table.

"This is a letter I found in the footlocker I brought back from my mother's in Houston."

Keith took the letter and read it. "It's addressed to Timothy Hudson, giving him legal adoption of the baby Georgette Farmsworth, together with the sum of one hundred dollars."

Debbie nodded. "And it's signed Kyle Muller."

"You're related to Kate?"

"Georgette married Daniel Dillon. I'm Kate's great-great-granddaughter. I'm the first girl since Georgette."

"Well, I'll be damned!" Keith laughed and picked up the envelope he'd dropped on the coffee table. He took out a letter and a picture. "This is a letter my great-grandfather wrote long ago." He handed Debbie the miniature picture of Kate. "He tells how he's going to try one more time to contact Kate, even though all his other letters have been returned. It seems Kyle and Henry caught Matthew the night of July 3. They beat him up so badly he barely survived and then they dumped him on a stagecoach going north. There was no way he could meet Kate. Later, to stop his attempts to contact her, Kyle wrote that Kate had married. Of course, from what we read in the journal, she hadn't married yet, but Kyle didn't mind pulling a few more shenanigans to get his way. This letter tells her Matthew will always love her and wishes her well. Needless to say, the letter was returned."

"So now we know the story," Debbie whispered, and, staring into the burning fire, lost her thoughts to the tragic pair of lovers long ago.

Several minutes passed before Debbie spoke. "I've seen Kate, but do you think she really spoke through Cressie at the séance?"

"I think Cressie and Sal are very unusual people. Certainly an ideal study for a book. As to how much of the séance was real and how much they put on for show, we'll never really know. That's how those things work. It's a manipulation of the mind and the senses until you'll believe anything."

"Then you still don't believe in ghosts?"

Keith grinned. "I'm a critic of ghost stories. How can you even ask? Now, I have something very important I want to say to you."

He pulled Debbie onto his lap so that she had to

look directly at him. One hand encircled her back and the other stroked her cheek. "I've been offered a job teaching in Virginia next year."

"I know."

"I asked them if I could teach in summer school instead. I thought we might get married over the Christmas holidays. We would live in your house and spend next summer in Virginia. It could be a sort of paid teaching vacation and an opportunity to do research for my next book. I thought you might be my special assistant, my passionate lover, my helpmate wife. Then we'd come back to teach here again next fall."

Tears of surprise and happiness filled Debbie's eyes. "I love you," she whispered. "I'd love to marry you."

"Good. Because I don't think I could exist without you now that I've known you."

Keith kissed her with all the passion Debbie could wish for, but as their emotions started to burn out of control, the room turned icy cold. The musty odor became so strong, it drove Keith's lips from hers. Angrily he looked around, his eyes furious. "Go away, you old reprobate," he yelled. "You'll do no harm this time. I'll not let you. She's forever mine."

Debbie stifled her laugh and kissed Keith's dimple. The air filled with the scent of jasmine and the sound of wind chimes. A soft brush of air touched her cheek, as though from a loving kiss. The aroma and sound increased until the room seemed alive with them, and then they faded away.

Keith's frown disappeared, and he started raining kisses on Debbie's eyelids and her temples, accenting each with the whispered words, "I love you. I won't let him drive us apart as he did Kate and Matthew.

We'll be together from now on."

"You don't have anything to worry about," Debbie whispered. Looking around the room that held only the crackle of the fire and the aroma of burning oak, she sensed that the restless Kate had reached out of the past, down through time, and despite the difficulties caused by the local intrigue, she had bound a new set of lovers. As a result, Kate's ghost had finally found peace. And so would her father.

Suddenly Debbie laughed with her happiness. "I thought you didn't believe in ghosts."

"Well, it never hurts to have an open mind, just in case."

Later, when the fire burned low and the two lovers sat satiated and thoughtful, Debbie said, "Cressie told me today she has a niece who would like to come and work for us next fall."

She felt Keith catch his breath. "She did? Was this what you're supposed to think about and let her know tomorrow?"

"Uh-huh. It seems her niece has special psychic powers and would be wonderful with our daughter."

The sound of rich laughter echoed through the house, as Keith pulled Debbie tighter into his arms.

COMING NEXT MONTH

TAPESTRY by Maura Seger

A spellbinding tale of love and intrigue in the Middle Ages. Renard is her enemy, but beautiful Aveline knows that beneath the exterior of this foe beats the heart of a caring man. As panic and fear engulf London, the passion between Renard and Aveline explodes. "Sweeping in concept, fascinating in scope, triumphant in its final achievement."—Kathryn Lynn Davis, author of *Too Deep For Tears*.

UNFORGETTABLE by Leigh Riker

Recently divorced, Jessica Pearce Simon returns to her childhood home. Nick Granby, the love of her youth, has come home too. Now a successful architect and still single, Nick is just as intriguing as she remembers him to be. But can she trust him this time?

THE HIGHWAYMAN by Doreen Owens Malek

Love and adventure in 17th century England. When Lady Alexandra Cummings stows away on a ship bound for Ireland, she doesn't consider the consequences of her actions. Once in Ireland, Alexandra is kidnapped by Kevin Burke, the Irish rebel her uncle considers his archenemy.

WILD ROSE by Sharon Ihle

A lively historical romance set in San Diego's rancho period. Maxine McCain thinks she's been through it all—until her father loses her in a bet. As a result, she becomes indentured to Dane del Cordobes, a handsome aristocrat betrothed to his brother's widow.

SOMETHING'S COOKING by Joanne Pence

When a bomb is delivered to her door, Angelina Amalfi can't imagine why anyone would want to hurt her, an innocent food columnist. But to tall, dark, and handsome police inspector Paavo Smith, Angelina is not so innocent.

BILLY BOB WALKER GOT MARRIED by Lisa G. Brown

A spicy contemporary romance. Shiloh Pennington knows that Billy Bob Walker is no good. But how can she ignore the fire that courses in her veins at the thought of Billy's kisses?

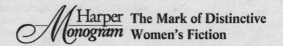

Harper Monogram The Mark of Distinctive Women's Fiction

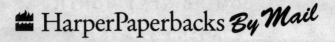

YESTERDAY'S SHADOWS
by Marianne Willman

Bettany Howard was a young orphan traveling west searching for the father who left her years ago. Wolf Star was a Cheyenne brave who longed to know who abandoned him—a white child with a jeweled talisman. Fate decreed they'd meet and try to seize the passion promised. 0-06-104044-4

MIDNIGHT ROSE by Patricia Hagan

From the rolling plantations of Richmond to the underground slave movement of Philadelphia, Erin Sterling and Ryan Youngblood would pursue their wild, breathless passion and finally surrender to the promise of a bold and unexpected love. 0-06-104023-1

WINTER TAPESTRY
by Kathy Lynn Emerson

Cordell vows to revenge the murder of her father. Roger Allington is honor bound to protect his friend's daughter but has no liking for her reckless ways. Yet his heart tells him he must pursue this beauty through a maze of plots to win her love and ignite their smoldering passion. 0-06-100220-8